Lucy Blue, where are you?
and
Hippy Chick

Louise Harwood is the author of the bestselling
Six Reasons to Stay a Virgin and *Calling on Lily*. She lives
in Oxfordshire with her husband and two young sons.

Praise for *Six Reasons to Stay a Virgin*

'Light-hearted, sexy, romantic comedy'
Observer

'Refreshing, light-hearted and emotionally intelligent,
Six Reasons says that it's more than OK to stand apart
from the crowd and follow your heart'
The Times

LOUISE HARWOOD

Lucy Blue, where are you?
and
Hippy Chick

PAN BOOKS

Lucy Blue, where are you? first published 2005 by Pan Books
Hippy Chick first published 2007 by Pan Books

This omnibus first published 2008 by Pan Books
an imprint of Pan Macmillan Ltd
Pan Macmillan, 20 New Wharf Road, London N1 9RR
Basingstoke and Oxford
Associated companies throughout the world
www.panmacmillan.com

ISBN 978-0-330-50793-6

A CIP catalogue record for this book is available from
the British Library.

Typeset by SetSystems Ltd, Saffron Walden, Essex
Printed in the UK by CPI Mackays, Chatham ME5 8TD

Lucy Blue,
where are you?

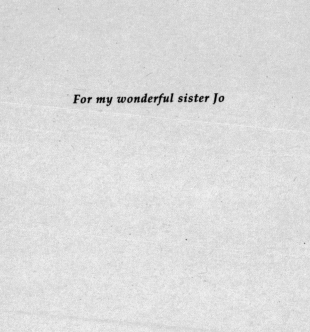

For my wonderful sister Jo

Acknowledgements

Special thanks to Imogen Taylor and the fantastic team at Pan, and to Jo Frank and Araminta Whitley for all their support and encouragement; to Russell Jones and Aileen Richards; to my family, especially Josie, for coming up with so many great ideas; and to wonderful Ant, Tom and Jack for looking after me so well and for making it happen.

1

Clutching a red duffel-coat in one hand and a telescope wrapped in silver paper in the other, nudging a heavy suitcase along with her knee, Gabriella struggled to keep walking, trying not to let the train's violent twists and turns throw her off her feet.

She didn't quite make it to the door to the next carriage. Just as she reached the last row of seats, and with Lipton St Lucy station only a few hundred yards away, the driver finally outmanoeuvred her, accelerating fast and then braking violently with a series of jolting lurches that lifted her first off one foot and then, a few long seconds later, off the other. Dropping the coat and the telescope on the floor, she landed in the last row of seats, deep in the lap of a surprised fifty-something business man. And as the train shuddered into the station, she felt his hand slide beneath her bottom.

'Stop that!' she snapped, but he pulled out a Mont Blanc fountain pen and pointed to the nib.

'I hope that didn't hurt?'

'Oh no!' She put her hands to her face, her cheeks hot with embarrassment.

'I'm sorry.'

He smiled at her and settled comfortably back in his seat. 'So, where did you come from?'

'Italy,' she said, misunderstanding, scrabbling for the ground with her feet and trying to stand up. The train was stopping now.

He nodded. 'I thought you looked Italian, all that dark hair. I was in Rome myself, back in 1976.'

She'd been born in Rome in 1976 but she certainly wasn't about to tell him so.

She put her hand on the table in front of them and began to lever herself upright, and he stared at her in disappointed surprise. 'Oh, are you getting off?'

'Of course I am!'

And then he glanced around and caught the amused glances of his fellow passengers, saw what a fool he was making of himself, and so, with a good deal of tutting and sighing, he finally helped her back to her feet. Knowing the train must be about to pull away again, she reached for the suitcase and telescope, praying it hadn't been broken by the fall, ran to the door and jumped off the train just as the whistle blew.

Standing on the platform, she slipped on her coat, grateful for its warmth in the cold afternoon air, then picked up her luggage and walked towards the exit, her carriage accompanying her for a few strides before the train picked up speed and pulled away.

She'd been the only passenger to disembark, and Lipton St Lucy station was as dark and deserted as she'd expected. She looked around and wondered where Jude was, hoping he wouldn't be late.

Gabriella had been aiming for the four o'clock train, but she had arrived at Paddington to find that an earlier one was still on the platform, just about to depart. She'd run awkwardly through the barriers and clambered aboard, and it was only after she'd settled down in her seat that it occurred to her that perhaps it hadn't been such a good idea, catching a train that would bring her into Lipton St Lucy forty minutes earlier than expected, with no guarantee that she could summon any of the Middletons to pick her up. Too late to change her mind, she'd called the house twice before anyone had answered the phone and finally she'd got Jude, dragging him from a deep sleep on the sofa in front of the fire. He'd been left all alone in the house, he told her. The rest of his mad family were out in the freezing rain, climbing Dixie Hill and working off their Sunday lunch. Of course he'd come to the station to pick her up.

But he hadn't come *yet*.

Gabriella turned away from the tracks, making for the bridge that led over to the station car park, then stopped and felt in her coat pockets for money for a cup of tea, thinking she'd be better off in the waiting-room than out in the open. And then she heard him, running across the bridge, his long strides ringing out above her head.

Just a few seconds later he leapt down the last five steps and all but collided with her, dressed only in jeans and a shirt, with a smile to soften the hardest of hearts.

'So good to see you.' He slipped an arm around her shoulders. 'I'm sorry, Gabriella. Don't look like that. I'm not late. Your train was early, it's only five to.' He pulled her against him and kissed her, catching the side of her head with his lips. 'You know I'd never be late for you.'

'Don't start, Jude.'

3

'But it's true. I'd spend my whole life waiting.'

'Shut up.' She reached up and kissed him on the cheek.

'Anyway,' he told her, 'there was this bull. A mad, dangerous bull, rampaging down the lane just outside the station.'

'A bull?'

'You know, one of those daddy cows.'

She pushed him away from her.

'And it might have hurt someone,' he said, replacing his arm round her shoulders and steering her towards the car park. 'You can imagine, a little kid, an old lady. There was no way I could leave it there.'

'So what did you do?'

He looked down at her and his arm tightened around her shoulders. 'Caught it, *of course.*'

'And then?'

'Found it a stable. Gave it some hay.'

'Bull-shit, Jude,' she said carefully, but laughing all the same. 'You went back to sleep, didn't you?'

'Sleep!' He laughed, kissing her again. 'With you here waiting? You think I'd fall asleep again?'

*

Three-thirty on the afternoon of 28 December and already it was nearly dark. They reached the car and then they were away, Jude picking his way carefully along the narrow lanes, through the dark afternoon towards Lipton Hall and the Middletons, where Luke and Suzie and James would surely all be back from their walk and waiting for them now. Gabriella thought of the belated Christmas

4

presents she was bringing for all of them: the backgammon board for James; the leather holdall for Jude, boring she knew, but she'd found herself struggling and failing to find the right present for him. She'd bought the telescope for Luke and a lovely set of carved wooden angels for Suzie that she'd found in a Christmas market in Rome. Five of them, hands clasped, heads bowed, tiny and beautiful. By rights she should have given them to her own mother, and if they didn't get her into Suzie's permanent good books nothing would. Guiltily, Gabriella thought how extravagant she'd been, how much more money and time she'd spent choosing things for the Middletons than she had for her own family. But they had been so much more difficult to choose for, and it seemed to matter so much more that she got these presents right. Next year, she silently promised her parents, next year I'll make it up to you. But for now she was in Oxfordshire, speeding through the countryside to give these presents away and to spend a few days with her lovely boyfriend and his gorgeous family, and she was suddenly filled with excitement that it was so.

She turned to Jude, about to ask if he thought the others would be back from their walk by the time they arrived, but the words never came, because, suddenly, out of the empty darkness there was now a car, arcing fast around the bend, swinging over on to their side of the road as it came towards them, crazy headlights dazzling.

We'll hit each other, Gabriella thought, but there was no time for fear. She heard Jude swear, felt him pull desperately on the wheel even though there was nowhere for them to go, and then she felt the breathtaking slam as the two cars collided. And then they were spinning, she and Jude, sharing a ride on a giant, malevolent waltzer that whirled them twice, then hurled them off the road. High in the air, she looked out and saw black clouds racing across the moon and glittering leaves swirling around the windscreen, caught in the wild beam of the headlights. And then they were hitting the ground again, forcing their way through a hedge before falling downwards, the ground now dropping steeply away beneath them.

And waiting for them at the bottom of the bank was a tree, slamming through the windscreen as they came. And then, of course, they were still and Gabriella felt the cold night air touch her forehead and heard herself whisper, just once, *oh please God no.*

2

A year later

'You're so soft,' whispered Gordon, drink-fumed breath tickling Lucy's ear. 'Your skin is soft as, soft as a . . .' He dropped two kisses on to her bare shoulder while he thought about it, and then, when nothing came to mind, encircled her with his arms, so that Lucy found herself being rocked gently and smothered by the scratchy wool of his dinner jacket at the same time.

He was quite sweet but very drunk. He was completely unfanciable, but this was better than sitting by herself watching everyone else dance. That was what she'd told herself, anyway, when he'd first taken her hand and pulled her to her feet. Now she was fast changing her mind.

'As soft as a pigeon,' he sighed, and Lucy felt his fingers slowly working their way down the bare knuckles of her spine, stopping abruptly when he reached her bottom. Obviously Gordon was a gentleman at heart, or perhaps simply gay? She pushed him upright and instantly he toppled forward again.

'Gordon?'

Now he was leaning so heavily against her that she wondered if he'd dropped off.

He didn't answer. She slipped her arm around him and

steered him away from the dance floor back towards the tables, kicking out a spare chair with her foot and pushing him down.

This was not why she'd come, Lucy thought, looking down at him as he stared, hypnotized by her cleavage. She'd not travelled five hundred miles, left behind Jane and all her other friends on New Year's Eve, only to meet a drunken arse like Gordon. He looked up at her with eyes so thickly glazed she could see her reflection.

'Lovely boobies.'

She looked longingly over to the door.

'Sorry,' he said immediately. 'Ver . . . ver . . .'

She patted him on the shoulder, left him there, and walked away, past the dance floor – disco had given way to yet another round of Scottish dancing and she was happier still to be leaving when she saw that – through the door and past reception, calling goodnight to the woman behind the desk and then running up the stairs, pulling her key from her mother-of-pearl evening bag as she went.

It was five to midnight. Reaching the second floor she turned left, stopped at the third door down and slipped her key into the lock, let the door of her bedroom slam shut behind her, bent and undid the straps of her sandals, kicked them off, wriggled and flexed her way out of her dress and tossed it over a chair, unhooked her bra and stepped out of her pants, then pulled back the bedclothes and climbed into bed. She took out her contact lenses, turned off the light, lay down, rolled on to her side, pulled her knees up close to her chin and closed her eyes. She hadn't even made it to New Year.

*

Next morning the Kirk Castle Hotel ballroom looked hungover and not at all pleased to be disturbed. The crimson velvet curtains looped across its windows gave the impression of heavy lidded eyes squinting irritably at the interruption, and on the opposite side of the room, in a huge stone fireplace, a burnt log poked up from the ashes like a dirty broken tooth.

When Lucy had left last night, the room had still been full of people, hoarse men and horsy women, drunkenly groping each other under the tables or twirling streamers into the antlers of the stags' heads mounted on the walls. But now it was silent in the dusty light, empty but for Lucy, standing there in the doorway, looking around to see if anyone had seen or heard her, wondering if anybody else was about.

It seemed that nobody was. She closed the door again and turned away, retracing her steps back across the hall to reception. At the desk she put down her overnight bag, laid her handbag on the scuffed wooden surface and fought the urge to lay her cheek down beside it and close her eyes. She'd fallen asleep at dawn, and now she was up again and it was much, much too early. Why had she booked a flight at ten a.m. when she could have slept half the day away?

Instead, she'd given herself to the very last second of

seven-forty-five, leaving five minutes to sit up, stick in her contact lenses, as scratchy and uncomfortable as Velcro, rub deodorant under each arm, pull on yesterday's jeans, shirt and cardigan and get out of the door, and allowing a further ten minutes to check out. Then one and a half hours to drive back to Inverness airport. Check-in nine-thirty a.m., flight departing at ten-thirty.

But five minutes had passed since she'd left her room and still nobody had materialized to help her, and if she didn't get a move on she was going to miss her plane. What was worse, as she'd walked down the ornate wrought-iron staircase, suitcase in hand, she'd looked out of the window and had been shocked to see the snow, falling thickly through the still-dark trees. This was snow that was going to slow her journey to a crawl and might mean she'd never make it to the airport at all.

Above her a wall clock ticked, and she bit her lip as the knot of worry tangled some more. She peered around the room again, as if by looking more carefully she'd magic someone to appear. This was where the party had begun last night, where she'd sipped her first drink and looked curiously around the room. But now the smell of old cigarette smoke and sweat seemed to be the only link with the evening before. In the candlelight the room had seemed romantic, but by daylight it was shabby and dirty, painted in a yellowing cream, shiny orange curtains hanging limply at each of the long rectangular windows. Orange, Lucy thought. Who could possibly have flipped through the sample book and chosen orange?

To the left of the fireplace there was a painting of a

flock of sheep standing in just the kind of blizzard she presumed was now raging outside, and below that was an armchair covered in green tartan and to the right of it a dinner gong made from brass and suspended on a wooden frame, with a padded wooden beater on a length of wire. She walked over to it. From the layer of dust, Lucy guessed this was a gong long since retired from active service, but it was too tempting to ignore. She brushed the beater gently against the brass, producing a muffled hum that wasn't going to summon anybody, and then, before she could change her mind, she struck it hard, whereupon sound crashed out across the silent room, growing louder and louder with each second, the echoes and reverberations falling in on each other, building into a tidal wave of noise. The whole room was sounding the alarm: here, waiting at reception, was the least patient, most obnoxious hotel guest imaginable.

Mortified, Lucy dropped the beater and placed a hand on the angrily vibrating brass to stifle the sound, then sat down in the armchair, overcome with the effort. She rested her head against the wall behind, and closed her eyes and waited. Slowly peace returned to the room.

The minutes continued to tick past and still Lucy continued to wait, and very soon she found herself yawning, unable to stop her eyes slowly sealing shut, seduced by her soft wool coat and the heavy warmth of the room, no longer worried about skidding off the road or missing her flight. Instead her mind was slipping back to the start of the party the night before, and she was catching again the sweet smell of hyacinths in the cold night air, pushing her way through a crush of people, all of them knocking back drinks, laughing and noisy, and she felt again the pang of trepidation mixed with excitement that had come from walking in alone. Apart from the host, an old school-friend, she had known nobody and nobody had known her. She remembered staring across the room at the wonderful kaleidoscope of taffeta and tartan swaying gently in the candlelight. At that stage, the evening had felt full of promise.

She had found her table, heavy cutlery laid out against white table linen, the stiff place setting announcing that on her left would be someone called Neil Armstrong, and she'd had to smother her smile because he was there already, pulling out her chair, with a buzz cut and a sweet, earnest smile.

She'd eaten hot-smoked salmon and drunk glass after glass of pale gold wine, ice cold and delicious. Sitting opposite her had been Neil's wife, Philly, and on Philly's lap their six-month-old son, Josh, who had made sure of both parents' full attention all evening. And on her right had been poor Gavin Singleton, fleshy and rather flashy too, more than happy to hold Lucy's attention and any-thing else he could get his hands on. But Gavin had choked on his salmon, his face turning fiery red, only recovering when the chunk of pink fish that had been blocking his windpipe had leapt out of his mouth in a perfect arc and into her glass of wine. Laughing, she'd said she'd never seen salmon leap so far, but after that he had barely been able to speak to her again. Not in itself a great loss, but from then on Lucy had had nobody to talk to on either side. And as the tables were so big, the people on the other side were out of range. It was then that she'd first thought wistfully of London and all her friends, dancing away New Year's Eve without her.

She opened her eyes and wiggled her bruised toes. She'd worn strappy silver sandals, not ideal footwear for Hogmanay with a crowd of twirling Scottish dancers, but they'd gone with her pale pink sequined dress. Not that the dress had been very suitable either. When Teddy had seen it in her suitcase he'd held it up and asked, dubiously, how it had got there. Teddy preferred his women well covered up.

She pushed herself upright in her chair. Why had she done it? Spent three hundred pounds on a beautiful dress and two hundred more to fly away from everyone she knew to wear it? Yes, she'd escaped Teddy, but with just a little effort she could have escaped him in London too. What had she hoped to find here? *Who* had she hoped to find here? Because from the moment she'd slipped the dress over her head, right to the moment when she'd pulled it off again, she knew she'd been waiting for someone.

And whoever it was she'd been waiting for, they hadn't turned up. Being in Inverness on her own, rather than in London with her friends, had proved not to be such a liberating devil-may-care experience after all. Fun at the beginning, to put proper make-up on again and to walk into the room in her new high heels and know she was free to behave as badly as she wanted, but that had lasted only as long as it had taken to see that there was nobody to behave badly with.

And now, sitting on her own on such a hard uncomfortable chair, looking around at the shabby walls, the peeling gilt picture-frames and the thick layer of dust on the table beside her, thinking of the snow cascading down outside, she felt let down and a little bit silly. She could almost hear Teddy's laugh. *Look how well you're getting on. Admit it, Lucy, it's not so much fun without me, is it?*

She leaned back against the wall and at that moment the door from the hall opened and at last someone appeared, a thick-set, frowning woman, striding across the room as the door slammed behind her, in lace-ups, a tweed skirt and thick, ribbed tights, iron-grey hair springing with each step. Lucy got to her feet and walked over to join her, but without acknowledging her at all the woman crammed herself between the reception desk and a swivel chair and then, only when she was ready, did she finally turn her attention to her guest.

'*So* sorry to keep you waiting . . .' The sarcasm was heavy in her voice and she was breathing heavily, her large body rising and falling to the rhythm. She settled herself down in the chair and began to check over some paperwork.

'And I'm sorry to have used the gong,' Lucy replied to the bent head, 'but I'm catching a plane. I have to check out.'

'No need to apologize,' the woman sniffed, 'but I'll be surprised if you haven't broken it, all the same.' She looked up suddenly and caught Lucy's amused grin, hastily smothered. 'I was in the kitchen,' she said defiantly, 'making everyone breakfast, breakfast in bed being rather popular on a Sunday morning.'

Oh, how mean of them, Lucy almost snapped back. How selfish they all are to want breakfast in bed on a Sunday *in your hotel*. But she bit back the retort because this was Mrs E. Sutherland, according to the plastic name badge on her lapel, whose thick brown foundation and floury face powder failed to disguise the grey skin and eyes sunken with fatigue. Mrs Sutherland, who had been there yesterday afternoon to check her in, had still been there behind the desk when she'd come down to dinner, and who had *still* been there when Lucy had walked up the stairs at five to midnight.

'Have you been to bed at all?' Lucy asked instead.

'For an hour or two.'

'How do you cope? When do you ever get a break?'

'When my son gets up. Thank you for asking.' She gave Lucy an unexpected smile. 'I'll kick his lazy backside out of bed after I've seen you off.'

She bent her head back to her computer and Lucy watched her work, fascinated by the way her soft fleshy neck folded and extended like a concertina as Mrs Sutherland alternately bent to scowl at her notes, then peer forwards at the computer screen.

'I'll have you know that you don't look so marvellous yourself.'

She said it suddenly, without looking up or pausing in her typing, jolting Lucy abruptly back to reality, and Lucy felt herself blush as she realized how she had been staring.

Not that she was in the least surprised to hear she didn't look so good. She probably didn't smell so good either, seeing that she hadn't brushed her teeth or washed since the evening before.

'You're in a great hurry to leave?'

'I wanted to catch the first plane back to London.'

Mrs Sutherland looked up sharply. 'Have you had a miserable time?'

Lucy smiled. 'Not great.'

'I'm not surprised to hear it.'

She took Lucy's key and turned to hang it on the row of hooks behind her.

'My room was very comfortable,' Lucy said hastily, 'but the party was . . .'

'Appalling!' Mrs Sutherland shuddered. 'And there was I thinking I'd seen it all.'

'Sorry,' Lucy said again.

'I understand your need to get away, but even so you should have something to eat or you'll be falling asleep on the road.'

Lucy swallowed uneasily as Mrs Sutherland started to rattle off all the different things she could and would prepare, the fried eggs, fried bread, potatoes, bacon, hash browns and pork sausages, pausing only to elaborate on the juiciness of the black pudding. She couldn't be sure whether she was doing it deliberately, turning Lucy's stomach into a butter churn, or whether she genuinely thought she was being kind.

She turned away, glanced out of the window, and Mrs Sutherland's voice faded away as she looked at the winter wonderland that lay before her. Suddenly the darkness had lifted and the world outside had been transformed. The cars, the roads, the little stone bridge just beyond the garden wall, were all covered in deep snow and still it was tipping out of the sky. Somewhere out there she knew there were hedges and a low wall that divided the garden from the car park, where she'd left her hire car, and further on there was a drive and a road that would take her towards the airport. But Lucy no longer recognized any of it, wasn't even sure where the garden ended and the car park began, couldn't have even said if she should turn left or right out of the hotel gates, couldn't even see the hotel gates.

'Who would have thought it?' Mrs Sutherland teased. 'Snow, in the Highlands, in January.' And she laughed at the dismay on Lucy's face. 'Don't you worry. It's a straight road to Scarth Ross. And once you get down there you'll meet the snowploughs.' She paused. 'Let's hope not head on.'

'Let's hope not.'

From inside the office Lucy heard a printer run through its routine and begin to print. When it had finished, Mrs Sutherland stretched her arm through the doorway and came back with Lucy's bill in her hand.

*

Outside, the fresh air made her feel a little better. The problem was that each of the vague white bumps looked identical and she wondered how she would ever find her car. In the end she pulled up the hood of her coat and determinedly marched from row to row, firing her alarm key at every bump until eventually she heard the satisfying sound of locks clunking open in response. Knocking off the snow, she rediscovered her little red car.

Driving painfully slowly, she slithered out of the drive, remembering that Mrs Sutherland had told her to turn right on to a tiny lane where the snow was already so deep it reached half-way up the hedges. For the first ten miles she drove very slowly, rigid with concentration, her shoulders hunched up level with her ears, leaning forwards, her eyes wide and unblinking, her hands gripping the wheel so tightly that her knuckles went white, convinced it was only a matter of time before she skidded off the road.

But mile after mile passed by and the crash didn't come, and slowly she realized that the brakes still braked and the steering-wheel steered, that the snow, while still falling, was no longer blizzard-like and that she could see perfectly well and then she started to relax and picked up speed.

An hour later and she still hadn't seen another car or any signs of life at all. She'd passed a few isolated houses and a handful of tiny villages, but they were all so tightly closed down against the weather that she doubted anyone could be living in them, and she wondered if she was right to believe that for as far as she could see and beyond, in every direction, she was the only person there.

She opened the glove compartment as she drove, fished out a bottle of water, unscrewed the top with her teeth and took a long drink, then dropped the bottle on to the map on the seat beside her and turned on the radio, guiding the car with one hand as she moved between the stations, letting her head fall back against the headrest, grinning to herself as the music filled the car. Now that her doom was no longer certain, she was even having fun.

She drove on, mile after mile, picking up more speed, gliding silently and smoothly through the endless white expanse of snow-covered highlands. And gradually, as the snow lulled her, hypnotized her even, she began to feel that here at last, on this journey home, she was free again and loving it: here, all alone, a stranger in a strange place, skiing along in this car, cut off from the world outside. This was what she'd been hoping to feel when she'd left London, this exhilaration, this enjoyment in her own company, the relief of being answerable to no one, least of all Teddy. But it had taken all this time, and now she was on her way home again and she wished very much that her journey wasn't going to end so soon. She dared to take her eyes off the road to look at the clock and saw that she'd be reaching Inverness in about half an hour, and even as she registered this the road widened into a dual carriageway and a huge green road sign, almost completely obscured by snow, flashed past with only the letters INV visible at the top. Seeing it, she took her foot off the accelerator and reached again for the water, willing everything she was feeling now to soak into her and last beyond this day.

And then, just as she had one hand on the wheel and the bottle of water back to her lips, out of the whiteness came a stag, leaping out of nowhere as quiet as a ghost, clearing her speeding bonnet with a foot to spare and disappearing again even before she had closed her eyes tight, stamped down on the brake and wrenched around the wheel. The car spun in perfect three-hundred-and-sixty degree circles, twice, three times, and left her pointing in precisely the same direction as before. She opened her eyes again to find herself travelling smoothly on down the road.

Oh my God, she breathed, as the shock caught up with her. She snapped off her music and slowed down to only a few miles an hour, feeling her heart slamming against her chest, her palms suddenly slippery with sweat. How could the stag not have hit her? How had she managed to stay on the road? Even the bottle of water had landed upright on the map, not a drop spilled.

Then, as she recovered and her pulse settled and she picked up speed again, it seemed as if the stag had shown her something important: that today, on this journey home, nothing bad could happen to her. That she could do whatever she wanted, that for now she was invincible. It was snowing harder than ever, but now she knew that however deep and impenetrable it became, however fast or slowly she drove, whether she kept her eyes open or closed, steered or didn't steer, it didn't matter. The car would somehow keep on driving, would follow the road, and she would be safe.

Signs of life returned as she approached the outskirts of Inverness. A snowplough suddenly looming in front of her, headlights full on as it noisily cleared the road, other cars idling at the traffic lights, all of them carrying heavy white duvets on their roofs and bonnets. Ahead of her she saw a bareheaded man in a suit and black leather shoes stepping daintily along the pavement, Sunday newspapers clutched to his chest.

Squinting through the snow for the road signs, Lucy reached the airport and found the Deals on Wheels car park where she was to leave the car. She found a space alongside a dark red Range Rover – surely far too smart to be owned by Deals on Wheels – and parked neatly, turned off the engine, unclipped her seat belt and stretched back in her seat. Just beyond her danced two excited little girls in matching pink ski-suits and bobble hats. Their parents, lugging heavy suitcases, staggered along behind them.

But she was not leaving for a holiday, she was returning home. She watched the holiday-bound family slipping one by one through the doors into the airport and thought how any moment now she would be walking through those doors too. And she thought about why she'd come here in the first place. How much she'd wanted it to mark the end of Teddy and the start of something new. She sat there for a few moments more, watching people walking all around her but not seeing them at all, aware only of how she was feeling: brave, happy, her own person again. How this was New Year's Day, a day for changes. How she was going to catch her plane and go home. And once she got there, how she was going to sort out her life. And how she would begin with Teddy.

3

The airport was busy, people constantly arriving, stamping their feet, shaking their heads free of snow. Lucy followed the signs for the Deals on Wheels desk and, having been prepared for a long queue, was relieved to see that there were only five people in front of her. She'd soon be handing over her keys and making her way to the check-in, she thought. In under an hour she'd be in the air. Impatience to be off overwhelmed her, making her clutch her bag in her hand and keep her eyes fixed on the woman at the front of the queue.

Ten minutes later, there were still five people between her and the desk. Lucy shifted restlessly from foot to foot and again cast her eye towards the front of the queue, where the woman in a shiny pink plastic raincoat was still arguing with the Deals on Wheels rep, hands waving furiously in the air, exactly as she had been doing since Lucy had joined the queue. Lucy swung her overnight bag off her shoulder and on to the ground and sat on it, telling herself again that she had plenty of time and the woman couldn't go on for ever. The nervous-looking couple behind her glanced at her uneasily, then craned their necks again to watch what was happening. Lucy shuffled around on her bag and saw that the woman was now leaning so far over the rep's desk that her feet, in high stilettos, had lifted clean off the ground and her pink coat had ridden high up her thighs, revealing more of the backs of her chunky legs than Lucy could stomach so early in the morning.

Next thing she knew, there was a rush of air as someone came striding past her. She glanced up and saw a man, dark-haired, a long black coat flowing behind him as he headed towards the front of the queue. Lucy stood up, interested, and wished that she'd caught a glimpse of his face. He touched the back of the pink raincoat and the woman dropped back to her feet and turned around to him in surprise. And then Lucy watched him move in on the Deals on Wheels rep, how threateningly he towered over the desk. She watched him lean in closer, the pink-coated woman nodding excitedly. And then, finally, the rep rose up from behind his desk, a small defiant-looking man in a navy Deals on Wheels blazer, and, as Lucy watched, he reluctantly placed something on the desk that the pink lady instantly snatched away, smiling jubilantly, first sideways at her rescuer, then turning to include the queue of people waiting behind her.

'I'm so sorry, everybody,' she giggled nervously, blinking sticky Barbara Cartland eyelashes at them all, still managing completely to block Lucy's view of the man. 'So sorry to keep you all waiting. But this man owed me fifty pounds and I didn't see why he should get away with it.' She nodded flirtatiously to her Knight in a Black Coat. 'Thanks to you, I'm glad to report he hasn't.'

Out of the way, Lucy thought impatiently, *let me see his face* – because of course he was going to be gorgeous. And, of course, once he finally turned around, he was going to notice Lucy standing in the queue (by now, her teeth would have miraculously self-cleaned and she would be looking great, better than she'd ever looked in her life before). And he'd come over, say something, make her laugh, and she'd say exactly the right thing back and then they'd check in together, sit beside each other on the plane, talk all the way back to London . . .

The pink-coated lady stepped aside but still the man didn't turn around.

No. Abruptly Lucy changed her mind. She should prepare to be disappointed. The expensive coat and the broad shoulders were sure to be misleading. When he turned around she'd see he had pitted skin and criss-cross teeth, less the kind of man to fantasize about sitting next to on the plane, more the kind of man to cross the airport to avoid.

And then, just as she was about to sit down on her bag again, he did turn around, slowly, taking his time, as if he knew that every eye was upon him. He walked back and took his place at the back of the queue and as he passed he caught her eye and flashed her a brief brilliant smile.

Lucy opened her handbag, peering deep and intently inside it, fighting the urge to laugh, because he'd been so shockingly good-looking and so obviously had known it too, with his carefully knotted scarf, just a touch of stubble and that dazzling super-white smile. He looked as if he'd just finished filming a commercial for Ralph Lauren, and all down the queue people were still turning their heads after him, as if it had been Prince William who had just strolled past.

Lucy turned her back on them and sat down again on her bag. With the pink plastic lady despatched it wouldn't be long till her turn. She opened her bag again, brought out the Deals on Wheels paperwork and slipped it into her coat pocket. She could see her flight ticket tucked neatly between her purse and the turquoise leather photo frame with the pictures of Teddy inside. Immediately she felt herself shrinking inside her skin and yet, even though it was the very last thing she wanted to do, she found herself reaching for the frame, lifting it out of her bag, opening it like a book, so that she could see the photos of Teddy, two of them, one on each side. Neither of them ones she had picked, certainly not ones she had ever liked. They'd been chosen by him, the photo frame his birthday present to her. On the left he was wearing a sports jacket and tie, and was standing alone, looking confident and determined, and on the right he was with Lucy, who'd been caught at a particularly bad angle, the wind that was making her tightly screw up her eyes lending Teddy a spirited, dashing air of vitality that he certainly didn't have in real life. Now, in both the photos, he seemed to stare back at her accusingly, a double dose of disapproval. She wanted to take them over to the nearest bin, throw them in among the cigarette butts and fast-food wrappers and half empty cans of drink, but she didn't want to lose her place in the queue.

She looked at them again. *You're history*, she whispered at them both, and the two Teddys seemed almost to start in surprise at her words. You're gone. You and your fuzzy hair and your big white teeth and your loud voice and your bad temper, and your Golf GTI and your snooty ridiculous parents and your control-freakery and your extra-strong mints. Gone, gone gone. She glanced up quickly. The man in the black coat was standing with his back to her, directly in her eyeline. And yes, Teddy, she thought defiantly, snapping shut the frame and dropping it back into her bag, he did smile at me. And yes, he is gorgeous, isn't he?

The queue was moving quickly now. Only two more people and it would be her turn. Lucy picked up her bag and moved a few more paces forwards. And at the same moment, the airport's PA system suddenly boomed into life, making her stop again in surprise, announcing that due to adverse weather conditions, all flights were grounded with immediate effect. The airport was closing until further notice and more details would follow shortly, but in the meantime could the airport authorities please advise anyone leaving the airport to do so in a manner in accordance with the treacherous conditions.

Groans rippled down the Deals on Wheels queue. How could this possibly be so, Lucy thought disbelievingly? Snow in the Highlands? In January? Was the airport not used to this? They'd got snowploughs and gritters, she'd seen them clearing the roads around the airport. In fact, she could see some more of them now, their headlights cutting through the blizzard that was hurling itself against the airport windows. And seeing what was now going on outside, Lucy reluctantly had to admit to herself that she was grateful not to be out on the runway in a plane, attempting to take off.

But what to do instead? How were they all going to get

home? It could be days before the snow stopped, weeks even. How was she to get back to London? She looked around the airport, at the rows of seats already full of people. She couldn't stay here, sitting it out with hundreds of others. She had work tomorrow and she needed to get back to her flat. She wanted to be home, beginning the new year, behind her desk the next morning. She wanted to be gone.

And then she looked down at the keys in her hand and pictured the red car waiting in the car park, remembered how it had felt to drive it, how she'd even wished for more time to drive. Now, here was the chance. Unlike most of her fellow travellers, she had a way out.

It seemed that everybody else in the airport simultaneously had the same idea. As the man ahead of her finally finished his negotiations with the Deals on Wheels rep and Lucy was nudged forward for her turn, she could see a dozen or so people, striding – but not quite shameless enough to break into a run – to reach the end of the queue first. Surely Deals on Wheels wouldn't have enough cars for them all?

She turned back to the rep, who immediately reached forwards and tried to snatch the car keys out of her hand before she'd even said a word.

'Don't do that!' She lifted the keys out of reach. He'd obviously been smarting ever since losing the battle with the pink raincoat woman and was dying for someone to push around. But it wasn't going to be her. She'd met him too many times before to be bullied by him now, dealt with him in the boiling heat of Nice airport and the sleety cold of Belfast, disbelievingly filled out his endless forms and argued over the hundreds of extra pounds in spurious supplements, the accidental-death-of-a-wild-animal insurance, the extra-large-suitcase premium, the using-all-four-seats-of-the-car premium. She'd been over them all.

'I would like to extend my rental for another day,' she told him firmly.

The rep shook his head.

'I'd like to extend my rental,' Lucy said again, 'and take the car back to London. I'll return it to one of your London branches tomorrow.'

'Not a chance, madam.'

'What do you mean?'

'Let me rephrase that. Your car has already been reassigned.' He held out his hand. 'Keys, please.'

Lucy reached into her pocket and brought out her Deals on Wheels documents. In her mind the little red car had taken on the lovable qualities of Chitty Chitty Bang Bang. She was not about to give it up.

'You can't reassign it. Look at the agreement – the car is mine until ten p.m.'

She handed the papers over. Behind her the queue had been listening to what was going on and now started muttering noisily, supportive of her, she hoped, even though they were being held up yet again. But the truth was, she really didn't care whether they were on her side or not. She was keeping the car.

'Yesterday's Deals on Wheels rep insisted that I paid for the whole of today, even though he knew I would be delivering the car back first thing this morning,' she told him. 'You've taken my money, so you can't reassign my car to someone else. Not before ten p.m. 'Stare at me as much as you like,' Lucy went on, seeing a savage look on his face, 'but I'm keeping the car.' Any more trouble and she would simply walk away, out of the airport, drive off and sort it out from London. 'I'll deliver it back by ten p.m. tonight.'

He studied the agreement and laid it down upon the desk in front of him. 'Very well,' he sighed after a long pause. 'Deliver it back by ten p.m. Any Deals on Wheels garage . . .'

Now Lucy wasn't sure whether or not to believe him.

'That is, any Deals on Wheels garage *in Scotland*. Because, madam, I would advise you not to drive over the border without insurance.'

'I've got insurance.'

'No, you haven't. You are insured to drive the vehicle *in Scotland*.' Now he was enjoying the chance to spell it out to her. 'Look at your agreement. If you want to take the vehicle over the border you need to pay the *international* insurance supplement. That'll be a further four hundred and twenty-two pounds and fifty pence, minimum forty-eight hours cover, payable in advance.' He looked her in the eye, gleefully taking in the doubt. 'Now, do you want to give me those keys?'

Behind her the whole queue came noisily to life, no longer a long thin snake of individuals but a cooperative and indignant huddle. As Lucy stood there, at a loss as to what to do, a smiley woman in a pompom hat stepped forwards and stood beside her.

'Hold on,' she said first to the rep, sounding polite and jolly, but with a don't-mess-with-me edge. 'I'll be with you in a second.' Then she gave Lucy a great grin. 'I've been hatching the most wonderful plan,' she said, nodding back to a group of triumphant-looking Deals on Wheels customers. 'We're going to give each other lifts. We can't believe there are many axe-murderers here among us, and it makes it all so much cheaper. And more fun too, don't you think? Is Manchester any good for you? There's a three who could do with one more. Then you won't even need his stupid little car.'

'I did want to get back to London tonight . . .' Was it such a good idea? Did she want to share? Lucy knew she had to decide fast but she couldn't seem to think it through clearly.

'Well, we've got three lots of four going to London already. And we've got a four sharing to Luton and a people-carrier going to Gatwick, but they're both full too, and I've agreed with the couple behind you,' the lady pointed to the nervous couple who'd been standing directly behind Lucy, 'to share a lift to Ashford. We've got room for one more for Ashford.'

'Did you say Ashford?' It was an old man, appearing from the very back of the queue, hobbling up to the pompom-hatted lady on a silver-tipped cane and giving Lucy a few seconds to think. 'Ashford would be marvellous.'

'Actually, I was just offering the space to this young lady . . .' The woman looked enquiringly back to Lucy.

'But you must have it,' Lucy told him.

'Are you sure?'

Lucy nodded. 'It's a great idea, but I want to go to London. Surely there must be more of us . . .'

'I could do you Kings Lynn,' a good-looking man in a pin-stripe suit came up and told her, giving a reassuring, trust-me-I'm-a-doctor sort of smile. 'Promise I won't bite.'

'I'll share with you,' replied a morose-looking woman. She had plaits and a nose like a bent finger and was sitting on her rucksack. 'But I can't drive.'

They'd moved so fast it seemed that Lucy had been left behind.

'Anyone else for London?' she called out loudly, taking the plunge. 'Share the insurance and I've got the car.'

'I do not approve of this. I do not approve of this *at all*.' The rep's face was mottled purple. 'Deals on Wheels does not sanction this action.'

'Hey, you nearly made it rhyme!' the woman in the pompom hat congratulated him. 'And we can do what we jolly well like. We're not breaking your silly rules.'

The man looked at her incredulously, picked up his telephone and urgently tapped in a number. 'You are being extremely foolhardy.'

'Oh, give up,' she told him. 'Just stop it.'

'I was going to London,' someone said to Lucy.

And of all the people standing in the queue, of course it had to be him, quietly arriving at her shoulder.

'London,' she called out again to the rest of the queue, not acknowledging him, hoping someone out there would come to her aid. 'Anyone want to go to London?'

'Yes, I do,' the man said agreeably.

She turned to him. 'I'm sorry, but I don't want to share with you.'

Had she actually said it out loud?

The rep turned to Lucy and put his hand over the receiver of the telephone. 'Have to say, madam,' he said with a gleeful smile, 'I think that's wise.'

Lucy looked away. She knew it would sound ridiculous to anyone she tried to explain it to, but it was the truth. She really didn't want to share with him. Ten, twelve hours alone in a car with him would be impossible. He was too pristine and perfect, with his shiny shoes and his cashmere coat. He made her feel hungover and out of her depth. If she had to share with anyone she wanted it to be some safe, comforting middle-aged couple who would listen to Classic FM and let her sleep on the back seat while they took on all the driving.

She glanced at him, wondering how he'd taken it, and was irritated to catch the amusement in his eyes, because of course he thought she was joking. He might even admit she was being quite funny, as long as she didn't keep it up any longer.

'Come on,' he said impatiently when she said nothing more. 'I'm just what you're looking for.'

Now he'd really blown it.

He waited for a moment more but when she continued to ignore him he shrugged and turned away.

'Anyone like to share a lift to London?' he called, standing shoulder to shoulder with Lucy, who then asked exactly the same thing, a little louder. Neither of them got any response.

'Gatwick? Birmingham?' Lucy tried, colour rising in her cheeks, feeling completely ridiculous. 'I've got the car.' There was still no response. 'Glasgow?' she said more half-heartedly.

'Looks as if it's just you and me.'

'I said I don't want to share a lift with—'

'Oh, go on with you!' The lady in the pompom hat interrupted Lucy in exasperation. 'You ninny, what are you shouting about if you don't want to share a lift with someone? Don't spoil everything! We're sorting it all out great, apart from you two. What's the matter with you?'

'It's none of your business,' Lucy told her, feeling stupid, because of course the woman was right. She was abruptly manoeuvred out of earshot of the man.

'I agree, it's none of my business,' the pompom hat lady whispered at her. 'But even so, I'll remind you that it is five hundred miles to London. On your own that's twelve, thirteen hours driving *at least*, non-stop and in this filthy weather. Just how are you planning to do it?'

Lucy shrugged. 'Slowly.'

'But I thought you wanted to be back in London today?'

'I do.'

'Then trust me.' Rather too enthusiastically the woman patted Lucy's cheek. 'Silly girl,' she said. 'I know he looks smoother than a jar of face cream but you'll be safe with him. I've stood next to him in the queue for the past twenty minutes and I can tell he's a gentleman.'

'I doubt he'd be interested in being anything else,' piped up the woman with the nose and the plaits, giving Lucy a critical once-over.

33

Lucy was quite hurt. She didn't look that bad. And what was this? Were all these people completely mad? Hadn't any of them heard that you didn't get into cars with strangers, especially strangers you had doubts about, whatever they looked like? And the truth was, she thought, looking glumly down at her feet, that it was precisely because he looked so smooth that he made her feel so rough. Because he was so assured and capable that she felt so stubbornly determined not to have him around.

'You know, I do understand.' He was looking over the pompom hat directly at Lucy, staring at her with what were now rather soulful brown eyes, and there was a new sincerity in his voice. 'I'd say the same thing if I was you.'

'Would you? Then why did you ask me?'

'I guess I was trying my luck. Because I do very much want to get back to London tonight. But it's perfectly OK. You don't know me. You shouldn't feel any pressure to share a car with me.'

Lucy nodded. Now, of course, he was getting somewhere. She dithered, wondering whether to relent or listen to the panicky voice that still gabbled on in her head about how it was too early in the morning to cope with someone like him, how she needed time to herself, time to think. She looked at him uncertainly.

'So I'm sorry I asked.' He turned back to the rep, who was still waiting for his call to be answered. 'I need a car for London. I'll take anything.'

'No, *sir*, you won't.' It gave the rep great pleasure to say so. 'We have no vehicles available. Very few of our customers made it back to the airport this morning. Perhaps you might like to come back in a couple of hours and try again?'

'Perhaps I'll do that.' He turned to go, then looked back at Lucy and gave her a nod of farewell. 'Drive carefully.'

Lucy reached into her handbag, found her purse and turned swiftly to the rep, presenting him with her Visa card. 'I'll pay for the international insurance,' she told him. 'Four hundred quid, whatever it was.' Perhaps her travel insurance would kick in. She doubted it. 'And put this man on the insurance, too.'

The rep put down his telephone. He looked so disappointed Lucy thought he might be about to cry.

'And name him as a driver. He'll definitely be sharing the driving with me.'

'Thank you,' the man said, coming back to her, looking genuinely surprised and relieved.

'No problem. What's your name? You need to tell the rep.'

He held out his hand and she shook it, noticing his shiny pink nails.

'It's Jude. Jude Middleton,' he told the rep.

'I'm Lucy Blue.'

He turned back to her. 'What a wonderful name. But people must say that to you all the time?'

Hey Jude, you're right. They do.'

He laughed, and as she found herself smiling back at him again she imagined telling her friend Jane about him the next day; how indignant Jane'd be. *What do you mean you nearly didn't give him a lift?* And then, *How come this kind of thing always happens to you? How come I never get to share a lift with a gorgeous man?*

But that wasn't why I did it, Lucy would insist, truly I did it because he made me feel sorry for him, absolutely nothing to do with that smile. She'd changed her mind and had offered him the lift because the pompom lady was right, it was ridiculous to think she could drive the whole way back to London on her own, and she would almost certainly be safer with him than without him. And what was more, now she'd be saving at least two hundred quid on the insurance. And then there was the bonus of being able to annoy the Deals on Wheels rep again.

*

'Do you mind if I make a quick call before we leave?' he asked, just as they reached the car. 'I had someone picking me up at Gatwick. I'd like to let them know I won't be there.'

He pulled out his mobile and walked away from her and Lucy stood for a moment, letting the snowflakes fall on her upturned hands, then tilted her face to the sky and caught a few more on her tongue. The wind had dropped away but the snow was still falling solidly, and she wondered whether she and Jude and everyone else in the Deals on Wheels queue were mad to think about driving through it. She guessed they would find out soon enough. She turned back to her car and unlocked it, swept an armful of snow off the windscreen and wiped her wing mirrors, opened the boot and threw in her overnight bag before slamming it shut again and dislodging a great heap of snow from the roof on to her feet as she did so. She walked around to the driver's side, shaking the snow away, then took off her coat, climbed in and started the engine, turned on the heating, took the map off the passenger seat, dropped it on to the seat behind her and prepared to wait.

She watched Jude through the windscreen. Now that they were out of the airport terminal and the journey was about to begin, she was regretting it all over again. She wished she'd at least put on some make-up to combat the effects of the night before. She wondered if this made her a very superficial person and decided that it probably did, but she had fair skin, and eyelashes that came to life with a little mascara and disappeared without it. Of course what she looked like hadn't mattered when she'd got out of bed. And it hadn't mattered when she'd entered the airport because she'd thought she would scuttle through, meeting nobody. But it was mattering now, now that she'd set eyes on Jude Middleton.

She ran her hands through her hair and checked herself in the mirror, then surreptitiously breathed on the back of her hand and sniffed. How long would they be on the road? She'd guessed ten hours, but the pompom lady had said thirteen. She was going to be sharing a lift with this man until approximately eleven that night, no distractions, nothing for them to do but get to know each other, and the least she should do, and for Jude's sake not hers, was gargle with a bit of toothpaste.

She looked out of the window again, watched him sliding his fingers through his silky hair as he talked on his phone, smoothing and straightening it perfectly into place as he walked slowly away from the car, across the car park, disappearing into the snow, clearly completely absorbed. She wondered who he was talking to ... his girlfriend perhaps? *Baby, you won't believe it, my flight's been cancelled. Yes, I know, me too, me too ... But I'm driving down! I've persuaded someone to share a lift ... yes, darling, a girl ... God, don't worry about that, you're quite safe. Breath like a dead badger ...*

She opened the car door, crouching down and slipping to the back of the car, opened the boot and unzipped her overnight bag, finding her toothbrush and toothpaste, then rezipped the bag, shut the boot gently and slipped back to her seat again. Toothpaste on brush, swig of water, furious brushing, a surreptitious gargle and spit into the snow. She opened her handbag, and quickly stuffed in the toothpaste and brush and zipped it shut again just as Jude opened the door. He paused, seeming to sniff the air appreciatively.

'OK if I drive first?' she asked him as he took off his scarf, a pair of soft leather gloves, then carefully unbuttoned his beautiful black coat, folded it and dropped it on to the back seat. She wanted to be in control at least until she'd had a chance to get the measure of him. 'We could swap over when we stop for petrol.'

'Whatever you want,' he said, bending his head and climbing in beside her.

'I guess we should just head south?' she asked, starting the engine and thinking how big he seemed in the little car.

'We need to follow the signs for Fort William, and then

to Perth.' He leaned round and reached for the back seat, practically kissing her as he did so, and took the map from under his coat. He cupped his hands and blew on them, then opened it and started to turn the pages. 'We'll cross the Slochd summit and then go over the Drumochter Pass. We want the A9 and after that we'll drop down on to the M74 and join the motorways. I guess the snow won't be so bad down there.'

'You sound as if you know the route.'

'Some of it.'

Jude didn't elaborate, so Lucy started the car and tentatively followed her nose out of the airport and looked for the signs to Fort William.

'Got some petrol?'

She nodded. She could hear a deliberate formality in his tone now, which she supposed wasn't surprising after the awkwardness in the airport, and the megawatt smile was nowhere to be seen. He'd probably concluded that she was mouthy and charmless and best left alone. She wondered whether she should say something, try to explain, and then she stopped herself. No regrets and no apologies. She didn't have to make him like her. It was her car. She'd chosen to share it with him. And anyway, she hadn't really been rude to him, she'd just been honest, looking after herself, cautious about travelling with a stranger, a lone man. And she'd brushed her teeth for him, after all.

The car suddenly skidded in the snow, sending them sliding sideways towards the ditch, and belatedly she woke up to the fact that she was driving again. In the short time since she'd first arrived at the airport the snow had clearly deepened and become more treacherous. Even within the ring roads of Inverness, with the gritters and snowploughs working hard, the road was still covered in deep fresh snow. Turning corners would need care and attention and a certain degree of luck.

'It's OK,' she reassured Jude the third time his head shot up from the map in alarm. 'I had the same trouble all the way here, although perhaps it wasn't quite so bad. But as long as there's nothing coming the other way, I find it's best to let the car right itself.'

He nodded and swallowed but said nothing, watching with her as she waited for a space in the traffic before slowly pulling out on to a roundabout.

'I nearly hit a stag on the way here . . .' She flicked on the indicator and turned off to the left as she talked. 'Well, I say *nearly hit* but actually it leapt over the bonnet of the car.' She paused and glanced across to him, unnerved by the cold, flat look on his face. 'It was beautiful . . .' she tailed off.

'I'd put the headlights on,' he said, looking down at the map again, 'and speed up the windscreen wipers.'

'I was just about to.'

She carefully moved up into third gear, then fourth, and when he said nothing more she told herself it was perfect if he didn't want to talk to her, that silence was what she wanted too. But who was she kidding? Now that she and Jude were in the car together, Lucy desperately wanted to talk to him, to lay the ghost of awkwardness hanging over them since the airport. Already this journey was so different from when she'd been on her own. Then she had thrived on the silence, but now the two of them, sitting side by side but not talking, didn't feel good at all but awkward and spiky. Once or twice she opened her mouth to speak, to ask him what it was he'd been doing in Inverness, where he was going once he got back to London, even who it was he'd been calling on his phone, but each time the look on his face made her close it again and say nothing.

She drove on, thinking how unexpected this was. In her imagination he'd been charming and flirtatious, intimidating even, dominating the conversation and tying her sleepy brain into knots with his witty chat. Instead, as she peered through the windscreen, carefully giving him the mother of all lifts, having kindly saved him from hours and hours at Inverness airport, he looked as if he was falling asleep. And Lucy imagined the shock on his face if she suddenly pulled the car over and stopped, told him that it simply wasn't good enough, that his behaviour wasn't up to scratch, that she felt he'd misled her and if he wasn't prepared to contribute to the mood of the journey he could get out.

'Are you OK?' he asked suddenly.

'Yes. Why?'

'You sighed.'

'Did I?' She knew she hadn't made a sound.

'Or was it a sneeze?' She looked at him, eyebrows raised, and he nodded towards the windscreen. 'You should watch the road.'

'I am watching the road.'

'You're OK then?'

41

'I'm fine!'

'And you know we want the A9 at the next round-about?'

'Yes, I do.'

'Not too tired to drive me safely home?'

'I want to drive myself safely home, remember.'

'Sure you do. But any time you want to change over, you should let me know.'

She nodded and stared irritably through the wind-screen, keeping her eyes away from him. And when at last she did sneak a look, it was to see that he'd stretched out his legs and turned away from her.

'I don't think you should go to sleep.'

His looked back at her. 'Were you talking to me?'

'Of course I was talking to you. Who else is sitting in this car?'

'I'm sorry.'

'I was thinking it would be nice if you talked to me,' she said.

He pushed himself up in his seat. 'And I was thinking it was better to leave you alone. Because you're clearly not a morning person, are you?' He waited. 'Or is it me?'

How dare he say that? What a bloody cheek! Yet she couldn't stop herself beginning to smile as she stared straight ahead at the road.

'It's you,' she retorted. 'Falling asleep instead of keeping me company.'

'I wasn't asleep, I was just resting my eyes.'

'That's rubbish. And aren't you interested in finding something out about your chauffeur?'

He pretended to think about it, then shook his head. 'I don't think so, no.'

'I'll drop you off at a bus stop then, shall I?' It was almost impossible not to keep looking at him, but the road was twisting and turning and great gusts of snow were being ripped about by the wind. 'Let me concentrate on driving.'

'You're doing fine, as long as you remember to keep looking ahead and not at me all the time.'

'That's easy enough.'

'And of course I want to talk to you. I got the impression you didn't want to talk to me, that's all. Not yet, anyway. But I think it's wonderful, you and me, sharing a lift, not knowing each other at all. It's such a one-off, don't you think? We could get back to London and find that the drive down from Inverness, experiencing the entire M6 motorway along the way – was a wonderful, life-changing experience.'

She wasn't sure if he was being serious. 'Strangers share journeys all the time,' she said crisply. 'It's just that ours is going to be longer than most.'

'I think that's what I meant.'

She heaved a sigh. 'I'm sorry.'

'That's OK.'

'I had too little sleep last night.'

He nodded. 'So did you have a good time?'

'Awful.' She saw him start to smile, then think that perhaps he shouldn't. 'That's right, you're not allowed to laugh because, as far as I can remember, the evening wasn't in the slightest bit funny.'

'Mine was. I had great fun.'

'Good for you. The best bit of my stay was leaving this morning.'

'The best bit of mine was dancing to the Sugarbabes with my eleven-year-old-cousins.'

She laughed in surprise. 'How did you manage that?'

'My mother got her sister to invite me because she was worried I'd be on my own for New Year's Eve. So I came from Aberdeen last night, only to find the parents were off to a party and I'd been brought down as the babysitter.'

'How mean of them.'

'No. The girls were lovely. We made banana and rum milkshakes.'

'You fed them rum!'

'Just a teaspoon.'

Lucy risked a quick glance. 'And otherwise you'd have done nothing? Didn't you have hundreds of swanky parties to choose from?'

'Now why would you think that?'

'Because you look the sort.'

'Said with true disdain.'

She shook her head. 'Not at all.'

'So what is my sort? What do you think I do in Aberdeen?'

'I've no idea.'

'Have a go.'

'Are we going to have to spend the whole journey talking about you?'

'No. We could spend it talking about you.'

She shook her head. 'I don't think so.'

'No? Then I suppose we could talk about aquaculture in the Inner Hebrides, or the long-term implications of the Criminal Justice Bill? What would you like to talk about?'

'I'd guess you sell aftershave,' she said, just to shut him up.

Jude spluttered satisfyingly. 'You can't say that.'

'Yes I can. You asked me what I think you do and I'm telling you.'

'You mean I'm a model? I'm flattered.'

'Did I say that?'

'No,' he admitted. 'Actually I work on the rigs.'

This was obviously meant to silence her, but for a long moment Lucy couldn't imagine what he meant, wondering vaguely if The Rigs could be some trendy Scottish magazine.

'Doing what?'

'I fly the guys out and I bring them back again.'

'Fly them out?' she repeated, knowing she was sounding really slow. He even looked disappointed, as if he'd had high hopes for her and what a shame to find she'd only got half a brain after all. But right now, even her half brain wouldn't do its business and work. In fact her whole head felt as if it hadn't been screwed on properly.

'I fly helicopters on and off the oil-rigs,' he said slowly. 'I work off the coast of Aberdeen. North Sea oil, Lucy, maybe you've heard of it?'

But this fashion statement in his long cashmere coat, with his spiky eyelashes and his glossy hair, could *not* work on oil-rigs. He was tea-tree oil, not North Sea oil; cashmere coats, not oilskins. Oil-rigs had men in boilersuits with grimy faces shouting to be heard above the hundred-mile-an-hour winds. Oil-rigs had tiny cabins, with no room to balance a bar of soap let alone the several washbags worth of expensive products that Jude would no doubt need beside him.

'You don't!' she laughed.

'Yes, I do. Why do you think it's so strange?'

'You're too clean.'

'I live in Aberdeen. I don't live on the rigs.'

She nodded, taking it in. 'So, do you get to see any of the drilling?' she asked, trying to sound serious. 'Or is it all done by computer now? No need to get your hands dirty, just a question of moving things around on a screen?'

He shrugged. 'I fly the helicopters on and off the rigs. The men out there work two- or three-week shifts. They need bringing back to shore and the new shift needs flying out. I've been doing it for about eight months.' He leaned close towards her so that she could feel his breath warm on her face. 'And yes, sometimes I watch the drilling.'

Do that again, she thought. Involuntarily she touched her hand to her cheek.

'It must be so wet and so cold?'

'I tend not to land in the sea.'

'You know what I mean. It must be a hard life.' She'd wanted to say a windswept, miserable, lonely life. 'Surely there are other places to fly helicopters, warmer places?'

'I've done that too. I used to fly helicopters for the Navy. I left last year.'

That was more like it. A suntan, aviator shades, gleaming white teeth. She could picture him in the Navy.

'Why did you leave?'

'Fancied the change.'

And the suddenly clipped way that he said it told her not to ask why.

*

They reached the Drumochter Pass relieved to find that it hadn't yet been closed, then threaded their way painstakingly slowly between the mountains which, even on this day, with the sky low and visibility so poor, were stark against the snow and very bleak. Lucy could only glance up, awestruck, as Jude did, catching the briefest of glimpses of the huge wet boulders, the steep granite slopes, before the snow enveloped them again.

As soon as they'd crossed the pass the road widened again, but still visibility was so bad that Lucy had to concentrate completely on the road and neither of them spoke at all. All she could think, as she gritted her teeth and drove carefully on, was how very relieved she was to have Jude beside her. How scary and daunting this journey would have been if she'd been making it alone.

'Were you in Aberdeen over Christmas?' she asked him eventually, when she was able slowly to pick up speed again. 'I guess the rigs don't close down for the holidays?'

'Yes, I was, and no, they don't.'

'It must have been hard.'

'There was tinsel and a turkey,' he said flippantly. 'What more did I need?'

'Family? Friends?' She didn't want to let it go. 'Didn't you miss them?'

'Of course, but that's why I'm here with you now, heading home. And I expect there'll still be a Christmas tree and some leftover turkey.'

'So are you the prodigal son?'

'No, I think his mother *cooked* him a fatted calf,' he grinned at her. 'Mine will have been *burned*.' But even though he was joking there was an edge to his words. 'And then it will have had a bottle of wine poured over it, always my mother's solution to a crisis.'

So's that where the problems lie, Lucy wondered. And the way she'd stepped in to set up his New Year's Eve perhaps meant his mother was rather interfering too. Not surprising that Jude was wary of seeing her again.

'And my father will have planned a fun job for me, drainage pipes needing laying at the bottom of some freezing field, something like that.'

Perhaps his father liked keeping far out of the way too?

'I'm meeting my brother in London and then we're meant to be driving on to Oxford tonight. Three and a half days of family bonding.' He turned to her and grinned. 'You know what? It's my idea of hell.'

She was surprised that he'd admit such a thing, but she kept her voice light. 'You shouldn't have made such an effort to persuade me to give you a lift.'

He was still looking at her. 'I decided you were worth it.'

It was so unexpected that as she kept her eyes on the road she could feel herself start to blush, and hoped desperately that he wouldn't notice. Ignore it. Don't react at all, she told herself. Twelve more hours in the car with him could only be survived if she didn't react at all.

'So is it ages since they've seen you?'

'A few months, not so long.'

There was a long pause.

'Where does he live, your brother?'

'In Notting Hill, off Moreton Road.'

'How funny. I'm going to a party there next weekend.'

'Come and knock on my door?'

'We'll have had enough of each other by then.'

'You know that's not true.'

And immediately she felt it again, anticipation and excitement, and again she tried to stamp it out. But the tune had begun now inside her head and it wasn't going to stop. 'I could drive you back there tonight, if you like.'

'That would be very nice of you.'

She nodded, saying nothing.

'So where do you live?' he asked.

'Barons Court.'

'Deals on Wheels has an office in Hammersmith.'

'How do you know that?'

'I asked at the desk when I was filling out the forms.'

'Jude!'

'What's the problem? I knew one of us had to take the car back. I was being efficient. And, any other time, of course I'd be offering. But I haven't been home for such a long time. And we're going to be so late . . . And now they know I'm still coming, they'll be waiting up.'

Nothing about her plans, she noticed. It didn't occur to him that someone might have been waiting up for her too. But she had offered to drop him back.

'This trip home is such a big deal.'

49

'It's OK,' she said quietly. 'I don't mind taking you to your brother's.'

'Thank you, Lucy. Luke and I . . .' he paused again, clasping his hands together tightly on his lap. 'Oh, sod it. If I'd got stuck in Inverness, I know they'd have thought I was making some excuse . . .'

'Why don't you want to go home?'

He turned to her. 'Why does it bother you if I don't?'

'Because it's sad.'

'Don't say it like that. Everything's fine. I love them, they love me.'

But even as she heard herself apologizing, she was thinking it had been a natural enough question to ask. He'd made so little attempt to disguise his feelings, it was almost as if he'd wanted to provoke her into asking.

'I'm sorry,' Jude said. 'I mean, they're used to me being late, that's all, not turning up for things, forgetting birthdays, being unreliable.' He was smoothing everything over again, the charm back in his voice, the smile back on his face. 'And they'll be waiting up, telling each other how hopeless I am and what a shame poor Luke – my brother – has had to spend the whole day waiting for me. You know, family stuff.'

'But you couldn't help the snow.'

'I couldn't help the snow. Will you tell them that for me?'

'I'll tell your brother if I meet him.'

'I expect he'll be out on the steps the moment we reach his front door.' He looked at his watch, then back at her. 'An hour and a half down. What do you think, twelve more to go?' Restlessly he drummed his hands on his knees. 'Guilt,' he said shortly. 'That's what it is – the closer I get to them, the more guilty I feel.'

He veered between openness and evasiveness so constantly that Lucy was at a loss as to how to react.

'Tell me about your party,' he demanded, immediately moving on. 'Was it really so bad?'

'Terrible.'

'Why?'

'Honestly? Because I think I'd imagined myself waltzing into the room in my sexy pink dress, wowing everybody with my glamour and my air of mystery. And it didn't exactly work out like that.'

Seeing surprise on his face, Lucy cringed. What was she doing, telling him that? Honesty was so rarely the best policy and now she imagined him thinking, *How funny, you seriously thought you could wow an entire room?*

'Mad Blind Idiots of Inverness, was that who the party was for?'

She grinned at him gratefully.

'I'd have been wowed.'

'Oh, shut up. Just because I said I'd drive you home.'

'No, of course I'd have noticed you. And your sexy pink dress.'

'Someone called Julia Clegg, an old school-friend, invited me. But I hadn't seen her for years.'

'And then you remembered why.'

She laughed. 'Exactly.'

'So why did you go?'

'Because she invited me at just the right moment. I

needed some time on my own.' She glanced at him. 'You know that feeling, don't you? When it's time to get away for a bit . . .' *Of course he knew what she meant. It was why he was in Aberdeen, wasn't it?*

But Jude wasn't about to admit it. He simply sat there, silently, letting the momentum of the conversation die away. And Lucy drove on, thinking how every time she sensed he was about to take her cue and talk more openly, he moved out of reach again. And so she didn't say any more, although she'd like to have told him about Teddy. She'd have explained how she'd finally binned him just before Christmas to cheers from her family and friends, and to tears of relief from her friend Jane, who'd immediately announced that at times she'd wondered if she'd lost Lucy for good. She'd have told Jude how Teddy had refused to believe her when she'd said it was over. How he had persisted in calling her every day over Christmas, much to her family's dismay: clearly Lucy hadn't been quite convincing enough. Didn't she realize there was no point trying to be his friend? And how she knew she was going to have to be that bit more convincing once she got back to London, this time telling him so firmly that he'd have no choice but to believe it. She'd have told Jude how difficult it was because she and Teddy worked in the same company and how they had to continue to get on for the sake of their work, how he was bound to be there at her desk first thing the next morning. If Jude had wanted to listen, she could have spent the next hour telling him all about Teddy.

She remembered him as she'd seen him last, just before

she'd left to join her family for Christmas. He'd watched as she'd packed, occasionally commenting on the things he liked, or didn't like, dismissing her pink party dress, then flicking at a lovely black shift dress and asking where she'd be wearing *that*? And she'd told him: drinks party, Christmas Eve, friends of her parents, keeping her head down, thinking to herself over and over again that this was it. And she'd waited until she was standing in the communal hall of the mansion block where she lived, with her coat on and her handbag in hand, her suitcase packed at her feet and the taxi waiting for her outside, and then, out of the blue, she'd told him that she wasn't coming to Norfolk for New Year with his parents after all, she was going to Inverness, to a party on her own. And then she told him how she didn't want to see him when she got back to London again either. And once he'd got the gist of what she was saying, he'd talked loudly through every next word she'd said as if he hadn't taken in a thing. He'd held the door open for her and had steered her out on to the street, packed her into the taxi, refusing to listen, saying that he would call her that evening and that he'd see her when she got back on Boxing Day. And that he hoped she liked his Christmas present. And she'd stopped, in a way so elated that she'd said anything at all and so grateful to be getting away from him that she'd hardly cared he hadn't listened. But then, just as the taxi was preparing to drive off, her courage had returned, and she'd called out of the window that she wasn't coming back to London on Boxing Day, she was staying away until after New Year. She would go to Scotland for New Year's Eve, straight from her parents' house. And she'd seen from the way he stopped and stared back at her in surprise that finally she'd got through to him.

Now she looked across at Jude again and saw in frustration that he'd closed his eyes once more. Open them, she wanted to insist. I need you to tell me what to do with him when I walk into my office tomorrow morning. But closing his eyes was clearly Jude's way of cutting short a conversation he didn't like. Why he mightn't like it she didn't know, because surely she was demanding nothing of him? Was it that he was wary of getting personal? Or was it simply that he was afraid she was about to bore him, to pour out her heart for hours and hours?

With one hand on the steering-wheel she stretched to reach the back seat and her handbag, and beside her Jude opened his eyes.

'What do you want?'

'My phone. Can you find it in my bag and turn it off for me?'

He asked for no explanation. She watched him unlock the phone for her and switch it off, and she felt first relief wash through her – that Teddy was no longer able to burst in on them in the car – and then anger with herself that he could still make her feel anything at all. Then Jude put the phone back in her bag and dropped it behind her seat and moved forward to switch on the radio and music suddenly filled her head, drowning out all thoughts of Teddy.

He moved them from station to station, gauging her opinion of what was playing as he went – Radiohead moving into Simon and Garfunkel's *America*. Kings of

Convenience into the Alabama 3, the Black Eyed Peas and the Red Hot Chilli Peppers. And the music lifted her spirits again, helped her remember and rediscover the person she'd been on that journey to the airport. And they sat there silently together, gradually building up the soundtrack of their own road-movie, as another hour slipped by.

And when they turned the radio off again, it was as if the music had loosened Jude's hold on himself because finally he started to talk, still not much about himself but happy to tell her more about the oilfields and his life on board the rigs, how they towered hundreds of feet above the sea and how they could creak in storms like huge ships. And she would sometimes not even be able to hear what he was saying but she'd smile anyway and nod, enjoying the sound of the calm rise and fall of his voice against the mesmerizing hum of the car on the snowy road. And now she was relaxed because she knew that Jude was relaxed too, and sometimes she was leaning in to listen to him and sometimes she was hearing no words at all but was simply liking him being there beside her. And then occasionally he'd break into her thoughts and ask her something, and she'd turn to him briefly as she drove and would be suddenly acutely aware of him there, so close. Or she'd think he was about to speak and she'd glance across but he'd say nothing at all, would just be looking at her, waiting for her to look at him, and then she'd feel a fingertip of excitement slide softly down her spine, and she'd grip the wheel and fix her eyes straight ahead at the road and not at him.

4

'Don't you wish we'd found some Hip Hotel and holed up for a few days?'

She darted a look at him, and he stretched in his seat and raised his eyebrows back at her.

'I meant don't you wish you were taking advantage of the snow? It's a good excuse not to go back to work, isn't it?'

She kept her eyes on the road, forcing herself not to react.

'I don't mean like that. Although I'm sure like that would be good.'

'I'm responsible. I'm very hard-working. Don't talk to me about skiving off.'

'What do you do?'

'Headhunting,' she said crisply. 'First I trained as a vet but then I became a headhunter instead.'

'Why did you do that? Why did you change?'

'Because I realized I didn't like animals enough.'

He laughed in surprise.

'But when I say I don't like them –' she was smiling too, still going over what he'd said about the Hip Hotel – 'I mean I don't like *little* animals, pregnant gerbils and guinea-pigs with ingrowing toenails, that kind of thing. I like horses, cattle . . . but you don't get that many of them in London. So last year I changed direction and became a headhunter instead.'

'And who do you hunt? Are you good at it? Do you like it?'

'I hunt anyone – producers, directors, graphic designers, marketing directors. I could be hunting on behalf of someone who's ready to change jobs, or for a company with a space to fill. But I sometimes wonder if I'm making a mistake.' She nodded towards the window, out towards the distant highlands where the snow was clearing and they could now see light across the farthest hills, and for a moment she held her breath, it was so beautiful. 'No more Barons Court station at seven in the morning. Find somewhere like this to live instead.' She stopped abruptly, thinking of heels and fifteen-denier tights, of getting up at six when it was still pitch dark, of arriving at her office, of how the adrenalin cranked up her heart rate whenever she pushed her way through those heavy glass doors. 'But after a holiday the first morning's always a horrible experience, isn't it? By lunchtime I won't even remember I've been away. You must feel it too?' She glanced across to Jude but he had turned away, looking out of the window, and she wasn't even sure he was still listening and again she was left feeling excluded from what was going on in his head.

Then the road narrowed and darkened again and they entered a deep, dark forest of pine trees, adding a spooky edge to the muffled sound of wheels on snow, paths twisting between the trees where the snow had not yet reached, and then they were out on the other side, back in the daylight, grey light, once more, and it was clear that the snow really had eased off. At times it had been rushing at them, so aggressively gusting and beating on the windscreen with rage that it had been almost impossible to see the road, but now it was tumbling softly, the downy flakes taking their time to fall, and from the vague ache in the back of her eyes that heralded the lifting of the clouds, Lucy guessed that soon the snow would stop completely.

She thought about Julia, whose New Year's Eve party it had been and who lived here all year round, in an old hunting-lodge a few miles from the Kirk Castle Hotel. Julia Clegg, who could gut a stag where it had fallen, kneeling in the heather with her hunting knife, a velvet scrunchie holding back her fine blonde hair, but who had passed out last night after only a few glasses of wine. Four seasons in one day, Julia had said, while she could still talk, that's what she loved about where she lived. Lucy had arrived in darkness and hadn't understood but now she could look out of her windscreen and appreciate exactly what Julia meant.

Far in the distance, across the huge flat expanse of moorland and up towards the mountains, the clouds had broken and shafts of pale sunlight had started to fall upon the peaks, making the snow around them glow with an alabaster light. She could even see a sliver of cobalt-blue sky.

And then Jude said quietly, 'Such a perfect day,' and Lucy turned to him in surprise and he reached for her hand and squeezed it gently. 'I'm glad I'm sharing it with you.'

But a strange, inexplicable sadness reached into her at

his words and she found herself stretching for his hand again, but letting it go almost before she'd touched him.

'I'm glad I'm sharing it with you.'

He said nothing more, and for a long time they drove on in silence, but by touching her hand he'd reached something inside her too, so that whereas before she'd sat beside him so comfortably, so light-hearted, now she found herself disrupted, intensely aware of him there next to her.

They passed a garage that looked shut up for the winter, and Lucy checked the petrol gauge and saw that they had just under a third of a tank left. She flicked on the car's computer, to find that they had now travelled a hundred and eighty-seven miles at an average speed of fifty-six miles per hour and that the temperature outside was minus four. She drove on, thinking of sleety rain and an oily black North Sea, roaring and crashing against the huge oil-rigs, and wondered how Jude could have ended up there, what it was that had taken him from the Navy, whether he'd been asked to leave or had chosen to go. She wondered about his life, whether he had a girlfriend, and if he did, how serious it could be with him away so much. She wondered where he lived in Aberdeen, whether he was planning on staying for another year, whether he might be thinking like her, that New Year's Day was a day for changes. And then he coughed, shifted in his seat and turned towards her, and she looked and saw that he'd fallen asleep, his mouth a little open, his head wedged between the headrest and the seatbelt, and when he didn't stir she looked again, in snatched glances as she drove.

She wanted to touch him. Asleep he was so defenceless

and sweet and alone and tired, his closed eyes sunk deep into their sockets, his full lips chapped and rough and the skin beneath his stubbly cheeks a pale biscuit brown, as if he'd seen a lot of sun but a long, long time ago, with a faint smattering of freckles there below his eyes. Awake, he was perhaps too vain, and it annoyed her that he barely listened when she talked about herself and did the disappearing act on her once too often, that he was flippant and evasive and that she could hardly say she knew him any better now than when he'd first got into the car. But asleep, her hand so badly wanted to stroke his face that she had almost reached his cheek before she realized what she was doing.

He was wearing baggy dark jeans but all she could see were the long muscular legs beneath them, and a heavy zip-up jumper she wanted to unzip. She took in the breadth of his shoulders and the narrowness of his waist. No doubt his mother would tell him he was far too thin, would bring him a huge breakfast in bed and inedible suppers of leftover, over-cooked turkey and Christmas pudding. She looked at his sleeping face, at the soft black hair cut close to his scalp, and wondered what she looked like, what kind of mother would have such a beautiful son as Jude. And then, what kind of girl might have a boyfriend like him.

They were approaching another roundabout now, with signs to the motorway ahead of them, and she changed down a gear and slowed ready for the turn, and Jude stirred with the movement and stretched out his arms. She wondered if they'd ever see each other again after she dropped him off at his brother's house, whether they'd swap phone numbers, at least pretending that they'd stay in touch. And she knew even then that she wouldn't want to. That Jude was part of this strange one-off day and it wouldn't be the same to see him again.

Then he swallowed and shifted again in his seat, turning to face her and at the same time his hand fell into her lap, palm up, where it stayed resting lightly on her thighs. And by the time she realized what she was doing she'd crossed both lanes of the roundabout and veered back in again, just missing the kerb, before finally righting the car and driving on. *You silly bugger*, she whispered at him. *See what you made me do?* But Jude didn't stir, his head stayed just where it was, and all Lucy could think was that Teddy had never, ever had that effect on her.

She looked at his long fingers still there in her lap and imagined them coming to life, wondered what they'd do, where they'd go next, and her stomach flipped over at the thought. She lifted his hand off her legs and dropped it back on his own. He was just a good looking man hitching a lift, taking advantage of the fact that they were alone together to have some fun, see how many knots he could tie her into, he wasn't going to think about her once he got home. And so she couldn't let him get to her. She couldn't, mustn't behave in the wholly predictable way he expected her to.

But why not? a little voice asked inside her head. After all, they'd been in the car alone together for nearly four hours *and now he was lying asleep beside her* and he wasn't so much good-looking as walk-into-a-lamppost gorgeous.

Of course her mind was bound to wander and she was bound to wonder. Since when was that so wrong? She looked across at him for a third time, and he seemed to smile up at her in his sleep.

But then as she drove over the brow of a hill she saw another petrol station ahead, this one lit up against the snowy road. And she knew that it would be the last before the motorway, that she would have to stop to fill up the car and that that would wake Jude again, and that the daydream was coming to end before it had even really begun.

*

He opened his eyes as she turned into the empty garage, driving across the spotless pristine snow and pulling up beside a pump.

'Welcome back,' she said, feeling his eyes upon her.

He stretched and yawned lazily. 'I was dreaming about you. We were on a beach, sitting in the surf . . . You had no . . .'

'If only,' she said, turning off the engine, and Jude sat up in his seat.

'I'm sorry,' he said, rubbing his eyes and making a big deal of looking all around him. 'How could I have fallen asleep, how could I have left you all on your own? Were you all right?'

'You only had about half an hour.'

He reached on to the back seat for his coat and pulled out his wallet.

'Stay here and keep warm,' he said. 'I'll do this.'

Which was the right thing to say.

She watched him through the window as he stood beside her door and filled up the petrol tank, his back turned to the wind. They were the only people there apart from an old man sitting huddled behind the counter in the brightly lit shop; she could almost believe he was there specially for them, as if they truly were the only two people travelling that day.

She watched Jude jog over to the shop to pay for the petrol and then, as if he knew she was watching, he suddenly turned and grinned at her. She waved back at him and felt her heart stop. *Don't*, she told herself, bringing her hand down on to her lap, clasping hold of it with the other. Fancy him but don't fall for him. That way danger lies.

She opened her car door and got out hurriedly, gasping at the icy cold but enjoying the movement after sitting still for so long. She walked round to the other side, slipped into the passenger seat, still warm from his body, and sat waiting for him. When he returned he waved a floppy hot-dog in a bread roll at her through the window, and she wrinkled up her nose at him. He opened his door, leaned across and went to hand it to her.

'What's the matter?' he asked when she shook her head.

'I can't eat that.'

'Are you sure? Aren't you hungry?'

'I've never seen anything so bright.' Her stomach was clenched tight as a fist. She didn't think she could ever eat anything again.

'Or a Twix?' He pulled it out of his pocket.

She shook her head, remembering the time Teddy had

removed a Twix from her fingers just as she was about to take a bite. *You're getting fat*, he'd told her cheerfully.

'I'll have your hot-dog,' Jude decided. 'Give it back to me once we're on the motorway. I need both my hands.'

I could use both your hands, she thought, and she took it from him, held it, smelled it, and felt what little breakfast she'd had rising again in the back of her throat.

Jude started the car and pulled out on to the road, testing the windscreen wipers, flicking the indicators, adjusting the seat as he went. They climbed a hill, dropped down the other side, and immediately ahead of them saw a huge green destination board with signs to the M74 and the M6, with Gretna Green as the first destination at the top of the list.

'Lucy, look, we could get married!' Jude said, laughing, turning to her. 'Please say yes.'

'I'll need a very big diamond.'

He glanced at her again. 'Are you always so demanding?' He was challenging her, asking her in such a way that it was perfectly clear diamonds were not on his mind.

'Sometimes, if I have to be.' She could feel the heat in her cheeks, her heart starting to race and she looked away, out of the window, because it was as if something had happened to him while he'd been asleep, as if he'd had a dream that had shown him how she'd been thinking and was now matching her, challenging her to take it further.

'Here,' she said, sounding so calm she almost convinced herself. 'Have this disgusting thing before it goes cold.'

The hot-dog sausage had fallen half out of the bread, and ketchup and vivid yellow mustard were dripping on to her fingers. He saw the distaste on her face and laughed. 'Go on. Eat some.'

'Take it off me,' she insisted, holding it out to him, and he took the hot-dog in her hand and lifted it carefully to his mouth and then let her go.

'Any more?' she asked when he'd finished the mouthful, holding it out to him again, but he shook his head, opened his window to an icy blast of cold air, took it out of her hand and flung it away.

When the window was shut and the car warm again she put her arms above her head and stretched in her seat, and thought about how the next few hours might map out. It had been deliberate, the way he'd taken her hand just then, no mistaking the way he'd looked at her, how it had felt when they'd touched each other, and yet, despite what he'd said, she suspected that that was as far as he would want to go. The reticence in him, the way he turned away from her as often as he came close, made her suspect that there was more going on than she knew, and that the rest of the journey would now turn into a marathon flirt that would end when they got back to London, when they'd walk away from each other without a backward glance. All too easy to spend the rest of the journey alert to every move that he made, watching him talk, watching him laugh and blink and swallow, watching his hands grip the steering-wheel, imagining how they would feel if they were touching her, brushing the hair from her face, stroking her cheek, imagining but never finding out. And she thought how she'd trade never seeing him again for him to stop the car and kiss her here and now.

'Are you asleep?' Jude asked.

She almost told him.

'I'm daydreaming.'

'Are they nice daydreams?'

She nodded.

He rested his hand lightly on her shoulder and there had been no reason to do that, no reason at all but that he'd wanted to, and that he'd known she wanted him to.

'You had your eyes closed.'

'I was a million miles away from being asleep.'

'You should try. You look tired.'

'That's sweet of you to say so.'

'You know what I mean. Go to sleep,' he insisted. 'I promise I'll drive you safely home.'

'But I should keep you company.'

'I've slept, remember? And there's time for us when you wake up.'

Time for us? Anticipation leaped inside her again and she felt sparklingly, electrifyingly awake.

She lay there with her eyes tightly closed, her body rigid. What was he doing? Why did he want her asleep? She imagined Jude looking at her, checking her out, taking his time like she had with him, studying her hair, the curve of her hip, the shape of her lips . . . She licked them, then stopped abruptly, feeling colour stealing up her cheeks again, and had to fight the urge to open her eyes.

And lost. She opened her eyes, to find Jude wasn't looking at her at all but was staring straight ahead, concentrating on the road and tapping the steering-wheel to some imaginary beat.

She turned slowly away, disappointed, still alert to every flicker of movement he made, every sound, and then she took herself in hand, listened to the scolding voice telling her to stop getting everything out of proportion, to stop acting like a lovesick teenager.

She stared out across the flat expanse of snow-covered fields stretching away on either side of the motorway. There was a train in the distance and she watched as it dipped in and out of view, keeping pace with them, and felt herself floating away on the sea of sleep, half-conscious, half-drifting. Through half-open lids she took in a cluster of houses, chimney-smoke hanging in the air.

Having been the only car on the road, they were now one in a multitude of others, most of them no doubt full of people travelling home from the Christmas break, in every sense changing gear, mentally limbering up for the Monday morning onslaught. As far as Lucy was concerned, Monday morning seemed still to be light years away.

Mostly Jude drove much more cautiously than she had done, staying well below the speed limit and hugging the inside lane even though the motorway was gritted and the snow, still falling in fits and starts, was causing them no problems, but occasionally he would put his foot down and overtake another car and then she would take a good look as they passed, checking out the luggage and what the passengers looked like. A family, their estate car piled high with duvets and dogs, then a clapped-out Golf with four men squashed inside, heads bent at right angles against the roof, and then a glamorous-looking man and immaculately groomed woman in a Mercedes sports convertible, both of them looking fixedly ahead, neither of them speaking. Definitely a couple, Lucy decided, peering at them nosily. They matched each other so perfectly. And then the woman caught her eye and looked curiously back at her and Jude, and sleepily Lucy wondered what conclusions she might be reaching about them, convinced she wouldn't come close to the truth.

'Where are we?' she asked, opening her eyes again and stretching slowly as she woke.

'About half-way down the M6. You've been asleep for the last two hours.'

'No!' she said in disbelief. 'I couldn't have been.' She looked at the clock and saw that it was nearly six o'clock, registering belatedly that it was dark outside and that the dashboard lights were on.

'I had no idea,' she said, stretching again. 'I could do with a break and a cup of tea.'

'We'll stop soon.'

She sat there watching him drive, unable to stop herself grinning into the darkness – it was so damn nice to wake up and find him there.

'I have to say,' she let out a giant yawn, 'that I feel miles better for having slept.'

She reached into the glove compartment of the car for the bottle of water and drank some then passed it to him, watching him tip back his head, his lips round the top where hers had just been. He handed her back the bottle.

'I missed you, while you were sleeping.'

She wondered if she was wrong to be reading an entire

romantic novel into that one line. Jude waited but said nothing else, only left the silence hanging there in an utterly disconcerting kind of way, and when she looked across to him again he didn't react at all.

'Do you know why people got married in Gretna Green?' she asked, suddenly very keen to break the silence.

'It's bothering you, isn't it? That you could have had me and you turned me down.'

'In your dreams, Jude.'

'I don't know. Why did they choose Gretna Green?'

'Because it's so close to the border. The laws changed in England, you see.'

'That's very interesting, Lucy.'

'It was some time in the mid-eighteenth century. Suddenly you had to be twenty-one to be married without your parents' consent. But gallop over the border and you could be married in Scotland at sixteen.'

'How reckless and irresponsible of them.'

'Don't say that. It must have been exciting, eloping with your true love, parents in hot pursuit.' She looked at him. 'Trust me, the girls would have found it exciting.'

'Are you asking me to turn around?'

'I am not.'

'Sure?'

'Someone who used to work in my office got married there last year. She had a piper and a chimney-sweep, very traditional apparently. And she was married in a blacksmith's shop, just like in the olden days, because the blacksmith's shop was where they always aimed for. And the man who married her was called an anvil priest. And afterwards, I suppose they probably went on honeymoon somewhere in Scotland.'

She knew she was starting to burble, recounting details of a wedding she hadn't even been to and had had no great interest in at the time. But her mouth was suddenly running away with her, her heart starting to race again, because although the thought of kissing him still seemed illicit and dangerous, now she knew it was going to happen.

'Loch Ness, perhaps? Or I suppose they could have flown anywhere from Inverness? Or maybe they crossed back over the border.' She paused briefly. 'Did you know ninety-seven couples got married in Gretna Green last Valentine's Day?'

'I'd rather shoot myself.'

'You're so unromantic.'

'No,' Jude said.

She looked across to him. 'No what?'

'I am romantic.'

She turned away from him, not sure what to do, what to say.

'Tell me some more,' he said.

'You're not interested.'

'I am. I like hearing about Gretna Green. I like the sound of your voice.'

'But you've talked the whole way down. Gretna Green's all I've got to talk about.'

'Lucy?' He reached for her hand.

'Yes?' she whispered.

'I wondered if you know any good games?'

'Games?' she repeated. 'I don't understand, like *Botticelli* or *Twenty Questions*?'

'Yes,' he said, 'or *I Spy*?'

'You are joking?'

'Yes.'

'Why?'

'Because I was about to say something else, but then I thought I shouldn't.'

She stilled. 'What was it? Please tell me.'

'I want to kiss you.'

'I thought you did,' she managed to whisper back.

'And I've been sitting beside you watching you sleep, eat, talk, laugh, wondering if it would be the last thing you wanted to hear. Chuck me out of the car if you have to, I can't not tell you any longer. Is it such an awful thought?'

'No!' she cried. 'The best thought I've heard for ages.' She laughed, then reached out for his face with a shaky hand. 'I badly want to kiss you too.'

'I was thinking it most when you were asleep,' he said. 'And the way you stretched just then, as you woke up. If I wasn't driving this crappy little car . . .'

'Perhaps we could stop . . .' she ventured.

He caught her hand against his cheek. 'Lucy, darling. Why didn't I tell you five miles ago? That's what I want to know. Because we've just passed a turn-off and there probably won't be another one for a hundred miles.' He banged the steering-wheel in frustration and she leaned forward, laughing because he sounded so cross, brushing his cheek with her lips, breathing in the scent of him.

71

'Don't.' He stiffened. 'I have to keep you safe.'

She drew back again and sat beside him, quietly, feeling so alive, aware of the blood in her veins, the weight of her limbs, a strange languorous heaviness in her body that made her want to lie down, and at the same time doubting it was really happening, because everything that day had felt so dreamlike and strange ... She looked over at Jude. He was there, beside her. He had just said something that felt momentous, and now he was about to turn off the motorway. And then what was going to happen? She imagined them together in the car, steaming up the windows, it getting farcical as they were jabbed by the gearstick, or accidentally sat on the horn.

'What's the matter?' he asked. 'You're having second thoughts?'

'No.' She reached to stroke back his hair, loving it that she could, and with the knowledge that she could came a recklessness, and a determination not to doubt, not to hesitate, but to go wherever the moment took her.

5

Fifteen minutes later and they had still not come to a motorway junction. And because it was dark, and Jude was having to concentrate on the road, they had slipped into an easy silence, their hands, gripping tightly, binding them close.

'Did you expect this to happen?' Lucy asked suddenly.

'You know I hoped it would. Did you?'

'I thought about it.' She looked at him in the darkness. 'But I didn't believe it.'

'I knew you were thinking about me.'

'Oh, yes?'

'When you nearly drove us off the road when I touched your hand.'

'I thought you were asleep!'

'Of course I wasn't.'

'You're such a schemer.'

'But I had to *know*. You were being way too cool and it was driving me nuts.'

'All that yawning and stretching when you woke up. Remind me never to trust you again. And why were you so keen to get me to sleep? Why didn't you say anything?'

'I guess I felt I could take my time.'

As he spoke he braked to join a long queue of traffic, three HGVs in front of them, spread out across all three lanes of the motorway. Lucy looked ahead to see three long trails of red tail-lights, stretching away as far as she could see. This felt so disappointingly wrong, still to be talking, talking, talking, when all she wanted to do was stop the car and grab hold of him before the heat of the moment cooled and all the excitement and spontaneity passed them by.

'We're going to stop as soon as we can,' Jude said. And then he looked at her again. 'Bloody fucking traffic.' And he picked up her hand and kissed it tenderly.

Finally the traffic started to move again, crawling at first but eventually picking up speed, and then at last a sign for services flashed past them. And all at once the steady tick-tick-ticking of the indicator seemed to be counting down the seconds to when they would stop.

Jude drove them between crudely landscaped traffic islands, past a children's playground and into the lorry park, stopped the car, pulled on the handbrake and turned to her.

'No,' she cried, looking out of the window in panic. 'Jude, we can't stop *here*. I don't want a bunch of lorry drivers watching us though the windows.'

He looked around. 'No one can see us.'

But he started the engine again and pulled away, taking them down the slip road towards the brightly lit service station.

'Go left,' she told him, and immediately he swerved left, towards a completely empty car park. He stopped the car.

'Choose a space.'

'Shut up,' she muttered.

He rolled the car forward into the first space in front of them, then turned off the engine and undid his seatbelt, Lucy did the same, then turned to look at him. Keeping his eyes fixed on hers, he reached beneath his seat and then, with a terrible scraping sound, shot it backwards, away from the steering-wheel.

'Oh, you're so cool,' Lucy said, laughing, and barely a second later she was sitting on his lap, her arms around his neck.

'I'm glad you think so.'

He pulled her closer, holding her, both of them understanding that what was happening was still precarious and still so unexpected and all the more exciting because of it. And then he was kissing her gently and insistently, opening her lips with his tongue, holding her face in his big hands, and then suddenly kissing her much harder, all the waiting, the drawn-out longing, finally able to find its expression so that they were lost in their kiss – lost to the car park, to who they were and where they were going and what they were doing. Just kissing and kissing, unable to stop. She closed her eyes to the hot smell of him, ran her fingers through his soft black hair, felt his hands, hard and strong, as they held her close, and his mouth, warm and addictive, sending her shivery with lust. And hearing him sigh, feeling him shiver, seeing how he stared at her, tipping up his face to her kiss, she felt powerful and desirable and reckless, so that the last thing she wanted to do was stop.

She had slid half-way down the passenger seat, twisted at the waist, and somehow had her head resting against the door handle with one leg bent over the gear-stick and under him.

'Is that a groan of pleasure or of pain?' he asked.

She winced and pushed him away. 'I can't bear to stop you but I'm in pain.'

He swivelled to kiss her again. His upper body was bent towards her, with his legs still facing forwards beneath the steering-wheel. 'I am too.'

She felt her way underneath him. 'That's because you're lying on the handbrake,' she said against his mouth.

He whispered back. 'What are you going to do about it?'

'Take you inside, I think, as we're parked outside a Milestone Motel Travel Lodge.'

She hadn't planned on saying it, and she could see how much she'd surprised him.

'Are you sure?'

And she could see doubt there just for a brief moment, a bedroom and a double bed being a whole lot more serious than a romp on the back seat of the car. And then she saw the surprise turn to excitement, as if he couldn't quite believe his luck, knew that he wouldn't have dared to suggest it himself. This is it, she thought. Do or die.

He glanced out of the window across the dark car park, the lights of the Milestone Motel Travel Lodge winking at them brightly, and then he turned back to her.

'That was not what I expected you to say.'

'You mean you're thinking *what a slapper*?'

'No. You're incredible.' He pulled her towards him again, burying his face in her hair. 'I would like to walk,

76

sprint, leap into that Milestone Motel with you more than anything in the world.'

'But?' She waited for what it might be, dread spreading through her. A girlfriend? An illness? An embarrassing disability?

'I'm thinking that soon we'll be back in London.' He gently touched his nose to hers. 'I feel I should remind you that tomorrow you'll be starting your day, going to work. I don't want you wondering what the hell you were doing.'

She looked steadily back at him. 'Will you?'

'No.'

'Then neither will I. Tomorrow has nothing to do with it.'

'But I can't say I'll—'

'And I won't be wondering,' she cut in, 'if I'll see you again. Because I know that I won't.' She said it impulsively but she meant it definitely. 'Not that I don't think you're amazing because I do, you know I do. But it could never be like this again, never as good. Don't you agree? This is New Year's Day and I want to grab hold of it with you. And let whatever we want to happen, happen. And then let it go again. Because I think if I walk in there, wondering about tomorrow, it will be spoiled.' She kissed him softly. 'We don't know anything about each other, Jude. We're not part of each other's lives, and that's good. We don't owe each other anything.' She leaned over to him, and he put his arms around her and held her close. 'I want to keep it like that.'

For a long moment he held her, saying nothing, and then he stirred, his breath hot against her neck.

'Has someone been talking to you about me?'

'Why?' she smiled.

'I can't believe you said that.'

'That's because you were thinking it too.'

*

They stood close together for a few moments in the dark of the car park, the snow falling lightly around them, neither of them wearing a coat, Jude looking more handsome than ever, snow settling on his dark hair as he looked down at her. And then he turned back to the car, leaning into the back seat and feeling in the front pockets of his overnight bag, and Lucy glimpsed the silver foil of a condom packet. This was a reality check, bringing her up short, and she stood rather warily watching him rezipping his bag and tucking the condom into his pocket. Then he slammed his door shut and turned back to her.

Lucy led them through frosted glass swing doors, across a purple carpet to where two girls in purple jackets and skirts waited behind a partitioned reception area.

'We'd like a room,' she said.

One of the women gave them a bright smile, the other didn't look up from her magazine.

'Of course. How long would you be staying for?'

'Just the one night,' Jude said.

The woman nodded. 'The room rate is forty-five pounds plus VAT.'

She took Jude's credit card and handed him back a registration form to sign. 'Thank you, sir, and if you'll be wanting supper, Milestone Motel restaurants serve a fine selection of both hot and cold foods, available twenty-four hours a day. Take the next left after the signs for petrol.'

'Thank you.'

Behind her Jude slipped his arms around Lucy's waist and she leaned back against him. 'You wanted a cup of tea, Lucy, didn't you?' he murmured against her hair.

'I don't think I do, not any more.'

'And will you require an early morning wake-up call?' Jude's arms tightened around her. 'Definitely not.'

'And will you need to fetch any luggage from your car?' They both shook their heads.

'Right then,' she said brightly. 'I'll show you up to your room. If you'd like to follow me.'

She took them in a tiny lift to the second floor, standing with her back pressed into a corner, eyes carefully averted, and marched them down a narrow, windowless corridor, walking so fast she was almost running and Lucy was twice nearly overcome with giggles.

Out of breath, they stopped at the last room, number 25, and the woman pushed a keycard into the lock, opened the door and walked into the room.

'Check-out is at eleven. There's tea and coffee on the table. There's an en suite—'

'It's great,' Lucy interrupted her, standing with Jude in the doorway and looking through to a square room with a purple nylon carpet in the centre of which was a double bed covered in a striped purple and green counterpane. 'We'll find it all out for ourselves.'

They went on into the room, making way for the woman, who turned back at the door. 'Dial zero for reception if you need anything and we'll do our best to help you.' She was obviously nearing the end of her spiel.

'I think we'll be fine, thank you,' said Jude, walking over and sitting down on the bed.

Lucy closed the door after the woman, locked it, then leaned back against it. 'What's your name again?'

'Come here.'

She stood in the doorway and didn't move.

'What's the matter?'

'I need the loo.'

'At last,' he laughed. 'I was worried about you.'

When she came out of the bathroom she stopped against the doorway again and Jude, misinterpreting the doubt on her face, reached across the bed to a small bedside lamp and turned off the light, leaving the room lit only by the soft glow of the car park outside.

'Are you OK?'

'I'm great.'

She sat down hard beside him, wincing at the jolt to the base of her spine. 'Don't you think that this has to be the hardest, most uncomfortable bed you've ever sat on?'

'Lain on,' Jude said, rolling away from her and on to his back, and Lucy moved over to join him, stretching herself out beside him, both of them now lying on their backs, staring up at the ceiling. She slid her hand into his and breathed deeply, letting her brain calm down and concentrate on the fact that Jude was lying there beside her. She moved her hand away from his and stroked his collarbones, then pushed herself close against him, nestling against his neck, breathing him in. She could feel his heart beating against her chest, one long leg sliding over hers.

'You've got glitter on your cheek,' he told her, touching it with the edge of a finger.

'Party last night.'

'I wish I'd been there. I'd like to have seen the pink dress.' He reached forwards and kissed her. 'I could have helped you with the buttons.'

'No chance.'

'Why, was it a zip?'

She looked up into his eyes. 'You have to realize, Jude, that I only feel like this on very, very special days.'

'Which days are those?'

'It has to have snowed for at least ten hours.' She kissed him slowly on his warm soft mouth, lust rising up so fast it was difficult to keep speaking. 'It has to be dark. I have to have eaten nothing since breakfast . . .'

'And then, only then, someone might get to undo your buttons?'

'Yup,' she said weakly, because his fingers were now on the button of her jeans, undoing them, tugging down the zip.

'Then I am the luckiest man, to be here with you at just the right time, in just the right place.'

'Only you,' Lucy whispered. 'This could only have happened with you.'

He didn't answer, just tugged up her shirt until it was clear of her jeans and he could spread his hands across her bare back. Then he groaned, reaching for her mouth, covering her face with slow, soft, open kisses. She stared up at the ceiling, seeing a sparkling glittering sun dancing on a blue sea, felt heat slide up through her legs, unable to move other than to twist the counterpane in her fingers and curl her toes inside her socks.

And then they were kicking off shoes, pulling at each other's clothes, and what had begun cautiously and hesitantly became more daring and purposeful, her hands undoing the zip on his jeans, a finger tracing the edge of her pants, a fumble of buttons and belts and zips as they pulled free of all their clothes and then the bliss as hot, naked skin touched skin and her whole body started to beat and she thought, *I want him, I want him, I want him.*

'Lucy . . .' he stopped suddenly, leaning back and somehow looking at her with such incredulity and tenderness in his eyes that she stilled. 'You are wonderful, amazing. I can't imagine this is true, can't believe you're here.'

*

The curtains were still open but the light from the car park outside was not bright enough for Lucy to see his face clearly. She knew that he was lying on his stomach facing her and that his eyes were open. As she lay there naked next to him, staring at the shadow of his face, feeling his breath gentle on her cheeks but not touching at all, she felt her body slowly coming back to her again, her heart steadying, and a languorous sleepiness stealing over her. She stroked his cheek with her fingertip, searching out his eyes in the darkness, but at her touch he rolled on to his back and sat up, then reached across to the bedside lamp and turned it on, so that she had to cover her eyes with her hand.

'Time to get up,' he said, looking down at her.

She lay still in the pillows, half-expecting him to fall back beside her, but then he jumped out of bed, pulling half the covers with him, and walked across the room to close the curtains. Lucy pulled the remaining covers back over herself again and watched as he prowled round the room, picking up his socks from the floor and sitting down on the end of the bed to pull them on before setting off again with nothing else on, bending down beside her to search under the bed.

'What time is it?'

He looked at his watch. 'Ten past seven.'

And they'd walked in, what, an hour before? Less perhaps. She watched as he continued to look for his clothes, for the first time looking at him properly, taking in the breadth of his shoulders, his sturdy thighs and well-muscled calves. There was a heaviness about him that she hadn't noticed before. It was ironic, thought Lucy, watching him turn away, that he should seem less familiar now than he had done before. Even his voice and his face seemed different now.

'Don't go all off-hand with me now. Please, Jude.'

He stared back at her, and in the movement of his body and the way he held himself at such a deliberate distance she could see none of the tenderness that had radiated from him before. He came back to her, bent his head and kissed her briefly on the cheek. 'I just think we should get up.'

Was this the horribly predictable ending she hadn't seen coming at all? She watched him moving around the room, waiting for him to say something else, anything at all.

'I've lost my trousers.'

'And your pants?'

'Pants I can do without. Trousers and I think people might notice.' Once again he returned to the bed and kissed her, and at his touch she relaxed. She was being way too sensitive, she told herself. It wasn't her he was suddenly desperate to get away from, it was the horrible purple hotel room. She looked around, taking in her surroundings properly for the first time. In the bright electric light the purple seemed to emit a toxic glow. But even so, she didn't want to leave quite so fast. She wanted time to take in the fact that they were here, take in what had just happened. After the long journey in the car, she felt like a bath.

She asked him to run her one and immediately he disappeared into the bathroom. Seconds later she heard the crash of water as the taps were turned on, then the door closed and she was left alone.

She was in a motorway service station off the M6, wrapped in a purple sheet, in this strange room with this strange man dressed only in his socks who was running her a bath, and yet however he behaved now, she was feeling more real, more comfortable in her own skin than she had done for years. Because just for once she'd broken free and done what other people did, let instinct and passion and devil-may-care recklessness sweep her up and carry her away. And if there in the background was the timid under-confident Lucy who was still trying to get her attention, who couldn't help but notice how effortlessly Jude was detaching from her, who couldn't help but think it strange and rather sad that they wouldn't ever see each other again, she could ignore her without a second's hesitation.

She got out of bed and walked around the room, picking up her jeans from the carpet, untangling her knickers from the sheet at the bottom of the bed, finding her long wool cardigan and pulling it back on, hiding her nakedness in preparation for the moment when Jude came back into the room. It wasn't that she wanted him to declare undying love, she thought, laying her bra and knickers and jeans neatly on the bed for when she'd had her bath. And she certainly didn't want him to plead with her to see him again. All that would sadden her would be if, now, they'd lost the easy relationship they'd had before they'd walked into this room. And she wondered if that was inevitable, whether she was stupid to think it might be otherwise.

She jumped back into bed, turned on the television and, as she guessed, it immediately drew Jude out of the bathroom.

He had damp hair and a towel around his neck and another in his hands. He walked around to the other side of the bed and sat down. 'I've run you a bath, I've even found you bubble bath. Guess what colour it is?'

She smiled at him, lifted the covers and stepped out of bed, wrapping the cardigan round her, and went into the bathroom deliberately leaving the door open, not so that he could look at her but so that he wouldn't think she was shutting him out. She tested the water, dropped the cardigan on the floor and climbed in, sliding down so that the bubbles came up to her chin.

'I cannot believe my purple bath,' she called out to Jude, and immediately she heard him get off the bed. Then he was there, standing in the doorway, dressed and ready to go.

'Your purple what?'

She turned to look at him. 'Bath.'

He grinned back at her, and now it was the same old smile but this time with a shared understanding and new knowledge of each other, an intimacy in the look that hadn't been there before. 'OK in there?'

'Yes, thank you.'

And then he was gone again.

Lucy looked down at her two white knees pointing up through the foam, listened to the bubbles popping against the sides of the bath. Then she found herself slowly flexing her toes, rolling her ankles round and round, slowly and methodically, and, even as she thought how silly it was, she knew she was doing it to try to find out if she was the same person she'd always been, checking that everything about her was exactly the same. All day she'd felt like a different person, an actor playing out a day in the life of Lucy Blue, free of any sense of caution, ballsy and determined to do what she wanted to do. And now, she thought, opening the rectangular packet of soap and sliding it around in her hands, she was not going to change back into the old Lucy again, the Lucy who could be manipulated by Teddy, crushed by some of her friends, daunted by evil bosses at work, easily silenced by everyone else. She liked this Lucy who'd not run away, not thought too much about what was best, but had followed her instincts. She liked who it had made her be.

She turned on the hot tap with her foot, flinching at the scalding burst of heat, then washed quickly and with a whoosh of water stood up and climbed out of the bath. Reaching for a towel she found that Jude, thoughtful guy that he was, had taken both of them, leaving her with a tiny square of hand towel. His problem, then, if she walked back into the room and reminded him of exactly what he wasn't ever getting again. She dried herself as best she could and came back into the bedroom.

Jude was sitting on the bed waiting for her, hands folded in front of him.

'Was it much too quick?' he said as soon as she came through the door. 'I'm sorry. I could tell you wanted to take your time and I rushed you, didn't I?'

'I didn't mind at all. I was flattered.'

It was only then, when he opened his mouth and then shut it slowly, looking completely taken aback, that Lucy realized that of course he'd been talking about her bath. She ran across the bedroom and threw her arms around him, bursting into giggles.

'Oh no, ask me again!'

He sat there stiffly. 'I can't believe you said that.'

'Please, please ask me again.'

'I'm crushed. I am a ruined man.' He looked mournfully across at her.

And the new Lucy didn't care. 'Shut up and go and get

my bag for me from the car, please,' she told him, dropping a kiss on to his head. 'I really need some clean clothes.'

He nodded silently and turned around, and he reached for the car key from the bedside table and let himself quietly out of the room.

While he was gone, she lay back on the bed and channel-hopped idly. But once she'd dried off completely and Jude still hadn't come back, foreboding slowly rose up inside her.

Stupid man, she thought, getting up off the bed and walking around the room. Surely he hadn't been so offended by what she'd said that he'd left her here? But what if he had – taken the car and abandoned her in this horrible place? How would she get home? She imagined the humiliation of asking the woman at reception for a taxi to the nearest railway station, rifling through her purse for enough cash, then hours of sitting on a snowy platform waiting for a train. And what about the Deals on Wheels car? She'd be responsible if it disappeared. She'd probably be interviewed by the police. *So what exactly were you doing in the Milestone Motel with Mr Middleton?* Perhaps she was only one of many other girls. *You do realize that Mr Middleton has done this before? Don't think you're the first to be tricked like this.*

Jude might nick both the bathtowels but surely he wouldn't do that to her? She leapt out of bed and peered down through the curtains into the car park below, and saw with relief that he was there, standing next to the car, talking on his mobile. As she looked down, holding the curtain to cover her naked body, he looked up, caught her eye, waved to her and grinned. She raised her hand back to him and turned away, not wanting him to think she was spying on him. She sat down on the edge of the bed and wrapped her cardigan around her.

After the fear of thinking he'd left her, why did the sight of him smiling up at her fill her with such sadness? Was it simply because he was on the telephone to someone she definitely didn't know and was certainly never going to meet? Because, whatever she told herself, it made her aware of the whole huge life he had that she knew nothing about at all. And perhaps she wasn't that woman after all, who could walk away from him now without a backward glance?

Soon she heard him walking back down the corridor and then the door opened and he appeared in the doorway with her bag. She didn't move from the bed. Her cardigan was pulled around her, reaching half-way down her pale thighs, her hair spread out on the bed, her feet bare. Jude stood for a long moment, looking at her.

'Hello, gorgeous.'

'I thought you'd driven off.'

'You silly softie.' He came and sat beside her on the bed, dropping her bag on the floor beside him. 'Why would I do that?'

'I don't know. Thanks for bringing my bag.'

He dropped his hand and gently stroked her hair back from her forehead as if saying goodbye. But he didn't go, just sat beside her on the bed, playing with a thick strand of her hair.

'It's the colour of barley.'

'Wet straw, someone told me.'

'Trust me, I'm a farmer. It's the colour of barley.'

'You're not a farmer, you fly helicopters.' And as she said it she wondered if everything he'd told her was true. Then, if anything he'd told her was true.

'Farmer's son, then.'

'Where was your farm?'

'It's still there, as far as I know. In Oxfordshire, near Woodstock, a little village called Lipton St Lucy.'

'It's my name.'

He nodded. 'So you see I won't be able to get away from you after all.'

'Lipton St Lucy. Do you like it there? Is it a nice place?'

'It's a beautiful place. There are soft, undulating, kind of curvy hills. Deep valleys, secret paths, places you can get lost in.'

'Stop it,' she said, laughing. 'And you're going there tonight?'

'Yes. I was just calling Luke when you looked out of the window. I wanted to let him know where we are.'

'Not *exactly* where we are, I presume?'

'No,' he agreed.

And although he was still sitting beside her on the bed, teasing her and stroking her hair, she knew he was a long way away from her at that moment. Still it was the same, the restlessness whenever she tried to get him to talk about his life, his unwillingness to reveal anything about himself, the way he persistently dodged getting personal, and she knew, even after everything that had happened between them, that she wasn't going to get any more out of him now.

'Jude.' She wished her voice wouldn't wobble when she said his name.

'Yes?'

She could see the sudden wariness in his eyes.

'You're not sitting there worrying I'm going to tell you I love you or something?'

He laughed, still playing with her hair. 'No, because we both know that's not what this is about, don't we?'

She nodded.

'Although, I want you to know that if I was looking for—'

'Don't say it,' she interrupted him crossly. 'Let's not hear the crappy cliché, please. In any case I'*m* not interested either.'

He let out a long sigh. 'Fair enough.'

She sat up on the bed. 'But that doesn't mean you can't kiss me again, doesn't mean you can go the rest of the journey not talking to me.' Four more hours in the car with him, Lucy was thinking. Keep it light. 'And you've got to meet my eye, too. After you got out of bed, you wouldn't even do that.'

'Not true!'

'It is true. And you leapt out of bed like the building was on fire.'

'All guys do that. Didn't you know? Girls rest, guys leap out of bed. We have to be alert, keep an eye out for danger.'

'Or girls like to have a bath.'

'They do,' Jude agreed, standing up abruptly. 'And now we should both be going.'

*

Lucy was driving again, and Jude sat quietly beside her as she backed the car out of its space and drove out of the car park. As they rejoined the motorway he returned to the radio, both of them understanding that music would release them from any pressure to talk.

By the time they had left the M6 and joined the M40, the snow had turned to sleet that spattered hard against the windscreen and sprayed out in great arcs of dirty slush, making passing lorries a test of nerves and will, and from feeling as if she was on fire at the thought of him beside her, now she was aware of an impatience to have him out of the car. It had gone on too long, this awkward postscript to what had happened in the Milestone Motel. Far better if they'd been able to go their separate ways at the front door.

The constant concentration made her gritty eyes ache, and the long hours sitting in the car were taking a heavy toll on her back, so that as they finally swished through Shepherd's Bush towards Notting Hill all she could think about was how soon he'd be getting out of the car, how soon she could finally be separated from him.

Finally, just after one o'clock, they pulled up outside Jude's brother's home in Moreton Street, an impressive four-storey midnight-blue house just off Elgin Crescent.

She turned off the engine, tired to the bone, listening to the sudden silence, the stillness after so much noise and constant movement, and she turned to Jude, who ran a practised hand through his hair.

'It's harder than I thought. Are you sure you don't want me to call? Not even just once?'

She shook her head, surprise making her stumble. 'You know it wouldn't work.'

'You don't want to come and say hello before your party next week? Luke and I will be coming back from Oxford that evening. I could make sure I'd be in.'

'It wouldn't work.'

He sighed deeply and reached for her, pulling her close. 'I know. But I won't forget you, Lucy. I really won't.'

She pushed him away again and looked towards the house, feeling irritation because it was so obvious he was trying to say all the right things in these last moments together when, truth be told, he had already moved on and away from her. It was clear in the way he was looking out through the window at the rain, in the hasty unfastening of his seatbelt even as he spoke. And in the way he hardly waited for her reply but snatched his coat from the back seat, dropping his wallet into the pocket as he did so.

She folded her hands on her lap and he caught her stare.

'One day we'll be old and decrepit and we'll be able to remember this year and that long, long drive down from Inverness. And every time you see a Milestone Motel, you'll have Milestone Motel thoughts about me.'

'Every time I drive to Lipton St Lucy I'll think of you. I'll tell my grandchildren about us.'

'Don't. They'll think you're a dirty old man.'

He leaned towards her and kissed her, once, twice, on the lips. 'You know that after you've gone it will be too late?'

'For what?'

'For either of us to change our minds. If we've got this wrong how would I ever find you again?'

'We're not wrong. Anyhow we'll probably get introduced to each other at some party in a few weeks' time.'

'I don't think so,' he said quietly. 'I'll be back in Aberdeen by then.'

'Yes, of course, hundreds of miles away. No chance of meeting then.' She paused again, then added awkwardly, 'Goodbye, Jude Middleton.'

'Goodbye, Lucy Blue.'

He opened the door, got out and slammed it shut. Then he walked round to the boot to get his bag and slammed that shut too. And seconds later a light came on in the hall of the house and the front door opened.

Even if she hadn't been expecting him, she would have known this was Jude's brother, Luke. Not simply because they were the same height and had the same dark hair – the similarity was there in the way Luke walked, coming down the flight of steps, then striding towards Jude with keys in his hand, wearing socks and jeans and a white T-shirt, his arms wrapped around himself for warmth.

'I'd given up on you,' she heard him say. She watched him hesitate, then move forwards, swinging an arm around Jude's shoulders, and she saw how Jude immediately stepped away.

'You knew where I was. I told you what was going on.'

'I know, I know.'

Jude would be glad if she drove away quickly now, Lucy thought. And she wanted to. Her time with him was over, but even as she was thinking it, Luke had turned curiously and Jude was coming back to the car.

'Lucy,' he called, 'come and meet Luke.'

And so she had to undo her seatbelt and get out of the car, walk into Luke's interested gaze, dipping her head against the rain, then take his hand and shake it.

'Luke, meet Lucy.'

'Would you like to come in?' Luke asked her politely.

Lucy shook her head. 'I have to get the car back to the hire company. And, you know, after thirteen hours, I'd like to get home.'

'Jude, you're not leaving Lucy to take back the car on her own?'

Jude nodded at him sheepishly. 'I thought we wanted to get to Oxford tonight.'

'You lazy bastard. That's our problem.'

'I'll be fine,' Lucy insisted. 'Get inside. It's horrible out here.'

'But how will you get home?' Luke asked her, concerned.

She hadn't thought about it. Deals on Wheels probably wouldn't even be open this late. 'It's just up the road in Hammersmith. I'll get them to call me a cab. Seriously, I'll be fine.'

'I'll follow you in my car,' Luke told her. 'You go and wait in the house,' he instructed Jude, then he turned back to Lucy. 'I'll drive you home.'

'No,' Lucy insisted, knowing that was absolutely the last thing she wanted.

'There's no point arguing with her,' Jude told Luke. 'Is there, Lucy?'

She shook her head. She didn't want a lift with his fierce-looking brother, but she would have been happy if either of them had offered to find her a taxi, right there and then, if either of them had offered to take over responsibility for the car. But they were going to Oxford so of course they weren't about to do that.

She went to open the door of the car and then, suddenly, Jude was back in front of her, blocking Luke's view, putting his arms around her and swooping down to kiss her hard on her half-open mouth.

'I'm sorry I didn't think about the car and getting you home,' Jude whispered. 'And don't drive away from me now, regretting what happened, thinking I'm a selfish bastard like Luke says I am, someone who doesn't care about you at all. Because I do, I think you're wonderful. Remember me fondly, please.'

She was surprised to hear such sincerity in his voice and to see such an urgent look in his eyes.

'I will do. And you do the same for me, OK?'

She pushed him away from her and opened the car door, not wanting him to see the tears in her eyes. And then she climbed in and drove away.

6

By the time the cab pulled up outside Lucy's mansion block in Barons Court it was twenty past two. She stepped on to the pavement and felt her whole body buzzing with the exhaustion of having travelled for so long, a thousand headlights flickering and dancing in her head.

She unlocked the door, kicked her way through the usual rainforest's worth of junk mail and slowly climbed the two flights of stairs to her flat, dragging her bag behind her. The taxi had been much too warm and by the time she reached her own front door she could feel her knees buckling with exhaustion. She opened her door and staggered theatrically inside, overwhelmingly relieved to be back. Letting the door click shut behind her, she switched on the hall light, edged off her shoes, dropped her coat over the back of a chair and looked gratefully round, breathing in the wonderful stillness and peace after the movement and noise of all those hours on the road.

She'd rented the flat six months ago and was surprised to find how much she liked living alone. Not that she'd been alone very often, with Teddy staying over at least two or three nights every week. But there'd be no more of that now. And with that knowledge there in her mind, she looked around and the whole flat felt different, hers in a way it had never been before.

She pulled off her socks and the coolness of the painted wooden floorboards felt blissful against the soles of her feet. She wandered into the bathroom, filled the basin with warm water and splashed her face, then caught her own eye in the mirror and couldn't stop smiling at herself because now, here at home, everything seemed to have settled back into a new sense of proportion. She'd had a great one-night stand. She'd celebrated her New Year with Jude, unexpected, unbelievable Jude. Jude who she was surprised to discover was already receding in her mind, becoming less and less real, leaving only a new confidence and sense of purpose in his place.

She left the bathroom and took the two strides necessary to reach the kitchen, through an archway at the other end of the hall. In the dim light she poured herself a tall glass of orange juice, visions of her soft bed with its cool white sheets drawing her towards her bedroom. She went back to the hall to pick up her bag and then, at long last, pushed open the bedroom door and walked in.

Teddy was in her bed.

He was lying asleep on his back, his arms stretched out wide as if ready to grab her the moment she came close enough, the light from the hall falling straight on to his face.

Teddy was in her bed. If she hadn't been so desperate not to make a sound she'd have cried. Instead she turned swiftly round, reached for the hall light and switched it off, returning the room to inky darkness, then closed the door quietly behind her and tiptoed quickly away, back down the hall to the sitting-room. She shut the door behind her and dropped on to the sofa, immediately aware of the horrible familiar churn in her stomach, the fluttery panicky need to pacify him even in sleep.

Bloody buggering hell, she thought, dropping her head onto her arms. He was not coming back. She'd allowed their mess of a relationship to begin and then to continue. And she thought she'd finished. She'd tried to get out – but clearly not hard enough – how could it possibly be that Teddy *still* thought he was in with a chance? And, worse, how could she not have remembered to ask him for his keys to the flat?

She rubbed at her face with her hands. She wanted to be asleep in her lovely bed, which she'd been waiting to fall into for so long. How *could* he do this to her after all that had happened? And yet, if she'd thought about it before, she might have guessed that he would do this. It was perfectly timed and exactly the sort of stubborn, defiant thing Teddy would come up with.

She stood up again, wandering around the room, racking her brain for some brilliant way of emptying him out of the bed and out of her flat too, preferably without him knowing what was happening. Because at that moment there was nothing in the world she wanted less than a conversation with him. But short of knocking him out with her Le Creuset frying-pan and dragging him feet-first down the stairs, there was no clever Plan A.

And so she came around to Plan B, which was to open the sitting-room door for a second time and creep back to retrieve her bag. She took it over to the sofa, unzipped it and started to pull everything out on to the floor, finding her toothbrush, her contact lens case, her pyjamas. She'd make up the sofa-bed and sleep on that. And in the morning, in all of five hours' time, she'd wake and ... Lucy shuddered at the thought of her and Teddy getting ready for work together, standing shoulder to shoulder in the tiny bathroom, brushing their teeth, because he'd know, he'd look at her, and without her saying a word he'd know exactly what she'd been up to. But it was so different now, she tried to tell herself . She was none of his business any more, and at some time before they left for work she was going to have to remind him of that and in a way he'd never heard before.

How could they ever have got close, she thought despairingly as she unbuttoned her cardigan and pulled off her jeans. How could she ever have thought it was funny and sweet that he was called Teddy and looked so like one too, with his golden fuzz of body hair and that little disapproving smile permanently stitched to his face?

The office softball team had everything to answer for. If she hadn't been pressganged into playing she'd never have met him. He worked with her at Barley & Bross, but it was a huge company – she'd been there a year and had never even set eyes on him – then someone came up with idea of forming a softball team, to join one of the company leagues that played in the London parks every Tuesday night.

He'd joined the team and she'd fancied him simply because he'd been so good, making the most impossible catches without really trying at all, cracking the ball the length of the park and beyond, scoring them a home run every time he strolled up to the plate. Slowly he'd become part of those long summer evenings, lying beside her watching the shadows lengthen across the grass and the sun dip behind the tower blocks of Kennington or the neat redbrick rows of houses in Wandsworth and Fulham. And then, sitting with her and the rest of the team outside the pub after dark, he'd surprised her one evening by taking hold of her hand under the table. And that was how it had begun. She wasn't to know then what she was letting herself in for, just how far from an uncomplicated summer romance theirs would turn out to be. She would have laughed in disbelief to hear that Teddy would soon be buying her clothes for a weekend with his parents, would not only feel free to take a Twix from between her fingers but would wipe off her lipstick at the same time with his thumb. The depressing part of it was that she'd let him get away with it for so long. The force of his will, his occasionally furious loss of temper when he didn't get his own way, coupled with her hopeless inability to confront him successfully, meant that they'd still been together right up until Christmas, right until that moment outside her flat when she'd told him she didn't want to see him after she got back – and had managed to forget to ask him for his keys.

And now he was here again, and his timing really couldn't have been worse.

*

In the cupboard in the hall was a spare duvet, kept for when she had *invited* friends to stay. The sofa would fold out into a bed but she couldn't be bothered to do it tonight.

Despite Teddy's presence, she knew that the second she curled up on the sofa, under the duvet, she would be asleep. So she tiptoed back into the hall a second time and dragged the duvet out of the cupboard and back to the sitting-room. She needed the loo but she couldn't take the risk that Teddy would hear her, so she ignored that and instead spread the duvet out on the sofa and set her alarm for work the next morning.

She laid out her T-shirt and pyjama bottoms on top of the duvet, then took out her contact lenses, pulled off her knickers and bra and stretched to pull the T-shirt over her head. And then her heart leapt in alarm because, through her blurry eyes, she could just about make out that Teddy was no longer asleep in her bed but was standing in the doorway watching her.

This time she couldn't help but cry out. Not a full-blooded yell that would have roused her kind and well-meaning neighbours, but a strangled yelp, of fright and anger that he should see her naked, and despair that whatever she did it seemed she couldn't get away from him. She leapt onto the sofa, pulled the duvet high around her shoulders, then fumbled for her glasses and put them on. As if he'd been waiting only for her to see him properly, Teddy took two quick steps towards her and dropped to his knees, skidding across the polished floor-boards like an amorous ice-skater to kneel beside her makeshift bed.

'Please, Lucy, I know I shouldn't have let myself in but I've been missing you so much and I've been waiting for you to call.' He was giving her what he clearly thought was a winning smile, trying to turn the awful invasiveness of what he had done into some kind of grand romantic gesture.

She gave him a hard stare back. 'I want you to get dressed and get out of my flat. And give me my keys back while you're at it.'

The winning smile flickered and died. He hadn't ever heard her talk like this, so cold and calm, so certain.

'But I was so worried,' he retaliated, recovering fast.

'You didn't need to sleep in my bed.'

She paused, knowing she should be following up her advantage, leaping off the sofa to manhandle him out of the door before he got any more words in. But she was lying on the sofa with no knickers on and that put her at a huge disadvantage.

'I wanted to be sure you were safe, that was all.' And then, awkwardly, he leaned forwards and kissed her cheek. 'Hello darling, happy New Year.'

If he'd been hoping for a sudden melting of her heart he didn't get it.

'Go home, Teddy.' She gritted her teeth and pulled the duvet higher up her shoulders.

'I can't go! It's nearly three o'clock in the morning.' He rubbed at his face. 'Come to bed?'

'You're joking.'

'Lucy, please,' he pleaded. 'What's the matter with you tonight? I wanted to talk to you, to tell you how terrible I felt when you left in that cab, what you said . . .' He shook his head, looking at her sorrowfully. 'I know you didn't mean half of it. You were stressed out and I wasn't making it any easier.' He shook his head again. 'But you were off before I could explain. And there was so much I wanted to say.'

'Teddy, listen to me.'

He looked at her warily. 'I don't think I want to.'

She stopped, aware that this time she had to get it right. And perhaps he'd already sensed what was coming, had seen in her eyes how much she'd changed in so short a time.

'Don't, Lucy. I know exactly what you want to say,' he ploughed on, no longer dominant, no longer certain, wobbly-voiced, pleading. 'I think I was as angry with you as you were with me. And I'm sorry about that, really sorry. You were probably right to give us a break, it certainly gave me time to realize how much I missed you ... But I was hoping that now you've had a chance to think things through ... you might have had time to miss me, too, just a little? Even if you didn't call.'

She shook her head. 'I didn't miss you.' She surprised herself by how absolutely definite she sounded. She stretched out an arm and pulled her jeans off the chair, dragging them under the duvet, taking her time to find the leg-holes with her feet and feeling such relief when she did because now she would be able to pull up the zip and do up the buckle of the belt, then get up and walk straight over to the door.

'I wish you'd called. We should have talked.'

She stayed where she was. 'I didn't want to speak to you.'

'What's happened to you, Lucy? Why are you being so

tough?' His voice was still very quiet, none of the fast-boiling anger she sometimes saw. 'Last time I saw you I was still allowed to talk to you, to come to your flat. Last time I saw you I was still allowed to care about you and worry. My gorgeous honey, my beautiful girl, of course I'm going to care. I don't understand what's changed.'

'Yes you do.'

'Oh, what was it you said? Some dreadful cliché. *You don't allow me space to be myself,* was that the one?'

Had she really said that? He was right, it was a dreadful cliché.

He pushed himself to his feet but made no move forward. 'It wasn't like you, Lucy, not to call. Whatever was said, however angry you were.'

Why wouldn't he let the telephone call go? It was almost as if he had a sixth sense telling him that this was his best chance of getting to her. And yet he couldn't possibly know that by asking her this one question he was sending her straight back to the little car on the darkened road. Of course she hadn't called, and she'd switched off her phone so that he couldn't call her, because at that moment nothing had mattered but Jude.

'I didn't call because . . .' she dared herself to say it, *because I was with someone else, and I was just about to shag him in the Milestone Motel service station, just off the M6, somewhere near Walsall, I think*. That would sock it to him between the eyes, end this ridiculous pretence that he was in her flat because he had been worried, when they both knew that it was only because she had finally slipped from his grasp and he hated it. But she couldn't bring herself to do it, partly because despite everything she didn't want to hurt him, partly from fear of what she'd provoke him into doing in response. 'My battery went flat.'

Her phone was on the table in front of him and she watched as he reached forward, picked it up and switched it on. And of course she knew from his bitter smile, and the way his face hardened when he looked back at her, that the phone had betrayed her with its full five fingers of power.

'It must have recharged. Anyway, I missed my flight. I've just driven down all the way from Inverness.'

He nodded, saying nothing, then walked over to the armchair in the corner of the room and sat down facing her. 'Tell me more.'

'Don't act like you've caught me out.'

'Then don't act guilty. Tell me about the party.' His voice was rising and getting louder. 'Did you have a good time?'

'I'm not in the mood for a chat, Teddy.'

'In your flimsy fuck-me dress, did you meet someone there? Is that why you didn't call?'

She shook her head. 'My business, Teddy, what I choose to wear. And I didn't call because I didn't want to speak to you.'

'I don't think that's true. I think you met some Scottish bastard.' He waited, then looked at her incredulously. 'You did, didn't you? I can see it in your eyes. Even better, I can see it on your little chin. Someone hadn't shaved, had they, Lucy?'

'I didn't meet anyone at the party, not that it's anything to do with you.'

'I don't believe you.'

'You should. The party was rubbish. There was no one to talk to at all.' Don't tell him anything, she told herself. Shut up. He has no right to know anything at all and if he knows any more it'll only make him explode with anger. But so much had happened to her that day that her brain was simply too full, and all the thoughts she wanted to keep safe were starting to spill back out of her mouth.

'I didn't even last until midnight. And then I was up again early this morning, and I have just spent the last fourteen hours driving five hundred miles home. I'm sorry I can't speak to you tonight but understand that I am tired. And yes, I forgot to cleanse, tone and moisturize before I walked through my own front door but, silly me, I didn't think there'd be anyone here.'

He hardly listened. 'Tell me there's not another guy,' he demanded. 'Tell me of course you couldn't have forgotten me so fast. Not when we had so much together . . . Lucy?' He stood up, crossed the room in two strides and took hold of her hand. 'Please.'

And she knew then that there was only one way to make him listen.

'I can't tell you that,' she said steadily. 'Because you're right. I did meet someone. Not at the party but in the airport coming home. We drove back to London together.'

'You drove back to London with him?'

She nodded.

'And?'

She stared impassively back at him and saw the anger unfold slowly in his stunned white face. He stared at her, silently, for long, horrible seconds.

'So where is he? Why isn't he here? I'm surprised you haven't brought him upstairs – you weren't to know I'd be here after all.'

'I won't be seeing him again.'

'Oh.' Momentarily Teddy was thrown. 'So nothing happened? It was no big deal?'

'Actually yes, it was a very big deal, to me,' she said, holding his stare. 'So you see, you really should go home now.'

She opened the door for him.

He stood there swaying slightly, giving little barely perceptible shakes of his head.

'You know what?' he said eventually, very quietly. 'You're going to regret telling me that.' And then he walked out of the room and back to her bedroom and closed the door behind him.

She waited for him in the sitting-room, shivering and sad, and when he reappeared, dressed, he walked past her, not looking at her once, opened the front door and shut it quietly behind him. She heard his footsteps clattering down the stairs.

She took her bag and her dress, walked with them back to the bedroom and saw he'd left his keys on the bedside table. She walked over to the cupboard and hung up the dress, trying to make sense of what had happened, to evaluate how high up the Richter scale Teddy might have reached, what the implications might be for her next day in the office. But she was simply too tired to do it. She numbly laid out her clothes ready for the morning on her bedroom chair, a pair of soft grey wool trousers, a high-necked black jumper and shiny black boots, forcing herself to think about anything but him. Then she looked at her watch and saw that it was now twenty past three. She climbed into the bed, still warm from Teddy's body, and sleep rose up and enveloped her.

7

Lucy arrived at work at eight-fifteen, showing what she felt was an impressive commitment to her job. In the past she'd arrived at work feeling so much worse than she did today. There'd been a very irresponsible day after Jane's birthday when she'd passed out in the lift, and in comparison to that morning she felt almost good. She was aware of a certain light-headedness, due as much to lack of food as to lack of sleep, which meant she still couldn't seem to pull her thoughts together, and a sick dread when she thought about seeing Teddy again, and she had a bruise on the base of her spine from landing too hard on the bed with Jude, therefore reminding her of the Milestone Motel every time she sat down, but otherwise she felt fine.

It was a beautiful day too. The tinted glass of the Barley & Bross building reflected the perfect turquoise blue sky and cotton-wool clouds, and the air was crisp but warm enough to remind Lucy of springtime and floaty cotton skirts and sunglasses. She imagined sitting outside a café with Jane at lunchtime, and hoped desperately that she would be able to escape her office and meet her.

She pushed open the doors, waved at Zoe, their office receptionist cum agony aunt – warm-hearted, unfailingly nosy and, Lucy suspected, more than half in love with Teddy too – and walked over to the lifts.

'Teddy's in,' Zoe called after her, just as the lift arrived and the doors glided open. 'I saw him about half an hour ago.'

And from the look on her face she'd heard something.

'He looked terrible.'

She had heard something.

Torn between jumping into the lift and returning to Zoe's desk to hear what she might have to say, Lucy hesitated and Zoe saw her chance and pounced.

'He's feeling really bad.'

Was he? Did she care? Lucy turned to look back at Zoe and Zoe's eyes pleaded with her to come back and talk.

Since Lucy and Teddy had started going out together, Zoe had enthusiastically monitored the state of their relationship from her vantage point just in front of the main door, logging their arrivals and departures, taking special notice of the times when either of them arrived or left alone, completely unabashed when it came to passing comment on either of them. *Such a sleepy-head, isn't he?* she'd usually offer to Lucy when she arrived in the morning before Teddy. And *Bounced out of bed this morning, did he*? when it was Teddy who had got in first. It certainly wasn't by chance that Zoe's remarks always seemed focused on Teddy in bed. The few mornings when they had arrived together had produced little more than a subdued *good morning*.

'I asked him what was wrong.'

The lift doors closed again and Lucy turned back and walked over to reception, staring into Zoe's huge, elaborately made-up eyes.

'I couldn't help it, he looked half-crazy.'

'What did he say?'

She shouldn't be asking. She should be walking into the lift. She should be opening the door to her office, sliding into her chair, preparing to behave like the responsible, conscientious headhunter extraordinaire she was supposed to be.

'Far more than he should have done.' Zoe shook her head disapprovingly.

You loved hearing every single word of it.

'But there was absolutely no stopping him,' Zoe went on eagerly. 'It all came pouring out.'

And it's not as if you'd tell anybody, apart from the hundred and twenty-seven members of staff who walk past this desk every day.

'You see, I'm a good listener, everyone tells me so, although, quite frankly, sometimes it can be a bit of a curse.'

'What did Teddy say?'

Zoe looked sharply right and left. 'Lucy, I'm sorry but he told me stuff I'm sure you'd rather I didn't know.'

'Oh God, tell me.'

'It doesn't seem right, so early in the morning.' Zoe swallowed awkwardly. 'He told me, well, why you two split up. How impossible it would be for him now—'

'Oh, yes?'

'Now that he knows. OK,' she went on, taking a deep breath, 'he said how you two had been happy together, in many, many ways, but that you'd never hit it off,' she dropped her voice, '*in the bedroom.* And until yesterday he never knew why!'

'And now he does?'

'Look, I know it's none of my business, I know you'd never have dreamed of telling me something so personal, but Teddy did, OK?'

Lucy shrugged helplessly. 'I don't blame you at all.'

'And don't blame yourself either.'

'Zoe, what did he say *exactly*?'

Zoe stopped, looking at her uncertainly.

'I'd really like to know.'

'Teddy said . . . Teddy explained . . .'

'Yes?' Lucy leaned closer in towards her. 'Tell me.'

'That you like to have sex with strangers,' Zoe whispered. 'Strangers, low-life, high life, you don't know and you don't care.'

Lucy leapt back from the desk in shock.

'Pick them up off the street, day-time, night-time, the less you know about them the better,' she went on with relish. 'And Teddy explained . . . that yesterday, he found out about it.' She looked at Lucy warily, then judged it was safe to go on. 'Well, you told him, didn't you? And he couldn't take it.' She looked at Lucy sympathetically now. 'He says he feels terrible because he knows he should forgive you – that you can't help it, that it's not your fault. He said perhaps he will forgive you eventually.'

'He said that?'

'Lucy, to tell you the truth I wouldn't try too hard to get him back. You and Teddy? Let's face it, you were never quite right for each other, were you?'

Wordlessly Lucy shook her head.

'And you know what? I take my hat off to you.' She

113

grinned. 'I suppose it's not something I'd like to do myself, but if you've found out what makes you happy ...' She leaned forward, looking at Lucy, and her face dropped in concern. She took her hand. 'Take care, love, won't you? Lucy?' She looked at her closely. 'Lucy, if you're not happy, there's lots of things you can try.' She nodded enthusiastically. 'Lots of things. There was a seaweed I was reading about only last week, from Zanzibar I think it was. It was in a magazine. It's meant to make you just *explode* inside.' She paused again. 'Perhaps that way you might find you can have a meaningful relationship with someone – someone else? I thought I'd try some myself,' she added encouragingly as she took in Lucy's uncomprehending face. 'No? You don't think it would help?' she hesitated, uncertain now. 'Then maybe it's just a question of talking it through with someone? Somebody you really, really trust? I mean, there's all sorts of things to try. You shouldn't feel there's nothing you can do about it. Lucy?'

'Oh, no. I don't feel that.' Abruptly Lucy started to laugh, making Zoe start with alarm. 'I can't believe he told you that. He really told you?' She shook her head. 'But I know *exactly* what I'm going to do about it. I'm going to go up to his office and kill him.'

She walked quickly towards the lift, then turned back and saw the doubt, the dreadful uncertainty there on Zoe's face.

'I'm joking, Zoe.'

'Of course you are,' Zoe said emphatically.

'And you know Teddy was too?'

Lucy looked quickly round the reception area to ensure

it was empty and then said loudly, *'Zoe, I do not have sex with strangers.* You know he's always been a terrible fantasist. He's pissed off because we split up last night, that's all. The truth is this is just his cheap, rather sad way of getting even.' She jabbed at the lift button with her finger. 'The seaweed sounds fun, though,' she added, as the lift doors opened and Zoe gave her a tentative, rather crushed smile back. 'Did you get an address?'

So this was what Teddy meant by revenge, Lucy thought as she was flown at lightning speed up to his floor, and yet how unlike him to show such imagination.

She found him crouching down beside the bottom drawer of his filing cabinet, half-hidden by his desk, and from the wary look on his face she guessed that he knew exactly why she was there.

'I was joking.' He stood up, protecting his face with a file, and then bent over his desk, not looking at her. 'Let's call it quits, shall we?'

'If you go down and explain that to Zoe.'

'What? Why would I do that?' He stood up and moved round her, then suddenly set off across the open-plan office floor, walking so fast she almost had to run after him.

'Because I don't want the whole of Barley & Bross thinking it's true,' she hissed back, striding as fast as he was, aware that he was making for the double doors at the far end of the floor that took them out on to the staircases. If he thought he could lose her, either by running up or down them, he was mistaken. She was far fitter than him.

It was as if he had the same thought at the same moment, because he stopped suddenly and turned around again and she was immediately painfully aware of where they were, standing in the middle of the eighth floor. She took in the watchful faces all around her, people stopping what they were doing, lifting their fingers off their keyboards, aware they mustn't miss this, whatever it was about.

'It is true. You're a thrill-seeker, Lucy. A cheap, sleazy thrill-seeker,' Teddy said, coming up close. 'Admit it. That's why you don't even want to see him again.' He looked round the room, aware of everyone listening, seeing how much he could do to damage Lucy's reputation – new, young to the job, not nearly so established as him – but then he stopped. 'Go back to work. Leave me alone.' He turned dismissively away.

'How dare you do that to me?'

He swung back to her in surprise. 'Oh, I dare. It's you who should be careful.' He nodded around the room.

'Teddy.' She leaned in close to him. 'Don't threaten me.'

And there must have been something of her fury in her face because he looked, suddenly, rather taken aback, as if he simply hadn't expected her to come at him again – little docile Lucy, who never usually answered back – let alone here, amidst his colleagues. And now that she had, he didn't quite know what to do next.

He shook her away, sidestepping her, and started to walk back across the room. She followed him silently until they returned to his desk.

'Go away,' he said, once again not looking at her, pretending to be searching for a piece of paper on his desk.

She waited but he didn't stop, so she put her hands on his desk and leaned close to him once more.

'Once and I'm prepared to let you off. But if you say this again you are slandering me and I will stop you.'

She waited for a few seconds more but he didn't move, so she pushed herself upright again and walked away, looking straight ahead, until she'd reached the double doors, swung them apart and arrived safely on the other side. Then she stopped, breathing deeply, aware that she'd been terrified the whole time but triumphant too, because she'd never ever behaved like that before, never dared to take him on.

Once outside her own offices, she put him out of her head, bracing herself for all the bustle and energy waiting for her on the other side of the swing doors, giving herself time to let calm, professional Lucy settle upon her. As the doors opened the smile was already breaking across her face, and she walked across the large open-plan area towards her desk, calling out hellos and Happy New Years, waving at her boss, Jon, who was sitting cross-legged on his desk, talking on the phone – and was she paranoid to think his beaming smile back at her was just that little bit too knowing?

She had a sudden fear that Teddy hadn't just talked to Zoe but had already targeted other significant members of Barley & Bross too. She looked across to her desk, wondering whether anonymous gifts of blindfolds and crotchless knickers would already be piling up, but when she stared more closely at Jon he gave her a surprised, what's-up-with-you, kind of look, so that she had to grin reassuringly and shake her head.

What's up with me, she wanted to shout across to everyone within earshot, is that *Teddy Arnold is a wanker* and you're not to listen to a word he says.

She went to her desk, sat down, switched on her table lamp and her computer and waited for it to boot up. Everything would be better once she'd spoken to Jane, tipped everything that had happened over the last couple of days out of her head and into Jane's lap.

By midday she'd drunk three cups of coffee, deleted several hundred spam emails, worked through fifty-six genuine ones, opened her post, gossiped and caught up with Jon, and started to pick up the threads of the two major projects that were still hanging over from the previous year.

First, Golden Mile Books. She'd been approached just before the Christmas break by the highly successful, highly aggressive Mr Galen, Director of Publishing, Sales and Marketing for Golden Mile Books, Edinburgh, who had finally decided to learn the art of delegation and hire a sales director. Lucy knew him by reputation, and during their first phone call it had become crystal clear how hard it was going to be persuading anyone to work for him, how unlikely it was that he would ever give someone enough space and responsibility to make the job work. She suspected that he knew it too. Even so, she'd spent the last week before Christmas making notes, working her contacts, sifting through CVs, and now that she was back she would shortly be putting together a list of potential candidates, then beginning the delicate business of the first approaches.

The second project had begun in the autumn and should have been over by Christmas. It had involved the placing of a new head of graphic design for Stillman Sound, a fast-growing multimedia company in Chelsea led by the fantastically cool Stuart Stillman. They had approached Lucy back in October and almost immediately she'd found them someone called Greta Dolland. Greta had loved them, they'd loved Greta, Lucy herself loved Greta. They'd gone through the motions of wrangling over her starting salary, her package and her start date, and then, just as Lucy had thought she'd managed to put the whole deal to bed, Greta's current boss had thrown a wobbly and insisted on holding her to the letter of her contract, having verbally agreed to waive her three-month notice period so she could begin with Spillman Sound at the start of the New Year.

She sat at her desk, scrolling back through her December phone notes to remind herself exactly where they'd got to before the Christmas break. But ten minutes later Lucy realized that, although she was peering in what looked like complete concentration at her computer screen, she could just as well have been playing Spider Solitaire for the amount of information she was taking in. She got up impatiently and walked around her desk to the meeting-room, the only place where she could get some privacy. She closed the door and sat on the sofa, neatly hidden from view, tucking her feet up, mobile in hand. She had to speak to Jane. She'd tried to be motivated, she'd tried really hard, she'd even managed to do some good work, but now she just had to call Jane.

She curled around her mobile, imagining the signal from her phone in Hanover Square zipping through the atmosphere to Jane's in Broadwick Street in Soho, and then, just as the line crackled ominously and she heard Jane's tinny voice say 'Hello,' she remembered with a sinking heart that of course Jane wasn't in Broadwick Street. She was in the Lake District on holiday with her boyfriend and his parents, and wouldn't be back in London until the following week.

'It's me,' Lucy said, 'and I've just remembered where you are. And I can't bear it. I thought you were going to be able to have lunch with me today.'

'Oh, Lucy,' she just about heard Jane cry, '. . . sorry. Really . . . was.'

'I don't know how I could have forgotten.'

'Cold as a witch's tit . . .' came back Jane. 'Too choppy, sick inside . . . but . . . games of Risk . . . my head in.'

Despite her disappointment Lucy laughed, then held the phone away from her ear, checking that it wasn't her mobile struggling, and tried again.

'Jane, you can't hear a word I'm saying, can you?'

'. . . signal . . .'

'But you're having a good time there, playing Risk with old Robin?'

Grisly and monosyllabic at the best of times, Robin Barraclough was Jane's boyfriend's father and in the early years she had despaired of ever holding his attention for longer than twenty seconds. But then had come the fateful day, the turning-point in their relationship, when Dillon had suggested Jane ask his father to teach her how to play Risk, because that was the game that made Robin come alive. *Do you secretly desire to conquer the world?* asked the back of the box. In Robin's case, yes, definitely, as soon as possible, and he executed his bold military manoeuvres with a precision and competitiveness that usually wiped his opponents off the board in record time. But not Jane. Jane, who was as competitive as he was, had proved a worthy adversary, and Robin's dad had decided he rather liked her company after all. He had no shame in bringing out the box every night when she came to stay.

'Sometimes six . . .' Jane crackled, but even so Lucy could hear the outrage in her voice. 'Believe it! . . . mother . . . Cashmere . . . Fucking way I am . . . she said that?'

'No! Yes! Whatever!'

'How was Inverness?' Jane asked, suddenly crystal clear.

'Life-changing. Amazing.'

'God . . . Done!'

'You'll be proud of me.' But she knew it was hopeless, that Jane was perhaps hearing perhaps one word in six. 'And Teddy is being awful. And I need you to tell me what to do – again.' She waited. 'Did you hear any of that?'

'And . . . flights . . . sure . . . today.'

'No, I didn't think you did.'

'. . . wait to see you.'

'Listen to me, Jane.' Lucy raised her voice as loud as she dared. 'I need to see you this lunchtime in Mr Wa's, please.'

Jane didn't answer. 'And I think if you explained to Dillon and got a train in the next hour or so you might still make it. Did you hear that?'

'Some . . .' she heard Jane laugh, and then the phone cut out again. 'Can't . . . No point, is there . . . when I get home.'

Fuck it, Lucy hissed at her phone, holding it in front of her and glaring at it angrily. Couldn't the signal appreciate just how important this call was?

'Teddy . . . cunt.'

'I know.' Lucy closed her eyes.

'Another . . . days . . . Come home.'

'Jane, I met someone on the way home.' She tried again. 'I wish I could tell you about him.'

'. . . say that . . . nice?'

Lucy paused. 'Very nice. But this is driving me crazy. I'm going to have to wait to tell you about it, aren't I?'

Silence.

'I don't know if you can hear me any more. And I know that you don't have a phone in your lakeside prison, so I can't even expect you to call me back.'

There was another pause, then Jane said, '. . . talk about Dillon.'

'No, please don't tell him.'

'. . . Not that . . . him and me.'

And then the signal died completely.

Lucy slipped the phone back into her pocket and then rubbed tiredly at her face. What had Jane meant about Dillon, about talking to her? Nothing could be wrong with the two of them, could it? Surely nothing beyond the usual moans and groans that Jane liked to fall back on every now and again? They were the most romantic couple Lucy knew, and seeing them together was all the proof she ever needed that there was such a thing as true love.

She stood up. She was imagining things. She was physically tired from all the driving the day before, emotionally drained from all that had happened, and she was therefore leaping to all the wrong conclusions. She pictured Jane, way too gorgeous for the freezing, dismal little living-room she'd be trapped in, cocooned in several layers of jumpers and huddled over the Risk board, convincing herself, as usual, that she was in the wrong house, with the wrong boyfriend.

'I'm going to the Lake District with Dillon and his parents for Christmas,' she'd announced glumly to Lucy as they'd fought their way up Oxford Street, battling it out with all the other Christmas shoppers. 'And we're going on a Christmas Day cruise.' With every day that passed she'd only looked forward to it less.

But the problem was that whatever she did with Dillon, whether it was a fantastic weekend at Le Manoir aux Quat' Saisons or the not-so-inspiring trip around freezing Lake Windermere, Jane carried the same question around with her wherever she went. *What am I to do about Dillon?* And it was a question she had never answered, no matter how many times she'd tried.

In Lucy's opinion it was very clear. Jane should stop asking and accept that there was nothing to do about Dillon. That Dillon was the love of her life and the fact that she'd met him at seventeen rather than later on, and had therefore never gone out with anybody else, was just one of those things. Yes, it meant that she'd had to alternate Christmases with his family and her own, trading her warm, exuberant parents for the difficult and strait-laced Robin and Dorothy. Yes, this would continue for countless years ahead. And yes, there were all those other men she was never going to get her hands on. But what was she getting instead? The brightest, most endearing, funniest, sweetest man she could ever hope to find, who loved her to distraction, who positively revelled in the fact that he'd found her so soon and could therefore misspend his youth with her as well as his responsible middle age. How much better, he believed, to do all the crazy, exciting things young people were supposed to do *with* her rather than before her. And when he talked about it like that, of course Jane was lit up too. It was when Dillon wasn't around that she became less certain, when she was out with Lucy (not that Lucy ever did anything other than tell her how lucky she was), when she heard about other people's see-sawing love affairs, which she'd never have, when she watched her friends light up with the dizzy excitement of new love. Even when her friends were weeping into pillows or losing weight with the misery of being dumped, she sometimes felt overwhelmed with jealousy simply because they were feeling so much, while her own cosy, familiar love for Dillon simply didn't compare. It was then that Lucy would give Jane a kick, remind her how she'd feel if she lost him, tell her to stop being self-indulgent, and Jane would shut up for a while.

They'd been friends all their lives. Lucy and Jane's

mothers had lived in the same village in Dorset and had had their baby girls within a few months of each other, and until the age of eleven Lucy and Jane had played together nearly every day. But then, with many doubts and regrets, Jane's family had moved to London and Jane had been sent to a high-flying, exclusive girls' day school, turning her skinny and beautiful and neurotic almost overnight.

While Lucy continued to fumble around at the Chilton and District Pony Club disco and play variations on tennis on the bumpy grass court at the bottom of her friend Miranda's garden, Jane was having private lessons at the Harbour Club and was already catching her first glimpses of seventeen-year-old Dillon as he was being put through his paces by his father, rather more athletic then, not yet reduced to playing out his competitiveness on a board game.

Jane and Dillon had started to talk. Then they'd started playing doubles together, first on opposing sides but all too quickly as partners. Both sets of parents were delighted by their children's new passion for the game, neither of them realizing there was an ulterior motive. And then one day they'd found themselves in each other's arms, kissing behind the curtains that separated the courts from the walkways, and Robin had caught them *the very first time*. Jane had graphically described her agonizing embarrassment. How she'd been standing with her back to Robin, how he would have seen her knickers, thanks to Dillon and his big hands rucking up the back of her tennis dress. And she knew that Robin still remembered it, now, nearly ten years on, every time they met. She could see it in the rather speculative look he always gave her whenever she reached forward to kiss him hello.

And so the long girly letters that they wrote to each other, funny letters that they'd both kept and reread when they were feeling drunk and sentimental, charted their teenage years and revealed that by the time she was eighteen Jane had only ever kissed two men, the second of whom was Dillon, the first a man she'd met at a Saints and Sinners party. It still galled her that the only other man she'd ever kissed had been dressed as a nun.

When Lucy had started university, Jane had got a job at LWT and a flat in Waterloo, sharing with a school-friend, and still she and Dillon had hung on together, at times only by the thinnest of threads, at other times so in love that Lucy wouldn't have been surprised to hear that the two of them had got engaged.

Two years on, Jane had jacked in her job and she and Dillon had done what he had always wanted them to do, taking a year off to travel around the world together. They had worked whenever they ran out of money and the rest of the time they'd lazed, doing exactly what they liked, crossing countries on a whim, climbing mountains and snorkelling on coral reefs, lazing around on a hundred beaches, canoeing down the Zambezi and climbing Mount Kilimanjaro. And then, finally, they'd come home, and at almost the same time Lucy had arrived in London and she and Jane had found themselves working only a couple of miles apart from each other, Jane at a production company in Soho, Lucy in Hanover Square.

Six months earlier, Dillon had suggested that Jane move

in with him, into his flat, because it was bigger, even though it was in Balham rather than her rather more upmarket Gloucester Road. I don't want to live in blinking Balham, Jane had moaned to Lucy. And then had come the inevitable question, what am I going to do about Dillon? Chuck him simply because she'd met him too soon? When he was in every other way perfect? And, struggling as she was at the time with Teddy, Lucy had felt uncharacteristically livid with Jane for taking so much for granted, for not understanding how lucky she was. And for talking about it the whole bloody time.

Jane wasn't going to react well to the story of the Milestone Motel. It was going to make her feel more boring and predictable than ever, and realizing that, Lucy even considered not telling her about it at all – but she dismissed that straight away. It was inconceivable that something so huge was not going to be discussed with Jane, her closest, dearest friend.

Still, it was going to have to wait until the following week. Impatiently, Lucy drummed her fingers on her desk. She opened the door and saw that her floor was almost deserted. She looked at her watch and saw it was one o'clock, lunchtime. She thought about how the sales had just started, Selfridges, Fenwicks ... There were ways of getting over the disappointment of Jane. She got up from her desk and slipped on her coat.

8

If she didn't care about him, what was she doing looking at his house? Or, more accurately, what was she doing sitting in her car in the dark, squeezed into a space almost directly opposite his brother's house, watching a man in a dinner jacket make his way along the street towards her, a girl in a glittery black evening dress trailing along behind him? The man stopped for a moment to let the girl catch up and Lucy watched him slide an arm around her waist and then they disappeared down the road behind her, the clackety-clack of the woman's sandals slowly fading to silence. Lucy turned back to the house.

She'd only been parked in the space for a few minutes – surely that didn't qualify her as a stalker? Anyway, she was having supper in the next door street and was lucky to find a space so close by. And she really wasn't there to see *him*, she just wanted to see the house again, sit out on the street and look at it, just for a few moments. She went to open the car door but instead wound down the window and breathed in the cold night air. It had stopped raining, but the look of the glistening wet pavement caught in the orange glow of the streetlights and the wet stone steps leading up to the front door that shone like silver were just the same as she'd remembered. Last time the door had opened under the weight of her gaze and Luke had

come out on to the steps, Jude rushing to get out of the
car to reach him. Now it was a shadow of a house, an
empty space between its two brightly painted, brightly lit
neighbours. She looked at the windows, three rows of two,
black shadows within the dark blue, the faint reflection of
the glass, saw that the downstairs curtains were undrawn
and one of the sash windows was open at least a foot, so
that anyone who wanted to pinch anything could have
peered straight in. It looked empty and probably was, and
staring at it inspired no feelings of excitement, longing or
regret, no rush of blood to the head. If anything being
there made her feel exposed and a bit silly, not so far
away from the stalker after all. She unclipped her seatbelt;
she should go.

But then, as if she'd worked some magic just by starting
to move, a light came on in a downstairs room. She stilled,
drawn to it like a moth, and then suddenly there was Jude
coming into the room with Luke standing behind him in
the doorway.

And it was a rush of blood to the head to see him again,
moving around the room, looking so exactly the same and
yet so unfamiliar too. At times during the week she'd
struggled to picture his face clearly, and seeing it again
now she wondered how she could possibly ever have
forgotten it. Not just because it was such a strong, lively
face, but because it was Jude's face, the face she'd held in
her hands and kissed.

She watched him come to the window and stare out
into the street, then turn back and say something to Luke.
She saw Luke hold out a can of what looked like beer, Jude

shake his head and turn back to the window, and she saw then that he was angry, was glaring out into the street, his hands clenched by his sides. She watched Luke move forwards, walk across the room to touch Jude lightly on the shoulder and Jude irritably shake him away.

She didn't want to see this. It was one thing to come back to look at an empty house and remember, but another to sit and watch them come to blows. She started to open the car door, planning on slipping past the window and out of the way, then changed her mind, turned on the lights and started the engine, went into reverse and began to edge backwards, wanting the car to hide her from their stare. And then her heart stopped because Jude's voice was now so clear and so close by that her first thought was that he'd seen her and was coming to get her, and she looked up to see him coming fast down the steps, just across the road from her, his long black coat slung over his shoulder, a bag in one hand and Luke just behind him.

'Leave me alone,' she heard Jude shout over his shoulder.

With a trembling hand she turned off the engine, flicked off the headlights, pulled on the handbrake and then, without consciously thinking what she was doing, undid her seatbelt and slid down in her seat until her head was level with the bottom of her window and half hidden by the steering-wheel. She could hear her heart pounding in her chest, could feel every muscle of her body tensing as she sat there, so still, keeping her eyes down because she knew that if she looked up it would be straight into Jude's disbelieving eyes.

Silence. Eventually she risked a quick glance out of her window and saw that Jude had paused on the bottom step of the house to turn back to Luke, who stood in the doorway, at the top of the steps of his house.

Start the engine. She must get away before he turned around and saw her. Because now that he was outside, what else was going to happen? She was a sitting duck, not even discreetly parked any more, but with the front of her car protruding out into the road. And what would Jude think but that she was a loopy stalker after all? Lucy cursed herself for ever coming here. And, having come, for getting into a space so minutely small that the only way to get out quickly would be to shunt the car in front and then reverse hard into the one behind.

Then things began to get worse. Jude turned his back on Luke and crossed the street towards her. He was walking fast, shrugging himself angrily into his coat as he approached, looking as if he might head-butt the next person who came close. No longer the dreamy, gorgeous Jude she'd known but far more compelling now.

'Stop!' she heard Luke call.

Go, Lucy begged him, shutting her eyes and slipping further down into her seat.

And then, just when she thought he was going to walk straight past her, Jude stopped right beside her car. Lucy winced and turned away, and then, when he didn't notice her, cautiously turned her head back and looked through the window at his jean-clad thigh, so close to her nose that she could see where the seam was white around the pocket and beginning to fray.

'Why?' Jude demanded.

'Because you can't just walk off. I want you to finish what you started. I want to know what you meant.' Luke was insistent, calling down the street. 'And I can't come after you or I'll lock myself out.'

'Stay there then.'

'Tell me, Jude.'

Walk on, Lucy begged.

'Lipton St Lucy,' Jude called back, as he moved down the street, and this time Lucy saw there was a new purpose in the way he was walking, a lightness in his step. 'Mum's party. Two weeks' time. I'll be there.'

'Stop, Jude. Don't do this.' Luke was still standing at the top of the steps. 'Think of Mum?' he called.

'Good one, Luke.'

'You're running away.'

Jude stopped abruptly. 'No, I have a job to do.'

'That's such crap.'

Jude turned around. 'Fuck you.'

For a moment Lucy thought he was going to go across the road and up the steps to hit his brother, but he stayed very still.

'Don't you tell me how I think, what I feel. You have no idea.'

'Then you tell me. Come back in the house . . . You won't, will you? Suddenly Aberdeen needs you.'

'You don't want to know what I think.'

'I know already. You want me to start behaving more like you, don't you? Pick up a girl like that one with the nose like a rabbit.'

Lucy uncoiled one clenched fist to bring her fingers slowly up to her face.

'That would be a start,' Jude agreed. 'That would definitely be a welcome change, if you think you could manage it. That would definitely lighten us all up.'

Lucy couldn't imagine where the punch in the words had been, but suddenly Luke was standing there at the top of the steps, looking so crushed and lost for words that she wanted to open the car door and fly up the stairs to him, spread her arms like wings to hold and protect him from Jude.

'I'm sorry.' Jude apologised immediately. 'I shouldn't have said that. I'm a bastard, you know that.'

'Is it too late?' Luke asked after a long time. 'Are you not allowed to change your mind?'

'I'll sort it out.'

'You won't. You'll go back to Aberdeen.'

'Forget about it,' Jude insisted. 'I'm not asking you to do anything. I've told you what it's like sometimes, that's all. And I shouldn't even have done that. My plane gets in at twelve, OK?' All the aggression had gone now from his voice. 'I'll be with you just after lunch.'

'Fantastic, Jude,' Luke said flatly. 'I'll see you then.'

And in response Jude turned away, so that he seemed to be looking straight at Lucy without seeing her at all. At the last moment he glanced back at the house over his shoulder as if he wanted to say something more, but Luke had already closed the door, and so he slowly walked away.

Far from putting the Middletons to bed, as it were, new questions were now falling over each other to get to the front of Lucy's brain. Watching Jude walk away down the street, she wanted to climb out of the car and run after him, to grab his arm and tell him he had to go back to Luke, try to put right whatever was wrong between them. She wanted urgently to ask him if the girl with the rabbit nose was or wasn't her. And what it was he might he have changed his mind about. Even as she told herself that of course she wasn't the girl and he wouldn't have changed his mind about her, and whatever their fight was about, it was none of her business. She could wish them well, hope that the two of them would sort out their differences, that the party would be a huge success, binding up the wounds, but she'd never *know* because it was nothing to do with her and she would never see them again.

And yet, suddenly now, sitting there in the car, she *did* want to see them again. She wanted to see where they lived, what they ate, the clothes they wore, the way they lived. She wanted to meet the glamorous mother who pined for her son and who did or didn't drown her troubles with wine, and the father who spent all his days outside as far from the house as he could be. She wanted to know why Jude and Luke had fallen out and whether they would ever put it right again. Wanted to know but couldn't. She unclipped her seatbelt and got out of the car, locked the door and turned back to the house. Goodbye, she thought, staring at it one last time.

And then she turned away, walked away, following the route Jude had taken just a few moments before her, but immediately breaking left into Moreton Street, towards number 27, where her supper and her friends were waiting.

9

'It's a sweet little nose,' Jane told Lucy firmly as they sat outside Mr Wa's sushi bar at lunchtime, five days later, and in answer Lucy wriggled it gently.

'Although, when you do that . . .'

'Which I don't ever, do I?'

'You do, actually, when you're thinking hard.'

'I do not!'

Mr Wa himself interrupted her, bringing to their table the red Perspex bowls of endaname, and saucers of pickled ginger, wasabi and soy sauce, then laying down square red plates of sushi and sashimi. Passing their table again a minute later, he surreptitiously dropped them two unordered Japanese beers because, he told them, Jane and Lucy were his favourite girls. Every time they had lunch there – at least once a week – he'd arrange for something extra to arrive at their table.

Lucy picked up a piece of endaname and slid her teeth down it, popping out the green beans. 'He was not talking about me. I was not that girl.'

'Don't be sad,' Jane looked across at her in concern. 'I'm sure it wasn't you.'

'But maybe I want it to have been me.' Lucy sighed. 'Bugger him and bugger Teddy too. Stick to Dillon, Jane, whatever you do.'

Jane reached across the table to squeeze Lucy's hand. 'You didn't feel any of this until you went back to the house. You've been so cool. And I'm so envious. Don't spoil it now by wishing you could see him again.'

'It's more complicated than that.'

Jane put down her chopsticks. 'Think about everything that's happened to you recently.' She stopped. 'All of it's good.'

'You think?'

'Of course!' She paused. 'How can I say this without getting it wrong?'

'Try.'

Jane nodded. 'OK,' she said, 'I will. When I said I nearly lost you, I think I meant it.'

Lucy looked at her sharply.

'With Teddy, you moved out of reach so fast. I used to see you together sometimes and I'd think I don't know her, doesn't she realize how much she's changed?'

'But in what way?' Lucy demanded defensively. 'You could still talk to me, we still had a laugh, didn't we?'

'Yes, when Teddy let you out, in your new knee-length skirts and your sensible shoes.'

'Don't say that. If you felt it so strongly you should have told me. Why didn't you say?'

'Because I thought you were happy. And I didn't think it was right to try to stir you up.'

Lucy looked down at her plate, dragging a chopstick through a trail of soy sauce.

'I'm not criticizing you, Lucy. I'm just telling you how

it was, for me. And I'm only telling you that because I want you to know how lovely it is to have you back.'

'I knew.' She looked up at Jane again. 'And I'm not angry with you, I'm angry with myself for taking so long to do something about it.'

Jane smiled in relief, raised her beer in salute. 'So thank God he wanted you to go up to his mum and dad for New Year.'

Lucy nodded. 'Thank God he thought *it simply wasn't fair to leave them on their own*. Because that was it, when suddenly I understood. Realized that I didn't have to go. I'd had that invitation from Julia Clegg for weeks, but I hadn't thought once about going. And then, I suppose I just thought sod it, sod him. And that was it.'

Lucy looked at her. Jane was wearing a cream wool coat and she had pulled the collar tightly around her neck so that her thick shiny auburn hair, newly streaked with dark red highlights and cut shorter than when Lucy had seen her last, was curled around her face. She looked lovely and hugely sympathetic, but still Lucy wondered how much she really understood. Because to Jane it must have seemed the simplest thing in the world to walk away from Teddy, who, after all, she'd only been with for a few months.

Impatiently she scraped back her chair and stood up. Seeing Jane's concerned face, she nodded at the gas burner that was standing tall above them, like a parasol, barbecue-ing them hard. 'I'm hot.' She quickly undid her buttons and ripped off her coat.

'I thought you were about to walk out on me,' Jane said.

'Of course not!' Lucy sat down again. 'I'm far too hungry.'

Jane grinned back at her. 'I want to have sex with some gorgeous stranger in a Milestone Motel.'

'Jane, you don't,' Lucy exclaimed. 'Don't start on that again.'

'How many times?'

'What!'

She nodded. 'How many times did you do it?'

'That's a very personal question.'

'Which you can surely answer for me.'

'Why?'

'Because I'm thinking that if it was once you were only doing it because you liked the idea. Twice and you two really had a good thing going. Three times and, quite frankly, Lucy, I'm a bit shocked.'

'Once,' Lucy said in a small voice. 'And we were out of the room again in an hour.'

'There you go. It's a good thing you're not seeing him again.'

Jane helped herself to a piece of sushi, poured over a little soy sauce, deftly picked off the salmon with her chopsticks and popped it into her mouth, then looked back at Lucy. 'I wonder if he had a girlfriend.'

'No, Jane. Listen to me, he might have done but that wasn't the problem. And anyway, if he did he wasn't going to tell me. Nothing in our real lives mattered that day. That was the whole point. He didn't want me to know anything about him. Right from the start, he didn't want to talk about his family or why he was working in Aberdeen. And he didn't want to find out anything about me, either.' She shrugged. 'He doesn't know how old I am, doesn't know where I come from, where I live, if I have a boyfriend. Doesn't know I have a fourteen-year-old brother competing in the National Swimming Championships next month. Doesn't know that my dad's thirty years older than my mum, or that they met on a ship sailing to New York, doesn't know I . . .' She stopped and smiled. 'Oh yes, he does know I trained as a vet and he does know that I'm a headhunter. But he doesn't know the name of the company I work for. He knows I catch the tube at Barons Court but not where I get off. He doesn't know about you or my other friends . . . And I barely know anything more about him.' She thought back to the weekend, sitting outside his brother's house in the rain. 'Well, I didn't until I sat outside his house on Saturday night. I know a bit more about him now. I know he's having a hard time with his rather sad older brother and that he's somehow hurting his mum's feelings. I think he's holding out for something she wants him to give up on.' Lucy heaved a huge sigh, running out of steam abruptly.

'He's stirred you up, made you catch a glimpse of a new exciting world you'd like to see more of. Take advantage of it. Let it take you somewhere new.' Jane shrugged. 'I don't know, go travelling, jack in your job. See the world if you're suddenly so restless here.'

Lucy looked at her, surprised. 'Are you talking about me or you?' She waited, but Jane didn't answer. 'Since we sat down here today you've not been right. And talking to me like that – something's happened, hasn't it?'

'Mmm,' Jane admitted, sighing deeply.

'Oh, God, Jane, tell me what it is! Something awful? Something exciting? Are you getting married? Are you pregnant?'

'Dillon's asked me to move to Australia with him. Three years, he says it would be, and more if we liked it.'

'Australia?' Lucy said in a quiet awestruck voice. 'That's a very long way away.'

'He's been offered a great new job,' Jane explained tonelessly, looking down at the table. 'And it is very exciting, even I can see that.' Slowly she raised her eyes to Lucy.

'And you don't know whether or not to say yes because you think this is it, if you say yes to this, you're saying OK, I'm ready to settle down with him.'

'And you know how I feel about that! I'm twenty-five. I can't help thinking there's still time for so much else.'

'We've talked about this so many times, Jane. You know how I feel, that you'd be crazy to lose him. That this is *grass is greener* taken to dangerous, dangerous lengths.'

'I know, I know. Of course I can see that too. And I love him and I don't want him to be with anybody else, ever. But, oh God. Call me a fool, self-indulgent, greedy, all the things I know I am, but I still can't look him in the eye and say yes, I'm coming with you. And it's like this awful test. He's thinking that by hesitating I'm proving to him that I don't love him like he does me. And I do.'

'I can see why he thinks that. He's had to put up with it so many times before, too, hasn't he?'

'This is the last time. I have a week to decide. Dillon's

going away on a conference all this week. And when he gets back I have to tell him what I'm going to do.'

Lucy nodded. She couldn't say what she should have said straight away, that of course Jane should go for it, that they were the best couple together she'd ever known, that they inspired her, made her see how good it could be, because she'd told her this so many times. And perhaps all the doubt that Jane expressed time and again meant something beyond her fear of commitment and insecurity, perhaps it did mean that she didn't love Dillon enough.

'You decide this one, Jane. Whatever I say, it's only what you think that matters.'

'I know.' Jane sighed, then reached again for Lucy's hand. 'The worst bit would be leaving you behind. How would I cope without you?'

'You won't have to cope without me. I'll be there, on the end of a phone. I'll come and see you, I'll email you. It won't be the same, but we'll still be there for each other, you know we always will.'

She glanced down at her watch. It was late, past three o'clock, time to return to their respective offices, no time at all to talk through everything in the detail it deserved. And seeing the look on her face, Jane nodded and pushed back her chair. They stood up to go, both of them feeling that the lunch hadn't worked as well as it should have done. That for such close friends, they'd come unstuck, neither of them being able to say what the other really wanted to hear, both of them wishing they'd had a little longer to talk.

'Don't worry about Jude,' Jane said again as they

reached Milton Street and the point in the road where they went their separate ways. 'He's sorted you out without you even realizing; just give it time and you'll see it's true.'

'And don't you worry about Dillon, either.' Lucy reached forward and pulled Jane into a hug, holding her tight. 'You know you had to arrive at this moment. Something had to force you to decide what you want. It's good that it's happened.'

Jane nodded.

'And we'll talk about it. We'll go out for supper – yes?'

Jane nodded again, turning away from Lucy and starting to walk away. 'And I hope Teddy leaves you alone now. I hope nothing else happens.'

'Nothing is going to happen apart from him going completely crazy and demolishing my reputation in Barley & Bross, which he's tried to do already.'

But then, the following Tuesday morning, exactly a week since the drive down from Inverness, something did happen.

*

That morning Lucy walked into Barons Court tube station at eight o'clock, barely aware of what she was doing because she'd done it so many times before. She bought a paper from the same newspaper stand and read the headlines until it was her turn to push through the ticket barrier, keeping her head down and rerunning a conversation she'd just had on the phone with her mum about whether she was going to make it home for the weekend.

She collected her ticket and moved seamlessly to join

another queue moving to the steps to the platform, one person in a sea of others. And then, just as she stepped on to the first step and looked back to her newspaper again, she passed a poster, an A3 sheet of dark green card with a cartoon car drawn in red at the top of it, seen out of the corner of her eye, and some words in bold black letters, taken in by a corner of her brain, so that she stopped, momentarily disconcerted, and looked up, wondering what it was that she'd seen. But then the tide of commuters was carrying her down onto the platform and she put it out of her mind and went back to her paper.

There was a train already waiting and she could see three or four empty seats in the carriage ahead of her. So holding her paper and her bag tightly at her side, she walked straight in, found a seat and sat down – and then in her head, she saw the poster again, the little red car at the top, and the words underneath, and she found herself whispering them disbelievingly, aghast that she hadn't taken them in properly before: *Lucy Blue, where are you?*

It felt as if everything inside her stopped. And then her heart began to pump again, leaving her lightheaded, as if she might be about to faint, and she stood up and turned to get off the train. But it was like one of those dreams where you're trying to run but can barely move at all, and even as she was forcing her legs forward towards the doors they were slowly closing in front of her, sealing her in, and then the train was starting to move, and then it was accelerating fast until it hurled itself headlong into the tunnel with a roar.

She clung to a pole, finding herself swinging and falling

again against the door as it swept her around corners at breakneck speed, further and further away from the poster. She looked at her bewildered face in the juddering reflection and felt nothing but alarm, not that he'd tried to reach her, but that the poster would be gone before she could get back to it.

Whereas the District Line from Barons Court to Earls Court stays above ground, the Piccadilly Line takes you deep underground, and as she was swept on, and she began to think coherently again, she started to plan what she would do once she arrived in Earls Court, trying to remember if it was simply a question of crossing directly from one platform to another to take her back or whether she would have to climb to the exits and then turn back. At this time of day the trains would surely be only a few moments apart; either way she could be back in Barons Court in what, ten, fifteen minutes time? Surely it would still be there. It had to still be there.

Finally she felt the train start to slow down, and around her other passengers left their seats and joined her to face the door. Lights from the platform appeared through the windows, and finally, with a hiss of air, the doors opened and Lucy left her carriage, slipping through the crowds of people, following the signs for the westbound Piccadilly line, hearing her harsh breathing as she pushed and dived her way past people, people everywhere, briefcases and rucksacks and feet. She had only to cross from one platform to the other but she could feel the hot air blowing up from the tunnels, telling her that a train was approaching, and still the people in front of her hardly picked up speed, so that when she finally reached the platform she was skating across the polished floor, long-jumping on to the train just as the doors shut again behind her.

Surely only five minutes since she'd left Barons Court station? Surely nothing could have happened to it in such a short time? She kept her head down, gritting her teeth, unable to look at anybody, unable to bear any distraction. He would have left her some way of contacting him, wouldn't he? And she'd answer him, wouldn't she? Whatever she'd said to Jane, whatever she thought about not wanting to see him again, he'd tried to find her; she had at least to to find out why, what it was he was wanting to say.

Finally the train pulled into Barons Court station. She was back above ground again now, and this time as the doors opened she was aware of the cold air as she walked quite calmly up the few steps and was back where she'd begun, just in front of the ticket hall.

And the poster had gone.

She knew it was true but she couldn't accept it. She could see exactly where it had been, pinned above the tube map. She could even see a tear of green paper left behind whenever whoever had pulled it down. But still she thought perhaps she'd got it wrong, that she'd walked into a different part of the station, that she hadn't retraced her steps in exactly the right way. She paused for a moment, trying to get her bearings, waiting for that moment when she'd realize where she'd gone wrong, but of course the moment didn't come because this was exactly as it should be, this was where she walked in from Palliser Road every morning. It all looked exactly the same as it did every morning of every day that she went to work.

She walked over to the wall where the poster had been, reached forward with her hand and touched the square of torn dark green paper and a piece of sellotape.

She placed her hand flat against the wall. It had gone, and it felt as if this were proof, if ever there was, that fate did not want the two of them together after all. Trying not to let the sense of anticlimax overwhelm her, she told herself how the right thing to do now had to be to get on the next train and put him, even temporarily, out of her mind.

But there was someone behind her, she could hear their breathing, and she spun around, for one crazy moment thinking that it was going to be Jude. But it wasn't, it was a girl, coming through the ticket barrier to stand close beside her considering her, head on one side, thin and pretty with dyed red hair and very pale skin and piercing blue eyes.

'Who are you?' Lucy asked.

'I'm Aileen Richards, Lucy Blue.' The girl grinned. 'It's you, isn't it? I could tell it was you from the way you touched the wall.'

She was looking Lucy critically up and down, obviously trying to decide if she warranted such an effort on her behalf, and Lucy wished she was wearing something more original and romantic, something more deserving of the poster than tights and a long blue coat.

'But it's gone,' Lucy mumbled.

'Lucy Blue.' Aileen Richards shook her head and smiled. 'Are you blind?'

Lucy turned around. Was he really there, hiding behind the ticket machines, about to jump out at her with a bunch of red roses? She looked, feeling sick with nerves, but there was nobody there. And then the girl took her arm and led her back through the ticket machines away into the middle of the ticket hall, where she stopped and started to look slowly around at the walls, and then she caught Lucy's eye and smiled again and looked again, and unsure whether she was looking for another poster, or even still looking for Jude, Lucy followed her gaze, staring round the shiny lime-green tiled walls, that in all the time she'd been using the station she'd never noticed before.

And suddenly, leaping out at her, Lucy saw the posters. All of them dark green, all of them with the little red car cartoon at the top, all of them saying the same thing. There were three of them stuck to the tiled wall in a line just in front of her, another over the top of a tube map. She turned again and saw two more, one above another, right in the entrance to the underground station, positioned so that she couldn't possibly miss them as she walked in. But she had.

She looked back to the girl and found herself starting to laugh. 'Thank you so much.' She walked to the nearest poster and read again *LUCY BLUE WHERE ARE YOU?*, saw that there was a telephone number beneath it, ripped the poster off the wall and held it in her hand.

'So how did he lose you?' the girl asked curiously, back at Lucy's side. 'Did he lose you on the train? Did he get to

Barons Court station and think *Sugar, where's that Lucy Blue got to?'*

Smiling at the thought that it could be so simple, Lucy shook her head and read the poster again, touched that he could have gone to such lengths to find her.

'You do like him, though?' the girl asked curiously, shoving little white hands into her pockets. 'I haven't been persuading the London Underground staff to leave them up for nothing, have I?'

'Did you do that?'

'Of course! It's so romantic, what he did for you. But you are pleased to be found?'

She turned back to her distractedly. 'Yes, Aileen, I am. But I can't believe he's done this for me. It doesn't make sense.'

'It's the loveliest thing I've ever seen. Not that I ever saw *him*. I wish I had.'

Lucy held the poster close against her.

'You realize he's the one,' the girl said wistfully. 'You do know that, don't you?'

'Perhaps!'

'What do you mean?' the girl cried, outraged. 'Anyone who does that for you ... He's definitely the one.'

'Shut up!' Lucy said, laughing now. 'You don't know what you're saying.'

'I don't need to know any more. You're going to make that call, that's all that matters. And when you find him you'll see I was right.'

She held out her hand. Lucy found herself gripped hard. 'You'll see,' she said again. Then she smiled at Lucy once more and was gone, slipping back through the ticket machines and disappearing out of sight.

Lucy found herself walking slowly out of the station, following the road for a few hundred yards until she came to a wet bench on a patch of muddy grass and sat down. The poster trembled in her hand as she held it out in front of her and keyed the number into her mobile.

'Hi,' said a voice after the second ring.

She tipped back her head and smiled at the sky.

'It's me,' said Lucy.

10

For the second time that day, Lucy leapt for a train. This time she left the platform with a good three feet to spare, and forced herself through an opening just a few inches wide, only to be greeted on the other side by a crush of soggy, steaming, irritable bodies, none of them remotely pleased at having their last few centimetres of space invaded by yet another thoughtless, pushy passenger.

She wriggled forward, aiming for a space just in front and to the left of her, about one foot square, where, if she stood on one leg, and kept her head bent at ninety degrees, she reckoned she'd be able to wait out the rest of the journey home. She looked up and caught the eye of a girl staring back at her disapprovingly, swinging on the end of a pole with a briefcase wedged between her ankles. Lucy gave her a what-a-hell-hole-this-is kind of smile but the girl scowled and immediately looked away.

If I told you what I'm doing tonight, maybe you wouldn't toss your head like that, Lucy wanted to say. Then you'd understand why I had to catch this train.

She looked at her watch and saw that it was nearly six-thirty. She'd known she was crazy to try to get home and change before she went out again to meet him, but she had to go home. She wanted to be out of her work clothes when she saw him and she needed just a few moments in her flat, alone, time to gather herself up before she saw him again, to quickly dry her hair from the rain, to go through her wardrobe, take deep breaths, persuade herself that she could cope with anything he might throw at her.

She'd spent almost the whole day thinking about what that might be, and then just as she was about to slip unobtrusively away there'd been a call from Greta Dolland, picking her moment to announce suddenly that she wasn't going to take the Stillman Sound job after all. And Lucy had had to swing into action and put Jude out of her mind, so that she'd ended up leaving the office half an hour later than she'd planned and with only seconds left to change her clothes before she'd have to leave again.

How mad was she still to be trying to get home first? It would have been so much simpler to have gone straight to the bar, which was what Jude imagined she'd be doing, the reason he'd picked Meat, a restaurant bar in South Ken because he'd thought it would be easy for her to reach by tube. But she'd order a taxi from the flat. If she was lucky it would only take ten minutes to get to the bar, and that way she'd add on twenty minutes to her time at home, plenty of time to get changed.

She'd wear jeans, she thought, as the train pulled to a halt in Earls Court station and then went very quiet, leaving only the disconcerting ticking sound that told her it was not about to leave again in a hurry. She clamped down on the rising feeling of panic in her stomach, ignoring it, thinking about Jude. He wasn't about to choose what he was going to say depending on what she was wearing, after all. He knew what he wanted her for. But what could it be, she thought again for the hundredth time, how could she think it was completely out of character, when the truth was she hardly knew him at all. Even so, he'd have to explain why he was going back on everything they'd agreed. Come to think of it, why he was even still in London? Hadn't he said he'd be back in Aberdeen by now?

She'd got no further on the phone, he'd sounded pleased that she'd called but cautious too, and so to-the-point that she hadn't liked to question him. He'd asked only if she'd meet him and when she'd said yes and had suggested that evening – she'd figured the shorter the time he left her wondering, the better – he'd mentioned a bar and restaurant in Arundel Street in South Ken that she'd never heard of, and had asked her what time and she'd said seven-thirty, and all he'd said then was *Good. See you then*, and had gone before she could even say goodbye. Hardly the grand romantic reunion she'd been expecting.

Forty minutes, she thought as the train finally arrived at Barons Court station. And then she'd find out what was going on.

On the street outside, she saw that the rain had got harder still. She paused for a moment in the dry of the station, wondering why it was that whenever she met Jude it had to be snowing or pouring with rain. And then she turned up her collar and ran into the street, shielding her head with her arm and leaping over the puddles.

She reached her block, unlocked the front door, ran dripping up the stairs and opened the door to her flat, undoing the buttons of her coat at the same time, pulling it off and leaving it in a damp heap on the floor, slipping out of her shoes, pulling her jumper over her head. Standing in her bra and pants, she rang three taxi companies before she finally found one free to pick her up and then, when the cab was finally booked, she walked through to the bathroom and stepped into the shower, rubbing shampoo into her head and tipping back her face to the rush of hot water. Minutes later she was sitting on the floor of her bedroom drying her hair, then she put on some make-up and pulled on her clothes. And by seven-fifteen she was ready to go, looking out of the window impatiently, waiting for the taxi.

When the intercom buzzed, she didn't even register that it was strange she hadn't seen the taxi arrive. She moved from the sitting-room to the hall and picked it up.

'Hi, I'm coming down,' she said.

'Lucy?' said a voice, Teddy's voice. 'I'll wait down here then.'

'No,' she gasped, leaping away from the intercom.

And then the anger pushed her forward again because Teddy was not going to do this to her. How could he possibly have known to come around now? She'd told nobody, not even Jane, that she was seeing Jude that evening.

She leaned back to the intercom. 'What are you doing here, Teddy?' She made her voice sound normal, calm.

'What do you think? I've come to see you.'

'No, but that's such bad timing! I'm going out, any minute now.'

'Lucy, I wanted to apologize. How I behaved . . . It was intolerable. I wanted to tell you face to face.'

'Thank you, Teddy, but I'm going out. Why don't we get together at work tomorrow, we could go out for lunch if you like.'

'You must be very desperate to get rid of me if you're offering to do that. Where are you going, anywhere nice?'

She shook her head, wondering what she was to do. Not just now, but for every day that followed too.

'Let's talk tomorrow, like I said. I really don't have time now.'

'Five minutes of your precious time.'

'But there's no point,' she couldn't help crying out in frustration. 'There's nothing to say.'

'How do you know that if you don't talk to me? Lucy?' He waited but she didn't reply. 'I'm not going to let you go out until you do.'

This was Teddy as he used to be. Insistent, not stopping until he'd trapped her into a corner and made certain she'd do what he asked.

'You are not going out without seeing me. You owe me that. At the very least you owe me that.'

'I owe you nothing,' she hissed, and slammed the receiver back into its cradle.

Immediately it buzzed again and furiously she picked it up.

'You owe me that,' he insisted furiously.

She waited.

'Lucy . . . Who are you seeing? Is it him?'

Her heart sank. Now she could see him waiting there all night.

'Perhaps tonight you might find out his name.' She heard him kick her door and alarm rolled through her. Perhaps now he'd go further, force his way upstairs?

'Let me in.'

'No, Teddy. I will not let you in.'

'Then I'll huff and I'll puff . . .' He started to laugh, and she imagined herself still in her flat an hour later, calling the police, watching from her window as he was dragged away. And then his laughter stopped abruptly and she heard the unmistakable sound of the taxi pulling up beside her front door.

She dropped the receiver back in its cradle, ran across to the window and looked down at the street, and with disbelief she saw him turning towards the taxi with a newspaper shielding the top of his bare head from the rain as he opened the door with the other hand.

'No! Wait!' she shouted. She turned away from the window, reached for her coat and her bag and her keys, and was out of the flat in just a few seconds, running towards the stairs.

But even as she descended them, clattering down as fast as she could to the front door, she heard the taxi's engine start to change, moving from a rumble into gear and then the inevitable awful sound of it moving off. She opened the front door to see it heading away fast, rainwater curving out from its wheels as it cut through the puddles, a figure, unmistakably Teddy, sitting tall in the middle of the back seat. And she thought, wretchedly, how she'd told the cab firm where she was going and that there was surely no chance at all that Teddy wouldn't now be heading there too.

It was seven-fifteen. No chance of booking another cab. She'd have to hope she found one on the street, in the rain.

All around her people were running for cover. But Lucy walked on, down her street, passing the tube station and walking out on to the Cromwell Road, surprised by how much better it felt to be outside and walking, rather than trapped in a tube, or waiting restlessly in her flat for a cab. What could Teddy do? What had he ever actually done but bluster and shout? He'd controlled her by suggestion, not action; he'd shouted at her once or twice in public, enough to make her nervous of it happening again, but he'd never done anything physical. And if he was there, waiting for her in Meat, Jude would be there too, and so would a crowd of other people. How bad could it be? Or perhaps Teddy wouldn't be there at all. She hadn't ever had him down as the particularly courageous sort. He'd arrive at the restaurant, perhaps, look inside. But then, more than likely, he'd walk away ... Wouldn't he?

And meanwhile, there was Jude, waiting for her. He was the one, the girl had said; how much better that she was walking to him through the rain. Weren't the most romantic reunions always in the rain? *Breakfast at Tiffany's, Cinema Paradiso, Singin' in the Rain.* Perhaps he'd be waiting for her outside Meat, and at the sight of her, wet as she was, he would open his arms and hug her tight, all explanations unnecessary after all.

Five minutes later, she wasn't so sure. The rain was too cold, numbing her cheeks and sliding down her neck and under her warm clothes, soaking her hair and sending dissolving hair mousse running into her mouth whenever she took a breath. And she was suddenly ravenously hungry too, images of hamburgers and chips pushing aside even those of Jude. She walked on, sidestepping the puddles, and all the time the seconds ticked away and she had to wonder how long before he gave up on her.

And then, when there was only five minutes to go before she was due to meet him, the orange light of a taxi magically appeared in front of her and she charged out into the road, madly waving her arms so that it barely had time to stop before it ran her over. She climbed in, apologizing for the pools of water she was bringing in with her, and breathlessly told the driver where she wanted to go.

*

Ten minutes late, she stood in the street looking up at a blue neon sign flashing Meat. With her heart in hands, she pushed through the door into a large dark T-shaped room, with a long bar running all across the back wall and tables and chairs lining each narrower side. It was dark, lit only by pencil-thin strips of electric-blue light that ran around the tops of the navy-blue walls.

People sat together chatting at the bar, or eating at the tables, and she took a few seconds to look around slowly and swallow the relief that Teddy wasn't there among them. Then disquiet began to build because she had to acknowledge, with bitter disappointment, that Jude didn't seem to be there either, certainly hadn't materialized at a run the moment she'd appeared in the doorway.

She scanned the bar for a second time, the chocolate leather and blue glass bar, with a mirrored wall running across its back. There were two or three couples in the middle and two solitary men standing like bookends at each end, both of them with their backs to Lucy and the doorway, one short and blond, one tall and dark-haired, neither of them Jude.

She turned to the rest of the room, trying to see the faces of the people sitting at the tables, thinking surely he hadn't given up on her? Not so fast, not after such an elaborate ploy to track her down? She looked at her watch again. She was fifteen minutes late, barely enough time for Teddy to have got in before her, let alone time for him to have deduced which man was the Scottish bastard who'd pinched his girl, and *persuaded* him to leave.

A waitress appeared at her side, a butcher's apron tied around her waist, but Lucy mumbled that she was looking for someone and edged closer into the room, searching even more carefully, peering into all the dimly lit corners, the strange blue light making it hard to distinguish anyone clearly, but seeing enough to know that everyone sitting down was with someone else, and that Jude wasn't there.

And it was only then that she walked forward a few more paces and scanned the bar for a second time. And this time met the eyes of the tall dark man who'd turned now and was looking at her, looking for her. And looking back at him, she finally acknowledged what she'd sort of known from the start but hadn't been able to accept. That

Lucy Blue, where are you?

Jude wasn't anywhere in Meat and never had been. And that the man who'd caught her eye, who was now walking towards her, full of purpose, as if he knew what her reaction would be and wanted to catch her before she fled, was his brother, Luke.

11

Lucy knew exactly what she should do. And yet she stayed, rooted to the ground, and waited for him to come to her, swamped with disappointment and with the knowledge that somewhere along the way she'd been made to look a complete fool.

'I needed to talk to you,' was the first thing he said, stopping in front of her.

And she was surprised that he wasn't even attempting to apologize, that it didn't even cross his mind that maybe she might not want to listen to him.

'I take it he's not coming?'

'No.'

'He never was?'

'No.'

'So you put up the posters?'

'Yes.'

She nodded. 'Then I'm going home.'

'No, you're not.' He shook his head. She'd have found him rather intimidating if anger hadn't been boiling up inside her. 'You can't,' he insisted. 'I have to talk to you.'

'Get off me.' She shook off the hand that had dared to touch her arm. 'You give me the creeps. You and your creepy posters.'

'No,' he spluttered, jerked into life by her words. 'It was the only way I could find you.'

'*Lucy Blue, where are you?*' she spat out furiously. 'You deceitful bastard. Making me call you like that, letting me think you were Jude. What were you *doing*?' She'd spoken his name aloud and immediately there he was in front of her again. And it was so hard to accept that she wouldn't be seeing him after all. In the course of the day she'd fast-forwarded to this moment a thousand times, had imagined him so clearly, how he would kiss her, his eyes alight with the excitement of finding her again. And now, she thought, glaring back into Luke's dark unsmiling eyes, she'd got this, this twisted, heartless man who bore no resemblance whatsoever to his lovely younger brother. She looked at the hard line of Luke's mouth, his high wide forehead and dark springing hair, at the uncompromising look on his face, and found herself taking two steps back from him.

'I had to be sure you'd come. The only way was to mislead you.'

'Why? For a game? Some joke you're planning?' Even as she said it she knew it wasn't that. No one as full of purpose as Luke was ever going to play a joke. 'Didn't you think I'd care?' She was aware of the rasp in her voice, loud in the little room, people starting to stare. She shook her head, dropping her voice again. 'No, you—' she paused briefly, searching for the right word, 'you *egotistical* man, you know what? Forget it. I *don't* care.'

'Jude doesn't even know I'm here.'

'So what? Is that meant to make me feel better or worse?'

'Better,' he insisted.

'It doesn't.'

He nodded, raking a hand through his hair. Belatedly it seemed to occur to him that stage two of his plan wasn't going quite like he'd expected it to, and that some degree of soft talking was necessary after all.

'But you're so wet,' he said, looking her critically up and down. When she didn't respond, he shrugged impatiently. 'OK, aren't you hungry? Thirsty?' He peered closer at her face. 'Oh, for God's sake.' The sweet talk ended abruptly. 'Stop being so damned stubborn. Stay for one drink, and then I'll take you home.'

'I've already shared a lift with your brother and that did me no good at all,' she snapped back. 'And whatever it is you want to say, every single bit of me is saying don't hear it, that the Middletons are not good news. Steer well clear of them. I came here tonight against all my better instincts, and I was wrong.'

'You make it sound as if we're a couple of psychopaths.'

'I wouldn't be surprised.'

'Don't be ridiculous.' He sighed heavily, gazing around the room for inspiration, found none, and turned impatiently back to her again. 'Look what I've done to find you. Doesn't it count for anything? Won't you lie awake at night wondering what on earth it might all have been for?'

'I'll never think about either of you ever again.'

'I don't believe you.' He leaned towards her, clearly now as irritated by her as she was by him.

'I don't give a damn.'

'Why come if you didn't care?'

'I nearly didn't.'

'Stop it!' Luke cursed, making her jump. 'Why won't you listen to me? Once I found you . . .' He shook his head. 'Why didn't I think what a major disappointment I'd be?'

'I have no idea.'

She turned away, towards the door.

'Just fancied a bit of room service, did you, in your Milestone Motel?'

She stopped, turned slowly back to him. 'Fuck off.'

'I want you to listen to me, Lucy.' Then, belatedly, he saw the hurt on her face. 'Lucy, I'm sorry.' Desperately he scrunched his hair in his hands. 'I didn't mean that, I'm not trying to taunt you, bringing that place up again. I'm sorry if it makes you so uncomfortable that I know all this about you.' Now he was speaking much more quietly and gently. 'I've been behaving badly.'

She looked at him.

'I'm rude and insulting. No wonder you don't want to listen to me.'

'This is the charm offensive now, is it?'

He shook his head. 'No, I mean I really have been behaving like an arse.' He folded his arms again. 'But what if I'm here to tell you that you were right to come, that he does really care about you? What if I can explain why he can't tell you himself?' He went straight on. 'You know what? I'm going to tell you, right now, whatever you say. I'm going to tell you standing here if you won't sit down.' He paused. 'And my feeling is you want to listen. I don't think you're quite ready to walk out of the door, after all.'

That was the moment to go, but, of course, she couldn't bring herself to do it.

'The first, most important thing, Lucy,' Luke said steadily, 'is that Jude does badly want to see you again. He talked about you an awful lot on the way down to Oxford.'

She shrugged, as if she couldn't care either way, even as her heart did a great flip of pleasure at his words.

'And if you'll listen I'll tell you why he hasn't told you himself.'

She shifted from one foot to the other, hitched her bag back over her shoulder, self-preservation still insisting she should go, curiosity making her stay, then looked up at him again.

'He was relieved to get out of the car and I was relieved to see the back of him,' she told him. 'We may have liked each other at the time, but we both knew it wasn't going to turn into anything more.'

'But don't tell me you two didn't *care*,' he insisted. 'Because I know that's not true – at least I know it's not true for Jude. If you could have listened to him after you'd gone, you'd understand why I'm trying to talk to you now, because there's so much more to know about Jude. And if you'll let me, I'll tell you what I mean. Nothing scary. Nothing awful,' he added hastily, seeing the sudden dread on her face. 'Just some things I think you'd be glad to know.'

Finally he'd got to her, and he knew it. He stood there quietly, waiting for her to tell him so, and as if to tempt her further at that moment the door from the kitchens swung open and a waitress appeared with a sizzling roast chicken on a wooden tray, with two wooden bowls of thin French fries perched on either side of it. Despite herself Lucy felt her stomach rumble, and tried to remember when she'd last eaten. She watched the tray make its way across the room to a couple sitting at a table at the edge of the room, and the girl picked up a chip in her fingers and bit off the tip.

'Are you hungry?' Luke asked immediately. 'Why don't we have something to eat? Come on, Lucy, it's the least I can do – buy you some supper while you listen to me.'

'OK,' she agreed, thinking what a good idea it sounded, but ashamed of what a complete pushover she was.

Instantly he sprang into action, grabbing a waitress, then steering Lucy, frogmarching her, across the room to an empty round table and two chairs in the corner. He helped her out of her coat and handed it to the waitress, pulled out her chair and practically pushed her down. He sat down opposite her, and while around them the bar buzzed with laughter and chat, and before they'd even talked about drinks or food, barely before Lucy had settled herself into her chair, he took a deep breath and started to talk.

And the first thing he told her was how, just over a year ago, Jude had been in a car accident and the girl he'd been with had died.

Luke was right. His news punched her in the stomach and changed everything. And as she listened, as Luke explained how Jude had picked the girl up at the station to bring her home, how she'd flown back from her parents' home in Italy to join them all for a second Christmas in

Oxfordshire, Lucy slumped in her chair with the shock of what he was saying.

'What was her name?' Lucy whispered.

'Gabriella.'

'Was it Jude's fault?'

'No.'

He sat back, waiting for her to take it in, and she looked away, unable to hold his stare, and sat quietly, trying to imagine how it must have been for Jude but knowing she could come nowhere close. Then she looked back at Luke, lost for words for him too.

He saw her stricken face and leaned towards her, full of concern.

'I know it's a shock.' He looked at her kindly. 'But I had to tell you. We couldn't have talked about anything else until I'd got it out of the way.'

She could see a waitress making her way towards them, the same one who'd caught her eye earlier, in her long white butcher's apron, coming through the swing doors from the kitchen with menus in her hand and a smile on her face, and Lucy willed her away, thinking not so soon, we've only just sat down. How can we hear about the dish of the day after Luke has just told me that?

'Can I interest you two in any drinks?'

Luke turned to her. 'Two minutes?'

The girl nodded and was gone.

'Sitting here, in a place like this,' Lucy looked around the room, 'I can't believe I'm hearing something so sad.'

'I'm sure.'

But of course, no longer a shock for Luke and for Jude.

They had to be carrying the knowledge of what had happened with them for every minute of every day, into whatever they were doing, wherever they were and far more acutely than she ever would.

And it was as if Luke hardly needed to tell her any more, because she'd seen the consequences for herself. How guilt had made Jude leave the Navy. How the loneliness of Aberdeen had become so attractive. How he could hardly bring himself to talk about home. How missing Gabriella had become such a part of Jude that it was there even when he'd been joking and laughing and sweeping Lucy off her feet. How easy it must have been to let Lucy go again, when all his thoughts had still been focused on somebody else.

And meanwhile, back in Oxfordshire, the whole happy Middleton family was slowly being broken apart. She'd seen him and Luke at each other's throats, after all, as she'd sat in her car in the street outside the house in Notting Hill.

'It's over a year ago now.' Luke was speaking again. 'It's a terrible cliché, I know, but Jude needs to move on.'

So that was why Luke had found her. It was his mother's birthday in two weeks' time and meanwhile Jude's misery was grinding them down. Time to find the girl Jude had talked about, the girl who perhaps might make him forget. After all, Luke had no doubt reasoned, how much longer was Jude going to take? Didn't he see he had a responsibility to the family to pull through now? She could almost hear Luke's voice telling Jude just that, wondered if that was what he'd been telling him when she'd watched them arguing outside the house in Notting Hill. He was the older brother, used to pushing Jude around, and now he was getting impatient. *Yes*, he'd have told Jude. *It was awful. Yes, Gabriella was a lovely girl.* Perhaps he'd even argued that Jude had to move on because *it's what Gabriella would have wanted.*

'I understand you'd like him to be happy again,' she said, carefully picking her words. 'I'd like it too. But surely he's got to be happy on his own before he's ready to meet someone new? Don't bully him into something he's not ready to do.'

'But he told me,' Luke insisted, 'all about you. Just by talking about you he was the happiest I've seen him. He was lit up by you, Lucy.'

Could it really be true? Could she really do that for anyone? And what did she feel if it was? She looked down at the table. She felt complicated and confused, flattered but panicky at the pressure it put her under.

'I hardly knew him.'

'But you knew how you felt?'

'I suppose, but ... I don't want to have to persuade him. Jude and I,' she shrugged, remembering he had heard it all anyway. 'Despite everything that we did, at the time, I ... It sounds so silly but it was like a fairytale day. I thought it was all to do with the snow.'

'The snow?' he repeated.

She heaved a deep sigh, aware that it wasn't just the shock of what Luke was telling her that was making her feel as if she might pass out.

'Are you all right?' He shook his head, staring at her worriedly. 'Lucy, you need to eat something.' He caught the eye of a waitress and almost immediately hot crusty French bread arrived at their table, then butter and knives and forks and thick linen napkins.

She broke off a piece of bread and ate it gratefully, then ate another piece smeared with butter, then smiled at Luke and he grinned back at her.

'I'm coming back to life now,' she said through a crumb-filled mouth, and stopped. 'Oh God, Luke, I'm sorry. What a terrible thing to say.'

'No,' he reassured her. 'It really doesn't matter.'

'What I should have said is if I'm coming back into Jude's life. If he cares as much as you say he does, then I should be certain that I want him and I'm not.' She swallowed the last of the bread, wiped her mouth with her hand and looked at him seriously. 'I hardly know him, Luke. And it wouldn't exactly help, would it, if I met him again and then I turned him down? We had an amazing time together. And yes, he's a very attractive man and that has a lot to do with why it happened. But that doesn't mean it's going anywhere. I don't think I ever thought it was love at first sight.'

'And when you thought it was him who'd put up the posters, how did that make you feel?'

'Confused, because I didn't think he cared enough. We never seemed to be on that level. But then I understood I'd probably got him wrong, that neither of us had given the other a chance to be how we really were. And he was showing me now . . .' She looked at him, rubbing crumbs away from her mouth. 'The most romantic gesture of my life, and it was you.'

'Forget about it,' he said briskly. 'How about love at second sight? Given what you know about him now. And there'd be no secrets between the two of you any more. Couldn't that happen?'

'But, Luke.' She felt better now, and something was occurring to her that surely should have been the very first thing she had thought of. She couldn't believe how stupid she'd been not to think of it before. 'Of course it can't work like you're saying it might. You're saying come back and make my brother happy, but the fact is, he's still in love with Gabriella.'

'No.'

'And you shouldn't be trying to rush him,' Lucy insisted. 'Jesus, a year, it's not exactly long. And in any case, surely it's up to Jude to know when he feels ready for somebody else? Who are you to tell him how long he needs to get over her? Maybe he never will. I can understand it's uncomfortable for you all, and time's pressing with the birthday party coming up and all that,' she paused, 'but what are we thinking! Of course it won't work. I can't believe you're even trying to put us together again.'

'Listen to me, Lucy,' Luke interrupted, then added in a rush, 'You've got it wrong. Jude was not in love with Gabriella. I was. She wasn't his girlfriend. She was mine.'

*

For the second time Lucy felt physically winded by his words, shocked that she'd got it so wrong. How could she have been so wrong?

'Oh, Luke,' she said, her voice choking on his name. She reached for his hand, but he flinched and pulled it away.

And now, for the first time, he was losing his cool. It was as if he'd been able to keep everything perfectly together as long as he wasn't the subject of their conversation, but now that they were talking about him she could see that he could hardly bear to talk, all the loneliness and battered spirit that she'd imagined for Jude there in Luke's sad dark eyes. How can it be true, she thought miserably, that everything I've just been thinking and feeling and saying about Jude is really about you?

'I'd have gone to meet her myself,' he said, talking calmly enough but unable to keep his hand from gripping the edge of the table as he spoke, 'but she caught an earlier train and I wasn't home. So Jude went instead of me. She must have thought it was brilliant, she was going to see me a whole hour earlier than she'd thought she would.'

'I'm sorry,' Lucy repeated the same useless words.

'Thank you.' And then he looked back at her squarely in the eye. 'But the point of telling you this is to explain why Jude has to have his life back. I want him to stop feeling guilty whenever he sees me. I want him to be with you, if you'll make him happy, if you want him. I'm this awful, malevolent shadow, hanging over him, stopping him meeting someone, bringing them home. I want him to feel free to walk into the kitchen at Lipton St Lucy and introduce his new girlfriend to Mum and Dad and me. But he thinks he can't, not while I'm still half-dead with grief.'

'Did he say that?'

'Yes, his exact words, in the middle of a fucking awful row last weekend.'

'And are you half-dead with grief?' she whispered.

'Don't ask me that.'

'I'm sorry,' Lucy said hastily, looking at his dark head as he bent to unfold his napkin and spread it slowly on his lap. Of course you are, she thought. I don't even need to ask. It's there in every word you say, every look you give me. It's there in your black eyes, in the way you flinch if I touch you, in the way you're so fiercely determined that your little brother should be freed of it, even if you can't be. And she thought of the lengths he was going to, to help Jude, and wished desperately that there was a way to help him too.

'And so you thought if you found me, delivered me back to Jude, that that would somehow make it all better?'

'Something like that,' he agreed. 'I want to prove to him that I mean it when I say I don't blame him and that I don't want him to suffer because of what I'm going through. It would be good for all of us if Jude, at least, was able to move on. And I think the fact that I've gone to all these lengths to find you will have an impact on him. It has to.'

'I do understand.'

'I'm sorry if I snapped at you then, but I'm not very good at talking about her.'

She looked away, and understood better than before how impossibly hard it had to be for Jude. 'And you really think it could work?'

Luke shifted in his chair, and then surprised her again with a smile. 'I wouldn't be here otherwise, would I? I think it would be wonderful. Honestly Lucy, more than anything you have to believe that he was completely bowled over by you. I think I had the full thirteen hours' worth of your conversation replayed back to me over the weekend in Oxfordshire.'

'Oh God, no.' She grimaced. 'Not all of it, please.'

'No.' He gave an embarrassed half-laugh. 'You're right. Perhaps not all of it. But what I'm trying to say is that you must know that this has come from Jude's heart. I want it to work for that reason more than all the others.'

'Any other reasons?'

He grinned. 'What, apart from the fact that he's never shown any taste before?'

'Oh, great,' she laughed. 'Sell him to me, why don't you?'

He shifted in his seat. 'Have you anything to lose? Is there someone in your life already?'

'No,' she said. 'Definitely not.'

'Thank God for that.' He stretched back in his chair. 'And thank you, too. I really didn't think you were going to stay.'

She laughed. 'Because you gave me the creeps, didn't you?'

'I don't think I'll ever forget it.'

'I'm sorry.'

He grinned back at her. 'You're forgiven, just.'

Inexplicably she found herself starting to blush.

'So,' she said brightly, twisting her napkin in her hands. 'When were you thinking I would see him again? I suppose he's back in Aberdeen now?'

'I've been wondering about that . . .'

'Oh no, not another plan?'

'Yes, another plan,' he said apologetically. 'Can you bear to hear it?'

But the smiley waitress was back at their table, explaining their choices. A half leg of roast lamb, rib of beef or roast chicken. Potatoes, fried or dauphinoise.

'I'm guessing you're not vegetarian?' Luke said, looking at her across the table, and she shook her head and smiled back at him, feeling suddenly a bit shy at the prospect of a whole meal with him, now that the reason for them to be there together was out of the way.

They ordered chicken and chips and another bottle of wine.

'Cheers,' Luke said, clunking his glass against hers when the waitress had left them alone again. 'So, what are you doing the weekend after next?'

'Could I be meeting Jude?'

He nodded. 'My plan was that you should come to my mother's birthday party. Black tie, bit of music, bit of dancing, it will be big and noisy enough for you and Jude to get lost in it together. I think it would be perfect.'

Lucy took a great gulp of wine, feeling the kick of excitement course through her as she swallowed. The thought of seeing Jude again made her feel warm and jittery. But go to the party? Meet him with his family all around him? If it worked, Luke was right, it could be perfect. She could see herself in her pink dress, dancing with him cheek to cheek, him looking unbelievably gorgeous in black tie. But what if it was a disaster? Surely meeting him again amid a crowd of others would make it even worse?

'You could come down in the morning,' he said reading her thoughts. 'Lucy should come to Lipton St Lucy in the morning. Don't you think it's fate that you have the same name? That you're here with me now? That I'm bringing you home?'

She blushed, remembering the conversation she'd had with Jude about her name and the name of his village as they lay on the hotel bed together. But Luke didn't notice her discomfort. He leaned towards her, his eyes bright, his face that had once seemed so hard now alight and warm and full of enthusiasm. 'Don't you think it's perfect?'

'You are a romantic,' she said, looking away.

'About this I am,' he nodded, unabashed. 'I feel as if you were meant to come into our lives. In my head you've become our talisman.'

'No.' She shook her head. 'Too much pressure, Luke.'

'It's all right, I'm joking, sort of. If you and Jude don't work out, that's fine. I just want him to see you again. I want him to see I meant what I said.'

She nodded.

'So perhaps you should turn up at Lipton Hall in the morning before he arrives? Meet my mother and father, if you want to, and I'll be there, and as soon as Jude arrives at the house I'll talk to him, so that by the time you see him he'll understand that you haven't just turned up uninvited. Otherwise,' he frowned, 'I think he might give you a bit of a hard time.'

'Of course he would. He'd hate it. He'd think he was being stalked.'

'And he's stubborn, and he won't like being set up, especially by me. But trust me, Lucy. It will all work out. Once he's realized why I found you for him, once he sees what a leap of faith you took, he will be so chuffed . . . It's the most flattering thing in the world. And then you could celebrate finding each other again, have fun, watch the fireworks.'

'Fireworks?'

'Fireworks. My father doesn't believe in doing things by halves.'

'It all sounds terribly grand. I'll be terrified.'

He smiled, realizing that, implicitly, she'd said that she would come. 'I'll look after you.'

And he would, too. She knew already that she could trust him to do that. But what about Luke himself? Wasn't all this the wrong way around? Shouldn't Jude have been looking after Luke? I'll tell him, she vowed. We'll work on Luke together. We'll find someone to make him happy again too.

'Jude will behave himself, you'll see.' Luke rolled the stem of his wineglass between his fingers, considering her. 'And if he doesn't . . . then he doesn't deserve you.'

'Thank you.' She laughed, awkward again, and she

picked up her glass and downed the rest of the wine. No more, she told herself, immediately feeling it take effect. But then she looked back at him again, unable to resist. 'I have to ask, Luke. What sort of girls does he usually go for? Are they so different from me?'

'There have been a disproportionate number of blondes,' he said carefully. 'Tiny little blondes . . . and they're usually allergic to dogs. And they always have very long hair.'

'Personalities, Luke?'

'Not so far.'

'You're so disapproving. Do you tell him what you think of them?'

'If he asks.'

'What, marks out of ten? Look at the moustache, that one had a nose like a rabbit, that kind of thing?'

He stopped in surprise, his glass of wine half-way to his mouth. 'What did you say?'

'That one had a nose like a rabbit.'

He put down his glass. 'Which one did?'

'I don't know which one it was.'

'How do you know any of them did?'

'Just a guess.'

It was satisfying, in a reckless kind of a way, to see how far she'd thrown him. But even with the wine loosening her tongue she knew that she wouldn't go any further and that she shouldn't have said anything at all.

He let it go. What else could he do?

'I suppose we talk about a few of them.' He winced. 'And OK, I know it's incredibly pompous to say and you must never tell Jude, but what I'm trying to tell you is that Jude's girls have always been of a type and they're nothing like you.'

And why did she care? Why was she so pleased to hear he thought her different?

'Food,' she said decisively. 'Where is the food? I have to eat.'

She turned away from him, searching the room for a waitress, and saw Teddy making his way towards their table. His face was pink with sweat and wet with rain, his hair and his suit soaking, and he was breathing hard, his eyes darting between Lucy and Luke.

'Whatever he says,' she hissed urgently to Luke, catching his sleeve, 'you must not believe him. Please.'

'Who?' he asked in surprise, then followed her gaze and saw.

'Hello, you two,' Teddy said with a tight, fixed smile, crouching down between them and wiping his face with his hand. 'I thought I'd find you here. I gave you a head start, Lucy, I've been hanging around outside. Sorry I'm a bit wet.' Then he held out his hand to Luke. 'Lucy didn't tell me your name. Pleased to meet you . . . ?'

'Luke,' Luke introduced himself, grasping the damp hand.

'And I'm Teddy. No doubt Lucy's told you nothing about me at all.' He turned to her. 'Lucy, close your mouth. I can see all your food.'

Luke pushed himself back from the table.

'Who are you?' he demanded.

'How about I pull up a chair and explain?'

'No,' Lucy groaned.

Was this to be the pattern now? Teddy appearing like a spectre at the feast whenever she was with another man? And yet, at the same time, looking at him standing there blustering and soaking wet, seeing the wild look in his eye, she felt responsible, and miserable too, that he could be behaving like this because of her.

'Oh, I think I should explain.' Teddy turned back to Lucy. 'Because in all your excitement I think you might have forgotten to mention me.' He balanced his hands on their table, then looked up again at Luke. 'And I think Scottie here should know that while you two were busy driving off into the sunset together, I was lying in bed waiting for you in your flat, half out of my mind with worry. I'm Teddy,' he said, and his lips twitched at the shock on Luke's face, 'Lucy's boyfriend. At least, I was. I've probably scuppered my chances now. '

'Please, Teddy,' Lucy said desperately.

'Please what?' he demanded. 'Please go? Please don't make a scene? Please don't tip this glass of wine over his head?' He tapped it with a finger, making it sing. 'Please don't tell Luke here what an untrustworthy bitch he's having dinner with?'

And she heard what he said and realized just how much had finally changed after all. That although Teddy could threaten, and might indeed do just what he said, she could turn away from his words. She *had* cut loose and he couldn't get to her now. She was still concerned about the kind of scene he had in mind, embarrassed by the fact that Luke was watching it all, but it was not as it used to be. Now she could hold her ground.

She turned quickly to Luke, who hadn't moved a muscle. 'It's OK,' she told him calmly, 'it's OK. Let me deal with this.'

'If you can.'

And then she moved back to Teddy. 'What are you doing this for? Why are you here?'

'Because I'm a little pissed off, Lucy. Can't you tell? And I want you to leave your delicious dinner, and Luke here, and come with me now because I want to talk to you, and you refuse to talk to me, and this seems to be the only way to get your attention.' He waited, but she didn't move. 'And if you don't come with me now, I'm going to make even more of a scene.'

'Make a scene then. Tip the bottle over, throw the chairs around. Get arrested. What good is that going to do?'

'It might make me feel better.'

And at that point Luke stood up, towering over Teddy who was still crouched down, level with Lucy. 'I want you to leave us alone,' he told Teddy. 'Up and out. Right now.'

And immediately Teddy rose to his feet too, turned to Luke, who was still a good head and shoulders taller, and defiantly clenched his fists, looking up at him aggressively. And Lucy could see it all playing out in front of her, the swinging punch from Luke that would send Teddy sprawling on to the table among the chicken and chips, wine-glasses smashing, everyone starting to scream.

'Get out.' Luke said it calmly and with easy, quiet authority.

'I'll get out. But Lucy is coming with me.'

'No, she isn't. She's going to finish her meal.'

'Yes, I am, Luke,' Lucy interrupted softly. 'I have to go with Teddy.'

All the uncertainty and doubt that Teddy had sought to create was there suddenly on his face, and she hoped so badly that she'd be given another chance to explain.

'We've talked enough, haven't we?' she pleaded. 'I've said yes, completely yes. You know I'll do it.' She saw the hesitation still there. 'And I haven't misled you about anything at all, please believe me.' She turned away, reached for her coat.

She could see the waitress coming towards their table now, with a tray of food, knives and forks wrapped in white linen napkins, a fresh bottle of wine. How badly she wanted to stay with Luke and share their meal together. They'd had so little time. But now Luke was standing to meet the waitress, explaining that he wouldn't be staying either, reaching for his wallet.

Lucy slowly did up the buttons of her coat, and Teddy, knowing that he'd won for now, stood there quietly watching her.

'Will you be all right?' Luke asked, coming between her and Teddy and standing close beside her, full of concern. 'You're not frightened of him?'

'No.'

And so, reluctantly he stepped aside to let her go.

'Thank you, Luke,' she said. And she looked back at him

one last time, as Teddy took her by the arm and steered her away then out through the doors and into the street.

'You humiliated me in there,' he said as soon as they reached the pavement outside. 'Made me look a fool.'

'You did that yourself when you came in to find me. And it was awful, Teddy!' She shook her arm free. 'How could you?'

'Because I thought I wanted you back. I thought I didn't want to lose you. I thought if I fought for you, you'd realize how much I cared.'

'You thought?' she said bitterly.

They were walking slowly down the street, going any-where. She watched people hurrying along on either side, saw the pavement shining pinks and reds and golds from the lights of the passing restaurants and shops.

'And then, when I saw you in there, with him . . .' Teddy gave her a tight smile, of relief and triumph. 'I realized how cheap and insignificant you are and that I didn't want you after all.'

'So why didn't you leave?'

'Because so far this has all been about you and what you want. And nothing at all about me. I thought it was time to redress the balance.' He stopped walking and turned to her, and Lucy saw something wild in his eyes and wondered if she'd been wrong to walk so freely out of the restaurant and away from the security of Luke.

She looked away from him and saw that the street, after being so crowded with people entering and leaving the restaurants around Meat, was now almost deserted.

'Our relationship only worked when I did exactly what I was told,' she said, trying to sound brave and firm. 'And now I can't be like that any more.'

In answer she felt his hands suddenly gripping her shoulders hard, felt herself being walked across the street and shoved up against a wall.

'And I am telling you not to speak to me like that!' he insisted, inches from her face.

'Let go of me, Teddy.'

'I am telling you to listen because I do not want *you*. Understand?' Is it clear? I do not want *you*.'

He gripped her head in his hands, reached forward and kissed her hard on the mouth, then stopped, only inches from her face. 'Goodbye, Lucy.'

Lucy stood there, arms at her sides, looking at him, making no attempt to push past him and run away, still so calm, because she had almost known from the start that this was where everything between them had been heading, ever since their relationship had first begun. That there would be an end and that Teddy would desperately need to control it. And in a strange way she was glad to be confronting it at last.

'Is that all you wanted? Just to feel as if you'd won, this one last time?'

'Maybe.' He patted her cheek with his hand. 'This way I am not being tipped out of your flat into the rain at three-thirty in the morning. I am not being interrogated by Zoe. I am not being forced to talk to you via intercom because you're in such a hurry to reach that arsehole back there.

Now, *I* am telling *you* how it is and *you* are standing here and finally *you* are listening. And when *I* am ready *I* will walk away.'

'You're crazy.'

'No, I'm not. Crazy would be wanting you back and I certainly don't. I probably won't even have to set eyes on you again – we didn't before.'

She would see him again, she knew she would. They'd probably find themselves sharing a lift together the very next morning. But she didn't care, she knew she could bear it, because after all that he'd said, she knew now it was finally over.

After he'd gone, she waited for a few moments more in the dark doorway and then moved back into the street-light and looked around. She turned back the way she thought they'd come, unsure about how far they'd walked, wondering if she could see the entrance to Meat there in the distance and if there was any chance at all that Luke would still be waiting for her.

As she walked hesitantly back, she realized that she and Teddy had not moved so far from the restaurant. She turned a corner and straight away she could see its glowing blue sign lighting the street. And there, standing beside the doorway, Luke was waiting for her, and even as she was telling herself she'd hardly got the right to do it, she was moving forward quickly, straight into his arms, and she let him hold her tight, closed her eyes to the warmth of his body against her cheek, feeling the relief wash through her and then the tears start to spill.

'I shouldn't have let you go.'

'No.' She shook her head, keeping it buried so that he couldn't see her cry. 'It was the best thing.'

'Poor Lucy. He didn't want to lose you, did he?'

She shook her head.

They stood there together for a few moments more and then she felt his arms loosen and he gently let her go.

12

The following evening, Lucy was sitting on the sofa in Jane's sitting-room with Jane's dog Pablo curled up beside her as she looked at Jane's photographs of the Lake District and worked her way through a bowl of pistachio nuts.

'Dolly the sheep,' said Jane, passing Lucy a photo of Dillon's mother, who was standing square on, feet planted firmly, giving the camera a glassy smile.

Lucy took it and studied it more closely. 'But look at her face. I think she's feeling nervous of you, Jane.' She meant it too – Dillon's mother's eyes were wary and the smile was trembling around the edges as she stood, in her bottle green Guernsey jumper and her tweed trousers, a light silk scarf knotted carefully around her neck. 'I expect you were being horrible.'

'Not all the time.'

'How much?'

Jane rubbed her face, looking just a little uncomfortable. 'Most of the time I was nice, but occasionally I got a bit irritable, I suppose. I know she thinks Dillon's getting a raw deal with me. No breakfast in bed on a Sunday morning, like she gives Robin. She was dying to do it for Dillon too, but couldn't quite bring herself to come into our bedroom with the tray. She asked me if I'd like to prepare one together one morning *for our boys*.'

'And you put her straight?'

'Of course.'

'Poor Dolly. Poor Dillon too. Why shouldn't he get breakfast in bed?'

'He can. He does, when I've not been told to do it by his mother.'

'Jane,' Lucy admonished. 'It was only a few days.'

'And most of the time I was very nice. Dillon never complained.'

'But you say they're so thoughtful and sweet to you.'

'They are – bought me a dustpan and brush for Christmas.'

Lucy moved on to the next picture, which was one of Dillon and Jane sitting together, arms round each other's shoulders.

'Look at the two of you! This is what matters.'

'Robin took that one.' She picked it up off the table. 'When we were having lunch the day we were coming back. It was freezing, but we all agreed we wanted to eat outside.'

And watching her face, listening to the wistful note in her voice, Lucy was so sad for Jane that she had to force herself not to touch her, not to say anything, because after so many years together her instincts were good, and she knew that at that precise moment Jane was holding herself together and did not want to break down.

She looked at the photo again, at the way Dillon was smiling at Jane with such pride in his face, such delight that she was standing next to him.

'I'm wound up about Australia,' Jane said defensively.

'We hardly talked about anything else. Robin and Dolly don't think we should go. But then, Robin's seventy-four and of course they don't want their only son moving across the world.' She gave a sad laugh. 'I don't think I want him to, either.'

'Three years isn't a lifetime.'

'But it is. This is me saying yes. I'm with him for the rest of my life.'

'And what's most bothering you most? Is it simply the fact you've never tried anyone else?'

'I know it's hard for you to understand,' Jane replied darkly. 'But I can see myself in a few years' time, married to Dillon. And I fear that one day I'd be really, really stupid . . .'

'That's the fear everyone has. What will we be like in years ahead? Knowing you won't both feel the same as you do now, but hoping it'll be even better, not worse.'

'Stop talking about it then.' Jane leaped to her feet in agitation.

'Poor Jane.' Lucy looked up at her from the sofa and grabbed her hand. 'This is horrible for you, I know. And I'm trying to be helpful, being the voice of reason, but I understand what you mean. For God's sake, I don't know what I'm doing either, do I?'

Jane squeezed her hand and let it go. 'So will you go to his party?'

'I did tell Luke I would, but it would be easier if I knew what I was letting myself in for. If I was going somewhere I knew.'

'Luke's on your side.'

'Yes,' Lucy agreed. 'Of course. And I like him very much . . . and I trust him . . . I mean he's . . .' She faltered, aware of the colour rising in her cheeks. 'I wouldn't go there without him.'

Jane looked at her sharply.

'What?' Lucy asked defiantly. 'I can say that can't I? It doesn't mean anything.'

'You tell me if it does.'

Lucy shook her head. 'Of course not, and stop smiling at me like that, Jane. Stop looking like you've got everything all worked out, because you haven't.'

'You like him, don't you?'

'No,' Lucy cried. 'Of course I don't.' She stopped for a moment. 'And if I thought I did, I'd have to bury it again, wouldn't I? What else could I do?'

'It depends what he wants.'

'Jane! Don't even go there. Don't tease me as if this is all one big game. It's not. It's so important that I get this right, for Jude and for Luke. I know just what Luke wants and it's certainly not me.' She paused. 'If I go to the party, it'll be to see Jude, not Luke.'

'Oh, bloody hell, Lucy.' Jane laughed, sliding an arm round her stiff frame, as Lucy sat hunched uncomfortably on the sofa. 'Teddy did turn up at the wrong moment!'

'And definitely don't mention him.' She pushed herself back on the on the sofa. 'I'm sure I imagined it. I'll see Luke again and I'll wonder what I was thinking about.'

'And if you do, we'll forget you said anything. But you

do see you have to go? You do realize that, don't you? There's no question about it. You absolutely have to go to their party.'

'Don't you think I should know what I want to happen when I get there?'

'Nothing has to *happen*. You've agreed to see Jude, that's all. To *see* Jude,' she repeated. 'Not jump straight back into bed with him. That's not the deal you made. From what Luke told you, all he needs is for you to be there.'

Lucy dropped her head in her hands. 'And am I allowed to say that perhaps I will still jump back into bed with Jude? That I'm still hoping if I see him again, I'll realize that's all I want to do.'

'Of course, because that would be the perfect happy ending, wouldn't it?'

Lucy stood up restlessly. 'Oh, Jane, what am I going to do?'

'You can come and talk to me while I get us some supper.'

Lucy followed Jane through into the back of the flat, where in daylight the kitchen looked out on to a pretty rectangle of lawn and terracotta pots. Jane reached behind the sink and dropped the blind, and Lucy went over to the scrubbed pine table pushed up against one wall and pulled out a chair, watching Jane pick out parmesan cheese and pancetta from the fridge, then put water on to boil for some pasta, then reach for a handful of fresh thyme from the windowsill.

Whatever Jane liked to think and to say, seeing her here, pottering around, moving to the cutlery drawer to find

forks and spoons, reaching up into the cupboards to pull
out a couple of plates, there was no doubt in Lucy's mind
that Jane had to stay with Dillon. Not because cosy domes-
ticity so suited her but because she was so clearly happy to
be there with all the touches of Dillon about the room. His
muddy trainers by the back door, a hooded sweatshirt laid
across the back of one of the kitchen chairs which, instead
of moving out of sight, she slipped on herself, rolling up
the sleeves. Jane was happy, but she couldn't seem to see
it for herself any more.

'We'll go and check out the house,' she said suddenly,
spinning around, knife in hand and looking at Lucy as if it
was the simplest idea in the world. 'We could go on
Saturday. I love snooping around houses, and Pablo would
like a nice country walk. We can look up Lipton St Lucy
on the map and work out which one we think their house
is. There can't be that many to choose from. It would be
fun, wouldn't it? Let's go!'

'We can?'

'Of course!' Suddenly Jane was uplifted again. 'We're
not exactly talking about an overnight flight to Australia.
It's an hour away, two at most. We could find some lovely
country pub for lunch.'

'Because, of course, darling, we only ever eat out.' Lucy
laughed. 'Heaven forbid we buy some sandwiches and eat
them in the car for a change.'

'Whatever. We could eat our sandwiches, walk Pablo,
check out the house and come home. It would be so easy.
Of course we have to go.'

'But they might see us. I've already stalked my way

around their London house and got away with it. I can't imagine doing it again.'

'No one will know. And if Luke saw you? So what? Anyone would understand why you were there. It's huge, what he's asking you to do. And you're contemplating staying with them all on the strength of what, one brief conversation with him?'

'And thirteen hours and a shag with his brother.'

'Oh, yes. That too.' Jane laughed. 'So we'll wrap up in our Barbours and green wellies and we'll look just like everyone else. Put a big hat on and a scarf around your face and even if he does see you he won't know who you are.'

*

So the next day, Saturday, a week before the Middletons' party, with Lucy driving and Jane navigating, Pablo at her feet, they sailed out of London at about ten-thirty in the morning on a cold, windy, blue-skied day, accelerated over the Hammersmith flyover, exhilarated by the lack of traffic, and picked up the M40. Less than an hour later they were following the tiniest of undulating turnabout lanes that plunged and climbed through the Cotswold hills. And barely before Lucy had had time to feel panic-stricken at how close they were getting, they found themselves making their way down one final steep-sided lane, following a white-painted signpost to Lipton St Lucy, and then they were there, in the centre of a clutch of five or six tiny stone cottages and a church.

The road forked in front of them. Straight ahead it

wound on up into the hills, and to the right it circled around an old stone war memorial. They pulled up beside it and Lucy turned off the engine and listened to the silence, wondering if their arrival had been noticed by anybody, but there was nobody in sight.

She looked towards the perfect, turreted church, following the line of the path that wound between great clipped boulders of yew towards the nave, where centuries-old lichen had splashed the dark stone creamy white. And then she looked at the cottages, with their stone mullioned windows and tiny front gardens, their thatched roofs bending almost to the ground, but even by the greatest stretch of imagination there was no way any of these could be Lipton Hall.

'But this has to be the right place,' said Jane, looking at the empty hills all round them.

'Then where is the house?' Lucy murmured back.

'And why are we whispering?' whispered Jane.

Lucy started the engine and backed the car until they could rejoin the road, but as they set off again it was clear that they had immediately left the village – more a hamlet – behind them, and that if Lipton Hall was in Lipton St Lucy, and Lucy was sure that Luke had said it was, then they had to have missed it. So they turned in the entrance to a field and made their way slowly back to the war memorial. And it was then that Jane noticed another lane branching off from the road just before they reached the cottages, with an old wooden signpost that said *Nether Lipton Gated Road*.

'This is where it'll be,' Jane said confidently.

'How do you know?'

'I can feel it in my fingers and in my toes.'

Lucy turned down the gated road and almost immediately, and unsurprisingly when she thought about it, they came to a closed gate.

'Do we drive through?'

Jane shook her head. 'No. This is where we start walking. The house will be somewhere down there and a gated road is a public right of way. Dogs, kids, ramblers, you can be sure they're used to people passing all the time. Lucy,' she insisted, seeing yet more doubt on Lucy's face. 'Stop it! You used to do that look with Teddy. You're coming with me now. This is what we planned, remember?'

Jane clipped Pablo on to his lead and they set off, side by side, their breath unfurling in the cold clean air. They opened and closed the first gate and walked on, and Lucy was aware that the wind had dropped and there was a silence and an absolute stillness all around them. She looked to her right, across empty meadows, recognizing the remains of the medieval ridges and furrows that meant, hundreds of years later, the field still rose and fell in deep, perfectly symmetrical ripples. And then she felt rather than heard Jane gasp beside her and she turned and looked to her left and saw that they'd found the house.

It sat behind tall cedars that spread out across its lawns, built of the same weathered gold stone as the village cottages, long and low and beautifully symmetrical, serene and dependable, as if nothing bad could ever have happened there.

'Oh, wow,' breathed Jane. 'Please marry him so that I can come and stay.'

'Listen!' Lucy said, laughing. 'Can you hear that?'

From an open upstairs window came a heavy drum and bass.

'Now I really like him,' Jane told Lucy with satisfaction.

'Please don't start dancing.' Lucy moved away.

Jane walked to catch her up. 'But that can't be Jude's music. He's not here, is he?'

'Perhaps it's Luke's?'

'Isn't Wagner more his style?'

Lucy laughed ruefully. 'I have sold him to you well, haven't I?'

'Perhaps it's the mother, dancing in her bedroom with a bottle of gin?'

'No! Don't say that. It was only the tiniest thing Jude said in the car. I'm sure she's great.'

'Very defensive, Lucy.' Jane caught her eye, teasing her. 'That's a good sign, it shows you're feeling very committed to the whole family.' She turned back to the house. 'And who wouldn't be, because that house is enchanting. Grade II at the very least, seven bedrooms, wouldn't you say?' She swung slowly around, looking out across the empty fields. 'And *idyllically* situated on the edge of the village, amid the most *wonderful* Cotswold countryside.' She looked back to Lucy. 'Price on application but definitely worth investigating further.'

Lucy walked on again, leaving Jane a few paces behind her. Jane's merry quips were not what she wanted to hear, because the truth was, seeing Lipton Hall had done just what Jane had thought it would do. It had made everything snap almost painfully vividly into life. As her eye followed the straight gravelled drive to the wide oak front door, she could picture it opening, Jude and Luke emerging amid a crowd of barking, excited dogs, talking and laughing, their voices carrying on the still air. She saw them walking to the end of the drive, then turning back expectantly to the house, waiting for someone else. And then she could see Gabriella appearing hesitantly in the doorway, long black hair tied back in a plait, huge Penelope Cruz eyes breaking into a smile at the sight of the two of them waiting for her.

How unbearably sad it was and how inadequate it made her feel, to think of the three of them together like that. She barely knew Luke, she'd almost forgotten Jude, and yet she was being fired into this wounded family having been given what was surely an impossible task. Luke, in his misery, could so easily have misjudged Jude; what if he'd heard only what he wanted to hear?

She looked back to the house again, this time imagining how it would look at night, on the evening of the party, lights on in every room, shining out into the dark garden, a steady stream of cars winding their way up the drive, glamorous women emerging in silk and taffeta, the men handsome in black tie. Would she really ever find herself inside that house with them all, standing there in her pink dress, Jude beside her, his arm around her waist, steering her around the guests?

She turned away, walking past the house and towards the barns, built of the same old stone. There were stables with a row of horses looking out at them. She wondered if Jude could ride, and thought again how little she knew about him.

'How do you feel?' Jane demanded, catching her up and taking her arm. 'Does it make you want to face the music . . . disco or maybe a little bit of jazz? Perhaps they'll have a band?' She caught the woebegone expression on Lucy's face and squeezed her arm sympathetically. 'It doesn't, does it? It makes you want to run away and hide?'

'Because it's so daunting,' Lucy insisted. 'I look at their house and it makes me feel even worse.'

'You wimp.' Jane smiled at her.

'I know I am.' Lucy bowed her head.

'So call him.'

'What?' Lucy's head snapped back up again.

'Now. Tell Luke where you are. Tell him you need to talk to him. Sort out the details.'

'No, no. I couldn't.'

'You could.' She breathed in the cold air. 'Being here, seeing where you'll be coming back to. It's made it all real. You have to call him. You need to make plans. If he's in, you could talk about them now.' Jane reached into Lucy's pocket and pulled out her phone. 'Call him.'

'But I should know what I want to say.'

She took her phone and weighed it in her hand, feeling as if she was about to leap not so much off a diving board as off the side of a mountain. Beside her, Jane bent down and undid Pablo's lead and immediately he streaked off down the lane. Then she stood up again and looked at Lucy.

'Call him.'

'Walk with me for a moment first.'

They walked on, picking up speed and quickly leaving the house behind them.

'This began when you went into that Milestone Motel with Jude. And now you've got no choice but to see it through. And you're not scared, you're strong now. You want to know what happens if you don't walk away but you go inside – just like when you walked into the Milestone Motel.'

'You make it sound as if I have nothing to lose, but I do. Being here . . .' Lucy opened her arms, stretching out towards the bare winter fields on either side. 'I can feel it. There's lots more going on that I know nothing about. I know I could hurt them and they could hurt me. It's not just a question of being daring or not. There'll be consequences.'

Jane suddenly stopped again. 'Call Luke now.'

'Don't make me.'

'It's like me and Dillon. Once the momentum starts to build you can't take time to decide what to do. You have to get on with it.'

'So have you decided what to do about Dillon?'

'Call Luke,' Jane said determinedly. 'And then I'll tell you about that.'

Just then, swinging around the corner towards them

came a galloping black spaniel and two small boys on very big bikes, riding side by side, very fast, all three of them aiming directly at Lucy and Jane.

Lucy and Jane stopped abruptly in the centre of the lane, no time to dive out of the way, no time to do anything but stand and pray and then, with a skid and a heart-stopping wobble, both boys managed to divide around them and then were gone, cycling away, shrieking with laughter. Far, far away, Lucy could make out a couple of figures, could hear their cries on the muffled air.

'Tom! Jack! You've gone too far! Come back! Come back!'

Have you, Jane? she thought. *Can you come back? And have I gone too far. Can I come back now?* She put her hand in her pocket and brought out her phone, searched for his number, waited, bent around the phone, then slowly turned and walked away from Jane, back the way they'd come.

And Jane could tell from the way Lucy's back suddenly straightened exactly the moment that the phone had been answered and she waited, anxiously, for about ten, twenty more seconds, as Lucy walked further and further away from her up the road, picking up the pace so that for a moment Jane had to wonder if she was being abandoned there and then, if Lucy had even remembered she was still with her.

And then Lucy's call was finished and she was swinging around, her face alight.

'I think it's going to be fine.' She came running back to

Jane. 'He was a little surprised that we were here, but pleased too. Now I'm so glad I called him.' Lucy paused. 'What's wrong? Why are you looking at me like that?'

Jane came forwards, took hold of her arm. 'You're all sparkling. I think you know exactly who you're coming back to see.'

'No, please don't tell me that. It's not true at all. I'm pleased he wants me back here, that's all. He's hurt and sad. He doesn't want anyone. Truly, I'm coming back for Jude. I am, I am.' She bit her lip. 'But he's insisting we come to the house ... now. So, you'll meet him, if you want to ...' Lucy's enthusiasm slipped away as she took in the doubt on Jane's face. 'I told him you were here with me. Is it OK that I said yes?'

'He needs to see you, Lucy, not me.'

'No, both of us, of course!'

'But I'd be in the way.'

'You wouldn't be. Jane!' Lucy caught her arm. 'You being here with me makes all the difference. You being here made it happen. I'm only here because of you. You have to come too. Now that he knows we're outside his house, we don't really have any choice.'

Jane shook her head.

'What's the matter?'

'I'm thinking. Pablo's not had much of a walk. And I could do with some time to myself, and so could you two ... I could come and find you later on.' Jane looked down at her feet. 'Do it my way, Lucy, please.' She turned and gave an ear-splitting whistle for Pablo, then walked away from Lucy, shoulders hunched.

Lucy jogged after her and slid her arm around her shoulders, pulling her to a halt.

'Are you all right? What's wrong?' Because Jane was suddenly crying, in great heaving sobs, and Lucy looked at her in alarm, then pulled her close and hugged her tight. 'Jane?'

'I don't understand what's made me cry. I was fine and then . . .'

'I don't understand.'

'I can't talk about it now. Luke's waiting for you.'

'He can wait.' Lucy shook her head, dropping the phone into her pocket. 'Are you crying about Dillon? Jesus, Jane. When were you going to tell me?'

'Today. Now. After we'd sorted this out.' She gave Lucy a wobbly smile. 'I told him last night. He's going to Australia without me.'

'Can you change your mind?'

She shook her head. 'I don't want to. And I was going to tell you about it in the car but then I couldn't. We were thinking about you and being here . . .' She turned away. 'I didn't want to talk about him.'

'But it's Dillon!' Lucy couldn't help herself crying at her, even as she knew it was the last thing Jane wanted to hear. She took hold of Jane's oilskin-clad arm, wanting to shake it. 'You believe leaving him's the only thing you can do. I was so worried that it would come to this, and now it has and it's so awful. Australia would have been your big adventure together. You were so lucky . . .'

'You really thought so, didn't you?'

'I still do.'

Jane stopped abruptly and stared hard at Lucy, her face set. 'Changing countries won't sort it out. I don't love him enough. How come you can't see that?'

They'd reached a second gate and she angrily wrenched it open and let it slam shut behind them, the metallic crash echoing out across the fields. Then she stopped. 'We're going the wrong way, aren't we? You're meant to be meeting Luke.' And she immediately turned round again, opened the gate and led them both back through, Lucy following quietly behind.

'He's definitely going without you?' Lucy said in a little voice as Jane again set off up the lane without her.

'Yes.'

'And Robin and Dolly?' She'd caught up again now, striding as fast as Jane. 'Has he told them yet?'

Jane shook her head.

'I'm so sorry,' Lucy said desperately. 'I'm so sorry I didn't realize how you really felt. That I didn't understand better and help you, because it must have been so hard.'

Jane finally slowed down and then she turned to her. 'You were telling me what you thought I should do. And I don't blame you for that. But look at my face and you'll see I'm OK, because you know what, I'm so *relieved*, Lucy, you have no idea. I could hardly bear to tell him but . . .' she looked down at the ground, 'now I'm free, for better or worse.'

'Is he all right?'

'I think he will be. I don't think he was even that surprised.'

Lucy nodded, still wanting to cry out to her, *But it's so*

sad. Whatever you say to me, I still think you're wrong. But she really knew Jane was right. She'd only been seeing what she wanted to see.

They walked silently down the lane towards Lipton Hall, only the sound of a lone crow cawing on the top of a telegraph pole breaking the peace, and all the time Lucy was waiting for the moment when Jane would start to pour out her heart. She was so used to Jane talking to her about Dillon, telling her how she felt, asking her what she should do, involving Lucy in every detail of their lives together, that this silence between them felt horribly unfamiliar and awkward. And then she realized belatedly that this was how it was – that now, after all these years, there was nothing more to say.

'Isn't it silly? I only started to cry . . .' Jake gave a big sniff, 'because you looked so happy.'

'Scared you mean!'

'No, you're happy.' She gave Lucy a smile. 'You know what you've got to do. And I'm better now.' She wiped her eyes again. 'Do I look awful?'

Lucy shook her head. The truth was that Jane's was one of those enviable faces that could cry and cry with barely a visible sign, her skin was just as pale, her eyes just as clear, no telltale blotches on her cheeks.

'Good,' she sniffed again, 'but I'm still going to walk for half an hour. Then I'll meet you.' She turned agitatedly and gave another whistle. 'Pablo!'

'I don't want to leave you now.'

Jane shook her head. 'Honestly, Lucy, I want you to.' Already she was sounding stronger, brighter. 'I need to have a walk on my own. Here is just the perfect place to do it. When I come back to the house to find you I'll be a different person, you'll see.'

'Where's your dog?'

'I'll find him.' She pointed back down the lane, smiling now. 'Go on, Lucy, before Luke comes looking for us. Back to the house now, back to the house, there's a good girl. Stop dithering,' she added sharply, when Lucy still didn't move. 'You know you want to go.'

Lucy nodded and turned away, and then she heard Jane cry out and spun round again to see that Pablo had finally appeared and was making his way proudly back across the field towards them with a cock pheasant in his mouth. The bird, alive but perhaps not so well, had one wing fluttering wildly as it fought to free itself from Pablo's jaws.

'Here, Pablo, here!' Jane yelled at him.

'Drop it,' Lucy commanded and Pablo abruptly changed direction and galloped up to her, then stopped at her feet, the pheasant jammed in his mouth, wagging his tail.

'Not me, you stupid fool of a dog! Go and give it to your mistress.'

'No, give it to her.' Jane shrank away. 'Sort it out Lucy.'

'Drop it!' Lucy commanded, striding over to him. 'Drop it, Pablo!'

'You're the vet. You've got to sort this out, make the bird better,' Jane insisted.

Lucy grabbed Pablo by the muzzle and forced open his mouth, which only made Pablo adjust his grip and hang on harder, whereupon the bird set up a sustained flapping of its one free wing, making Jane shriek and leap away in fright.

Lucy moved towards Pablo again, who immediately leapt away, and then her heart stopped because there, coming down the road to meet them, was Luke.

She glanced quickly back at Jane. 'Get Pablo to drop the fucking bird. Luke's here.'

'But I daren't.' Jane practically wept at her.

'Luke's here.'

Lucy marched over to Pablo and jammed her fingers into his mouth, prising his jaws apart. 'Drop it, Pablo!'

The bird dropped limply to the ground and Pablo sat beside it, guarding it, ears cocked, watching it intently. Lucy could feel Luke at her shoulder and she turned to him first anxiously, then unable to stop herself smiling at the sight of him.

'Is this your dog?'

'No, it's hers.' She pointed an accusing finger at Jane, who immediately came forwards with an outstretched hand.

But for the moment Luke ignored her, picking up the pheasant and swiftly breaking its neck. As the pheasant set up a sustained flapping, Luke held out his other hand to Jane. 'Hello.'

Lucy watched Jane step warily around the beating wings and reach out and take hold of his hand.

'If you let your dog run loose,' he said, letting go to scratch Pablo behind the ears, 'that's what will happen. You should keep him on a lead at this time of year.'

'Yes, yes, of course,' Jane said, seriously. 'One less to shoot tomorrow, what a terrible shame.'

Luke laughed, then he turned back to Lucy. 'I was thinking about you. Isn't that strange?'

'I hope you don't mind we came this morning?' she asked him, not sure whether or not to kiss him hello, suddenly feeling very polite.

'Mind? No! I've been waiting for you to call, hoping that you'd call,' he corrected himself, 'hoping you were OK.' He seemed not to care in the slightest that Jane was standing beside them, listening to everything he said, but even so Jane turned and walked away, out of earshot.

'No more hassle from Teddy?'

She shook her head and smiled at him, suddenly relaxing. 'But I dream about the chicken and chips.'

'We'll Meat again, perhaps?' He stopped abruptly. 'I'm sorry, did I really say that?'

She laughed. Luke nodded over to where Jane had wandered, a few yards away, and was staring down at a brook that ran parallel to the lane.

'Is she all right?'

'You saw us?'

'I was in the lane. She was crying?'

'She'll be fine. She's better now.'

He called over to her. 'Jane, would you like some coffee? Why don't you come back to the house?'

Jane turned back to them, not coming forward, standing a little awkwardly. 'No, I think I'll walk Pablo, at least to the end of the lane.' She fished out the lead from her coat pocket and swung it in front of them. 'On the end of this, of course. Pablo,' she commanded, without a pause, 'over here!'

Eyeing the lead, Pablo slunk reluctantly over to her.

'I'll give you half an hour,' she told the dog. 'And that's it. It's too cold for any longer.' Then she turned back to them, gave Luke a grin and a wave. 'We think we worked out which is your house. I'll come and find you soon.'

13

Luke held out his hand. 'Come with me?'

'Sure,' she nodded, slipping her hand into his, and felt again that immediate connection with him, as if she'd woken up after years of being asleep.

They walked across an immaculately tidy yard towards a low stone building.

'Come and meet our old ladies.'

She raised her eyebrows at him questioningly, but she had a good idea what he meant.

'They're all in calf, not that any of them are due yet. That's why we're keeping them close by.'

She waited as he heaved open the door, still holding her hand. They went inside and he switched on a light and she stepped cautiously after him, to find herself in a warm dark space with low raftered ceilings, looking into the soft, liquid eyes of about forty Friesian cows.

But you're holding my hand was all she could think. *Surely you shouldn't be doing that.*

The cows were divided from Lucy and Luke by a low metal rail with diagonal struts that they could stick their heads through to reach their food on the other side, and they were knee-deep in golden straw, several of them lying down.

As Lucy and Luke entered the barn, a few of them

turned away; most of them simply carried on slowly chewing and looking. To Lucy, they all seemed completely blissed out.

She moved forward cautiously.

'Let them sniff you,' Luke said quietly, finally dropping her hand. 'They won't bite.'

'No?' she whispered back. 'Really?'

She walked forward a few more paces, then slowly dropped on to her haunches and stretched out her hand to the nearest cow, who tossed her head and snorted at her warily and then stepped cautiously forwards, nudging at her sleeve with a very wet nose, back and forth, back and forth, before starting to lick the back of her hand with a scratchy and extremely long tongue. Lucy slowly reached up to rub the cow's broad forehead.

'Hey, Luke,' she said in a low voice, 'you know how to show a girl a good time.'

'Oh, you'd be surprised, Lucy Blue.' She looked up and saw that he was standing directly above her. 'Remember, please, that you were the one that called when I wasn't expecting you. I do have jobs to do here, you know. I can't stop just because you decide to turn up on my doorstep.'

She smiled and stood up, wiped her hand on her jeans and looked around the barn. 'So is this what you do? You're a farmer?'

He shook his head. 'Kind of, but not really. Dad's the hands-on farmer here. He hopes I'll take it over one day, when he's about a hundred and ten and I'm eighty-six. But in the meantime I work in the same world, only more in theory than in practice.'

'Meaning?'

He came over to her and stood by Lucy's side as her new friend continued to reach for her sleeve.

'I'm an agronomist.'

'I'm so sorry.'

'Shut up,' he smiled. 'I work at Imperial College. I'm studying wheat, specifically the best sort of wheat to grow in Africa, where, as you know, they don't get enough rain.'

'That's wonderful. How come I didn't think to ask you that before?'

'Because we had other things on our minds, I suppose.'

She couldn't think how to reply, couldn't even turn away, and for a long moment it seemed neither could Luke.

'And you love it, presumably?' she said eventually. 'I'm thinking headhunting isn't perhaps so rewarding.'

'I love the travelling. I get to spend a few months of the year in Africa.'

'Everyone must miss you so much while you're away.' What on earth had compelled her to say that?

'Do you think so?' He sounded amused. 'I'm not sure all my family would agree with you.'

'No. Probably not,' she gave him an awkward smile, 'knowing what an *egotistical man* you are.'

She turned away from him self-consciously, looking around the barn. 'So, what needs doing around here? Shall I roll up my sleeves and get on with some examinations?'

His lips twitched just short of a smile. 'So you'd know how to do that, would you?'

'Can't be that hard.'

He walked behind her and vaulted easily over the low bars dividing them from the cows, landed gently and then walked slowly among the them, slapping them gently on the rump to push them aside so that he could get a closer look. 'I'm not usually here at a weekend.' He glanced up at her. 'You and Jane were lucky to catch me.'

'That's not what we were setting out to do.'

He grinned back at her. 'Humour me, Lucy.'

'So, why are you here?'

'My parents are away so I said I'd come down, keep an eye on everything.'

'And that's what you're doing now, is it, casting an expert eye?'

'Don't sound so doubtful. I'm giving each of these cows a sound and thorough health check. I might look as if I'm not paying them much attention but that's not the case. Not that you'd know.'

'That's where you're wrong, actually, because I trained as a vet.'

She laughed at the startled expression on his face. 'So, just pass me an apron and a pair of wellies. When are this lot due? March? April?'

He came back to the rail and rested his arms on it, looking up at her with a smile. 'You're full of surprises, aren't you, Lucy Blue? If you're a vet, what are you doing headhunting in London?'

'Career change, but I like to think I could come back to all this again one day.'

Again she felt herself staring at him, felt herself move closer.

'There's another thing Jude didn't tell me about you.'

She stepped back again. Saying Jude's name was as if Luke had physically pushed her away. 'So,' he went on briskly, 'they're all looking good, wouldn't you agree? And now, if anything goes wrong on the night of the party, we'll know who to turn to.'

'Let's face it,' Lucy couldn't stop herself adding darkly, 'if there's trouble at the party, I don't think it'll be this lot causing it.'

He didn't answer, just climbed back over the rail then snapped off the lights, returning the barn to its wintry gloom, and she dropped under his arm and stepped outside.

'Lucy?'

'Yes?' She turned to him quickly but his face in the darkness was completely unreadable.

'You're definitely coming back? You still want to see this through?'

'What do you mean?' She stopped, feeling herself go light-headed and giddy. 'Are you saying you don't think I should any more?'

He shook his head. 'I want you to come back.' And then he stopped and added deliberately, 'For Jude.'

'Then I'll be there,' she told him. 'After all you've told me, everything you've done for me, for Jude, how could I be anywhere else?'

14

Clutching her overnight bag in one hand and a bunch of hyacinths in the other, Lucy staggered down the carriage, just about managing to keep on her feet as the train rocked and rolled its way towards Lipton St Lucy station and then, with a long, thin squeal of brakes, finally pulled to a halt.

She reached for the door of the carriage, opened it, then stopped, unable to make herself step down. She felt weak, wobbly and sick with nerves. Why was she here? How would she feel when she saw him again? And then almost as if someone behind her had impatiently shoved her forward, she found herself jumping down on to the platform.

Straight away she saw him, looking for her at the wrong end of the train. And she was completely unprepared for the sight of him. *Oh God*, she thought, watching him, watching for her, peering so hopefully, pushing back his dark hair impatiently, turning this way and that as he sought her out. *This isn't how it's supposed to be.*

For a moment she stopped, unable to walk forward because she wanted to run, throw her arms around him but eventually he turned in the right direction and saw her and then he stopped too, and waited as she walked stiffly towards him.

'Hi, Luke,' she said, and stretched up and gave him a quick peck on the cheek.

'For a moment then I thought you'd decided not to come after all.'

She shook her head, but just as she was about to step away from him again, he reached out for her, gathered her up in a great bear hug and pulled her hard against him, and she felt herself breathing in the warm scent of his body, felt her legs disappearing beneath her. It was as if now that she'd allowed herself to acknowledge how she felt she was giving free rein to her body to react as it wanted to.

'I thought you might have changed your mind.'

But I have. Oh God, I have.

He held her away from him. 'Nervous of seeing him again?'

'Yes.'

'Remember you're his *golden girl*.'

Remember why I am here.

She shook out her flowers. 'Look at these.'

'Oh, you shouldn't have done. Thank you.'

'You know they're not for you.'

'I suppose I guessed they weren't for me.'

He seemed high on her being there. But how could she know why? Perhaps it was just because, by the sheer force of his will, everyone and everything was finally fitting into place.

He took her arm, picked up her bags and pointed her towards the steps leading out of the station.

'Thanks for coming to pick me up,' she said, trying to match his mood, trying to sound happy and normal and unfazed. 'How's everything back home?'

'We're all OK. So far, Mum's only burst into tears once and Dad not at all.' She looked at him uncertainly, unsure whether or not he was joking.

When they reached the station car park he took her bag, dropped it in the boot and opened her door. And then they were leaving the station behind them, turning right into a little lane, immediately dropping over a humpbacked bridge and disappearing into a tunnel of leafless trees.

'How far to the house?'

'A few miles.'

She sat quietly, the hyacinths wrapped in pink tissue paper damp on her lap, watching his big hands on the steering-wheel. She looked at his face, the leanness of his cheeks, his high cheekbones, the way his dark wavy hair sprang up from his forehead and how his wide brown eyes with their thick dark fringe of lashes stared unblinkingly at the road ahead. At first she'd thought it was a hostile, angry face. She remembered thinking how unfair it was that Jude was so beautiful in comparison to Luke, but now she thought it was an inspiring face, full of strength and purpose. And she wondered again what the hell she was going to do.

She looked out of the windscreen at the frost-swept fields, so beautiful, cold and grey, imagining the great house waiting for her at the end of the journey. How on earth was Jude going to react to finding her in his house, waiting for him? Had she been crazy ever to believe there might have been enough between them to set up a future together?

'How long is Jude staying for? Did he say?' She had to say his name. She was aware of her foot tapping frantically against the floor of the car. She looked across at Luke, and watched his smile slip away.

'That depends if you give him something to stay on for . . .'

She flinched at the cold tone in his voice. 'I'll come up with something,' she said, biting her lip.

He stopped at a tiny T-junction, waited for a car to pass and then pulled out, taking them down another tiny, twisting lane, high hedges on either side. 'I'm sure you will.'

'What's the matter?' She turned to him in surprise. 'Why did you say it like that?'

'I didn't mean to say anything in any particular way.'

'Because this is exactly what you wanted, remember?' she said. 'You planned this. Now you're making me feel as if you wish I wasn't here.'

'Don't say that, Lucy. Stop thinking this is all about you.'

'I'm sorry, but I'm sick with nerves about seeing Jude again. I really want to get this right, for you and for me. And this is probably the last chance we get to talk before he arrives.'

Still he didn't reply, just drove silently, staring unblinking at the road ahead. And then she understood. And as soon as she'd thought it, she cursed herself for not taking a taxi and finding her own way to Lipton Hall, because of course this had to be the same way home that Jude and Gabriella had taken almost exactly a year earlier. No wonder Luke had gone so quiet. Perhaps they were driving the very same stretch where the accident had happened?

She glanced across to him, saw his hard face and thought how he had to be thinking about Gabriella, as he surely must do every time he drove this way. If only he hadn't been out walking when she had called. If only she hadn't caught the earlier train, it would have been him rather than Jude who had come to meet her. And the car that had met them so catastrophically would have safely passed by a good half-hour earlier.

And then, she thought, looking miserably down again at the bunch of hyacinths in her hands, it would have been Gabriella sitting beside him in the car, Gabriella he'd be bringing home for the party. She looked at him, imagining herself for just a moment in Gabriella's place, how it might feel to have him turn to her, his face happy, soft and loving. She imagined them laughing, talking non-stop, filling each other in on their time spent apart, Luke sliding his arm around her shoulders and pulling her close, and she saw how stupid she'd been to read something into their moment in the barn, how unlikely it was that Luke had been even remotely aware of how she was feeling then. A year, that was all it had been.

'He hasn't arrived yet. He said he'd be with us by lunchtime.'

'What?' She was startled to hear his voice.

'I'm saying you've got a little time to settle in.'

She nodded. *Good*, she was supposed to say, wasn't she? *How excited I am to be seeing Jude again.* But she couldn't bring herself to say it. The truth was that in the last few days, whenever she'd tried to remember what Jude looked like, she had hardly been able to bring his face to mind. 'Whatever happens, you will make sure you talk to him before I do?'

'Of course I will.' He paused, then heaved a giant sigh. 'Lucy, everything is going to be just great. At least, far better than you're expecting.'

'I'm so nervous I can hardly think straight.'

He nodded, misunderstanding. 'I tell you, Jude will be fine. More than fine, he'll be over the moon.'

They bounced over another bridge, climbed a hill, and mile upon mile of undulating Cotswold hills rippled out below them, as far as she could see. But then, immediately, they were plunging down again, the road twisting and weaving through more woods and bringing them out into a tiny village of heart-stoppingly sweet houses, all built of the same rich gingerbread-coloured stone. She saw a duck pond, the village church, signs for the school, and then they were out the other side, climbing again, meeting the same lane she'd driven down with Jane. Luke slowed down once more, indicated right, and they turned again, down a lane so narrow the car could barely slip between the high banks on either side, and she recognized the same little crossroads with the old stone war memorial in its centre. And her heart gave another giant leap as she realized that they had arrived. Luke turned right into the gated road, the gate open this time, and there, waiting for them, was Lipton Hall.

'It doesn't look real,' she said in a whisper, stunned at the sight of the house transformed for the party.

It had been one of the most beautiful houses she'd ever seen, and now it took her breath away. Great swathes of holly and tiny white fairy lights had been built into a spectacular arch around the old oak front door, and all around the garden the majestic clipped yew trees were also covered in lights that glittered and twinkled in the grey daylight and were only going to look better once darkness fell.

He nodded briefly, taking them over a stone bridge and into the drive that cut in a straight line between the smooth flat lawns to the front door of the house, but instead of parking there he drove them around to the back, pulling up between a Range Rover with blacked-out windows and a convertible Porsche with the roof down.

'You've got other people staying?'

He glanced across at her. 'One or two.'

'Friends of yours?'

'Sort of.' He shrugged.

Some of the surprise she felt must have shown, because he reached across and took her hand. 'I'm sorry this is so hard for you, Lucy. I know you think I'm completely certain about what I'm doing but I'm not. I'm sitting here too, wondering what the hell I was thinking bringing you here, to face everyone, believing that you, who hardly know us at all, can sort us out in just one night.

But there's no going back, is there? We have to let it happen now.'

She nodded, taken aback by his admission, and sat there silently, aware of his eyes on her face, her hot sweaty palm pressed against his but not wanting to pull it away.

Then coming out through the door to meet them appeared two handsome black Labradors, bounding out towards the car in ecstatic welcome, and behind them a tall, stunning-looking woman, with long dark grey hair swept loosely up into a clip, wearing velvet slippers and a long white nightgown and hastily throwing a jewel-bright shawl around her shoulders.

'My mother,' Luke said, 'who evidently hasn't found time to get dressed.'

His mother, Suzie. Nothing like Lucy had imagined her to be. She came forward, opening the passenger door for Lucy. 'I'm Suzie,' she said, leaning in and giving Lucy a warm smile. She reached out a hand to help her out of the car and Lucy caught the wink of the largest diamond she'd ever seen.

Luke got out of the car too and Suzie turned to him. 'And before you say anything rude, someone's used up all the hot water.' She had a musical, tremulous voice. 'So I'm having to wait for the immersion heater to make me enough for a bath.'

Lucy went to hand her the flowers but had them knocked out of her hand as both dogs decided to jump up at her at the same time.

'How absolutely lovely of you,' Suzie said, pushing the dogs away with her foot. 'Get off them, Parson, get off them, Wiggins.' She picked the hyacinths up one by one, along with the various pieces of soggy pink tissue paper, then bunched them together again and sniffed deeply. 'How wonderful.'

'I'll take Lucy upstairs, show her where she's sleeping,' Luke said from the back of the car, where he was lifting out her bag. 'Then you can interrogate her properly.' He swung the bag over his shoulder and, without stopping to see if Lucy was following him, strode into the house, the dogs following eagerly.

Suzie stared after her son.

'He's not told me anything about you at all,' she said, springing back to Lucy, her eyes now bright and warm. 'I didn't even know you were coming until this morning.'

'I'm sorry.'

'Heavens, I didn't mean it like that. I'm delighted.'

'Good.' Lucy grinned at her, relaxing for the first time since she'd left London.

'Have you known Luke long?'

'No.' She wanted to explain a little, but somehow guessed Luke wouldn't want her to . . .

'Mum!' Luke demanded through the open door. 'Stop that. Lucy, come inside.'

Suzie rolled her eyes at Lucy, and led the way through the kitchen door. Lucy followed her into the room and immediately caught the smell of something burning.

'Oh, Christ,' said Luke, seeing the look of alarm on Lucy's face and going straight to the Aga, where smoke was curling up around the edges of one of the half-opened ovens. He grabbed a tea-towel and pulled out a tray.

'Shit!' Suzie said, making Lucy laugh. 'Shit, shit, shit. I deliberately left the door open so I wouldn't forget them.' She took another towel and wrestled the tray out of Luke's hand, then took it over to the sink and shook it, releasing a shower of blackened crumbs.

Suzie turned, catching Lucy's eye, and grinned at her, sensing an ally. 'Croissants,' she explained. 'Would you like one?'

'I'm taking Lucy to her bedroom,' Luke insisted.

'Oh are you?'

But Luke was in no mood to be teased. 'If Lucy wants something to eat, she can brave it when I've shown her where she's sleeping,' he said sharply.

'Whatever you say, darling.' The fun had vanished from Suzie's face now. She walked over to the breadbin, turning her back on the two of them, lifted out a craggy rock of bread and silently started to cut a slice.

'We've got caterers for this evening, thank God. Never ever eat anything homemade here if you can possibly help it,' Luke told her as they left the kitchen. 'It's a golden rule.'

'Shhh, she'll hear you.'

'No, you don't understand. It's *her* golden rule.'

He led Lucy into a flagstone hall with an inglenook fireplace at one end, a fire already lit and burning brightly, throwing shadows around the dark beamed walls. Lucy barely had time to take it in before Luke disappeared again, leading her up an ancient oak staircase. They arrived at the top of the stairs and moved onto a wide landing with bare oak floorboards and a shining suit of armour standing guard at the far end, with a crown of silver tinsel and a dog lead hanging off one arm.

'This one goes for walks then, does he?' she laughed as they passed him by, but Luke immediately pulled the lead off and slung it around his neck instead.

Partly in response to his silence, she defiantly veered off course towards the windows and looked out. She could see across the garden towards the gated road where she and Jane had stood. She remembered being out there, looking in, and now she was inside looking out, and for the first time since she'd arrived she felt a tiny kernel of excitement growing deep inside her, and an inexplicable confidence that she was in the right place after all.

A moment later Luke came to stand beside her and they looked out together across the frosty fields, towards some dark woods and a hill in the distance with a tiny little church perched on top.

'You were horrid to her,' she told him, very, very aware of how close he was.

He looked sideways at her. 'It's how I am with everyone. Haven't you realized that yet?'

She laughed nervously, aware of her heart thumping in her chest, and she leaned forward on the wide oak window-sill in front of her, staring out of the window again but this time taking in nothing at all. Then he touched her shoulder with his hand and she stopped, frozen, then turned so that she was facing him and, looking up at him, thought for one ridiculous, heart-stopping moment that he was going to kiss her.

'That church is very pretty,' he said, nodding towards

the window. 'You should get Jude to take you to see it this afternoon.'

'But—' she began, staring up at him stupidly. 'Luke?'

'What?' He let her go and stepped back from her.

She was going mad. Imagining all the time that he was about to kiss her, pull her into his arms, crush her against him, tell her how ridiculous it was to think she could have anything more to do with Jude.

She turned away. 'Will you show me my room?'

He nodded, then took her to the end of the landing, turned right into another smaller corridor with doors on both sides and opened the first to reveal her bedroom.

She followed him in, finding herself in a large square panelled room with dark red linen curtains and wide oak floorboards covered with rugs and with the same heavily beamed walls. Luke brushed past her and dropped her bag on to a huge white bed in the centre of the room.

'Bathroom's through there.' He nodded towards another doorway. 'I hope this will be all right for you. Prince Charming's next door, so I thought this would be the appropriate bedroom for you.'

It hurt, and she suspected it was meant to, too.

'Do you want to unpack? Have a wash? Hang up a dress?'

She sighed, then walked over to the bed and sat down.

Luke moved over to a cupboard in the wall. 'There'll be hangers here, somewhere.'

'Shall I come down with you again now?'

'No rush. Stay here, sort yourself out. I'll come and find you downstairs.'

Now he looked so tense she thought he'd ping if she touched him.

'Lucy?'

'Yes?'

'I don't want you to tell my mother what's going on.'

She slumped again. 'Oh, for God's sake, of course I won't.'

She jumped off the bed again, walked over to the window and found she was looking down to where they'd parked, to the three cars standing in a line just beside the kitchen door.

'As I said,' Luke said, watching her from the doorway, 'Jude's bound to be late.'

She didn't turn round.

'And as soon as he gets here, I'll talk to him, before he sees you. And then he can come and find you.'

And my role in all this will be over. Lucy almost heard him thinking it.

She didn't reply.

'You can find your own way down, can't you?' he said and when she didn't answer he quietly left the room.

225

15

After Luke had left the room, Lucy turned back to the bed and sat down heavily on it, imagining how it would feel to see Jude arriving, to look out of the window and watch his dark head emerging from the car. What would she say to him? How could she explain why she was there when she didn't know herself any more? She imagined the moment when he saw her, and then, after that moment, every possible outcome seemed awful. How likely was it that she'd take one look at him and fall for him once more, when the only person she could think about at all was Luke?

She should leave, she thought. She should avoid what was undoubtedly going to be an excruciating reunion. So what if her presence here proved something to Jude? She could do that *in absentia* – Luke could regale Jude with the whole exciting story of how he'd tracked her down and too bad she'd ended up making a dash for it before the final chapter. Suzie Middleton could act as witness. Yes, Luke had indeed picked her up from the station and brought her here. And then all the Middletons could live happily ever after . . . And Lucy could go back to London, forget about them all. All of them but Luke.

Luke, Luke, Luke. She closed her eyes and breathed out his name. How had he managed to take over her thoughts so completely? When had it begun? You were aware of him right from the start, the voice answered in her head. It began right back to the very first time you laid eyes on him, when you dropped Jude home, but you're only facing up to it now.

At this thought, such crushing despondency overwhelmed her that she flopped back on the bed and covered her eyes with her hands. Nothing like this had ever happened to her before. She'd always despised people who talked of unrequited love. What was the point, she'd asked, not understanding until now that that had nothing to do with it. But now she did understand. She understood that she would stay, see the evening through, simply because being near Luke was better than being away from him. To go through the awfulness of her reunion with Jude was a price worth paying if it meant staying close to Luke, even though she knew that all Luke wanted her to do was fall into his brother's arms, not his own.

She went to her bag and got out the pale pink dress that she'd worn to the party in Inverness. The only dress she could have chosen for this night, unblemished and still lovely despite having been rolled up in her bag for hours. She wondered if Jude would remember her describing it as they'd lain together on the bed in the Milestone Motel, remember what he'd said about undoing the non-existent buttons. She remembered how she'd kissed him, how exciting it had been to be with him then. Perhaps . . . was there any chance that to see him was all she needed to make her fall for him again? Was there any possibility at all that everything she thought she was feeling for Luke was bound up in the confusion and uncertainty of being here, and in her fear of how Jude was going to react when he saw her again?

She took the dress over to the cupboard, feeling the soft, stretchy fabric heavy in her hands. She hung it up and immediately it slithered off the hanger and fell to the floor – very symbolic, she thought, picking it up, looking at how the sequins shone softly in the light. She hung it up a second time and shut the door on it.

She left the bedroom, heading for the staircase that would take her back downstairs, then changed her mind and followed the landing in the opposite direction instead, wandering down the long corridor, looking through the windows as she went.

At the far end was a huge planter of white hyacinths, sitting on a very beautiful little table that looked at least five hundred years old. She walked over and touched the stiff flowers, breathing in the sweet, heady scent and thinking how they put her own meagre bunch to shame. Then she walked on again, randomly turning left through an open archway and into another long hall, more rooms to the right and the left. It was a huge house, she was beginning to realize, wondering how she would ever find her way back to the kitchen.

Now she came to a heavy velvet curtain, dark red and trimmed with tiny embroidered birds, all different colours, and with beaks of silver thread. She pushed her way through and wandered on, past a rusting watering can sitting incongruously beside a bedroom door, and peeped around the corner to see a lion skin spread out across the floor.

'It jumps up at you when you go through the door,' a voice said at her shoulder.

Lucy spun around to find a girl standing close behind her, with fluffy blonde hair and wrapped in a fluffy white towel, holding a hair-dryer and looking at her with unabashed interest. 'There's a hot-air vent under the floorboards that switches on and off automatically. It absolutely terrified me the first time, but there, I've warned you now.' The girl stuck out a hand. 'I'm Sophia,' she said with a flash of white teeth. 'And I'm guessing you're probably Lucy?'

'Hello.' Lucy smiled, rather disconcerted that she should be known by name. 'I'm sorry. Is this your bedroom?'

'Absolutely not. I wouldn't sleep in there if they paid me.' The girl, Sophia, adjusted her towel and Lucy looked down at her bare feet. 'I've just been having a bath, getting hot water before everybody else uses it up. There's never enough in this house. If you're wanting to have one too, make sure you get it in early.'

'Thanks for the tip.'

Sophia stared at her again, not hostile but not particularly friendly either. 'Why don't you come and talk to me while I get dressed?'

It was more an order than a question and, without waiting, Sophia set off down the corridor. Lucy followed her rather uncertainly, trying to get over the surprise of finding her there, telling herself it was a huge house, probably stuffed full of pretty girl guests wandering around in towels, all with bleached blonde hair and spectacular tans. She guessed she should be thinking how nice it was to meet one of them.

She followed Sophia into another gigantic bedroom and the girl skipped across to her unmade bed and leapt up on it.

'So ... I know your name but that's all,' she said to Lucy, who was still standing rather awkwardly in the doorway. 'Luke is being very secretive about you.'

Lucy laughed warily. 'God knows why.'

'I have to be honest, I'm *dying* to know why!' Sophia exclaimed. 'He wouldn't even let me come to the station with him to pick you up. He told me to stay here and wash my hair.' She rubbed at her wet hair. 'Which was perfectly clean as it was. He can be such a bossy, can't he? But I always find I do what he says.'

Lucy nodded uncertainly.

'Still, I've found you now.' She winked at Lucy. 'So, spill. Who are you? Why couldn't I come and pick you up?'

Lucy didn't want to be rude. God knows, she could do with making a friend before the party, but this girl was so inquisitive and in-your-face. 'Probably because he's only got two seats in his car?' she ventured.

'Oh yes, I forgot that.' Sophia paused, then immediately came back at Lucy again. 'But it still doesn't explain who you are. I'm a very old friend of the Middletons and I've never heard of you. And I went through the guest list a couple of weeks ago with Suzie, checking to see who hadn't replied, and you weren't even on it.'

She tucked her feet under her and sat cross-legged on the bed, looking at Lucy expectantly.

'I'm a last-minute addition,' Lucy replied, knowing she sounded defensive. 'That's allowed, isn't it?'

'I suppose,' Sophia said. 'But I think I'll keep an eye on you, all the same.'

How could she respond to that? Lucy watched the girl slip back off the bed and walk over to her chest of drawers, the top of which was completely hidden by various pots and potions. She picked up a bottle of body lotion and tipped some out on to her hand, then let her towel drop to the floor, leaving her completely naked, and began to rub cream into her thin arms and legs.

So who did she have her eye on? Lucy wondered. Was it Luke or Jude?

'You know,' Sophia said, turning back to her, completely unbothered by her nudity, 'I just can't decide what to wear.' She put the lotion back on to the chest of drawers and wandered over to a cupboard, taking out an armful of coat-hangers and cellophane.

'Jeans, perhaps?' Lucy suggested. 'Something warm?'

'No, I mean tonight. I've brought three.' She rolled her eyes as if to say what a pain it was, having so many lovely clothes, then held the cellophaned bundle out in front of her, not that Lucy could see anything. She imagined tiny, wispy, backless, frontless dresses, looked again at the girl's long blonde hair and decided she was probably after Jude.

'Perhaps you should wear all of them, one on top of the other?'

'Oh, don't be silly.' Irritably, Sophia disappeared back inside the cupboard again.

Lucy gritted her teeth. 'I'm sorry,' she said. 'It's just that Luke's waiting for me downstairs. He'll be wondering where I am.'

'You hope,' said Sophia from inside the cupboard, and then she looked around the side of the door, eyes bright with mischief. 'Yes? You do realize there's no point lusting after him?'

'I don't lust after him.'

'Of course you do. Everyone does.'

Why was she blushing? And in front of this dreadful girl who'd now come out of the cupboard and was looking at her almost pityingly.

'No, I'm here with Jude,' Lucy said impulsively, regretting it immediately.

'You're not!' Sophia was hanging on to the cupboard door. 'Please don't tell me that!'

'I'm sorry,' Lucy said hesitantly, wishing very much that she hadn't.

'And that's why Luke thinks you should be downstairs, because Jude's about to arrive, isn't he?'

'That's right.'

Sophia saw the distraction in Lucy's eyes, the clear desire to get out of the room.

'Please?' she begged. 'Stay for just a second?' And before Lucy could respond she dived back into the cupboard, pulled out a pair of jeans, knickers and a T-shirt and kicked some boots out on to the floor with her foot. 'Tell me more.' She hopped on one leg as she pulled on the knickers. 'Because I have to know . . . Are you serious? You know you're nothing like his usual girls, nothing like me! And take that as a compliment. Oh Lucy!' Abruptly she sat down on the bed and looked her in the eye. 'There's no point me pretending. I'm gutted.' She laughed at herself sadly. 'I thought this weekend I could have been in with a chance. He's been away so bloody long – I haven't seen him for almost a year.'

She made Lucy feel more awkward than she could bear. *Have him*, she wanted to cry. *I don't care.* And she was tempted to tell Sophia the truth, that Jude didn't even know she was going to be there. That she was a fraud, that the whole undertaking was a complete sham. But loyalty to Luke and a dogged determination to see it through, at least for a few hours more, gave her strength. Sophia, sweetly honest as she was turning out to be, would have to be hurt.

'I met him at New Year.'

'At a party?' Sophia had stopped trying to dress and was hanging over the top of the cupboard door again.

'Something like that.'

'So, *is* it serious?'

'No.'

'Serious enough for you to be here now, though. You must be so excited about seeing him again!' Sophia gazed at her with big sad eyes and Lucy thought what a masochist she was. And yet how she'd been in similar situations herself, when every question is agony and yet not knowing is even worse.

'I don't suppose you understand the significance of all this . . .' Sophia went on. 'Last year, it was terrible.'

'Yes, I know.'

'But clearly Jude's feeling better. And I suppose, because, buried somewhere, I do truly have his best interests at heart, I have to say that's good news. Oh God,' she sighed theatrically, 'I don't mean it at all.'

'I'm sorry,' Lucy said weakly, wishing she was anywhere else, but Sophia hadn't finished with her yet.

'Luke? Luke?' she suddenly shrieked, looking over Lucy's shoulder towards the doorway. 'Is that you?'

Immediately alarm swept through Lucy and she spun around to see that yes, Luke was walking down the hallway towards them. He peered in through the bedroom door and shielded his eyes at the sight of Sophia.

'Luke, get out of the room!' Sophia said immediately, walking away from the cupboard to ensure he got a good look. 'Can't you see I'm practically naked?' Luke stepped back again, so that he was standing shoulder to shoulder with Lucy.

'Don't do that in front of my father,' he told Sophia, 'or he'll have a heart attack.'

'Of course he wouldn't. He'd love it.' She reached for the towel and pulled it back around her body. 'There. You can take your hand away from your face now.'

'I was just going downstairs,' Lucy said.

'And I was just saying she had to stay and talk to me.' Sophia looked from Lucy back to Luke. 'I was saying she wasn't allowed to leave the room until she told me *all* about Jude. I can't believe you, Luke. Why didn't you say?'

The smile was wiped from Luke's face. 'You two have been making friends fast,' he said.

'Lucy was just saying how excited she is about seeing him again. She's spent the whole time watching out of the window to see if he's arrived yet.'

Still standing close beside him, Lucy looked at Luke for the first time. 'I was actually saying that I needed to get downstairs because you'd be wondering where I was.' She could hear the defensiveness in her voice.

'But Jude's not arrived yet, has he?' Sophia said immediately. 'I'm sure we'd have heard the car.' She walked across the room to her window.

'No. Sorry, Lucy, no sign of him yet.'

Now she couldn't bear to look at Luke. What must he be thinking? That she'd tossed out the information like a bit of gossip that didn't matter to her at all? That she'd callously been passing titbits of her time with Jude to the one person who wouldn't want to hear?

She shrank back from the doorway and immediately Sophia came across the room and put her arms around Luke's shoulders. 'I'm making a great effort to be pleased for both of them. You are pleased for him, aren't you, Luke?' she asked, staring up into his eyes. 'You do see that it's great he's met someone? One of the Middleton boys has to be snuggled up with someone tonight, after all.'

'How do you know it couldn't be me?'

Lucy froze.

'Is that an invitation?' Sophia laughed, arms still draped around his shoulders. 'You know I'll be free.'

And Luke was smiling back at her.

'Lucy,' Sophia whispered, not breaking the gaze she was still holding with Luke. 'Would you mind? I think I need a private word with this lovely man.'

From being so impatient to go, now Lucy felt weighted to the floor. *Please, Luke*, Lucy begged him silently, *just say no. Tell her you want me to stay. Tell her that you badly want me to stay.*

Instead, Luke walked out of Sophia's reach, made his way across the room and sat down in an armchair by the window. Then he turned to Lucy. 'Why don't you go downstairs and find Mum?' he said dismissively. 'I'm sure she said she needed some help with the flowers.'

Lucy stared back at him, terribly hurt.

'That's a good idea, Lucy,' Sophia said encouragingly, verbally shooing her out of the room. 'Luke and I will come and find you soon.'

'Perfect,' Lucy said. 'I'll see you downstairs.'

She stalked out of the door and off down the hall and heard the bedroom door close behind her. Fine, you fuck-wit, she thought savagely. Shag her for all I care, if you're not quite so *half dead with grief* after all. She found herself in front of the red velvet curtain again and ripped it aside, furiously trying to think which was the way back to her fucking bedroom. Damn it, why did people have to live in such stupidly huge houses? She didn't want to be wandering around these endless corridors, she wanted to find her bedroom so that she could close the door and bang her head against the wall in private.

She turned around and walked backwards, trying to see

everything as she had done when she'd first walked in. But it didn't help. She turned round a second time, opened another door at random, turned a corner and found herself in a pale blue drawing-room, still and quiet, with a desk in one corner looking out over the garden and long windows looking out into the gardens. At least there was a staircase at the far end that would take her downstairs.

She started to move towards it but then realized that she couldn't face the thought of Suzie Middleton. She didn't want to talk to anybody, she wanted to sit on her own and think. She went over to one of the pale blue silk-covered sofas, sat down, put her hands on her knees and looked down at the floor.

She sat there for a few moments until the pain in her heart subsided and was replaced with sick determination not to let Luke, Jude or Sophia get to her any more. She would complete her task, and whether she ever saw Jude again after the night ahead didn't matter. This evening she was going to forget about Sophia, she was damned well going to kiss Jude right in front of the pair of them. Show Luke that he was just as invisible to her as she was to him.

She heard footsteps ringing out across the wooden floor, and looked up to see Luke. He sat down opposite her, stretched out his long frame and smiled. 'What were you doing in there?'

'I got lost,' she said. 'I was trying to find my way downstairs and I bumped into her. Would you mind showing me the way down? I was going to help your mother do the flowers, wasn't I?'

'I mean, what on earth were you saying?' Luke didn't move. 'I thought that was supposed to be our secret?'

'I'm sorry. It just burst out of me.'

'Yes, Sophia can have that effect on some people.'

'But not on you?'

'No, rarely on me.' He grinned. 'But I suppose it can't matter too much. She'll get over him. And you mustn't worry about Sophia, she's a drama queen. She'll have forgotten him by tomorrow.'

Lucy nodded.

'I didn't expect her to find you so fast.' He was looking more gently at her now. 'I should have warned you she was hunting you down.'

'I suppose I should have kept to my quarters.'

'Out of harm's way.' He ran a hand through his hair. 'Sophia was explaining to me how it was time I moved on.'

'With her?'

'I could do worse. If you're with Jude, perhaps I should help her drown her sorrows.'

'Depends what you're looking for.'

'Everyone keeps telling me I should be having fun. If everyone else is having such a good time, perhaps I should be trying to do the same.'

'Then I expect Sophia's your girl.'

He leaned closer. 'But I'm not looking for fun.'

She stared at him and saw the soft, sad look on his face, and suddenly he was rising up out of the chair, taking two steps towards her.

'Lucy,' he said urgently. 'He's my brother. After all we've done and everything he said to me, you can't dismiss him before you've even seen him again. Remember how it was between the two of you last time you met. How do you know it's not going to be like that again?'

And at that moment Suzie called up the stairs. 'He's here, he's here!'

Suddenly dogs were barking, doors were slamming, there was the sound of feet running across the hall below them.

'Luke!' Suzie shouted urgently up the stairs. 'He's here, for God's sake come down.'

'Does she know?' Lucy asked in surprise.

'Some of it, just a little.' He turned back to her. 'I'm going to talk to him, warn him that you're here.' He leaned forward and kissed her briefly, chastely, on one cheek. 'OK?'

Then he was gone, and she could hear him running down the stairs. She walked to the window and saw a taxi pulling up outside the front door, and her heart was beating, beating, beating, waiting for the moment when she would see him again.

But there, instead of Jude, was a sweet-faced, grey-haired old lady, climbing carefully out of the back of the taxi as Suzie came running around the side of the house, exclaiming, 'Felicity! It's you? Why didn't you call us from the station? Someone would have picked you up!'

On shaky legs Lucy returned to her chair, hoping Luke would come back for her. And she waited for long enough to know that he wouldn't.

*

Back in the kitchen she found Suzie and Luke chattering rapidly.

'Darling,' Suzie said as she saw Lucy arrive. 'Come and have a coffee.'

'And darling,' she turned to Luke, laying her hands on his shoulders, 'go and help the Butler and Rodd men bring in the wine. They insist they can do it themselves but there must be twenty cases.' She smiled at him, adding in a stage whisper, 'They look really old. I don't think they'll manage on their own.'

'Sure,' said Luke, glancing uncertainly across to Lucy.

'Don't you worry, Lucy can look after herself,' said his mother briskly. 'Take the white down to the cellars, it's cold enough down there, but leave the red in the dining-room. Stack it up below the window. And you could put all the extra champagne in the cold room.'

Suzie waited until Luke had shut the kitchen door behind him and then turned back to Lucy. 'And you can help me finish the flowers.'

She clearly wanted to talk to Lucy alone. She led her out of the kitchen, through the hall, gliding ahead of her like a ghost, still dressed only in the long white nightgown. She took them out of the house, along a little cloister, and then through a door at the far end that opened into a wonderful, long rectangular room with angels painted on the ceiling, and floor to ceiling windows running all down one side.

'Wow,' said Lucy, looking around. She turned to Suzie and raised her eyebrows. 'The ballroom?'

'Yes.' Suzie smiled. 'Isn't it a waste? We only use it about once a year.'

'For parties?'

'We used to, yes, lots of lovely parties. We've had one every New Year for the past twenty years. But,' she put her hands up to her cheeks, and closed her eyes, 'not this year. Not after Jude's accident.' She opened her eyes again. 'And now look at us, three weeks after New Year and what are we doing, we're having a party. I wouldn't have agreed to it but James absolutely insisted. I don't know why. I'm going to be fifty-four, for God's sake. Since when has that been cause for celebration?' She drew her hands slowly down her face and let them fall to her sides. 'Yes, if I'm honest, I like the chance to have my two boys home again and I like decorating the house and I enjoy choosing the flowers and the food.' She shook her head. 'But guests? And dancing? Alcohol and merriment? I certainly don't think I want any of that. I think how absolutely awful of us to be having a party on what's practically the anniversary of Gabriella's death. I'm looking around at all of us today and I can't help thinking what on earth are we doing? It feels so horrible, as if it happened yesterday.'

'Perhaps a party at this time of year is a good way to remember her,' Lucy ventured. 'You're all together. You're talking about her . . .'

Suzie shook her head. 'James doesn't talk about her at all, of course. And he absolutely adored her. Thought she was the prettiest girl he'd ever seen. Luke talks about her a lot. And Jude shouts about her, when he's feeling particularly angry with the rest of us.'

'Oh,' said Lucy, flinching at Jude's name, then added clumsily, 'I haven't met James yet.'

241

'You will. He'll be in soon. He's around the farm but I know he'll be wanting to get back for Jude. Because do you know, last year Jude came home the grand total of *once*, for Sunday lunch, didn't even stay the night. But we've done better with him this year, New Year, and now here he is again.' She smiled briskly, moving across towards the far end of the room. 'One good reason for having a party. We tempt Jude home.'

Lucy followed her to the far end of the room, where the wall was entirely taken up by a huge mirror, painted white and very plain, but with armfuls of pine and holly lying on the ground beneath it.

'I'm worried about seeing him again too, you know,' Suzie said unexpectedly, taking a chair and carrying it over towards one of the windows. 'We had such a bloody awful row the last time.' She stood up on the chair and reached along the curtain pole to pull down the remains of a yellow balloon tied to a piece of dirty, cobwebby string. She climbed down again and carried the chair back to the side of the room.

'He can't see that by behaving as he does, he makes it so much worse for everyone else, especially Luke.' She looked at the balloon distastefully. 'I think we had these at Luke's twenty-first. So, why are you nervous about seeing Jude again? Has he been beastly to you, too?'

'No,' Lucy said, 'not at all. It's just . . .' She paused, wondering whether Luke would mind her saying so, but unable to resist Suzie's interest. 'I'm here to see him, but he doesn't know it yet.'

'Oh, bugger,' said Suzie, crumpling slightly. 'And there I was thinking you were here with Luke.'

'Oh no,' Lucy said defensively. 'Not at all.'

'I thought it was too good to be true. And, to be honest, Luke did insist that you weren't.'

'I'm sorry,' Lucy said sadly.

'Can't be helped. And I must say I wondered how much longer Jude could last without a girlfriend.' She stopped. 'Now that sounded very rude, didn't it? What I mean is he's not a loner, Jude. He doesn't much like his own company, he needs to be the centre of attention.' She stopped again. 'Now, that was rather rude of me too, doesn't make him sound very nice at all. And of course he is. Terribly nice.' She shook her head. 'Ignore me. I should keep quiet. *You* can talk to *me* while we finish these wretched flowers.'

Lucy had imagined fresh flowers, to be artfully plonked into vases around the windowsills, but instead Suzie led her across to a couple of cardboard boxes. Lucy bent down, lifted the lid of one of them and peered curiously inside. Then she dipped in her hand and carefully brought out a flower with the wonderful loose floppy petals of a peony, on a long string with many, many others. They were all different colours, some pale olive green, others a dark crimson, the one in her hand a beautiful dark violet, all made out of some sort of stiffened linen and wire, and at their centre was a tiny lightbulb in the shape of a seed pearl.

'Where did you get them?' Lucy said, wonderingly,

touching one of the centre petals with her finger, seeing how they had been stiffened to keep the flower in shape. 'They're so beautiful.'

'I made them.' Suzie emptied the box on to the floor, gathering the long strings of flowers up in her arms and taking them over to the mirror. 'There are a hundred and fifteen.'

'How long did it take you?'

'Years,' Suzie laughed. 'I began when I was pregnant with Luke. But the most difficult part was finding someone who could put the bulbs in and get the lights to work. I ended up discovering a place in Shrewsbury.' She turned to Lucy. 'So now they can flash, dazzle or twinkle depending on your fancy.'

They worked quickly together, Lucy lifting and holding the branches of pine and Suzie artfully twisting and tying them on to the mirror, then together they picked up the armfuls of flowers and began to arrange them among the pine branches.

And suddenly Suzie started to talk about Gabriella again, the words beginning hesitantly and then picking up speed until they began to pour out of her, running away with themselves, and although Lucy knew that she had to have said it all before, could sense that she was the type of woman who talked easily and openly and who would undoubtedly have had many friends prepared to listen, still it was as if she was saying every word for the first time. And as if, in the year that had passed, the agony of that night had hardly lessened for her any more than it had for Luke or Jude.

She said how she couldn't breathe the smell of wood-smoke without thinking about that day. How she couldn't bear to hear church bells, because they had been ringing as the police car turned into the drive. She described the slow agonizing seconds when she'd first registered the awful fact that Jude was nowhere to be seen, how Luke had answered the door.

And then she told Lucy how, when Luke had heard what had happened, he'd turned back to Suzie and James. And seeing Luke's face, at first Suzie had thought Jude was dead. So that when he'd said Gabriella's name she'd felt such a wave of sick, guilty relief that she had had to turn away so that Luke couldn't see her face.

'What about Jude?' Lucy whispered.

'He wasn't hurt, although he'd have preferred it if he had been. It wasn't his fault at all, but of course that doesn't make the slightest bit of difference.'

As she spoke, Suzie bent to pick up one of the last branches of pine and then seemed to give up on it. She let her knees give way and sat down heavily on the floor. And Lucy silently dropped down too, so that they were both sitting facing each other, cross-legged, surrounded by the remaining branches and flowers.

'We could cope with grief. God knows we've learned that over the years, but guilt is a different one, isn't it? One year on and I feel we're falling apart. What happened was a terrible thing and Gabriella was the loveliest girl in the world and I'm not for a second trying to get my family to forget about her, but the guilt that Jude carries around with him is breaking us up. He's dealing with it far worse than

Luke. Luke's bereaved. It's understandable that he's taking his time to grieve for Gabriella, but Jude's lost. And he's lost who he was. There's no room for the person he used to be any more. His job used to be to make us all laugh.' She gave a cry, half laugh, half sob.

'I'm so sorry for you all.' Lucy swallowed hard.

'And of course he can't do that any more. And when I saw Luke sitting in the car with you just now, smiling and holding your hand, I thought, at last Jude is being set free. And I can't tell you what it was like.' She put her hand on her heart. 'My lovely boys. I felt this wonderful, blessed relief. Because if Luke could sit there outside the house holding your hand, I thought it meant that Jude would be freed . . . that everything was going to be better.'

'Everything is going to be better. Jude will be free.'

Suzie wiped her eye. 'I shouldn't have said that, should I? About Luke holding your hand.'

'Of course I don't mind,' Lucy lied. 'I'm here because Luke thinks I can help.' She gave Suzie a rueful smile. 'And he was holding my hand because he wanted to reassure me.' Now was not the time to confess all the doubts, the longings, the complications that ran through her visit that day.

'But I don't really understand, Lucy. You said that Jude doesn't know you're here?' Suzie looked at her quizzically. 'Forgive me for saying so, but when I last saw Jude, and it was only a couple of weeks ago, he was in such a filthy temper, and was so battered and angry with everyone. I really don't think there was much room in his head for a girlfriend. If he doesn't know you're here—'

'Luke asked me here,' Lucy interrupted. 'He tracked me down because he believes that the only reason Jude didn't come to find me himself was because of the guilt. Jude told him,' she shrugged awkwardly, 'that there *was* room in his head for me. And so Luke has asked me to come here. It's his way of pushing Jude forward, trying to make sure he moves on from all this.'

'Luke has done that for him?'

'Yes, Luke found me. We had met each other on New Year's Day, that night when the two of them arrived here so late? Jude and I had spent the day driving down together from Inverness.'

'Go on,' Suzie encouraged her gently.

'We'd decided, both of us, that we wouldn't see each other again. But then, on the way up here, I suppose, Jude told Luke about meeting me and how he wished . . . I don't know exactly what he said. But, Luke didn't want Jude to lose me because of him. And it was such an amazing thing to do, wasn't it? I couldn't turn Luke down, could I? I wanted to come. I wanted the chance to see Jude again . . . But now . . .' She looked at Suzie, listening so intently, caught the flicker of anticipation that told her that Suzie perhaps knew exactly how she was feeling now. 'Jude's lucky to have him as a brother and he should know it.'

Suzie picked up one of the flowers by its centre bulb and twirled it between her fingers.

'Jude has always broken everything Luke loved,' she said carefully. 'And Luke has always had to reassure him that he doesn't mind. I know it sounds awful to compare Gabriella's death with a broken toy, but it's true nevertheless. When they were little Luke used to have to lock his things out of Jude's reach, but he'd still always find them. And yet it's always Jude we have to reassure.'

She put down the flower in her hand and looked sharply towards the door. 'Hello, Sophia. Feeling lost?'

Lucy turned to see Sophia standing in the doorway at the far end of the room.

'I was wondering where everyone was. Have you seen Luke?' She must have caught the wary look on both their faces. 'But he's busy, is he?'

'No, darling, not at all. I think he's waiting for Jude to arrive, that's all.'

Sophia nodded, clearly too restless to stay; or perhaps intuition played a part after all, and she realized she'd butted in on a conversation she wasn't to be included in. 'I think I'll go and find him anyway,' she said, turning away from them abruptly. 'Keep him company, perhaps.' She looked back at the two of them. 'The room looks gorgeous,' she added as an afterthought. 'I'll see you both later.'

'Poor girl,' Suzie said, after she'd gone. 'She's a little lost today, isn't she?' She stopped, saw the guilt on Lucy's face and smiled. 'Now I'm going to say something else I probably shouldn't say. But somehow I don't think you'll mind.'

'What's that?'

'That she's far better suited to Jude than you are. Don't you think they're two of a kind?'

'No!' Lucy cried. 'You really shouldn't be saying that to me.'

'I can. I can say whatever I like.'

'So what else then, might you say?'

Suzie looked at her carefully.

'I could say that when he was younger, Jude was completely out of control. He made us laugh and we loved him for it but we – usually Luke – always had to pay for it. A few years ago he borrowed Luke's car and drove it into the bottom of our lake, but it was an accident and Luke would get it on the insurance, what was the big deal? With Gabriella, however much it was an accident too, in a way it fitted with everything that had gone before.'

'So you *do* blame Jude after all?'

'No, but I am saying that before the accident Jude was as charming and as selfish as it's possible to be and we've all grown up looking out for him, and looking after him, Luke especially, and if there's any doubt in your mind . . . about anything at all . . .' Her eyes were on Lucy, and her stare made Lucy think *She knows everything.* 'Don't ever think that Jude isn't plenty strong enough to cope, because he is . . .' She paused. 'Look at you all,' she said eventually. 'Trying to do the right thing.'

'But *trying* to do the right thing is *doing* the right thing, isn't it?' Lucy insisted.

Suzie gave a little laugh. 'We'll have to see, won't we?'

She stood up, picked up the last remaining branches and stuffed them into the empty cardboard boxes. Then she closed the lid and turned back to Lucy. 'I liked talking to you and I'm so pleased that you're here. Luke was right to bring you. I think you'll be the making of us.'

'I'm not sure he wanted me to talk to you quite as much as I did.'

'Probably not.' She smiled suddenly at Lucy. 'But he is

used to it, you know. He calls me the great interrogator, but I don't think he really minds. He knows I like to talk to people. But you . . .' she touched Lucy's shoulder gently, 'have talked and thought enough. You should stop worrying now, just let it all begin. In the end, you're not going to be able to control what happens next, even if you think you can.'

She carried the box out of the ballroom and led the way back through the hall to the kitchen. She opened a door to a scullery and disappeared inside, and Lucy went over to the kitchen table and sat down at a chair.

When Suzie reappeared, without the box, she lifted a saucepan off a rack above the Aga and filled it with milk from the fridge.

'I'll make us some lunch,' she said decisively.

Out of milk? Lucy wondered.

'Coffee, coffee,' Suzie sighed, seeing her face. 'I mean I'll make some coffee. We'll have lunch when Luke appears.'

Lucy stretched to look out of the window. It had to be getting close to the moment when Jude would appear too, and Luke was nowhere to be seen.

'He'll get to him, don't worry,' Suzie told her, seeing the tension in her face. 'Butler and Rudd have gone, and as Luke's not here with us now, he's probably outside. Don't you worry, he won't let anything distract him. He knows how important this is. After all he's done to set you up, he's not going to blow it now. He'll be outside somewhere, listening out for the car.'

Suzie passed her a mug of coffee and found a plate of biscuits and they sat down together at the kitchen table.

Above her the kitchen clock ticked.

'Where could Luke have got to?' said Suzie after a long pause. 'Now I'm getting worried too.'

Lucy shook her head. 'As you say, I'm sure he's outside, waiting for the car.'

And at that moment the kitchen door opened and her heart stopped because there was Jude standing in the doorway, all alone, looking weary and very handsome, with dark shadows beneath his eyes and two days' worth of stubble on his cheeks. And Lucy found herself frozen to her seat because he hadn't noticed her at all.

16

He walked into the room in the same familiar cashmere coat and scarf, holding a bag in each hand. He paused there for a moment without coming forward, staring across the room to his mother, sitting so still at the kitchen table.

'Aren't you going to come and say hello?' he asked, dropping his bags and holding out his arms.

Suzie leapt to her feet.

'Of course, darling,' she said, reaching him and hugging him tight. 'How are you? How was your trip down?'

'What's the matter?' He kissed her cheek, then held her back from him so that he could look at her face. 'Why are you talking in that funny voice?' And then he looked at her again, saw her unease. 'What's wrong?'

And then, finally, he came further into the kitchen and set eyes on Lucy.

He stopped dead, his eyes widening, the smile dropping from his face. And seeing nothing but shock and absolute dismay in his cold blank stare, all Lucy was aware of was the sound of the blood roaring in her ears, so loud that it was drowning out everything else in her head, everything that might have told her how to explain what she was doing there, sitting at his kitchen table, when Luke so clearly hadn't got to explain it to him first.

'Lucy?' he croaked.

'Don't say anything,' Suzie cried.

He turned to his mother incredulously. 'What do you mean *Don't say anything*?'

'Oh, Jude!' Suzie literally wrung her hands. 'I mean, let Lucy explain. I mean, please don't say anything horrible.'

But Lucy couldn't explain. She couldn't think how to start, so she sat there stiff and still, red with guilt and embarrassment, while Jude walked across the room until he was standing directly in front of her.

'Explain, Lucy,' he said icily. But then, before she could begin, he went on. 'Tell me what you're doing here. Because, as far as I remember, I didn't send you an invitation. I don't think I even told you where I lived.'

'Stop!' Suzie insisted. 'That's enough.' And she positioned herself between the two of them like a referee in a boxing match. 'She's here to see you.'

Out of the corner of her eye, Lucy glimpsed Sophia standing in the doorway, her mouth open in shock. As Lucy caught her eye, Sophia gave her a little, helpless thumbs-up.

Jude turned back to his mother. 'Oh, she's not here to see you? Or the dogs? Or Luke, perhaps? She's here to see me, is she? Yes, Mum, thank you. I think I might have worked that out for myself.' He turned back to Lucy, his face flushed and angry. 'What is it you want from me, Lucy?'

Lucy pushed back her chair, making a terrible screech on the terracotta tiles, and slowly stood up.

'Jude,' she said, her voice wobbling. She clung on to her

chair for support, then reached out her hand. 'Please, for God's sake, stop talking to me like this.'

He deliberately turned his back on her and walked over to the Aga, where a large saucepan sat bubbling furiously. He lifted the lid and peered inside.

'I'm not boiling your rabbit, if that's what you're worried about,' Lucy snapped at him, and she heard a hysterical giggle burst from Sophia at the other end of the room.

'Then what *are* you doing?' he asked, dropping the lid back again.

'Don't speak to her like that,' Suzie cried. 'Lucy's very nice.'

'Stay out of this, Mum,' Jude snapped. 'You know nothing. I can't imagine what crap she's been spouting but I'm telling you, this girl is weird, and seeing her here, sitting in *my* house, in *my* kitchen, drinking coffee with *my* mother, is fucking weird too. How did you find us, Lucy? How did you get here?'

'I'll tell you,' Sophia declared, coming into the room. 'Luke picked her up from the station.'

And then the kitchen door opened again and Luke walked in from outside, took in the scene in a second, first looked quickly to Lucy and winced and apologized all in one glance and then turned all his attention to Jude.

'OK!' he cried, walking across the room as Jude swung round, looking as if he might be about to punch him. 'One major cock-up clearly not averted.' He took Jude's arm and held on to it tightly. 'How did I miss you? I've been hanging around outside the house for the last hour and a half and yet I didn't see you arrive?'

'Tell me this isn't true, Luke,' Jude told him. 'Tell me you didn't bring her here.'

'Yes, I did.'

'But why?' Jude demanded. 'You must be mad.' He turned back to Lucy. 'What did you say to him?' he demanded, practically spitting the words into her face. 'How did you get him to do this?'

'Lucy did nothing. I invited her here because I wanted her to come to the party. And I'll tell you why if you stop shouting and behaving like a complete twat.'

Lucy could hear Suzie's voice rising in a quavering wail. 'Yes, Jude, remember who she is. It's *Lucy*, the girl you met on New Year's Day.' As if by reminding him, she would make it all better. *Oh, you mean it's that Lucy!*

'Have you looked at her once? Look at her now, look at her, you stupid, stupid man. See her face, see what you've done to her.'

At first, Lucy had felt terrible shock and agonizing hurt that Jude could behave like this, that no memory of their time together was softening his treatment of her now. But seeing him turn his poisonous glare on Luke, anger flooded through her, giving her strength. So this is what you're really like, she wanted to shout, wanting to punch him in his pretty-boy face. This is the man we've all been agonizing over for so long! He was the reason she was here, feeling more miserable than she'd ever done before, and she strode over to him, elbowing Luke aside and glaring up at him.

'I want to boil your head in the saucepan, let alone your bloody rabbit,' she told him furiously. 'You presume everything and you know nothing. Your family loves you.' She was shaking. She could feel deep uncontrollable shudders running through her. She would get out of this house, soon, soon, she told herself. It was nearly done. 'That's why I'm here, because they asked me to come, for you. Because Luke had some stupid idea that it might help you to see me again. I only came here because of Luke and you don't deserve him as a brother. And you certainly don't deserve me.'

Jude looked as if he'd been turned to stone but it didn't stop her. She leaned even closer to him.

'Look at me,' she commanded and he dragged his eyes to hers. 'Listen to me. You know what?' She spoke slowly and clearly, enunciating every word just a few inches from his face. 'Everyone has spent too much time worrying about *what will help Jude.*' She nodded into his startled face. 'Run away to your oil-rig, that'll make them worry about you, and it's worked hasn't it? Brilliantly well. You got exactly what you wanted, everyone spending all their time worrying about you, your mother, father, especially Luke.' She shook her head in frustration, turning to Suzie, who stared back in wordless shock. But she couldn't stop. No one else in this family of pussy-cats was going to tell him the truth if she didn't. 'How ridiculous is that, Luke having to worry about you? What about you worrying about him? Surely he's the one who's lost the most? You should be the one lifting him up, not pulling him even further down. And if that means being strong, *being here*, being positive, that's what you should be doing. Running away is what a self-pitying loser . . .'

'Stop!' Suzie commanded her, rising out of her chair. 'Who the hell do you think you are?'

Lucy looked at her furious face and abruptly ran out of steam, all the anger vanishing, so that she felt only crippled with embarrassment.

Suzie walked closer to Lucy.

'How dare you speak to us like that?' she demanded, eyes flashing with anger. 'How dare you walk into this house and tell us how to live our lives, talk to us about our grief, our private, horrendous grief, as if you can have *any idea* of how it's been. How dare you criticize my son? How dare you tell me how I should have behaved? Do I know you? Do you know us?'

'But in the ballroom, when we talked, I thought you understood.'

Suzie glared at her unblinkingly. 'You have no right to speak to us in this way, in our own house. How dare you?'

'You're right,' Lucy said falteringly. 'It was a terrible thing to say. I'm so sorry. I'll go. I'll pack my bag. I'll walk to the station.'

She turned away from them all, fumbling as if she couldn't see, and moved across the kitchen to the door.

'Lucy?'

It was Luke, taking hold of her arm. 'Don't go. Please wait for me . . .' But she shook her head, shaking her arm free, unable to look at him, unable to bear to look back at any of them again.

On the other side of the door she bumped blindly into

Sophia, who stepped in front of her, forcing her to stop. 'Wait,' Sophia insisted. 'Stop.'

Lucy looked up at Sophia with dead eyes.

'I didn't realize . . . that Jude didn't know you would be here.'

'Is that all you're bothered about? That now you've got free rein to do what you like?'

'No. Don't be ridiculous, of course that wasn't what I meant. Everything you said in there, it had to be said. It's what we've all been thinking but nobody could say it but you. I'm glad you said it. They need you, all of them. This is what they've become. Don't go.'

Lucy laughed bitterly, shook her head. 'At least you know Jude won't want me now.'

'Do you really think I'm so superficial?'

Lucy stopped abruptly, snapping briefly out of her misery. 'Of course I don't, I'm sorry.' She took Sophia's arm. 'I've been feeling awful for you the whole time I've been here.'

'You shouldn't have done, it wasn't your fault. I've wanted him all my life but I know I'm never going to get him. I've had years to get used to it.'

'Somehow I don't think I'm about to get him either.'

'Do you really want to?'

Despite desperately wanting to go, Lucy stopped and stared at Sophia.

'So stay and be brave,' Sophia told her. 'Don't run away. Don't be a wimp. Stand up to Suzie and Jude. Jude's behaved like a pig. Let him come back and apologize – he will, when he's realized just how much of what you said was true. And Luke? How can you think of running away from Luke?'

'The truth is I can easily think of running away from all of them.' Lucy stopped, fighting back tears. 'It was difficult enough before, waiting all the time for Jude to come home, but now that he's back . . .' She shook her head, walking away, towards the hall and the stairs to her bedroom.

Once in her bedroom she threw her bag on the bed, then opened the cupboard, gathered her dress up in her arms, picked up her shoes, and swept her make-up, wash-bag, nail varnish and hair-drier off the chest of drawers beside the bed and into the bag, chucking the dress and shoes in on top. She zipped it shut, picked up her coat and slipped it round her shoulders, took a deep shuddering breath and closed her eyes. A couple of minutes, that was all it had taken. Another five and she'd be gone. Free of the lot of them.

She sat down heavily on the bed. Free? Free wasn't the word. Wherever she went she wouldn't be free at all.

17

Lucy walked back into the kitchen to find Suzie waiting for her alone. She immediately took Lucy by the shoulder, steering her to a chair, and Lucy sat down, staring at Suzie warily.

'I'll take you to the station.'

'I'm so sorry I said all that.'

'There's a rule that you clearly don't know. It says that mothers are allowed to criticize their children, but nobody else can. Luke says it was good for Jude. He's with him now. Perhaps you might talk to Luke again before you go?'

'Why?'

'Because he made me promise not to take you to the station until you had. And Luke's done nothing wrong, and he's done an awful lot right, and I think you owe him that and I think you owe it to me too.'

Lucy nodded, and immediately Suzie's face cleared a little. 'Thank you.'

'Luke's plan rather backfired, didn't it?'

Suzie gave her a wry smile. 'Or perhaps you being here has had exactly the effect Luke wanted it to. It's forced everything into the open, after all.'

She got back to her feet and picked up their two empty coffee cups, then went across to the Aga and opened one of the ovens, half-heartedly waving aside another cloud of smoke. 'Are you sure you won't stay for lunch? You must have heard how a meal at Lipton Hall is always an experience? And it is a quarter to two.'

'You want me to? You can face having me in your house?'

'Just about,' Suzie said, cocking her head to one side like a bird. 'I've enjoyed most of the conversations I've had with you today.'

'I would like to talk to Luke.'

Suzie nodded. 'Jude was deeply sorry, Lucy, once he'd got over the shock. It might make you feel better to talk to him too before you go?'

'I was meant to be a nice surprise for him. Surely if any part of him felt anything for me at all, he wouldn't have behaved like that?'

'Jude is extremely sensitive about being made to look a fool.' Suzie lifted the lid off one of the saucepans and peered inside, then jumped back in surprise. 'And he felt trapped by us all, so he behaved like a complete pig.' She picked a wooden spoon out of a pot beside the Aga and prodded cautiously, leaning well away from the saucepan as she did so. 'But I know he'll be feeling terrible about it now. Trust me, once Luke has finished with him, he'll be wishing he'd never been born.' She turned to Lucy. 'Luke can be rather good at making people feel like that.'

So can you, Lucy thought, watching as Suzie picked up a sieve and took it over to the sink, then went back for her saucepan, staggered over to the sink and tipped the contents through the sieve. Dark brown lumps the size and consistency of horse droppings plopped steadily out of the pan in a cloud of steam.

'That looks good,' Lucy said with a tired grin.

'It'll be fine once it's mashed.' Suzie stopped, listening intently. 'They're coming back now.' She gave Lucy a smile of reassurance. 'Nearly over.'

But it wasn't Luke who came through the door into the kitchen, it was Jude. He walked over to Lucy, still sitting at her chair, and crouched down at her feet. Suzie seemed to melt into the corner of the room and disappear.

'Luke's told me everything,' he said, dropping his head.

She sat there, looking down at his dark hair, and then, slowly, he looked up at her again. 'You're free to boil my head if you want to.'

'I think your Mum's used up all the saucepans.'

'It wasn't me, Lucy,' he said, trying to take her hands in his, but she pulled them out of his grasp and sat on them. 'I can't believe I behaved like that. I'm more sorry than I can begin to tell you. Can you ever forgive me?'

He looked up at her sorrowfully, and when she didn't reply he said, 'No, of course you can't. Why should you?'

'I knew you'd be surprised,' she offered. 'I knew it would be a shock. And Luke was meant to get to you first, to explain. But Jude, how could you have thought I'd do that? Track you down like some creepy stalker? You know what we said, how we left everything in London. You might have known I wouldn't have followed you here without a good reason.'

'Now I know why you're here, of course I understand. But when I walked through the door I can't tell you what a surprise it was. And you know as well as I do, we hardly knew each other at all.'

'So you had to presume . . .'

'Yes. No. Oh, Lucy . . . Of course I didn't have to. Of course I could have rushed up to you and said how fantastic it was, is, to see you again. Don't think that I don't wish I'd done that now with all my heart. I can't bear that I behaved like that, to you.' He pushed himself away from her knees and sat heavily down at her feet. 'Is there anything I can say or do that might make you stay? Please.'

She hadn't expected him to be so nice, and the sincerity in his words took her aback, so that yet again she felt the certainty evaporate, leaving doubt and confusion in its place. She wanted to stay . . . but was that simply because she could hardly bear to tear herself away from Luke? Luke who'd not reappeared and perhaps didn't even care any more whether she stayed or went. She wanted to go because to stay here with Jude, now, still felt like a sham. And yet she wanted to stay . . . and Jude wanted her there, Suzie wanted her there, and to insist that she was driven to the station, to leave under such a cloud, seemed perhaps unnecessarily petulant, not really her style.

'I need to get out of the house for a bit,' she told him quietly.

'Sure, sure, I understand. Let's go outside, walk somewhere, drive, anything you want to do, I'll do it. Let's go now.'

'But what about your lunch? Suzie's been cooking a welcome home special.'

'Then we have no choice. Lives depend on it. We must go right away.'

He grinned at her, climbed back to his feet and held out a hand. 'Come on. You've got your coat on. We'll go for a walk and a talk and then, if you still want me to, *I'll* take you back to the station.'

She nodded, starting to feel better. 'Down the lane and back again?'

'Wherever you want.'

'And then, I could come back to the house to say goodbye to Suzie and Luke?'

'Absolutely. No problem at all.'

*

And so, with the two dogs, Parson and Wiggins, oblivious to the tension and running ahead joyfully, Lucy and Jude opened the back door and stepped out into the cold winter afternoon, walked around the side of the house and down the gravelled drive, crossed the bridge and turned left down the gated road.

They walked to the first gate with neither of them saying a word and then Lucy, hesitantly, began to speak.

'I came here with my friend Jane just over a week ago. And we walked down here as I tried to make up my mind what to do about you.'

He nodded. 'Don't make me feel worse.'

'You deserve it, you know.'

He turned to her, seeing from her face that although she wasn't joking, she wasn't completely serious any more either. 'I'm still surprised you had to be quite so angry. I wasn't threatening you, was I?'

'You were very threatening in the kitchen just then.'

'Yes, I'm sorry about that.'

'Is that what you think? That I'm a loser?'

'I think it's wrong the way you make them tread so softly around you. And I meant what I said about you needing to look after Luke.'

'You think so?'

She nodded.

'It's very strange, hearing you talk about everyone this way. When I left you last, you didn't know them at all.'

'I do understand.'

'Luke seemed to think you needed looking after too.'

'He was angry with you. He wanted this to work.'

'Do you like him?'

'Of course.'

'You've spent time together?'

She shrugged. "Supper, when he told me about you . . . A coffee.'

'Fancy him?'

She flinched. 'Don't ask me that.'

Jude turned in surprise. 'Forgive me, Lucy, I was teasing you, that's all.'

She looked down at the tarmac, kicked a stone with her foot. Then looked back at him again.

'I'm sorry, I was messing around. Getting used to you being here, that's all.'

'I think it was a strange thing to ask.'

'And I apologized.'

They walked on slowly, matching strides, and came to a T-junction in the road where a lane wound up into the hills to the church. Get Jude to show it to you, she remembered Luke suggesting as they'd looked out at it through the upstairs windows of the house.

'Shall we see the church?' she asked him.

'Sure, we can do whatever you want.'

Then he looked doubtfully at her feet, at the trainers she was wearing. 'Although perhaps we should go the long way around, stick to the lanes, it's a little further.' He looked up at the grey skies, heavy with rain. 'But it's not raining yet and we're in no rush, are we?'

They skirted around the fields, the brook on their left, a light breeze in the air, and as they walked she found comfort in the rhythm of her steps and began finally to relax. They turned right, into the wind. She could see the church, shielded by trees at the top of the hill. She was aware of him looking at her, considering her, getting used to the sight of her walking there beside him.

They strode on up the hill towards the church and she could hear his breath coming harder as she pushed on faster and faster, feeling the muscles in her calves beginning to ache with the steepness of the slope. And then she had to stop, and she swung round and looked back down the way they'd come towards the house, tiny as a dolls' house now, in the valley below them. Jude came and stood beside her, then touched her arm and led her to a fallen tree-trunk and she sat down beside him.

He turned to her and opened his mouth to speak.

'Don't apologize again.' She found herself able to look at him calmly now, and the relief on his face made her smile.

'Actually, I was going to move on to the thank you for coming bit now. And then I was going to ask you ... before I blew it all by behaving like Mr Angry, how you were feeling about seeing me again?'

He should have said *before Luke got in the way*.

'Scared, and intrigued, I suppose, because we hardly know each other. And it was a strange time, our long drive, wasn't it? A million miles away from a place like this.'

He took a deep breath. 'It's probably the last thing you want to hear,' he said in a rush, 'but I have to tell you even so, even though it's probably much too soon. I always wanted to see you again. I thought you were great. I wished, very much that I would see you again. Is that so bad?'

'No. But I'm surprised.' She looked at his face, staring at her full of hope. 'It all seemed very clear at the time.'

'But that was your fault,' Jude said immediately. 'I knew, or I thought I knew, how you felt about me. You seemed very clear. I'd got you sorted too. I thought I knew exactly what you were like, what you wanted. I couldn't see you because of Luke. You didn't want to see me anyway. It seemed very simple. That was another reason why it was such a shock, finding you in my kitchen ...'

He waited expectantly and she knew what he was asking her. How did she feel now? And the truth was that everything she thought she knew and felt and believed was spinning round in her head, uprooted and out of control. And there was Jude, labouring under the misapprehension that it was all about getting her to forgive him for what he'd said in the kitchen ... But poor Jude, what else was he supposed to think?

'The truth is, I hardly know you, do I?'

What was it he was hoping for now? Could he possibly believe that she'd turn to him as they sat together on the tree trunk and confidently tell him that it would all be all right, kiss him maybe, here on the hillside, in this wonderfully romantic spot he'd brought her to?

And in spite of all the doubt, she was tempted to do it, to blot it all out simply by kissing Jude. After all, here was a man, such an attractive, handsome man, sitting beside her and telling her in a heartfelt way just how much she meant to him. Someone she'd once been so close to, had shared so much with, someone she'd once sat beside for thirteen hours, someone she'd felt good enough about to walk into the Milestone Motel with. And meanwhile, back home, there was Luke, who still seemed only to see her as a means to an end, who was difficult and still full of grief, who'd never said anything to give her hope, probably with no space in his life for her at all.

Was it so bad, to be tempted? Not for long, not with any commitment to the future, just for as long as the party lasted, because she wasn't going to leave now. She'd realized that almost as soon as they'd started to walk, that she was going to stay.

Beside her, Jude rose to his feet and held out his hand. 'Don't let's talk about it any more now. Let me show you the church.'

She stood up, wishing she could respond as she knew

he wanted her to, that she could be happy now, could turn to him and begin again.

They walked up a grassy path with a post-and-rail fence separating them from fields on either side, through an ancient wooden lychgate and into a churchyard. They walked between the headstones and she looked ahead to the beautiful little golden-stone church. She heard the distant whinny of a horse, carried to them on the wind, and Jude lifted the latch of the door and waited for her to go in first. She stepped inside, into the silence, breathing in beeswax polish and a faint smell of lilies, and left Jude and walked on down the tiny tiled aisle. Her footsteps were loud on the floor as she walked between the simple wooden pews, black with age, then looked up at the wonderful stained-glass windows that threw in a clear gentle light. *In memory of the dear infant Mary*, she read.

Then she turned back to Jude, still standing in the doorway, watching her quietly. And as she met his look he came forward to meet her.

'It's OK, everything's going to be all right.'

If he'd been awful earlier, he couldn't have been nicer now. And yet, as he took her in his arms and held her close, she still felt deceitful and troubled, the serenity of the church making it feel all the more wrong that she was here with him, unable to say what he wanted her to say. When Jude suggested they move on, she nodded quickly and they left the church, carefully shutting the door behind them, and she felt grateful for the wind in her hair, the openness of the sky.

As darkness began to fall, the rain came too, and they walked bareheaded back along a lane with high-sided hedges and down through fields of sheep, and as they neared the house again, she finally turned to him. 'Of course I'll stay.' And in response he slipped his arm around her, and this time it felt natural to fall into the fold.

They reached the gated road again, the house looming up on them, and just as they reached the last bend in the lane he touched her arm and stopped.

'What?' she asked. And in answer he pulled her into his arms.

'I said I'd forgiven you.' She looked up at him, half smiling, half scared. 'That doesn't mean you can get too close.'

'I want you to know how happy I am that you're here.' He smiled into her eyes, not making any move to release her. And then he leaned forward and brushed his lips against her cheek. 'How good it is to see you again, even more gorgeous than I remembered.' His eyes were full of intent and she looked back at him, her cheeks burning. What was she doing, letting this happen? How much more trouble was she setting up for herself now? But if Luke couldn't tell her he wanted her, Jude certainly could.

'Is that all right?' Jude asked, his arms holding her still.

'Yes,' she smiled. And she looked up into his eyes and this time he held her look and she thought she saw something like triumph in his smile. And then he dipped his head and kissed her again, this time softly but on the lips, and despite thinking so badly of herself, hearing a voice shouting in her head that she was deceitful and was behaving so badly, still it was lovely and she couldn't stop herself kissing him back, caught in the moment, remembering the past.

18

Lucy opened the kitchen door and cautiously looked inside, and Suzie spun around from where she was washing up.

'You're staying, aren't you?' she asked, though it was barely a question. 'Of course you are.'

'Yes,' Lucy agreed, smiling rather sheepishly. 'I'm too easily influenced, aren't I?'

'Thank heavens you are. I'd have been absolutely miserable if you'd insisted on going home.' She came over to Lucy and started undoing the buttons of her coat. 'Have a cup of tea. It's only an hour and a half before everybody starts to arrive.'

Jude had followed her into the kitchen and Suzie turned to him with a huge smile of relief. 'She's staying. Isn't that great?'

'Took a bit of persuading.' He glanced across to Lucy and smiled. 'But I think I've convinced her now.'

'Oh.' Suzie was clearly taken aback. 'So you're properly together again, are you?'

Lucy found she couldn't bear to look at Suzie.

'Perhaps if she'll have me.'

Suzie shook her head. 'You'd better get her upstairs.'

'Excuse me!'

'Hot water,' Suzie snapped. 'She'll want a bath.' It

271

was as if Lucy wasn't there. 'She'll want a hot bath and a clean towel and if she doesn't hurry up she won't get either.'

Lucy looked down at her jeans, caked with mud, felt the rain in her tangled wispy hair. 'I could wash and get ready and then perhaps there's something I could do to help?' she suggested awkwardly.

'It's all done, darling,' Suzie said airily, still not looking at her. 'Don't worry about that. The caterers are here. The band's setting up . . .' She looked out of the window. 'I can see the rain has arrived early.'

'But that doesn't matter, Mum,' Jude said reassuringly. 'We'll be inside, it'll be dark, the weather doesn't matter at all.'

'Yes, darling. I'm quite aware of that.'

She'd snapped at him, Lucy realized in surprise. But Jude, on his best behaviour now, didn't rise. Instead he walked over to Suzie and pulled the plug out of the sink. 'Leave this,' he said. 'I'll finish it off. You must have better things to do.' He smiled at her. 'It's your party, Mum, you should be painting your nails or reading the paper or something, not messing about in the kitchen.'

Suzie protested, but she allowed Jude to steer her away from the sink and then broke away from him and walked over to the door.

'Luke is at the bottom of Tindle Hill. Dad asked him to chop up a tree. Did you meet him, on your way back?' Now she was looking pointedly at Lucy.

'I saw him,' Jude answered for her. 'I was wondering

where he was going. What's he doing that for?' He looked out at the rainy night.

'Because it's fallen on a fence, Jude. You know Dad, nothing can wait until morning. But I wonder if you'd go and fetch him, please. As everyone's been invited for seven-thirty I think it's very inconsiderate of both of them not to be here.'

Luke was at the bottom of Tindle Hill. Not in the house, not anywhere she might find him. And she went cold at the thought that he could have seen her and Jude coming back from their walk. She bit her lip in agitation, then looked up and saw Jude watching her, a strange bright look on his face.

'I'll go and find him now,' he said slowly, still keeping his eyes on Lucy. 'And you,' he went on, 'your bathroom awaits.'

He led her up the stairs, along to the hall to her bedroom door. 'You'll be OK?'

She nodded quickly, moving to the door, but he stepped forward, took her gently by the shoulders and turned her round, and then his mouth was searching for hers, his arms holding her tight, and she had to step back, pushing him forcefully away from her.

'Hey!' He kept his hands on her shoulders, trying to see her face. 'Don't do that. Just tell me not to.'

'I'm sorry.'

He held her away from him, looking hurt.

'I'm sorry,' she said again.

'I'm not expecting anything of you, Lucy. Just because

of what happened before ... it doesn't mean that I'm presuming it's going to happen all over again.'

She laughed uneasily, trying to make light of it. 'You mean I don't have to dance the smoochy dances with you?'

'Yes, you *do* have to dance the smoochy dances with me.' He pushed open the bedroom door. 'Go and get ready. I'll see you later.'

*

Lucy drew the curtains, then pulled off all her clothes and stepped into the bath, which was wonderful and hot. After a long time she climbed out, wrapped herself in a towel, and went to the cupboard for her dress. She slipped it off its hanger and laid it out on the bed, then went back into the bathroom, brushed her teeth, returned to the bedroom, found some underwear and went to the dressing-table.

She dried her hair into a head of loose curls, then pinned up the ones over her face so that she could work on her make-up, determined to look her best, to put it on carefully, with none of the slapdash she usually got away with. She looked at her face, making herself smile as she started to work on her cheeks – foundation, blusher, a dusting of bronze. She moved on to eyeliner, eyeshadow, brow highlighter, mascara, then lipstick, the exact same pink as her dress. And then she stopped and looked at herself again and saw a fearful looking ballroom dancer staring back at her. She exhaled a long wobbly breath, found her cleanser and a tissue, and wiped it all off. Then she began again, this time only lightly brushing her cheeks and her shoulders with bronzing powder, leaving off the foundation completely, touching her eyelashes with mascara and adding just the briefest of gold lines to her lids. She shook out her curls, added a spray of scent, and went over to her dress, lifting it carefully over her head, reaching behind her to tug up the zip. It slipped over her body so perfectly, fell in exactly the right way as she walked, clung and stretched in just the right places, the sequins winking gently, that for the first time in a long while Lucy began to feel better. Give her a big glass of champagne and she'd survive anything.

She went back to the cupboard for her sandals and stepped into them. Then she went back to the dressing-table and looked at herself in the mirror. It was a party, that was all, it would be over, one way or another, so soon. And tomorrow she'd be back on that train, leaving them all behind.

She bent to her make-up bag and added another line of glittery gold to her upper lids, then headed to the door. She wished she had someone to walk down the stairs with. More than anything she wished she could magic Jane there beside her. She looked at her watch. Seven-thirty. Perhaps other people might already be there? Perhaps downstairs the rooms would be full of people and she could slip in unnoticed.

She trod carefully down the stairs and towards the hall. She could hear voices ahead of her, Sophia's high-pitched giggle, and she hesitantly pushed open the door and looked inside.

'It must be Lucy!' A grey-haired man who looked like a gnome leaped to his feet and rubbed his hands delightedly.

'And looking absolutely stunning, my dear.' He came over to her and took her hands in his. 'I'm James. What a pleasure it is to meet you at last. Such cold hands, come over to the fire.'

The elusive James. She gratefully allowed herself to be led into the room, catching sight of Luke and Jude sitting side by side on the sofa, Sophia standing talking to Suzie and every so often tossing back her hair, dressed in spiky high heels and a white backless dress that showed off her tan.

'Lucy, what a stunning dress,' Suzie said, breaking off her conversation with Sophia and joining her husband in front of Lucy.

'Thank you.' Lucy smiled, accepting a glass of champagne from James, thinking how his eyes twinkled as if he were constantly in the middle of a wonderful private joke. And yet he was clearly a force to be reckoned with too. Lucy could see where Luke had inherited his air of command and authority. If James wanted a tree chopping or a drain unblocking at the bottom of his field, she'd probably try to do the job for him.

Jude hurriedly pushed himself to his feet. 'Let me in. I want to see her,' he insisted, and when he'd manoeuvred his father to one side he stopped and looked at her. 'My God. But she's beautiful.'

'Don't sound so surprised.' Suzie laughed.

'I mean, you look amazing.' He came forward and whispered in her ear, 'It's the pink dress, at last I'm getting to see it.' He kissed her cheek then turned back to the others, his eye alighting on Luke. 'Doesn't she look fantastic?'

'Very nice.' He was staring back at her, unsmiling, swilling his champagne around in his glass.

And then suddenly there was a loud knocking at the door and immediately both dogs started barking noisily.

'Get it, James,' Suzie cried in relief. 'And Jude or Luke, would you shut these two dogs away? We can't have them barking every time someone arrives.'

Into the room came a tall grey-haired woman in a long velvet cape which she swung away from her shoulders to reveal a full-length scarlet dress and a spectacular diamond necklace. Behind her came two teenage girls, both in tiny dresses, both with impossibly long legs and long blonde hair. They were pink-cheeked and beautiful and giggling together, and looking at them Lucy suddenly felt terribly old.

'Bethany, Abigail.' Suzie greeted them warmly and put a hand on each of their shoulders. 'So you were allowed out for the night? Mum wasn't sure if school would let you come.'

'Oh yes.' Both girls nodded, eyes bright, and Suzie turned to Lucy to explain. 'Bethany and Abigail are at boarding-school near Oxford. Don't you worry,' she added in a stage whisper, turning back to the two of them, 'you'll find you're not the only two young ones.'

'Oh, yes, we know,' Abigail or Bethany replied enthusiastically, in a high-pitched, very posh voice. 'Sam and Josh Pemberton-Leys are coming, aren't they? And Miles Hadlow. And loads of other girls from school . . .'

And then, all at once, more guests arrived, pouring into the house in a steady stream, unwrapping themselves from velvet stoles and long fur coats, picking glasses of champagne off heavy silver trays, marvelling at the weather, the room, the fireplace, how wonderful it was to see Luke and Jude there too, and looking so happy and well.

Not that Luke looked well or happy. He looked unapproachable and dark. As Lucy sipped her drink and was introduced around the room, she was aware of him all the time, how guests would be brought up to him, or would cautiously make their own way over to him, and how they'd get a moment of his attention and then seconds later would move away.

Jude, on the other hand, seemed to be the life and soul, refilling everyone's glasses, laughing and chatting, circulating and cracking jokes, but always coming back to Lucy, gamely introducing her into one conversation after another. He was back in his old role, she realized, watching him as a horse-faced young woman leaned eagerly towards him and then burst back in delighted laughter. He was back where he was supposed to be, at the centre of attention, the dashing, electrifying charmer he'd always been. And she was amazed that the transformation could have occurred so fast, that it was all so simple for him.

He caught her eye and immediately came over to her and took her hand. 'Listen, the band's begun. Come and dance?'

'Jude!' She smiled at him. 'People are still arriving. You're on duty.'

'No, I'm not. Luke can do that.'

'But they'll still be doing sound checks, tuning up. They won't want us in there yet.'

He shook his head. Determinedly he took her hand and led her out of the hall, out of the house and along the dark cloister and in through the door to the ballroom. It was dark but for the flashing lights bouncing off the walls and the huge glitter ball that was now suspended from the ceiling. Self-consciously Lucy allowed Jude to lead her into the middle of the room, and seeing them there, the band immediately fell into a song, their lead singer, a bosomy middle-aged woman in a long split-to-the-thigh silver dress, stepping forward to the microphone and giving it her all.

And dancing with Jude turned out to be fun. For all her uncertainty, confusion, doubt, she was perfectly happy to be held against the scratchy wool of his dinner jacket, feeling his arms loosely wrapped across her back, letting him catch her hands to spin her around the room or guide her slowly left and right, never catching her eye with a meaningful stare, never trying to pull her towards him too hard. He was so sweet and undemanding, knowing intuitively what she wanted, and she found that she danced on, through one song and on to the next, and then on again, losing herself in the music and the rhythm, finally letting go.

'Thanks, Jude,' she said when the third song finished.

'But they've hardly begun. Wait till you hear what else is on my mother's playlist.' He kept his hands around her waist. 'You sure you don't want to rock around the clock?'

She smiled. 'Later on, we could. But don't you think we should be getting back to everyone now? You especially should be back in the house.'

'No.' His arms tightened around her. 'I'd rather stay here with you all night.'

Other people had heard the music and were appearing in the doorway, peering in uncertainly and then, seeing Lucy and Jude in the middle of the dance floor, following their lead and coming in to join them, starting to dance. Above them on the far wall the flowers flickered in time to the beat. Lucy could see people noticing them, pointing them out to each other. And then she saw Luke entering the room with Sophia, watched how he was dragged unwillingly across the dance floor, Sophia looking more like an angel in her long white dress. How stiffly Luke stood as Sophia danced gamely beside him, his hands loosely clasped around her tiny waist.

She found herself stopping, standing still on the dance floor.

'Are you all right?' Jude asked immediately.

'I'm fine.' She nodded. 'I think I need to sit down, that's all.'

He took her hand and led her away, back to the cloister, where there was a long bench running along the wall.

'Not too cold here?'

'No. Thanks.'

He left her alone while he disappeared to find them a drink, returning with a bottle of champagne, wet from its ice bucket, in one hand and a couple of glasses in the other. He sat on the floor at her feet, turning his back on the guests who passed them by, pulling off the foil and beginning to work out the cork. Then James chose that very moment to appear at the other end of the cloister, and Jude smoothly changed his aim and fired the cork at him. Miraculously James caught it and lobbed it straight back at him.

'So you've abandoned the party already, you hopeless pair?' He turned to Lucy. 'Don't disappear completely, because I'm expecting a dance with you later. And I would suggest you come and eat something soon, before it all disappears.'

'Was that an order?' Lucy asked Jude when they were left alone again. The truth was that while dancing with him had been fine, sitting with him out here all alone with nothing to say was proving much more difficult.

'Are you hungry?'

She nodded. 'Yes, a little.'

'Then we should eat.'

He rose to his feet again and for the first time she caught a look of impatience in his eye. She knew that she was being awful, lousy company, her hopeless inability to think of a word to say to him only too obvious. What must he be thinking of her now? She stood up, then caught the back of the bench.

'Are you OK, Lucy?'

'Yes.'

'I feel I'm asking you this all the time.'

'I know you are. I'm sorry, Jude.' She shook her head. 'Don't ask me again. Go and find someone else to talk to if you want to.'

'Is that what you'd like me to do?'

She looked back up at him. 'Give me another couple of drinks and I'll be fine.'

'I think I should find you something to eat.'

He took her back to the hall and left her alone sitting in an armchair, looking at the fire and listening to the wind, which had got up in gusts and squalls. She could hear it howling down the chimney in the main hall, and she rose to her feet and walked to the window and looked out at the black night, rain spattering at the windowpanes. She checked her watch. It was nine o'clock. She could see her face in the reflection of the window, and she touched her cheek with her hand. Then she went back to the fire and sat down again, leaning back against the chair and watching the flames.

'Hello.'

She turned fast, the colour rising in her cheeks, and Luke came towards her, bending down and briefly kissing her cheek, producing such a flood of longing that she could hardly pull her thoughts together enough to answer. He went towards the fire, spreading his hands to its warmth.

'Never ever let my father catch you at a loose end. There's a party? Forget it! He's just sent me to check on the cows. Our cows!' He smiled uneasily. 'And don't think wearing a dress will put him off. He'll have you out in your high heels mucking out a stable if he gets half a chance.'

'So I heard.'

He moved away from the fire and sat down in the chair opposite her.

'If Jude hadn't come to Tingle Wood to bring us back we'd probably still be there now.'

She nodded.

'You know he's a good-for-nothing bastard and he doesn't deserve you.'

'Are you joking?'

'No.' He leaned back in his chair, staring at her through half-closed eyes. 'But after all the work I've put in for the pair of you, I'm happy enough, I suppose.'

How could it be so painful to hear him talk so calmly, as if he really couldn't care either way?

'I thought about interrupting when I saw you kiss him outside the house, then decided I shouldn't.'

She flinched at the thought, feeling a guilty flush spread across her face. 'If you saw it, you'd know it was a brief insignificant little kiss.'

'No it wasn't.' He looked at her witheringly. 'Anyhow, I'm sure you'll find plenty of opportunity to pick up where you left off.'

'Luke,' she said desperately, 'I don't know what to do.'

'It's done. Don't think about me. Look forward now.'

'Is that what you want me to do?'

'Oh, Lucy,' Luke said quietly. 'Lucy Blue.' He shook his head. 'I guess I'll survive.'

She couldn't believe that he was standing up, leaving again before she'd hardly said a word. Yet with him like this, so utterly remote, she wondered what else she might have found to say.

'I wish you well,' he said quietly from the doorway. 'Having spent the last year ruining Jude's love life, I'm pleased for you, truly I am. Happy it worked out.'

And then he was gone, and moments later, Jude was back, with two plates piled high with food.

'Come with me.'

Like a puppet she allowed him to steer her away, following him as he shouldered open a door into another room that she'd not been into before and led her to the far end, pulling aside a long blue velvet curtain that revealed a wide windowseat, covered in deep cushions, that looked out into the dark garden.

'I know I'm supposed to be hosting this damn thing, but I need you to myself for a little while now, no interruptions.' He smiled at her. 'Do you mind? We can eat and then we can be sociable afterwards.'

She shook her head and went to sit beside him, thinking how she would not be being sociable afterwards; she would be leaving the party as soon as she could, waiting in her bedroom for morning. The window was wide enough for them to sit facing each other, balancing their plates on their knees, and once they were settled he let the curtain swing again in front of them, closing them off from the rest of the house.

'Hey, Jude,' she said, giving him a half-hearted smile.

'I think you've used that one up already.'

He waited, but she just looked down at her plate of rare roast beef, tiny Yorkshire puddings, roast potatoes and dark green beans, wishing she could think of something, anything to say.

'Lucy?' She could tell from the tone of his voice that he wasn't about to crack a joke.

She looked up at him.

'Try telling me what's changed. When we were out walking together today, it felt as if everything would turn out OK – better than OK, I thought it would turn out perfectly. And then you came down into the room this evening and you were wearing your pink dress and I thought it was some sort of sign for me. And you looked so beautiful and happy to be there with us all. And now, forgive the cliché, it's as if the light's suddenly gone out of your eyes. And try as hard as I can, I can't seem to turn it back on again, and I don't know why.'

And Lucy thought this is why I'm here, for this moment, to be here with him, sitting behind this curtain now. This is what I've been leading up to, for so long. I must not think about Sophia. I certainly must not think about Luke. This is the moment when I'm meant to reassure him, to do what I've come to do. She picked up their plates, leaned precariously down off the windowseat to place them gently on to the floor, then faced him again.

Evidently he decided it was all right to move forward, to put a finger on the line of her collarbone and slowly let it slide around the back of her neck, at the same time drawing her closer, closer, until he could touch her lips with his. Then he moved forwards on to his knees, bending over her and cradling her face with his hands.

'Why do I always have to kiss you in such bloody awkward positions?' he whispered, coming forward again.

And then the curtain was pulled wide open and Luke was standing there.

'Get away,' Jude said good-naturedly, grabbing it back and pulling it closed again. 'Silly bugger!' he said. 'Doesn't he realize a closed curtain has to mean someone is behind it?'

The curtain opened a second time.

'Luke, for God's sake leave us alone! What's the matter with you? What do you want?'

'I want you out of there. What the fuck do you think you're doing?'

'Trying to kiss Lucy,' Jude said simply.

'You should be with the rest of us, hosting this party.'

'Don't give me that crap.' Jude climbed off his seat and squared up to his brother. 'Leave us alone. Give us a chance to get to know each other again.'

'You can do that later. Right now you should be out here, both of you should. We have guests, Jude.'

'For Christ's sake, Luke! What's the matter with you?'

'I have to go,' Lucy blurted, startling them into silence.

They both stopped, looking at her in astonishment.

'Where?' said Jude.

'Anywhere away from the two of you.'

'Don't say that, Lucy.' Jude was turning back to her, reaching for her hand, pinning her to the chair and laughing at her, still misunderstanding how serious she was. 'Stay with me, please. I'll get rid of him again, watch me.'

But she was talking to Luke, not to him. 'I can't bear to watch the two of you like this,' she told him. 'And I'm making it worse now, not better. And I'm sorry I'm not turning out quite as you planned. Not for you, not for Jude. Not for Suzie, not even for bloody Sophia.'

'Lucy?' Jude was still trying to stop her but she was rising up off her seat, sidestepping the plates of food on the floor. 'I didn't realize. I didn't understand.' He was looking wildly from her to Luke. 'I'm sorry, I didn't know.'

Then he was turning back to her again. 'Why are you so upset? What's wrong? Both of you – Lucy? Luke? What's wrong now? I don't understand.'

She pushed past the pair of them, still hearing Jude asking again, 'What's the big deal? I don't understand.' And then she was escaping from the room, through the door at the far end and into the main hall. She slipped along the highly polished floorboards of the drawing-room, passing guests, turning left and right, running into and out of the rooms she now knew so well. She climbed the stairs two at a time, turning on a heel and feeling a stab of pain in her ankle but stamping down on it again grimly.

'What's the matter?' a stranger asked as she passed him on the stairs, his eyes full of concern. 'Are you all right?'

'I'm fine, fine,' she muttered, then stopped and turned back to him, to where he was still standing, looking after her anxiously.

'Would you tell Jude that Lucy's going home, please?' she asked him, politely enough. 'Tell him I'll call him tomorrow and I'm sorry I couldn't tell him myself but not to worry about me, please.'

The man nodded at once, as if he understood completely and wasn't surprised at all.

In her room she ripped off her dress, stepped out of her shoes, pulled on her jeans and her shirt and jumper, found her socks and trainers and pulled them back on to her feet. Then she threw everything else into her bag – bottles and wash-things, T-shirt and pyjama bottoms – pulled the sides of her bag together and zipped it shut, then shrugged herself into her coat.

Five minutes, that was probably all it had been since she'd left them both behind the curtain. She closed her eyes. *Please God let them still be there shouting at each other.* Would that man have found Jude yet, she wondered? Would Jude guess she was planning to run away? Not just to slip up the stairs to her bedroom but to leave the house and go for good. She knew what a coward she was being, slinking away into the night, and she felt hopeless and full of shame that she wasn't saying goodbye to Suzie after all they'd said and done together that day. But at that moment it felt as if it was the only thing she could do. Flee the house, out into the night, away from the lot of them.

She slunk down the stairs, anxiously looking ahead in case anybody noticed her, half expecting to see Jude or Luke or even both of them waiting for her, but although there was a throng of people down there, neither of the brothers was among them and no one noticed her slipping round the side of the banisters and quietly walking across to the front door. And once she had turned her back on the Middletons and had her hand on the door-handle, she didn't care if anyone noticed her leaving, if anyone was wondering who she was or where she was going. She saw a torch on the floor in the corner of the porch and picked it up. She'd send it back to Suzie from London. Then she shut the door quietly behind her and walked out into the night, looking up at the thousands of stars and the bright clear moon in the midnight-blue sky and feeling a certain poignant peace descend upon her. As crushed and hopelessly confused as she felt, at least she was getting away.

She ran down the drive, her feet crunching loudly on

the gravel, her bag swinging against her back as she ran, and then she turned right on to the gated road and began to walk, following the lane, past the war memorial, starting to climb the first long winding hill that led towards the station.

She was more than glad of the torch, realizing within a few strides that without it she would have had no hope of finding her way. Used to London, she couldn't believe how deeply black the night could be. She waved the torch into the hedgerows, imagining foxes and badgers staring at her silently as she passed, and felt the first ripple of unease. Then she reminded herself of what waited for her back at the house, told herself that she was glad to be there on the road, getting away, that anything was better than staying at the party, feeling so false and miserable. That however many miles she would have to walk, however long it would take her, however slim the chances were that she'd find a train going anywhere from little Lipton St Lucy station tonight, it was better to be beginning her journey home. She'd sit in the waiting-room, wrapped up in her coat. She'd sleep a little and she'd catch the first train in the morning, wherever it was going. She didn't care.

The certainty started to slip away after the first half mile but still she walked, swinging her bag on to her other shoulder, her footsteps very quiet on the tarmac road. With each step forward it got harder to imagine turning back, yet, with every stride it seemed more stupid that she was out there at all. And then with a rush she started to cry, silently, at the hopelessness of it all, the loneliness of walking on her own in the dark.

She reached the brow of the hill, lifted the torch again and could make out the lane snaking away below her, disappearing into a shadow of trees. She hefted her bag on to the other shoulder again, huddled into her coat, and walked on. Ten minutes later, at the bottom of the hill, she came to a T-junction she didn't remember having seen before, and a signpost with the names of two villages, neither of which she recognized. She stood uncertainly in the middle of the road, panic starting to rise inside her. How far had she come? She'd been walking for twenty minutes, perhaps, but the thought of choosing the wrong road, walking further and further into nowhere . . . She looked round again, feeling the night closing in all round her, even the road behind her, leading back to Lipton St Lucy, suddenly looking terrifyingly impenetrable. She looked back to the signpost, desperately trying to work out which route she should take, but she couldn't make herself go forward in either direction.

And then she shone her torch back along the lane to Lipton St Lucy for a second time and realized that she had only one choice: not to go back, slink through the front door and pretend she'd never been away, but to go back and find Luke. And immediately, from stepping out hesitantly, tentatively, she strode forward, wondering why it had taken her so long to realize that of course that was what she had to do. Why she had left at all? She thought back to the moment when he had pulled back the curtain. Why had she run away instead of confronting him? How was it that at that moment she'd become Teddy's Lucy again, so hesitant and uncertain? And suddenly the urge to be back there, to run into the house, not up the stairs to her bedroom but to find Luke, made her start to run, her bag bumping hard against her back.

Then, for the first time since she'd left the house, she thought she heard a car. She stopped, hearing it again, definitely coming closer, accelerating around the bends and bearing down on her fast, and she leaped up off the road in fear, leaning back against the hedge and holding her bag straight out in front of her as if it might keep her safe.

Headlights swept towards her and she lifted the bag further, shielding her eyes. But instead of passing her, the car slowed as it reached her and then stopped square in the middle of the lane just in front of her, its hazard warning lights suddenly starting to blink brightly in the dark. A dark figure leaped out of the car and came towards her and she saw that it was Jude.

'What are you doing? Where were you going? You silly fool.'

'I was going to the station,' she said sheepishly, then made herself look up at him. 'Jude, I'm so sorry. I thought I couldn't bear to stay any longer, listening to the two of you always fighting, losing your temper, Luke so sad, you so angry.' She shook her head. 'I know it was a stupid, horrible thing to run out on you without explaining ... and in a way,' she shrugged, giving him a helpless smile, 'this scary walk did me good. I'd turned around. I was coming back. I need to find Luke.'

'I came to find you.'

'Yes, thank you. I can see that. It was very nice of you. It was a long way to the station, further than I thought.'

He nodded.

'What's the matter, Jude?' She came forwards, unsettled by the stiffness in his face, the way he seemed to be holding himself so tight and still. 'Are you so furious with me?'

'Get into the car and I'll take you home.'

She came forward and gripped his arm. 'Is Luke OK?' She had a sudden thought that something terrible had happened.

'Going berserk looking for you.' He forced out a smile. 'But otherwise he's fine. Oddly, it didn't cross his mind that you might have left. But once I'd had a word with Colonel Everett – who passed on your message perfectly, thank God – I knew where to find you.'

'So what's wrong, Jude?' She still had hold of his arm. 'You sound so strange. What's happened?'

'There are two things I have to tell you.' He looked away from her, his handsome face tight with strain. 'And I don't want to tell you either of them. But I'm going to have to before I take you home.'

'Tell me now!'

They had reached his car, and he opened the door for her then started the engine and drove them further down the lane to a lay-by. He stopped the car again, turned off the engine and turned to her in the darkness.

Lucy sat, huddled in her coat, and waited.

'Somehow being in the car with you again, looking at your face – and it's dark, I can hardly see you at all – it reminds me of before, makes me think of our journey together. How close we were. I'm thinking perhaps ...

Well, I can hope at least that you might remember I'm not all bad.'

'Just tell me what it is, please, Jude.'

He nodded. 'Luke told you about Gabriella, didn't he?' he said.

'Gabriella?' She looked at him in surprise, but he was staring blankly through the windscreen. 'Yes.'

'There was something *I* had to tell Luke about Gabriella and me, about the night I picked her up from the station.'

'No,' she gasped. 'You weren't. Please God don't tell me that.'

'No,' he said, 'we weren't.' He paused, still not looking at her, and then went on quietly. 'But I suppose it would be fair to say that I'd have liked it if we were.' Finally he turned to her, caught the distaste on her face and immediately looked away again. 'Yes,' he said. 'I knew you'd look at me like that. But nothing ever happened between us, nothing ever would. She was too much in love with Luke.'

'So?' she asked cautiously. 'Why are you telling me this now? Why did you have to say anything to Luke?'

'Because . . .' He took a deep breath in, exhaled slowly. 'On that afternoon, when she rang to say she'd caught an earlier train, I was the only one home.'

Lucy nodded. 'Luke told me about that.'

'But what Luke wouldn't have told you, because he didn't know himself until just now, was that as I got into the car I saw them all coming home from their walk.' He was looking at her again, defying her to look away, but she held his gaze, transfixed. 'Luke had reached the gate. I could have called to him, I could have let him know, could have let him go to the station instead of me, but I didn't do it. *I* wanted to go. I wanted to go to the station and pick her up. I wanted to get her on her own.'

Wordlessly Lucy dropped her head into her hands.

'So tell me what you're thinking,' Jude went on. 'Tell me what a sad, fucked-up bastard I am, to try to nick my own brother's girlfriend.'

She shook her head miserably.

'And then we had the smash. And afterwards, I could never tell any of them, could I? How I shouldn't have been there at all.'

Lucy looked up at him. 'And now you find you can't be around Luke any more?'

'I suppose. At times I've kidded myself that it was no big deal – not compared with what happened afterwards – and that I hadn't been planning to *do* anything. I tell myself I just wanted the fun of flirting with her for a few minutes, that not calling out to Luke was a little misjudgement but not a major crime.' He paused. 'But I know that's not true.'

She looked at him, sickened by what he'd thought he was capable of and yet, at the same time, wanting to reach out to him, to tell him that it was all right, that he'd suffered enough, that everyone at times had thoughts they shouldn't have, behaved as they shouldn't behave. The tragedy was that Jude, because of the accident, had been forced to live in that moment for ever, to have that bad thought, be that shameful person, over and over again.

She touched his arm. 'How do you know that's not true? Perhaps a little misjudgement is all it was?'

'I know because I'd have done the same thing all over again with you.' He said it so quickly that she had to listen again to his words in her mind to take in what he had said, and then she felt the shock punch her. 'Because you were just like Gabriella, suddenly you became a challenge. You are the second part of my confession tonight.'

'How am I?'

'He's in love with you, Lucy, completely in love.'

'What?' She felt herself swoop and dive at his words.

'I saw he liked you straight away, but then, of course, I realized it was more than that, much more.' He breathed in deeply and then held his breath and closed his eyes. 'And instead of backing off, thinking how wonderful that he could feel such things again, for somebody else, it made me want you for myself.' His eyes flashed open again and he turned to her. 'Not that I hadn't always thought you were wonderful, fantastic. But it had always been about that one day, to me. Even when I saw you again, and then . . .' He laughed bitterly. 'I realized that Luke had his eye on you too.'

'You said something to him in Tindle Wood, didn't you? When you went to find him, what did you say?'

Jude turned back to her, staring at her in the dim light inside the car. 'I thanked him for finding you for me. I told him how happy we both were. How we couldn't believe we'd found each other again.'

'You are a bastard,' she said.

'Yes, over and over again.'

'But you're also here, telling me this . . . about Luke.' She started to laugh, tears in her eyes. 'And for that I could almost love you! Oh Christ, Jude, to be honest, all I can think of is him there, at home now, looking for me. Will you take me back? Are you sure it's true? You're not making it up?'

He shook his head. 'Tonight, when he pulled back the curtain and I saw his face, I can't believe you didn't see it too. And I felt sick at myself. I knew what I was doing to him. But it wasn't until you ran away that all the energy, all that determination to hang on to you, to make it work, just stopped. I stopped. And I realized I didn't want to be that person any more. That in a way I was being given another chance and that this time, instead of running away, I could put it right. Luke brought you here for me, thinking he was doing the right thing. And in a way he was, and now I can bring you home to him.'

He nodded, started the car again and drove them cautiously out into the lane. And Lucy suddenly, in her mind, saw the red-headed girl in the tube station, smiling at her, remembering the girl's absolute conviction that Lucy would be with the man who'd drawn the poster, how certain she was that Lucy would find him. 'When you find him, you'll know I was right.' And she was, she was.

Jude took her hand. 'You've come here and you've turned me round, sorted us out. And I owe you everything for that. I'm glad you forced me to tell Luke the truth.'

'Just out of interest, how was Luke when you told him all this?'

'He didn't hit me, if that's what you're wondering. But he didn't exactly hug me tight and tell me not to worry either.' He smiled. 'I don't expect him to. Perhaps he won't ever feel like doing that. But right now, that's OK. I can bring you back to him. Perhaps that will make a difference to him in the end.'

'It will,' she said. 'Of course it will.' She saw the pain in his eyes despite the smile of bravado. She thought of the long journey they'd made together, begun in Inverness airport only two weeks ago, about how far they had come since then.

'Find him, Lucy,' he said, turning briefly to her once more. 'Walk back into that party and find him now, that's all you need to do.'

And then they were in the drive, pulling up alongside the other cars, and Jude took her hand and helped her out of the car, keeping his arm close round her as they ran towards the front door and in through the hall, under the surprised stares of Suzie and Sophia, who was sitting on the edge of the sofa in front of the fire, hand in hand with a beautiful man. Lucy was aware that everyone stopped talking when she came in, their drinks frozen in mid-air as they took in her face, her jeans, her muddy trainers, but Jude's arm was protectively around her shoulders and in any case she really didn't care.

Suzie seemed to understand everything in an instant. She caught Lucy's eye, nodding her through the open door to the hallway beyond. And without a word, Lucy left them all behind her. There was another crowd of people in the next room but she didn't see any of them, only Luke.

As she stood in the doorway he turned, and for a long moment he didn't move, just looked at her with such love and hopeless longing that she wondered how she'd ever doubted it before. And then Jude came up behind her and nudged her forward, and the crowd around Luke seemed to step back from him to let her in. And she walked towards him, and it was as if he finally understood and a great exultant smile broke across his face and he opened his arms and pulled her towards him, crushing her against him as if he would never let her go.

'I've been looking for you,' he told her, his face so close to hers. 'In the barn, round the garden, down the gated road, everywhere I could think you might be. And then Jude said he had an idea – that he thought he knew where to find you.'

'I was coming back to you but Jude found me and he brought me home.'

She looked up at him, tight in the circle of his arms, and he reached down and kissed her softly on her mouth.

'Yes?' he asked in a whisper. 'Does that feel right?'

'It does,' she whispered back, hardly able to speak because it had felt so utterly, completely perfect.

He stroked her hair. 'Lucy Blue, I found you.' He looked down at her, tenderly stroked her face. 'Perhaps there'll have to be another poster?'

'No, Luke,' she told him, smiling back at him, coming forwards to kiss him again. 'This time, I found you.'

Hippy Chick

For my brother, Charlie

acknowledgements

Not surprisingly, Ibiza was a magical place to research, made all the better by beautiful Can Marias, my brother's house on the island (thank you, Charlie). But better still by the many friends I have made there who helped me so much with this book. Most of all I would like to thank Clare Bloomer and Toni Guasch, Victoria Durrer-Gasse and Hilly Shields, for all their advice and insights, and without whom Ibiza would be nowhere near such fun. And many thanks too to Kristiina and Jaume Guasch at the incomparable Atzarō, and to Tina Cutler, whose vivid and wonderful memories of growing up on the island proved invaluable.

Back in England I was comforted and tied down to my desk by my always perfect husband Ant, and by Tom and Jack too. Thanks as always to you. And thanks too to my many friends who tramped Ditch Edge Lane and Brancaster beach with me, especially Karen Heron, Caroline Seely, Sarah Walker, Candida Crewe, J. B.

Miller and Victoria Pougatch, all of whom valiantly kept on listening at the early stages of the book and helped me through to the point where at least I knew what I wanted to write.

And huge thanks, as always, to the sales, marketing and publishing team at Pan Macmillan, especially to Trisha Jackson, Steph Sweeney, Liz Cowen and of course to my wonderful editor, Imogen Taylor. And finally thank you to my agent, Araminta Whitley, who always knows exactly when to prod, reassure, inspire or calm me down. I'm very lucky to have her.

one

ibiza

HUGHIE BALLANTYNE took a quick sharp breath and raised his arms out wide. At the other end of the pool the woman was lying on her sunbed, one tanned leg bent at the knee, a lazy finger now running tantalizingly along the elastic edge of her bikini bottoms. Then, as if she'd heard him, she lifted her sunglasses high off her nose and smiled at him and he knew he'd got her. He looked up at the sky and rose to her challenge, clasping the edge of the pool with his toes, swaying slightly on the balls of his feet.

Skirting the olive trees on her way to the pool, Honey froze as she saw what he was about to do, and then she could only watch as her father launched himself into his swallow dive, his pigeon chest straining forwards so that for long seconds he hung suspended, motionless against the empty blue sky. It was only when he smacked into the water that she finally started to run, wine leaping free from the open bottle in her hand, marking her passage in spreading splashes across the limestone tiles. '*Dad*,' she yelled, her voice cutting through the gentle chatter of the hotel guests. '*Dad!*' And she ran to the edge of the pool, kicking off her flip-flops, leaped into the water and swam towards where her father had disappeared, grabbed a breath and ducked under, reaching forwards through the sudden silence with her hands. Then, within a few seconds, she was wrapping her arms around his waist, kicking them both back to the surface, bursting through the water into the brilliant sunshine with his enormous weight in her arms.

'Sweetheart, what has he done?'

'Is he dead?'

'Oh, Jesus, look at the blood.'

'Stupid fucker. How much has he had to drink?'

She started to drag him towards the voices gathered at the edge of the pool, but suddenly his bulk burst back into life and he pushed himself to his feet, then stood waist deep, swaying in the water, staring at the line of people watching him.

But now that they could see he was all right, that this dive into the Can Falco swimming pool was just another Hughie-mishap to be logged alongside the many, many others, people were even starting to laugh.

'Nul point,' she heard someone chuckle.

'Oh, much too harsh! I thought he was rather good.'

'Come on, Hugh-boy, let's help you out.'

He staggered silently on towards the steps while Honey followed a few paces behind, watching as he tripped up the first one and then allowed himself to be hoisted from the water by his friends.

She climbed out after him, wringing out her skirt, wiping her face with her hand.

'Dad?'

He turned at her touch, water streaming off him, blood dripping freely from his nose.

'Deep end good, shallow end bad.' She smiled at him, wiping the water from his face and gently smoothing back his hair. He was shuddering with shock. 'OK?' She peered closer at the shape of his nose and the smile turned to a wince. 'Are you? Can you tell if you've broken it?' He stared back at her with wild unfocused eyes. 'You know what? We might have to take you to hospital.'

Someone came forwards and dropped a heavy towel around his shoulders. A clean white *bath* towel, she couldn't help noticing, hoping he wouldn't get blood all over it.

'Let's go inside.'

She reached forwards and gently took his hand, but at her touch he suddenly cried out.

3

'Rachel!'

She was aware how everyone around them fell silent at the same time.

'No, Honey.' She said it quietly, trying to coax him away. 'Please, come and get dry.'

'Rachel!' This time it came out softly, full of wonder. 'Rachel! You can't be here.'

'Oh, Dad, for God's sake shut up.'

'Has Tora seen you?' He turned guiltily. 'Where's Tora?'

'She's got a class. Come on, beer-for-brains, you've hit your head. You've got concussion. You need to lie down.'

He looked back at the pool, then down at the blood-spattered stone at his feet. 'I'm sorry.'

'Don't worry about it. It was an accident. Claudio will clear it up. Come on, nobody minds.'

'You look beautiful.'

Behind her she heard someone laugh. Hughie heard it too and in answer he took a deep sobbing breath and fell dramatically to his knees, wrapping his arms around her legs.

'Let me go,' she whispered, patting his wet head.

'But I've been waiting to tell you.'

'Shut up, Dad. Stand up.'

Concern at what he might say next made it difficult to

speak gently. Who was she, this Rachel? Ex-girlfriend, or a current one? She'd never heard any mention of her, this Rachel . . .

Her father looked up at her pleadingly, still hanging on to her soaking wet skirt. 'Don't be angry. Oh yes, be angry. But hear me now, for God's sake, please, listen to me now. I'm saying sorry, Rachel, please.'

She glanced around at the captivated faces of his friends. They were used to devil-may-care Hughie, mad and bad and sometimes even dangerous to know, exuberant and noisy, as quick to cry as he was to laugh, but this was different and they knew it. And Honey did not want to share any more of it with them.

She bent her head to his ear and said in a whisper that only he could hear, 'Come inside with me now, without saying another word, and then I'll tell you why I'm here.'

'I'm taking him in.' She stood back up. 'Find him some dry clothes and a bandage . . . and a hospital.' She touched his shoulder. 'We'll go inside. You do know where we are, Can Falco? Home, yes?' Wide-eyed incomprehension stared back at her.

She picked a towel for herself off an empty sunbed and slung it over her shoulders, then walked him carefully away. He came with her docilely, allowing himself to be threaded between the wooden sunbeds that had been turned haphazardly by guests following the afternoon sun, muttering to himself as they moved up the gentle flights of stone steps and pathways that took them away from the pool and through the terraces, winding them on between the almond and orange trees, past his own cottage and hers too, and finally on to the main house itself.

As they arrived she saw with relief that Claudio was there ahead of them, halfway up a ladder, pinning a huge branch of purple bougainvillea back to the sugar-white wall. Twenty years old and with them at the hotel on a placement from the University of Palma, he was trustworthy, completely unflappable and right now exactly the person she needed. He turned as she came nearer and she caught his eye and went straight on, not wanting her father to break the momentum of walking, and immediately she heard Claudio rattling down the ladder behind them. She propelled her father towards the last flight of steps and then took him through a stone archway and out of the heat of the sun into a cool and shady courtyard that led them through the front door of the hotel – an arched and ancient studded door, wide open now – and then on into the front hall. She was taking a chance bringing him in here – regular guests would most likely take the sight of a raving and bloody-nosed Hughie in their stride, but new arrivals might not . . .

'You are taking your father to the hospital?' Claudio asked as he moved smoothly on to the reception desk at the far end.

She nodded. 'But I think I should find Tora first.' She said it quietly, not wanting to upset her father. 'Keep an eye on him while I look for her?'

'Your mother has a class in the Garden of Serenity.' He was rapidly opening and shutting drawers as he spoke, pulling out bottles, boxes of plasters and mosquito repellent, until he found what he wanted.

'Now then,' he said, coming around to Hughie with a large wad of cotton wool in his hand and placing it firmly on the bridge of Hughie's nose, 'Hold on to that.' He led Hughie over to a window seat and pushed him gently down, then squatted beside him, looking relaxed and in control in his immaculate white T-shirt and baggy brown shorts, leather flip-flops on his long brown feet. 'Are you OK? You'll feel better soon, I'm sure.'

Hughie shook his head but then his familiar wide-mouthed grin slowly broke across his face.

'Never felt better than Tora.'

Claudio nodded back benignly, misunderstanding or not quite hearing what Hughie had said.

'Sixty-nine and ninety-six, on the beach, in the sea, upside down, back to front. You name it, we did it. ' Hughie produced such a brilliantly shocked look on Claudio's face that Honey couldn't help herself letting out a great snort of laughter, but then her father turned at the sound and again started in surprise at the sight of her.

'Rachel? Christ alive, it can't be you!'

This time she decided to ignore him. She put out a hand and helped Claudio to his feet. 'Don't worry. He hit his head on the bottom of the pool. He's concussed.'

Claudio smiled with obvious relief. 'Of course.'

'So don't expect him to talk any sense.'

'The doctors will bring the old Mr Ballantyne back, I'm sure.'

'I don't think I'll ever be so pleased to see him.'

She went and crouched at his side and took his shaking hand in hers.

'Honeybee, that's the name you gave me, you and your equally mad wife. It's Honeybee, look at me!' She came closer, aware of the plea in her voice. 'Do you still not know me at all?'

He shook his head, retreating into his chair, then pulled his hands free and covered his face and she found she could no longer look at him either. She was

8

used to seeing him weepy and sentimental. She'd seen him distraught when he'd accidentally shot Bugger, his dog, and sufficiently off his face to walk naked through a packed restaurant in Ibiza town, but even then he'd somehow retained a degree of style and self-control, had never been as hopeless as he was now.

She pushed herself back to her feet. 'It's every time he looks at me . . . I don't know what to do with him.'

Claudio nodded, then touched her shoulder sympathetically. 'We will fetch him some dry clothes and I will just pick up my car keys . . .' – he returned swiftly to the desk, opened another drawer – 'And my wallet . . .' He closed the drawer again. 'And I will take him to the hospital and you will wait for your mother to finish her class. Yes? And then you can come to the hospital later and I will be here to check in our guests. And you needn't worry, not about anything at all. And tonight, you must take time with your daddy, yes? For once you take the evening off. You must stay with your daddy if you need to.'

'Thank you,' she agreed with relief, 'that would make all the difference in the world.' She touched her father's bent head. 'I'll follow as soon as I can. I promise. Will you go with Claudio now?'

Claudio put a hand under her father's elbow and

half coaxed, half pulled him to his feet and Hughie allowed himself to be turned and then led away, only stopping once in the doorway irritably to shake himself free of Claudio's arm.

As they made their way through the hotel towards the door that led out to the car park she found herself walking slowly along behind, keeping far enough back for them not to be aware she was there. And eventually the tall rangy figure of Claudio and her grey-haired, shuffling father reached the doors and then walked back into the hot dry sunshine of a late-August afternoon, Claudio keeping his hand beneath her father's elbow to support and gently guide him forwards. And then, finally, the two of them turned a corner and disappeared from sight.

Honey came back into the hall, held her head in frustration, thought about banging it against the wall, and instead went to straighten the cushions on the window seat where her father had been sitting. Then she moved on to her desk and her chair and sat down, as if by tapping at her computer she could somehow take control of everything that had happened. Perhaps she should go back to the pool and reassure everybody, tell them how Hughie had forgotten 'Rachel' as fast as he'd conjured her up? She could laugh it all off – of course her father's hallucination would be a beautiful woman, what else? But she didn't want to go back down there, to face the laughter or, even worse, the silence of a gang closing ranks, a gang who probably knew exactly who Rachel was but weren't going to tell her.

With her chin in her hands she watched the fine cotton curtains billow in and out, in and out, at the four-hundred-year-old windows, making dancing shadows on the polished stone floor. Out there, in the Garden of Serenity, her mother's class would be nearing its end. In her sexy rasping voice that six years of relatively clean living hadn't softened at all, Tora would be preparing her little flock to face the world once more. *Breathe in and breathe out again. Feel the joy in your veins, hear the laughter in your ears.*

But clearly there were to be no joy and laughter winging their way towards Tora. Whoever Rachel was she clearly mattered to her father and somehow Honey knew that all the undoubtedly messy, sad, private details were going to come out now. Honey remembered how everybody had drawn back when her father had shouted Rachel's name, embarrassed by the desperation in his voice. *Had* they realized who he was talking about? Did they know all those messy details? She pictured them, her father's friends, his motley crew, crumpled and creased from decades of too much sun and wild living. With insouciant style the men would sit together on the edge of the pool at tea-time, mingling with the other guests yet completely apart, feet dangling in the water, knobbly nut-brown knees all in a line as they ate their little lemon meringue pies and ordered endless rounds of tea that they'd never dream of paying for, talking their way through the sunny afternoons. This lot shared her parents' history. They'd been in Ibiza for over thirty years. They surely knew everything about Hughie. So what was it that they'd be saying about Rachel now? Were they talking about how much he loved her? The thought sent a shaft of sadness running through her because that was perhaps the worst of it – not that there was another woman, but that she had the power to make him cry.

And, at least as powerful as the sadness, there was irritation too. No, more than irritation, a real red-blooded anger that had burst into life as she'd watched his typically flashy, typically irresponsible dive. Of course he'd choose the shallow end. Of course she'd be on hand to jump in afterwards, to fish him out and patch him up. And now he'd presented her with 'Rachel' to contend with too, and that made her angrier still, not just with Hughie but also with her mother, Tora, for letting it happen, for being so away with the fairies that reality barely figured at all. Because if Tora had not been quite so self-obsessed, Rachel – whoever she was – would surely not have got a look-in.

So, at that moment, Honey wanted to tell her mother everything that had happened. She wanted to see the news of Rachel slap the rapt smile off Tora's face. She wanted a reaction, wanted to see her mother hurting and remorseful. Even better, she wanted to see her jealous. She wanted her taking control for once, driving to that hospital in a cloud of dust and fury, ready to fight for Hughie and prove after all these years that she did still care for her family and husband after all.

And then, perhaps, Honey would be free. Not completely, not forever, but just enough to walk out of the hotel without always having to call in someone to cover for her. Free to jump into her car on the spur of the moment, perhaps drive to a beach, somewhere small and unknown where she would strip off and spend the whole day sunbathing and swimming and rediscovering Ibiza, the island of freedom and love that for her had become an island of bills and broken boilers, bounced cheques and demanding guests, power surges that blew the electrics, water shortages, stroppy chefs and nymphomaniac waitresses. An island where, centre stage, stood her feckless, unfaithful father and her beautiful butterfly of a mother, who had left their daughter to shoulder Can Falco all on her own while they drifted through their days on a sweet-scented breeze of marijuana and patchouli oil, just as they always had, just as they always would do, with no sense of her increasing loneliness, and absolutely no understanding of how relentless running Can Falco could be.

Honey pictured her mother as she would be now, sitting in the Garden of Serenity – her perfect rectangular garden carpeted with the softest, greenest grass, protected by high hedges of jasmine and lavender, at the far end a massive stone fountain carved in the shape of a pair of cupped hands, gently spilling water. The hands were so huge it was possible to climb up and lie back inside them, and listen to music through speakers bored into their fingertips. Her mother could spend hours lying there contemplating the world. But now, nearing the end of her class, she would be sitting cross-legged on the grass, facing her pupils, palms turned upwards as she cast a last, loving look around their rapt faces.

And standing wearily up to go and find her, Honey knew that she had been conditioned by too many years of calming and reassuring to hurt her mother now. Her role was to act as a buffer between Tora and the nasty world outside, it wasn't to make things worse. She would go and find her and she would tell her about the accident and perhaps even mention Rachel's name, just to prepare the way in case it came up later, but in a breezy, light-hearted kind of a way so that her mother would instantly forget it. And then she would drive to the hospital and see her father and find out exactly what he'd been up to.

two

a week earlier

'YOU KNOW YOU want to.'

Edouard Bonnier was on the other side of Honey's desk, leaning in towards her on the flats of his hands, messing up all the invoices and letters that lay in orderly piles in front of her, certain he was going to get what he wanted, eventually.

'Let Claudio run things. Tell him you're having some time off.'

'I do take time off. It's just I don't like spending it with you.'

Edouard didn't flinch and she looked back at him steadily, her own hands folded neatly in her lap. 'OK, not you, your noisy, ugly, loud-mouthed friends.'

'Honeybee, I'm hurt.'

'But they were a bunch of wankers weren't they?'

'It's bankers, Bee, bankers.' He was still smiling but she knew that she'd rattled him. 'And you didn't give them a chance. They weren't so bad. They hadn't left work behind, that's all.' He pushed himself away from her desk. 'And I've already said I'm sorry that they danced on the table.'

'And poured hundreds of pounds' worth of wine in each other's hair?'

'Yes, and paid for it too. We went through all this last weekend. Do we have to do it again now?'

She shook her head.

'You know the strangest thing is they loved you. Took one look at your dirty feet and your toe rings and thought they'd found themselves their very own hippy. Obviously they hadn't expected you to be so bad-tempered but they still loved you.'

He went over to the window, looking out at the early-evening sun, and she stared at his broad pinstriped shoulders, his flight bag at his feet, and wondered why it was that she always had to try to knock him down.

'So,' she went on. 'Here we are on a Friday night again. Have you brought some more? Are they up at El Figo right now, waiting for you to take them out on the town? We can't look after them here tonight, we don't like plate smashing at Can Falco.'

She imagined him driving up to his beautiful house, stripping off his stripy shirt and diving into his spec-tacular navy blue swimming pool, joining his horrible friends, who turned him into one of them.

'That's why I want *you* to come to El Figo.'

'You'd like me to entertain them?'

'Yes.' He didn't turn back from the window. 'So put some flowers in your hair and bring your guitar.'

She laughed. 'That's what they'd expect, after all. And you know I haven't got a guitar.'

He came back to her desk, leaned in on her once more. 'So borrow one.' And she was glad to see that he hadn't minded what she'd said after all, that his eyes were warm and full of fun, so much the old Edouard that she nearly held out her hands for him to pull her to her feet.

But he kissed her briefly on the cheek, then stepped back, picked up his bag and hitched it over his shoulder.

'Imagine how impressed they'd be, the most beautiful girl in Ibiza turning up at my little party. If you change your mind, you know I'll be there. And you should give them a chance because this time I think you'd like them . . . I think you'd be pleased you came.' He paused, frowned, thought about it, 'Or perhaps, maybe not.'

And he was out of the door before she'd decided how to respond.

She didn't watch him go. Instead she spun on her chair and went back to her computer, forgetting about him as she checked emails and worked her way through the staff lists for the weekend, then moved on to the details of guests arriving that evening, double-checking them against the rooms that had been booked for them. Friday night, end of August. They'd been full almost every night since May and she could still see no sign of demand slacking off, even now, nearing autumn. The emails requesting rooms were flooding in every day. She sent off her regretful replies, thinking how the hotel could double, treble in size and she'd still fill every room. For a season at least, or perhaps even two, until she finally died of exhaustion, keeling over in the middle of the hall as she welcomed her ten thousandth guest through the door.

When she made her routine call to Ibiza airport she heard there'd been a six-hour delay on the flight from Gatwick, which meant she'd be staying up until three or four in order to check in the last guests. She ran her finger down the arrivals list and saw it was a family, chasing the late rays of sunshine before the start of the new school year and long winter back in England. Not the best of starts then, for them. Altogether there were fourteen guests arriving that evening: two families of four, a honeymoon couple booked in for a fortnight, and two couples out for the week.

At about six her mother appeared, floating down the

hallway in a gauzy see-through kaftan and bikini bottoms. She put her finger to her lips and gave Honey a wide berth, sending her a beam of a smile but not pausing and certainly not speaking because, for Tora, the first Friday of every month was always a silent day.

For her father, on the other hand, Fridays were always extremely noisy days, days to be exuberantly celebrated as the end of the working week – by Hughie, who had hardly done a full day's work in his life. Honey could hear the boom of his laughter from the bar.

And yet, without lifting more than an occasional finger to summon a bottle of wine, a great deal of the success of Can Falco was down to them. Honey had lost count of the times she had been told by enthusiastic and well-meaning guests how her priceless parents had made their holiday. Invariably they would go on to tell Honey in confiding whispers how special it was, in a world so tainted by greed and commercialism, to find somewhere like Can Falco; what a joy to be able to recapture something of their own hippy pasts. It was then that Honey wished she could check them into just that, an un-modernized bedroom, in a hippy chic Can Falco from the seventies – the derelict finca she'd been born in – complete with rats, no running water and no electricity, at the end of a two-mile dirt track that wound so steeply up into the hills that even a donkey and cart struggled to manage the climb.

Of course the truth was that these guests liked goose-down pillows and crisp cotton sheets, air-conditioning, power showers, imaginative and beautifully cooked food, carefully polished terracotta floors, colourful drapes and ancient furniture, but they would only have mentioned them if they hadn't been there. What guests remembered when they got back home afterwards, what they wanted to tell their friends about, was the delight of having Hughie and Tora as hosts because, although they'd never acknowledge it, even to themselves, Hughie and Tora made them feel rather raffish and fun. Through Hughie and Tora they could recapture a youth they'd never really known in the first place. And for all his noisy ineptitude Hughie had a gentleness and rare kindness about him that nurtured them and made them blossom; while Tora, for all her earnest chatter about Zoroastrianism and atomic essences, did indeed seem lit from the inside with a kind of radiance. And so, between the two of them, without trying at all, they gave people exactly what they were looking for and just what they'd hoped to find.

Then there were the other, mostly younger, guests who smiled politely at the way Tora and Hughie treated

Can Falco as their own private hotel – which, of course, it was – but were much more interested in Honey. She knew what they saw because they told her all the time. To them she was the smiling, sun-kissed Ibiza girl, free from the cares of the world, gold from the sun, glowing with the good life, the spirit of Can Falco. And they came back to see her time and time again, hypnotized by the near-perfect escapism of what she'd created there. After city fumes and skyscrapers, here they opened their windows in the morning and breathed in the scent of the pine forests, looked out over the spectacular view of the sea, or up into the flawless sky to watch the eagles that gave Can Falco its Catalan name circling lazily above their heads. They came for nights at Pacha and Privilege and Bambuddha Grove, to watch the sunset on Benirras beach, have dinner at La Paloma, sunbathe with the supermodels on Aguas Blancas, or simply to stay put and sleep and swim or wander lazily through the forests around Can Falco. And, refreshingly for Honey, they loved Ibiza for what it was now rather than for what it had once been and, in return, she loved having them to stay, basked in their enthusiasm, made friends with many of them, even if each time they left she had to cope with the fact that they made her feel just that little more restless – each one, in their leaving, emphasizing the big wide life beyond the shore.

hippy chick

At seven she heard a taxi pulling to a halt at the front of the hotel, the sound of slamming doors and raised voices. And then through the doors came Claudio carrying cases and with him a tall blond man, a sleeping child in one arm and a suitcase in the other, his wallet and passport clenched between his teeth. He made his way across the hall towards Honey and she came from behind the desk to meet him and carefully tugged the wallet and passport free.

'Thanks,' he grinned, 'Steve Kelly.' He unceremoniously dumped the child straight into her arms. 'And this is Joe.' Then he turned back to help his wife, who was now making her way through the door, gamely dragging with her another small, blond-haired boy, who was sitting on her foot and gripping tightly to one of her bare brown legs like a monkey around a tree. 'Charlie.' The woman grinned at Honey, tucking a long dark curl behind her ear, then gritted her teeth as her husband wrenched their son free of her leg 'And Freddie.' She reached forwards to take the sleeping Joe from Honey's arms.

Truth be told, Honey quite liked her guests arriving completely frazzled and therefore primed to appreciate the beauty and calm efficiency of Can Falco. With guests like these she could fly into action, whisk away their luggage, order them a herbal tea or a cold beer, listen

23

to their horror stories of delays and lost luggage, calm their shattered nerves and distract their kids. It wasn't nearly so satisfying to play host to people who behaved as if they spent their entire lives on holiday.

Immediately after the Kellys had been taken upstairs two couples arrived at the same time. But of course this was as Honey liked it best: the hotel full, running smoothly, seemingly effortlessly, laughter carrying down the hallways, footsteps clattering on the stone steps. She sat at her desk, swiftly checked in the four new guests and drove Can Falco seamlessly on towards the evening.

The desk had been her father's but she'd always thought of it as hers. It had been one of the few items to join her father at the start of his life in Ibiza, making the journey from Wiltshire to Can Falco in the back of a lorry driven by a friend of Hughie's. As with so many who made the journey over to Ibiza in the sixties and seventies, the lorry and the friend both ended up staying for good. And with the desk, carefully wrapped in cotton sheets, had come an eccentric collection of other things Hughie's parents knew their son couldn't do without. First and most importantly there'd been an envelope with details of the modest monthly payment that would be wired straight into his bank account. Then there was his bed, but no mattress, a watering can, a packet of pea seeds, a prawning net and a wind-up gramophone. Griffon and Meriel Ballantyne, frugal and hard-working, had taken a very dim view of their only son's decision to move to Ibiza, realizing quite rightly that it would herald a lifetime of lethargy and wanton indulgence. And yet, even so, they'd carefully discussed what to send him and they'd got him spot on, shipping over the only things he'd ever have missed, apart from themselves, of course, whom he missed most of all. In all the years since Hughie had moved to Ibiza they hadn't yet made it out. Honey knew that he still hadn't quite given up hope that they would.

To Honey, the desk had stood out like a jewel. She had found it on an April day in 1999, the same day that she'd returned from her first year at university in Barcelona to pay her parents a surprise visit . . . and had never left again.

What was it that had made her return to them that day? Not the disconnected phone line because that had happened so often it was almost more of a shock when she found it working. And it wasn't even the news, second hand and a couple of weeks late, that Hughie had spent a night in a police cell (on suspicion of stealing and eating a neighbour's goat) because that too had happened before and skirmishes with the neighbour (who lived half a mile down the valley and was, to use Hughie's phrase, 'a little Brit shit') took place almost every month. Instead it had been her parents' oldest and dearest friends, Maggie and Troy, who had brought her back. Maggie and Troy Ripley, who of everybody had been most determined that she should leave Ibiza, who'd badgered and insisted and persuaded through all the months when Honey had agonized; who'd searched through the various courses on offer at the university in Barcelona, and had even paid the fees for her first year, had then ruined everything by sending her a postcard, mentioning, among other things, how her father had asked to borrow their fishing lines. They weren't to know what alarm bells they'd sent ringing with that one innocent remark. Honey had returned the next morning, suspicious of what she might discover, but at that stage full of hope that she'd prove herself wrong.

But she'd been right. Honey had arrived home to find Tora in the garden. As Honey had quietly come up behind her, Tora had carried on what she was doing, unaware. She was bending over, tugging at a sprig of rosemary, but without quite enough strength to snap it free, and each knuckle of her spine was fascinating in its knobbly awfulness. Honey had been gone just six weeks and Tora looked as emaciated as if she'd been on hunger strike the whole time. In a way, perhaps she had: present Honey with her starved, pathetic body and she didn't need to say the words aloud, *look what happens when you leave me.*

At the sound of Honey's footsteps, Tora had turned slowly. She'd been collecting herbs for an omelette, she'd explained defensively. Back in the house the fridge was empty but for a bottle of cava and a paper bag full of stinking prawns. And then Tora had admitted of course there were no eggs for the omelette, no milk either, but it didn't matter because she wasn't hungry anyway.

At that Honey had exploded at her, demanding to know where Hughie was, and in answer Tora had collapsed weakly back into a kitchen chair but had still refused to wilt in the face of her daughter's fury. She explained that Hughie had walked to town the day before and now she didn't have any idea where he was. And yes, they'd run out of money. And what the hell, yes, as soon as Honey had gone they'd had a party, several joyful parties. And when next month's money came through they'd have some more because at least with boring Honeybee out of the house, finally they were having *fun.*

But what about surviving, Honey had pleaded, and Tora had looked back at her, infuriatingly calm. What could Honey mean, when they lived among so much plenty? They ate from the fruits of the land and the sea: there was fresh fish to be caught, wild asparagus to be picked, olives, there were figs from the garden, nuts and oranges, melons . . .

It was such a ridiculous fantasy that Honey had had to walk away, tears smarting at her eyes, because at that stage the land around Can Falco was completely barren. There were no orange groves, no fig trees, and as for the wild asparagus, Tora had eaten it once and had never forgotten it, because of how *romantic* it had sounded, *wild asparagus*, how perfectly it had conformed to her absurd view of her life. Left high in the hills, unwilling to drive and with only Hughie to look after her, Tora was as helpless and as irresponsible as a young child.

But that was OK, because instead of food they'd had *fun!*

Honey had stormed from room to room, opening windows, kicking over the discarded wine bottles, holding her breath at the old familiar stench of her childhood: blocked drains mixed with marijuana and damp, rotting rubbish and squalor. *The parties had been worth it, had they? Worth starving for were they? They thought this was fun, did they?* And alongside the rage at her parents' irresponsibility, at the way she was being given no choice but to take on the role of nanny and nag once more, there was also the hurt that they only saw her as a killjoy, not the saviour at all.

And then she'd returned to the kitchen and Tora had fallen into her arms because of course it wasn't true, of course Tora didn't really mean it, didn't truly want to live this way, of course she wanted Honey home: without Honey there, she hardly knew how to exist on her own.

And so Honey's choice had been a simple one: break away from them, grit her teeth and turn her back, this time knowing exactly what she was leaving behind; or stay and acknowledge that, for all her hopes for the future, her place for now was with her parents, her world was Ibiza and no further.

Some tiny part of her was even relieved that the decision was so clear-cut. That same day she'd scootered down to Santa Gertrudis to make calls to her tutor and university friends, and to pay the telephone bill and get the phone reconnected. And afterwards, when she'd returned, she had found the beautiful oak desk sitting on top of the logs in the wood shed and had brought it inside, wiped it clean and had sat down behind it, almost immediately feeling surprisingly enthusiastic and hopeful. And when Hughie had reappeared the next day and found her there, writing the first of many letters to the bank, he had expressed more surprise at seeing his old desk again than at seeing her. And the strange thing was that, from that day on, neither he nor Tora ever really acknowledged her decision to come home. Perhaps they were embarrassed by it, or perhaps it simply didn't occur to them that she'd sacrificed anything at all, because what, after all, could be better than a life at Can Falco?

But still, there was no doubt they'd changed as a consequence of her return, Tora particularly. Always the free spirit, childish and beautiful with it, with her blonde hair and huge blue eyes, Honey's return had signalled the moment Tora turned away from her old life and zoned in on the new. She started yoga classes, began to read books with titles like *Give Me Joy in My Heart* and *Here Comes the Sun*, and to talk of tasting the bliss and thinking outside her shell of mud, and within just a few months had embraced her new spiritual world with a speed and passion that Honey found both sweet and deeply infuriating.

Six years later Can Falco had, according to Condé Nast *Traveller* magazine, become a hotel worth crossing continents to visit and Honey had managed only two two-week trips off the island, once to Bali to stay with an Ibiza-born girlfriend and buy a ship's container worth of outdoor furniture for Can Falco while she was there, and once to England, to combine a friend's wedding with a visit to the land of her father. But even with two weeks and the freedom to go wherever she liked, she hadn't gone to see her grandparents – Hughie hadn't wanted her to.

The trip to England had been the winter before last, now over eighteen months ago, and since then she had not left the island again. Only in the past few months had she started to think about it, not least because of Claudio questioning her in the same way Maggie and Troy had done before, disbelieving when she denied she was bored, occasionally teasing her, forcing her to defend herself against the charges of all work and no play. Because there *was* play, of course, how could there not be, living in the party capital of Europe. But even so, she was light years older than the mad sixteen-year-old who'd loved her forty-eight-hour house parties, who'd bicycled to Marrakech and trekked across India, a different person to the Honey she'd been before the weight of Can Falco and her parents had fallen upon her shoulders.

At eight o'clock, the second to last of that evening's arrivals were shepherded gently towards her by Claudio, a honeymoon couple who'd got married in Barcelona that day, the girl, still in her wedding dress, carried through the door high in her husband's arms, a laughing, shrieking bundle of net and white silk, long dark hair cascading down her back.

Looking up from her desk, for once Honey had to force the smile of welcome. The girl was too noisy, too triumphant, too keen to sweep everyone else into her celebration. Fleetingly, Honey wondered about losing their reservation, then pulled herself together, welcomed them in perfect Spanish and waited patiently while they kissed and kissed some more.

'We want our bed,' the woman dragged her lips free just long enough to say.

Honey handed her their key.

'It's a big bed, yes?'

Honey nodded. And knew that it was only her own bad mood, and a healthy dose of jealousy, that was making her feel so irritable.

How had they made it as far as the hotel, she asked Claudio as they sat together afterwards, Honey with her bare feet up on the desk, a glass of wine in her hand. How had they negotiated customs, baggage reclaim and found their Can Falco taxi?

And Claudio looked at her with a big smile on his face and suggested she needed some fun herself, and why didn't she finish early and let him take over?

After Claudio had gone she'd left her desk and walked noiselessly through the gardens, right out to the boundary, to where the vibrant green Can Falco lawn ran abruptly into red Ibiza dust, where guests would say the fairytale ended and real life began, but where Honey would say the opposite. She stood for a moment, staring at the gigantic flaming sun as it slipped towards the horizon, then sat down on the grass to watch it go, still startled by how fast it moved, exploding across the sky in a way that took hold of her breath and her thoughts and forced her simply to sit and behold. And then, afterwards, she sat on, as every last fire died down and the embers disappeared, her bare brown legs and bare feet stretched out in front of her, feeling lonely and left behind, in her skinny white vest and long silk skirt, as the darkness of the evening immediately began to settle all around her.

She let herself fall back slowly until she was lying flat on the ground and she looked up at the midnight-blue sky and said in a low voice, each word clearly enunciated, 'Now I am sad.'

And as she heard herself say it out loud she immediately sat back up again, then jumped to her feet and looked self-consciously around though she knew there'd been nobody there to see or hear her.

The garden lights were all on now, little red raffia lanterns strung out across the gardens, dimpling and twinkling in the trees, marking out the pathways back towards the restaurant. With someone to walk with her, the garden at night-time was the most magical place to be, yet for so long there'd been no one and to be walking back alone now – with nothing but her work and her desk and another evening stretching ahead of her – it felt as if there was no more lonely place on earth.

She passed her cottage. Just two whitewashed bedrooms and a tiny garden of its own, shaded from the harshness of the sun by olive trees. It had once been a pigsty, and from the age of fourteen, when Honey had first imagined converting Can Falco into a hotel, she had eyed it up for herself, had run through the darkness to reach it, had camped out in it night after night with her friends. Then it had seemed the perfect hideaway, a den supreme. She'd moved in permanently when she was sixteen, years before she'd been able even to connect the water, and in time she'd made it exactly as she'd always imagined it could be, far more girly and pretty than Can Falco, with floating white lace at the windows and gossamer-thin mosquito nets around her bed, pale blue shutters and red geraniums growing in terracotta pots outside. But now in the darkness with no lights on to welcome her in, it looked cold and uninviting.

By contrast and just a few hundred yards further on, and far enough away not to disturb the hotel guests – it had been a strategic decision to site their cottage there – the lights were on in Angel's Wings, her parents' home. Honey took a few steps towards it, careful not to bump into the Portland stone bird bath, ghost-white in the darkness, and then she stopped abruptly as Mozart's exuberant Horn Concerto came bursting through the open windows towards her.

At this time of evening Hughie and Tora were always there and if Honey walked in now she knew exactly how she would find them. Her father would be in the bath, a large gin and tonic balanced beside him, soaking in his favourite Hermès bath oil, contemplating the evening ahead and conducting a random and at times incoherent conversation with her mother, who would be on her yoga mat, destressing at the end of what Honey presumed had been another completely stress-free day. Both of them would be surprised and delighted to see her, both of them would immediately arrive (naked) at her side, would hold her hands and ply her with drink. Then they would sit her down and her father would chat, chat, chat, twitter, twitter, twitter, bombarding her with that day's thoughts and observations. He would have met a beautiful new guest, her mother had a new and wonderful idea for a yoga class, he would relish the opportunity of telling Honey all about them.

But she couldn't face either of them, not tonight, and she slipped away again quickly before they saw her.

She sat alone, tucked away in the corner of the restaurant, eating a plate of prawns and potato salad and realizing with every delicious mouthful how hungry she'd been. And by nine thirty she'd been back at her desk for an hour and had checked everybody in apart from the guests arriving on the delayed flight from Gatwick, who wouldn't be getting to the hotel for another six or seven hours; she'd played several games of Solitaire on her computer and had ordered eleven hammocks for Can Falco from a new shop in Formentera and slowly her mood had improved again. And so when Claudio came in to find her and opened his mouth once more to persuade her to take the rest of the evening off, to let him stay up for the very last guests, she astounded him by smiling up at him and for once agreeing.

She left him while she went back to her cottage, stripped off her clothes and jumped into the shower and then changed into a dark green, thigh-skimming, daisy-printed dress and crocheted white sandals. Then, with her thick blonde hair hanging wet and heavy down her back and almost before she'd known she was going to do it, she walked through the ink-dark night to her car and climbed in.

three

EDOUARD MIGHT have known she'd come but, until the moment Honey turned left onto the San Miguel road rather than right towards the village of San Carlos, she hadn't acknowledged to herself where she was heading. She drove fast through the hills, roof down, the wind in her hair, and with every mile her mood improved further. She remembered making her way to Edouard's on the night of her thirteenth birthday on an old scooter her parents had just bought her – concluding she was better off driving herself than relying on lifts from other inebriates, themselves included. She remembered how she had wobbled her way up in the darkness to find Edouard and ask him to ride out with her to celebrate. She'd been met at the door by his mother, who'd looked at the rackety scooter and at skinny, defenceless little Honey and had promptly burst into tears at the thought of Tora and Hughie's irresponsibility. She'd fetched Honey a helmet, telling her sternly that Edouard had worn it for his first six months and she was going to do the same. Honey had nodded eagerly, thanked her enthusiastically and had thrown it into the first field they'd passed.

And she'd known even as it unfolded that this night was an important one, the night when all the fun began, the first night of being a teenager. As she'd raced Edouard along the narrow roads down to the coast to meet their friends, feeling the warm night air on her skin, she'd believed and she'd been right to believe that this night would mark the beginning of the best four years of her life.

They'd moved within a great group of friends, some Ibicencos, others ex-pat offspring like her and Edouard, the children of her parents' friends, mainly British, German or Dutch, who'd been part of the first wave of hippies coming out, like Tora and Hughie, in the late sixties and early seventies.

As they'd got older they'd followed in their parents' footsteps, making their own fires on the beaches, camping in the sand dunes or in the untamed gardens of Can Falco and El Figo. Like them, they'd drummed out the sunsets, slept out on the beaches and gone clubbing together, starting at Pacha and moving on to Ku, then the most famous, spectacular nightclub in the world. Edouard had had a succession of flings, usually with

hippy chick

British girls who lived on Ibiza, and Honey just one big love affair with a Spanish DJ working at the Café del Mar. They'd split up after the summer of her seventeenth year and the end of their relationship had marked the end of her four-year idyll, the end of a carefree and easy way of life, the last summer before she grew up and left Ibiza for university. The last summer she spent with Edouard and their gang of friends before they all went their separate ways.

The following year, when Honey had been forced to abandon her degree and return to Ibiza full-time, she'd been disappointed to find he could hardly make it out to the island at all. And from then on, as he emerged from university and began work in London, she saw him less and less, until it was barely more than the odd weekend, occasionally a full week, but never long enough to gather up with the others again and re-create the wonderful laziness of that one glorious summer. In any case the reality was that most of the others had gone too, leaving Honey almost alone as she embarked on the huge project of turning Can Falco around.

So over the next few years, El Figo stood mainly empty, Edouard's parents finally admitting that, hard as they'd tried, they'd never truly enjoyed the hippy lifestyle after all, preferring now to live in Geneva instead. Then when Edouard was twenty-five, they formally

passed the house on to him, shrewdly absolving themselves of the bills whilst still retaining a place to stay.
And because Edouard had become rich by then and had
no one other than the occasional high-maintenance
girlfriend to spend his money on, the house had been
swiftly upgraded. Overseen by Honey, landscapers got
to grips with the gardens, planted olive groves and
lavender walks, added a pool and a tennis court, and so
his parents' foothold on the island had become unexpectedly luxurious.

And with El Figo his own place, in the last year
Edouard had finally begun to return. But now he filled
the place with his London friends, work colleagues,
clients and hangers-on and juggled his three mobile
phones and was frequently so distracted she knew better
than to ask if he wanted to re-create a sleep-over on Es
Palmador or an evening sail to Es Vedra.

El Figo was on the range of hills next to Can Falco,
built high on a cliff and facing out towards the sea, and
was only five or six miles away as the crow flies. People
joke that every journey in Ibiza takes twenty minutes,
but it was at least that before her car turned off the
main road and began to bump and bounce its way up
the steep rutted track, dust billowing out behind her.
She eventually turned the final corner, shot through the
olive-green painted gates, and came up against a great

jam of tightly parked cars. She slipped in between a dusty jeep and an immaculate 4x4 and then sat in the car for a moment, listening to the sounds of the party in the gardens below her. She tried to run her fingers through her hair and found that the journey there had blown it dry too thoroughly. She imagined she looked rather wild – presumably just what his guests were expecting.

She left her car and walked between banks of lavender, the scent heady on the warm night air, the lights from El Figo twinkling in the dark and the steady beat of music and ripples of noisy laughter guiding her towards the house, white and stark and beautiful, three perfect sugar cubes shining in the light of the moon. She felt at home here as ever, even now that it was landscaped, smoothed over and upgraded to Xanadu. For so many years it had been just as untamed and tumble-down as Can Falco, both of them ancient fincas with the same whitewashed, metre-thick walls. Honey and Edouard's parents had moved in at the same time, had both been enchanted with what they'd found and completely disinclined to do anything to change them. Edouard's parents had built a mud bath, but for years that was as far as the home improvements had got.

And now here she was again, she who had never left, standing outside El Figo once more. And for a moment, as she stood at the top of the steps that led down to the beautiful white house, she could believe that time had stood still after all. Now another party was beginning, another group of people was there below her, sitting in candlelight, spread out around the house, listening to music, dancing under the trees, unwittingly re-enacting all those parties of the past. And despite her reservations about Edouard's guests, she found herself smiling down at it all because this was just as it should be, it was what El Figo was best for – providing a beautiful setting for a party.

She walked to the edge of the steps and looked down, and saw that there was a man, spotlit just below her, at the edge of the pool. He had a cigar in his mouth and was wrestling with a girl who was doing a good job of not falling in. He was wearing pinstriped trousers, a pink shirt and red braces and his bleached white feet were planted firmly on the ground. She was slight and blonde, wearing a short flouncy skirt and a shocking-pink T-shirt that said Gold Digger across the front. And there was something so determined, almost fer-ocious, about their battle, a complete absence of any shrieks or laughter, no cheers or clapping from the other guests, no noise from either of them save the odd grunt, that Honey hesitated for a moment, wondering what on earth she was walking into.

Seconds later the man's brute strength finally overwhelmed the girl and with a final shove she was shot backwards into the water with a high-pitched squeal and an almighty splash. Without waiting for her to return to the surface the man rubbed his hands on his trousers, turned his back on the pool and strolled to a nearby sun lounger and sat down. Beside him Honey could see there was another man lying flat out, also smoking and dressed incongruously in a suit. She imagined they'd caught the late plane over and had probably only just arrived, but still it seemed odd that they hadn't immediately wanted to change.

But she was transfixed by the surface of the rippling spotlit water, waiting, waiting, until finally the girl burst back into the air. Honey watched as she trod water for a few seconds, taking several deep breaths and wiping her eyes, then swam to the edge and gracefully lifted herself out. Honey couldn't see her face. Had it all been one big game, she wondered, or was she really pissed off?

Once out of the pool the girl walked stiffly towards where the man was lying. Soaking wet, she looked even smaller, her pink T-shirt stuck to her skin, running mascara giving her panda eyes. And as she got closer to the man, Honey could see she hadn't found it funny at all. The man, with his back to her still and now

43

engrossed in conversation with his friend, didn't at first realize she was there.

'You trod on my toes,' she told him in a high, shaking voice.

He held up his hand to her, still talking to his friend and didn't even turn around.

'Paul, look at me. You ruined my clothes.' She stood her ground and waited but he still didn't react. 'What's the matter with you, fucking bastard?' She walked around his sun lounger so that she could look at him and at the sight of her he slowly dropped his arm, placed his cigar carefully between the other man's fingers and got to his feet. 'The least you could do is apologize.'

And then, so fast that neither Honey nor the girl herself had time to register what he was about to do, the man had caught her wrists and manhandled her to the edge of the pool and pushed her hard. This time it was a nasty, shut-up-bitch-don't-hassle-me push and she went backwards into the water with such momentum that waves rocked angrily over the edges of the pool.

'Watch her,' he said to his friend, as he sauntered back to his chair for the second time. 'Two hundred pounds says she bursts into tears.'

'Three hundred pounds says you get a well-deserved slap across the face.'

'I don't think so.' He sat back down, then swung his legs up and grinned. 'Five hundred pounds I'll still get a blow job tonight.'

Behind him the girl again broke back to the surface but this time made her way slowly over towards the shallow end and the steps, where another girl was silently waiting to help her out.

Honey found she couldn't step forwards. Uncertain if she still wanted to join the party, she stood wavering at the top of the steps and then the second man sat up to hand back the cigar, and as he did so, looked up and suddenly caught her eye. He immediately got to his feet.

'Well, hello, eavesdropper,' he said, walking over and looking up at her. 'Enjoying the show?' He moved forwards as if he was about to come up the steps to join her but then, quick as a flash, the other man, Paul, appeared at his side.

'Do we know you?' he barked up at Honey.

'No.'

She made her way slowly down the steps and once on the ground gave them the briefest nod of acknowledgement and then made to walk away, scanning the area around the pool to see if Edouard was there.

'You realize this is a private party?' Paul stepped forward and effectively blocked her route.

She gave him a quick glance. Close up, he was

good-looking in a swarthy, heavy, bully-boy kind of way, with big dark eyes and a large well-shaped head, thick hair cut close to his scalp, high cheekbones jutting out from the flesh that had settled on his cheeks and around his neck.

'So are you going to throw me out, or throw me in too?'

He laughed at that and suddenly there was interest in his eyes.

'It depends who you are. Looking at you, I can't believe you're the entertainment.'

'Oh, Paul, don't be so damned rude,' said his friend.

'I'm saying she doesn't look like a fucking tart. She should take it as a compliment.' He folded his arms, enjoying himself. 'So what were you doing up there?'

Honey felt the heat of battle flaring inside her. 'As your friend says, I was eavesdropping. And I was watching you too, having such fun with that girl. I'm sure you wouldn't have wanted anyone interrupting. How do you know she didn't want another go?'

For a few moments he looked stunned but then he recovered and smiled as if, perhaps, he'd misheard the contempt in her voice.

'Are you saying you'd like a turn?'

'No, thank you.'

'Then don't tempt me.'

'You don't tempt me either.'

She said it recklessly, daring him on, and as if he knew she was in mortal danger, his friend let out a great burst of desperate laughter. 'Edouard,' he cried, directing his call to the far side of the pool. 'For fuck's sake, get over here.' He turned to Honey. 'Quick, what's your name?'

'Honey Ballantyne,' she told them both. 'I'm a friend of Edouard's.'

'Honey's here,' called the friend while Paul let out a great hiss of shock and clutched dramatically at his face. 'You're not? Honeybee Ballantyne? Oh Jesus-Fucking Christ!'

'Paul!' his friend laughed, staring at him in surprise. He grabbed Paul's hand and prised his fingers off his face. 'What's wrong?' Then he swung back to Honey. 'Who *are* you?'

'I'm so sorry,' Paul groaned. He let his hands slide slowly down his face and stared back at Honey. 'What the fuck was I thinking? Who else could you be? Was I very rude? Please don't say yes or Edouard will crucify me.'

'Who is she?' the friend insisted again.

'It's not a problem.' Honey gave them both a brief

dismissive smile. 'Excuse me now, there's Edouard . . .'
She made to walk away and immediately Paul held out
his hands to her.

'Of course you're her, look at you. Friends? Please?
Forgive me before you go?'

'Why does it matter to you?' she couldn't resist
asking.

'Because, Honeybee Ballantyne, you're only the one
person Edouard hasn't stopped talking about. Only the
one person I've spent the whole evening waiting to
meet.' He turned to his friend. 'This is the smartest,
most talented, coolest woman on the island, that's who
she is.'

The friend looked decidedly unconvinced.

'Shit I've practically flown over here to meet you.
Tell me I've not blown it.'

'What?' asked Honey.

'Come on and I'll tell you. Let's grab Edouard and
find you a drink.'

'But what about your friend?' Honey stayed where
she was.

Paul laughed. 'You mean this one?' He nodded at
his companion. 'He's not a friend he's a hanger-on.'
Then he grinned. 'Meet Carl.'

'No, I'm talking about that girl. You should be
worried about her not me.'

For a moment it was clear that Paul had no idea what she was talking about. He paused, looking at her in genuine surprise.

'The poor girl you threw into the pool,' Honey reminded him. The girl you wanted to drown, she thought.

At that, Paul sighed a long sigh and sadly shook his head. 'Oh, you mean Nancy. The thing is, Honeybee, Nancy had been a very naughty girl and I had to teach her a lesson . . .' He saw the distaste in her face and stopped abruptly. 'I threw her in a swimming pool not a vat of hot oil! We were having a laugh that's all.'

She shook her head. 'It looked very cruel to me.'

'I promise you Nancy is fine. You'll meet her in a moment and you'll see. It must have looked horrible to you but honestly it's what we *do*. Get to know us better and you'll see. I don't know, she must have thrown me in *fifteen times* since I got here. I *had* to do it.' Honey shook her head again refusing to believe it. 'But it's true,' Paul insisted. 'It was my revenge, that's all, Nancy loves it. It's how we are. I promise you. We've stuck around together so long we have to find new ways to keep each other on our toes – off our toes even. It's how we are, I promise,' he repeated. 'Edouard will tell you it's true.' He grinned at her again, all charm and innocence now, twinkling and laughing at her mistake, enjoying it even, so that she couldn't help but doubt what she'd seen, wonder if it had, after all, simply been a light-hearted tip into the pool and not a modern-day Nancy facing up to her own Bill Sykes.

Meanwhile Edouard had still not materialized but now Honey saw lights and a cluster of people sitting close together under a thatched gazebo and as she and Paul and Carl drew nearer suddenly he stood up among them, and she guessed it wasn't just pleasure at seeing her again that got him striding towards her in such record speed.

'Bee, you came! And you've met these two?' He kissed her cheek and gave her a quick concerned glance. 'Are they behaving?' He immediately started to steer her away from Paul and towards the house. 'They're not, are they? Come with me now, out of danger. How did I miss you?' He turned back to Paul and Carl. 'Wait for us. I'll bring some drinks out.'

'Hope they wait all night,' she whispered quietly, as she slid her arm around him.

'You're serious? Why what's wrong? What's he done?' Edouard looked down at her full of concern.

'Nothing,' she muttered, 'apart from behaving like a stupid bastard, a pinstriped arse. Why do you bring them here?'

He stopped in his tracks and turned to face her.
'Please don't say that.'

'Edouard! Come on. It's exactly what he was.'

'The pinstripes are a problem?'

'No! He's a bully, a thug. You surely see that? And I
don't understand why you let people like him stay here.'

'People like him?'

'Yes,' she retorted, 'people like him.'

'City wankers in their pinstriped suits? Honey you're
such an Ibiza snob. He's only just left work, he's had
no time to change. What would you like him to wear,
a sarong?'

'You know his clothes have nothing to do with it, for
God's sake.' She glanced quickly around. They were
so close to the house, to all his friends, she couldn't
believe he'd be so loud. She could see Paul disappearing
through the doorway into the house and Carl settling
down on the huge wide sofa. And there was a crowd of
people, some of them she recognized, others presumably out for the weekend from England, all of them
relaxed, sprawled together, talking and laughing, none
of them paying the slightest bit of notice to her and
Edouard. And now there was Nancy, lifting a hand to
Carl in welcome, grinning up at him as if she hadn't
a care in the world.

She stared at them all uncertainly. Was she wrong? Had she misunderstood the nasty intent that she'd seen in Paul's eyes, built it up out of all proportion? She turned back to Edouard, not sure whether to persist or to let it go, and saw on his face the wary half-smile half-frown that she hadn't seen for years.

Don't spoil tonight, he was pleading with her. Please don't let's fall out over Paul.

And looking up at him the outrage that had been bubbling up inside her calmed again and the words she'd been about to say dried on her lips and instead of explaining, telling him all about what Paul had said and done, her heart just softened and she reached up to his smooth brown cheek and kissed it, then took his arm and looped it over her shoulders.

'Everybody's here. Why didn't you say? When you said party I thought you meant a few people and some prawns on the barbecue.'

'And instead I've got a DJ and dancing girls from Pacha. Seriously. Mark Ure is DJ-ing on the beach. City wide-boys expect nothing less.'

'Shut up.'

He laughed, bent and kissed her cheek. 'But you know what? I have to say *pinstripe arse* is perfect.'

She was serious again. 'Then why is he here?'

'Because he's important to me.' He shook his head.

hippy chick

'And I'll tell you why, but not tonight.' His arm tightened around her as he said it and she wondered just briefly why not and then let the thought drift away, forgotten.

four

NANCY, THE GIRL from the pool in the Gold Digger T-shirt had appeared from around the side of the house and now she waved a bottle of wine at Edouard and Honey and grinned. 'Hi! Coming to join us?' She spoke in a light and happy voice and there was no sign of her recent dip, her pale blonde hair now smooth and dry and shining in the house lights. 'We're over there, please come!' And with a little smile, she was gone again. Clearly the girl knew who Honey was. Perhaps she'd caught sight of her as she'd swum out of the pool?

'We'll join everyone in a minute,' Edouard told Honey. 'First I must show you the house.'

She felt his arm tightening around her as he spoke and looked up at him in surprise.

'What about it?'

But now they were nearing the doorway and instead of answering he moved aside to let her see and Honey strode on and then stopped in shock because the first

thing she saw was that someone had cut out a large
rectangular hole in the sixteenth-century front door
and had inserted a piece of pink glass.

She turned back to him in wordless horror.

'Oh, good,' Edouard said drily. 'You love it already
don't you?'

'How could you do this?'

'I think we used a hammer and chisel. Apparently we
needed more light.'

She walked on in. El Figo was as familiar to her as
Can Falco. With her eyes closed she could have navi-
gated her way through the hall, turned left up the five
steps, then right into Edouard's den, could have thrown
herself confidently down on his sofa. But wide-eyed and
silent now she walked on in and looked around at the
complete transformation that had taken place since
she'd been there last.

Under the care of Edouard's parents, this hall that
she was standing in now had been an unconverted barn,
complete with owls raising families in its high-arched
ceiling. As a child she had often spent the nights here
on a makeshift bed, fighting sleep, watching the moon
through the gaps in the rafters, listening for the notes
of a piano or guitar, gentle laughter, quiet conversations, all the soothing sounds of grown-ups outside
having fun.

Then Edouard had taken on El Figo and the hall had been incorporated into the main part of the house and had been given a simple going-over by Honey that had left it plain and white, a spectacular entrance to the house but unadorned. Now, since she'd been here last, just a few months before, it had been transformed again, finally into a room rather than an echoing unused space, its white walls painted in a burnt terracotta, the floors painted white and covered in bold modern silk rugs. On one side the enormous fireplace had been painted dark red, logs stacked ten foot high beside it, while stretching out on either side were two long sofas built out of the walls, their cushions deep and covered in a thick purple velvet. And between the sofas there was now a square stone table, fat white candles grouped artfully together in a round stone dish. There were new paintings, huge modern abstracts, on the walls, and in front of her there was a polished oak dining table laid elaborately for dinner with twinkling silver and heavy-looking glass, eight chairs around it, candles seemingly floating in mid-air above. Altogether it looked like an extremely expensive and rather hip private members' club, but certainly not the beloved El Figo she'd grown up with.

Who'd helped Edouard make such astonishing changes? When had it happened? Why hadn't she known anything about it? And was it just a misguided possessiveness that made her want to shout how much she hated it? How unbearable it was. Because actually it was spectacular, she couldn't deny that. But it was just . . . she walked forwards and leaned across the table to touch one of the candles and it swung away from her, revealing the fine wire that suspended it from the ceiling . . . It was just that every trace of Edouard's past life there, and hers, had been painted over. Had he realized that was what he was doing? She turned to him but couldn't find the words to ask, and then a telltale prickle down the back of her neck made her turn suddenly and she saw a woman standing quietly in the doorway, hands clasped, watching her.

'Anna!' Edouard immediately left Honey's side and moved towards her and Honey took in the expectant, hesitant look on the woman's face as she stared back at Honey, and understood a little more.

She managed to summon up a big enthusiastic grin. 'You've done all this, haven't you? It's amazing. It's completely transformed.'

The woman, Anna, nodded. 'I saw you coming in and I couldn't resist joining you.' She waited until Honey reached her then held out a thin hand.

Honey was aware of how Edouard moved, no more than a foot, just the tiniest of movements, and yet now he was standing quite definitely beside Anna not her, and in the context of the house it felt hugely significant.

While Honey shook Anna's hand, her brain clicked and whirled through a hundred possibilities. The immaculate black linen suit looked so out of place here, and yet Anna herself seemed disquietingly at home. Were she and Edouard together? She wasn't his type – attractive, yes, with long shiny chestnut hair tied back in a ponytail, but so humourless, so severe.

'And I'm Honey. I'm a friend of Edouard's.'

'I know who you are. So, tell me, do you like it?'

'It's beautiful.'

'But really not your style?' Anna smiled graciously, clearly not caring in the least. 'Don't worry, I can imagine.'

'Have you decorated all of the house?'

At that Anna laughed unexpectedly. 'Eddie wouldn't let me do any more until you'd passed this. I think he cares more about your opinion than anybody else's. Don't you, darling?' she teased, turning back to Edouard with a smile.

Honey looked at her as much in surprise at the *Eddie* as at what Anna had said. 'That's definitely not true,' she retorted pleased all the same at the thought that it might be.

'Oh, trust me.' Anna gave another little laugh. She didn't sound jealous, if anything she sounded gently mocking as if she was teasing Edouard for being such a fool. 'So we've been out a few times this year, trying to get the place straight.'

'Anyway,' Edouard interrupted awkwardly. 'I should be getting Honey a drink. Bee, what'll you have? And Anna what about you?'

'You should have let me know you were here.' Honey told him off. 'I didn't even realize you were doing this. How could you not tell me?' At that Anna raised an amused eyebrow. 'I could have come around to see you, brought you some provisions.' Argued with this woman about putting purple velvet with terracotta.

Edouard didn't answer.

'We had everything we needed,' Anna said. 'I think we managed.'

Honey stared back at Edouard. 'Good for you.'

'Actually, we did come to see you at Can Falco,' said Anna.

'Did you? I'm sure I'd remember.'

'You weren't there. It was one evening, early, end of May. We only stayed for a drink.'

'I'm very sorry I missed you.'

'Edouard badly wanted me to see Can Falco.' And

again it was as if she was teasing, making the point, *not you, Can Falco.* 'He wanted to show me what you'd done there.'

'Did you like what you saw?'

'Yes, what a pretty place.'

She sounded so patronizing that Honey couldn't resist a quick glance at Edouard. He was waiting for her, with a look, a mix of wide-eyed innocence and the sparkle of laughter.

'I left you alone because you were adding fifteen bedrooms to Can Falco and I knew you didn't have the time,' he told her.

'I should explain – I'm an interior designer,' Anna went on, completely unruffled. 'I have a consultancy in Great Portland Street called Green and Pleasant. We're very eco-ware. I think you'd approve of us.' She caressed the smooth polished oak of the table with the palm of her hand, and now she narrowed her eyes. 'So what has he told you about me?'

'Nothing,' Edouard answered smoothly. 'Not yet.'

Abruptly Honey'd had enough. She looked longingly to the door. She wanted to be away, running back up the steps to her car, giving up on the lot of them, Edouard most of all.

But Edouard followed her glance and knew exactly what she was thinking. 'Don't go. There's lots of friends of yours outside, Honey, all waiting to see you. Please stay.'

'I'll go and find them.' She turned for the door.

'I'm so sorry, I should have asked before,' Anna exclaimed. 'Would you like a glass of champagne?'

A glass of champagne? She wanted to laugh because coming from Anna it sounded so pretentious.

'No, Honey's more of a cocktails girl,' Edouard told Anna. 'And tonight we have Danilo here, world-famous maker of strawberry daiquiris.' He turned to Honey. 'He's down on the beach waiting for you. He told me to tell you.' In his way, Edouard was apologizing for his awful woman, for letting her ruin his lovely house and be so rude. But still he couldn't bring himself to cast Anna adrift. 'Come and try one too,' he suggested, deliberately including Anna once more.

'Get one for me would you, Edouard?' Honey walked straight out through the door and didn't wait for an answer. 'I'll be outside. Do you mind?'

Skirting the side of the house, she told herself she was crazy still to be hanging around. What was she trying to prove by staying? Why didn't she simply walk away?

She stood at the top of the steps that led down to the first of many terraces. Below, the gardens looked like a lush and beautiful jungle, strings of lights swinging gently from the trees, the green grass of the pathways curving between spotlit palm trees and giant shrubs with leaves the size of elephant ears. And from far below, down on the beach, came the sound of seventies' soul, making her want to run down the steps towards it. And she knew there'd be friends to talk to, that if she made her way down she could pick up a drink and laugh and dance and talk and have a great time and probably carry on till the next morning without even seeing Edouard again. But she didn't want to do that. She wanted to know what he was up to because he was up to something. And what exactly had possessed him to turn to Anna for help?

'Honey!' a voice called and she spun around to see it was Paul's girlfriend, Nancy. She was sitting with her friend who'd helped her out from the pool, stretched out at opposite ends of a huge carved wooden sofa and beckoning her over to join them. Opposite them were two dark-haired men, and Honey wavered for a moment as she saw that one of them was Paul. They were laughing together quietly, their backs to the girls, and when Paul saw her he raised a hand at Honey's approach but didn't interrupt his conversation. And Honey saw that he'd changed into baggy shorts and a T-shirt, just like his friend, and the smoke that was curling into the air between them was now sweet familiar cannabis rather than nasty pungent cigar.

'Will you join us?' Nancy smiled. She touched her

hand to her chest, 'I'm Nancy,' and then she pointed to her friend. 'And this is Belle.'

'Aren't you coming down to the party on the beach?' Honey asked.

Nancy yawned and stretched back against the cushions. 'We *were* on our way, weren't we Belle?'

'Stay for a moment,' Belle offered and jumped to her feet, stepping around the low table to reach Honey. She was tall, full of smiles, with thick reddish hair cut artfully in a choppy untidy bob and interested olive-green eyes. Then before Honey could move she'd crouched down to peer intently at Honey's feet.

'Wow. Totally beautiful. Just as I knew they would be.' She touched one sandal lightly with one finger, then smiled up at Honey. 'Do you mind? There was an article on you in *Red* last year and you were wearing some like this.'

'And she's wanted a pair ever since,' Nancy explained, curling her feet up beneath her. 'I think she's engineered this whole weekend purely to be able to go and buy some.'

Belle turned back to her indignantly. 'As if I'd come just to look at shoes.'

'And dresses too, sorry.'

'She's being so unfair,' Belle told Honey. 'So, do you get them in Ibiza town?'

63

'And churches, and museums. You were saying you hoped to find some stained-glass windows, weren't you, Belle?'

'Ignore her,' Belle insisted, taking Honey's hand to guide her towards an empty chair opposite their places on the sofa. 'She's trying to make out I'm frivolous and silly and that she is cultured and classy, which, as you probably can see, could not be further from the truth. Here's to Ibicenco architecture – see, I can even say it right. And,' she went on solemnly, 'if there are any caves or churches I should spend some time in, on my *very short* break to Ibiza, I hope very much that you'll tell me where they are.'

'I will.' Honey laughed, overcome with the urge to stand up and hug her.

'But if I happened to pass the world-famous Las Dalias hippy market on the way, then I wouldn't object. And if there were any interesting little roadside shops, too, perhaps you could highlight them for me on my map?'

'Ideally little roadside shops with an authentic Ibicenco peasant woman inside, sewing tiny immaculate stitches and slowly going blind from the strain,' teased Nancy.

'In which case it would be thoughtless and selfish not

to stop and buy something,' Belle finished for her. Then she looked down at Honey's feet. 'Just fabulous, take them off, let me try one.'

Honey dutifully stepped out of one of her sandals and Belle slipped it on her own bare foot, pulled up her floor-length green skirt to get a better look and sighed. Then she caught Nancy's eye and started to laugh.

'Oh, for God's sake, stop looking so disapproving, Nancy. Yes, I want to look like her. Honey's gorgeous and so is her hotel. And please don't you pretend that you don't think so too and that you haven't been dying to meet her and wouldn't kill for a night at Can Falco.' She swung back to Honey. 'To be honest, Honey, I didn't come here to pick up shoes, I came to meet *you*.'

'How nice of you . . .' Honey looked at her uncertainly.

'We both wanted to meet you. We've been looking at Can Falco on-line,' Nancy joined in. 'We were imagining what fun it would be to come and take a yoga class in the Garden of Serenity.' She uncurled her legs and lifted her feet onto the low table in front of them, then reached for her glass and finished what looked like a strawberry daiquiri before she stretched back against the cushions. 'Hey! *You* haven't got a drink.'

'It's OK. I think Edouard's gone to get me one . . .'

Belle nodded. 'You know he was so pleased when he saw you were here tonight . . .'

Honey frowned. Of course it hadn't seemed quite that way to her.

'He was,' Belle insisted. 'I know how you don't get much chance to see each other now.'

'Not like it used to be. Now he has such a flat-out life.'

'I live with him in London, so I guess I know about that too.'

'You do!'

Belle grinned. 'I'm his lodger. I moved in with him about six months ago, into his flat in Islington.' She shook her head. 'You don't know the flat in Islington?'

'I guess I knew he had to live somewhere in London.'

'He bought it about two and a half years ago. It's gorgeous, especially now he's got me keeping it in order.' She leaned back, studying Honey. 'You should come and see us.'

'I know,' Honey agreed quietly, meeting Belle's stare.

Unexpectedly Belle held out her hand. 'I know, you can never get away,' she said. 'I've heard how hard you work to keep everything going. Edouard did tell me if I was ever going to meet you it was going to have to be here.'

'I must have sounded very boring.' Honey laughed.

'No . . . as if you need a holiday. It must be so hard having to work through the summertime, just when everybody else here is having fun,' Belle went on.

Her tone was still light and sympathetic but somehow she was making Honey feel as if she needed to defend herself. 'I love Can Falco,' she heard herself say, even though she wasn't sure if she did at all. 'And one day soon it'll start to run itself and I'll be able to travel again, take my holiday. Then I'll come to London and see you and Edouard . . .' She shook her head. 'And you live with him, and I didn't even know . . .'

'We worked together on Trade Secrets . . . You must have heard.'

Honey nodded, but the truth was that again she was on shaky ground and she imagined Belle probably knew it too. All she remembered about last summer was that she'd hardly seen Edouard at all, and when she had done he'd been more distracted than ever. But she'd let it go. She'd never thought to ask why, never tried to find out more.

'It was a big project he was involved in all last year. And now he's concocting evil plans with Paul.' Belle turned to include Nancy again. 'At least it means I get to spend time here with you! Nancy and I have been seeing quite a lot of each other, thanks to them.'

'The lovely Princess Anna introduced them,' Nancy explained. 'Have you met her yet?'

'Just now,' Honey said. 'Who is she?'

'She's a designer, with designs on Edouard's heart.'

'She'll have trouble finding that.'

'Poor Honey.' Belle laughed. 'Was she completely horrible?'

'Oh no, no, no. Yes.'

'You're a threat. Everything she can do you can do better.' Then she raised her leg to study her foot in Honey's shoe. 'And she's fallen for Ibiza. She says she loves the *whole vibe*. So you might find you're seeing more of her than you want to.'

'I'm sure I can keep out of her way.'

Belle smiled. 'Don't be. Not if you're in her sights. She's persistent. Look what she persuaded Edouard to do to this house.' She leaned forwards. 'You know he doesn't like it.'

'He doesn't?'

'He'll leave it a few months and then paint over it all. He's sweet, he doesn't want to hurt her feelings, that's all.'

'For that have my shoes!' Honey reached down to pull off the other one and handed it to Belle, laughing at the surprise on her face. 'Six euros at Las Dalias market. If you like, I'll take you and Nancy there tomorrow.'

'We *would*.' Belle turned to Nancy. 'Wouldn't we? You'd be able to come too? Paul doesn't have other plans for you?'

'Of course not!' Nancy brushed her aside. 'And we could see Can Falco on the way . . . Paul already said he'll be busy with Edouard all day.' She hesitated then and Honey saw the vulnerability in her face. 'You met Paul, didn't you?'

Honey nodded.

'Just as he pushed me in?'

'Yes.'

'Oh.' She nodded. 'You must have thought . . .' She looked up at the black night sky. 'It was no big deal. We were fooling around.'

Beside her Belle shifted in her chair.

'Don't worry, Honey,' Nancy insisted. 'I promise I'm in control and one day I will have my revenge on him. Now,' she went on brightly, 'how about we meet you at Can Falco tomorrow?'

'Perfect,' agreed Honey. 'We could join one of my mother's yoga classes if you'd like to. Then I'll show you Las Dalias.'

'Brilliant,' said Belle.

'I know nothing about yoga,' Nancy warned.

'Doesn't matter at all. Tora loves her uncorrupted beginners best of all.' Honey hoped Claudio wouldn't mind losing his free Saturday morning if she joined Nancy and Belle for the class. 'And in any case it's a method all her own. My mother has a very special style. You won't have tried anything like a Tora class before.' She leaned into Nancy. 'When the fairies join us we must be very quiet.'

'She sounds brilliant.' Nancy giggled nervously.

'You'll fall in love with her. Everybody does.'

'*Tora*?' repeated Belle.

'She's Dutch.'

'But why do *you* call her Tora?'

'Because she never liked words beginning with *M*. Words like Mama or Mummy . . . or mature.' Honey laughed. 'She likes T words, like Tora and Tanit and Tai-Chi.'

'And Tickle,' said Edouard, from somewhere above Honey's head. 'She loves being the tickle-monster. I rather like her being one too.'

At the sight of him Nancy opened her arms and then Honey felt a pair of hands land gently upon her shoulders.

'I'm very sorry about Anna,' he whispered, tickling her ear with his breath, 'I don't know what got into her. Here . . .' He passed her a tall pink cocktail then moved around so that she could see him. 'And Danilo says drink it slowly.'

'So where are ours?' Belle asked accusingly.

'Honey needed it more. Yours are waiting for you down on the beach. They're your reward for getting off the sofa and being sociable.'

'You need some time alone?'

'No, you can stay if you want to.' Now he was looking at Honey. 'I was wondering where you'd gone.'

'We're taking a Tora yoga class tomorrow morning,' Nancy told him. 'Do you think we'll survive? Do you want to come too?'

'Not sure I'm bendy enough for Tora.' He came and sat down between Nancy and Belle, tucked a strand of blond hair behind his ear and grinned across at Honey with warm brown eyes. Clearly absence had made his heart grow fonder.

'I never got the chance to ask. Do you like the house?' He stuck out his long legs on the table in front of him.

She sipped her drink. 'You know what I thought.'

'Subdued, classy, wonderfully tasteful?'

She prodded one of his feet with her bare toe. 'And I know you don't like it either. I'd have helped you if I'd known you wanted to change it. You should have asked me.'

'I didn't know I wanted to change it either. And, in any case, it turned out there was hardly anything to do, just an enormous lot of shopping.'

'And you know I'd never have managed that.' She leaned back, caught Belle and Nancy's eye and grinned at them.

At that Edouard threw his head back against the cushions. 'No. Stop those sneaky little glances. Nancy and Belle are *my* friends, *my* allies, Belle's *my* flatmate, Honey. What's going on?'

'Nothing.' Belle ruffled his hair sympathetically while sitting on his other side Nancy tried to uncork an obstinate bottle of wine.

'Poor Edouard,' Nancy said, handing Edouard the bottle before turning to Honey. 'He was very worried about what you'd think about his house. It's been bothering him all day.'

'No it hasn't,' Edouard insisted. 'Don't tell her that.'

He took the bottle of wine from Nancy's hands, uncorked it and then poured her a glass and handed another to Belle before settling back easily between the two of them.

There he was, Honey thought, with his beautiful handmaidens on either side, pouring them wine while they stroked his sun-streaked hair and hung on to his every word. As he took a sip, she watched Belle push herself that little bit closer, laughing at something he'd said. She wasn't flirting, only being affectionate, but still an unexpected and unwelcome pang of jealousy shot through Honey.

Don't touch, she found herself wanting to snap at Belle. It was ridiculous, she knew it was. She liked Belle and of course she was just the right sort of housemate for Edouard. Happy, good company, able to hold her own, she should be pleased to think of him living with someone so much fun. And yet she wasn't at all. Watching him sitting there between Belle and Nancy, Honey couldn't help but feel childishly jealous and fearful that she'd lost her status as his number one girl. She'd known him all her life, had never been presented with competition before, but now she wondered if she could still make him laugh like Belle and Nancy did. She doubted he ever looked as happy with her as he did right now, with them. She'd seen him fall in love with other girls, but what she'd never seen or even thought of before were the ones who might have been his friends because there'd never been any who could remotely compete with her. Until this funny bright affectionate woman who lived in his present not his past and made Honey feel she hardly knew him at all.

She downed her drink quickly and made to stand up.

'Danilo said *slowly*,' he told her. 'Don't go away.'

'I want to. Come with me, we should all go down. I keep hearing the music on the beach. Why are we sitting up here?'

'Go with her,' Nancy encouraged him, 'take her down. She's an Ibiza girl. She can't sit on a sofa all evening talking when there's music on the beach! It's not her fault she's just met the two laziest and most antisocial people here tonight.'

'Come with us.' Honey held out her hands to them although the truth was she wanted a moment with Edouard on his own.

'In a while,' Nancy insisted. 'We'll finish our wine and be right behind you. Then you can introduce us to all your gorgeous, glamorous, boho friends.'

Edouard placed his glass on the table, pushed himself back to his feet and held out his hand. 'You can show them to me too. Come on.' He led Honey down the steps then stopped as soon as they were out of earshot. 'What's going on?' he asked. 'Are you angry with me?'

'No, with myself.' She was impressed by her own honesty. 'It's rubbish that I didn't know about Belle. She lives with you. How could I not even have heard her name before tonight? What's the matter with us, with me, that we've let it come to that? And Trade Winds. What are they? Why didn't I know about them?'

'Trade Secrets,' he corrected gently.

'Whatever. And Anna too. I know you don't like what she's done, but how has it got to that? Why did you let her loose on El Figo?' She paused, then added deliberately, 'How could you let her near *you*?'

'She's not got that close. I'd been working with her in London and one day we were talking about here, and then she came out and saw the house and she wanted to have a go at it, that's all. She had all these ideas and they sounded great.' He shrugged. 'And to tell you the truth I really didn't care what she did. You know I'm not precious about El Figo.'

'But you should be! Why aren't you? I hate that you can say that.'

'Bee.' He came to a halt and took her hands in his. 'All I mean is I don't care what colour my walls are.'

She threaded her fingers through his.

'What else?' he asked.

'I think it's you. You and me. Tonight I felt as if I'd lost you and worse, it's as if you've been gone a long time but I've only just noticed.'

'Come here.'

He pushed her down gently onto the edge of the next flight of stone steps that would take them down another tier, to a lower terrace. Below them was the sound of people, a beat of music, but here for the moment they were alone.

'Don't you know you'll never lose me? That however hard you try it's not going to happen?'

She let her head rest against his shoulder. 'But how many times have you been out here this year? How many days? How many years since we've sat here like this?'

'Too many. I know it's dreadful, such a waste of a house.'

She turned to look at him.

He laughed quietly. 'I can't quite believe you're saying you miss me.'

'But I do, I am. I've missed you for years. I want you to come back. I want you to spend some time here without a crowd of City bums to keep you company or even lovely friends like Belle and Nancy . . . and Paul. I want you on your own. Because you need to spend some time here, you and me, together. You need to remind yourself of what you let go.' She could see it was the last thing he'd expected her to say and she felt suddenly self-conscious and yet at the same time relieved that she'd said it. 'I'm in a strange mood tonight.' She thought back to how she'd felt in the gardens of Can Falco, the restlessness and sadness that had forced her to her feet and sent her running to him and realized she'd been in a strange mood for weeks.

'Say some more. I like it.'

'I don't think so.' She stood up and held out her hand and he took it and stood up too, close beside her, and she thought he was about to say something else but then instead he silently led her on down the next flight of stone steps, along another path, past a square thatched gazebo, filled with people, more spilling outside. The music from the beach was louder here, she could feel the bass resonating beneath her feet and without thinking began to move in time to the sound.

As they rounded a corner they came across another group of people, her dear friends Claire and Tony talking to a tall woman with a capuchin monkey around her neck, who called out to Honey in delight when she saw her but Edouard held tight onto her hand and didn't let her stop.

'But that was Claire and Tony, and Juno too,' Honey protested as they rounded another corner and disappeared out of sight. 'I haven't seen them for ages.'

'I don't care. We're going to dance.'

He was moving faster now, almost running down the shallow steps, down towards the sea.

'Did you see her monkey was wearing a little scarf around his neck? He looked so sweet.'

He turned back to her briefly. 'But if we'd talked to her we'd never have got away and I'd like to dance with you more than I'd like to talk to Juno.'

Her heart was beginning to race with the exertion but her feet picked up speed again until she was flying down the steps behind him. 'You saw Maggie and Troy were here too?'

'Maggie and Troy are always here,' he called back.

'They're not, they live at Can Falco. You must know that.'

'Not when I'm home.'

'Even when you're home.'

'No, Bee, they like me most. They told me.'

He led her down another flight of steps and past another clutch of people. She saw her new neighbours, a couple called Inca and Nash who'd just bought a house down in the valley below Can Falco. They were artists, working on all their *expressions* together.

'But I wanted to see Inca and Nash. And there was such a good-looking man talking to them. Who was he? I think I should go back.'

'Another time.'

'Did you hear they've finished the work on their house?'

At that he looked back at her once more. 'Do I care?'

'Yes,' she laughed, 'because it's all made of green glass. Don't you want to see it?'

'Find them later.'

'Tora's been modelling for them.'

'I heard.'

'Naked but for drawing pins. But don't worry because they stuck drawing pins *to* her but not *in* her. How do you think they did that?'

Edouard didn't answer and she stopped beside him because now they'd reached the last flight of steps before the beach and they were both out of breath. For the moment they were alone, standing side by side while their hearts thudded fast and in front of them the round white moon hung huge and low over the sea.

five

I'M WITH EDOUARD, she found herself saying in her head, over and over again. How strange it's Edouard standing here beside me, holding my hand, and I really don't want to let him go.

Still holding her hand, he turned away again to check his path and then led her down the last few steps and onto the beach.

Inaccessible but from Edouard's garden or by boat, the beach was almost the best part of El Figo. Only little, no more than three hundred metres long, it was covered in pure white sand and because of its location was completely private and for that almost priceless.

There were flares caught between the rocks that lit the path to a cluster of colourful Indian tepees with jewelled cushions and rugs scattered beneath them, while further out to sea the moonlight flickered on the rippling water. She'd seen the beach a million times before but it had never looked as beautiful as it did tonight. Beside the tepees their friend Mark Ure had set up his music and was mixing tracks for the fifty or so people spread out around them. Many people were dancing, some ankle-deep in the water, a few had even started to swim. Edouard took Honey's hand and led her towards the others. Mark raised a hand in greeting as he saw them approaching and Edouard slid his arms around her waist and together they began to dance on the sand, both of them already barefoot, Edouard in his long trousers, Honey in her very short dress that kept riding up high around her thighs.

Then following them down onto the beach came a rush of gorgeous-looking girls and glamorous men, none of whom Honey knew, the girls with sheets of long shining hair and beautiful floating clothes, fluttering excitedly down the rocky steps like nocturnal butterflies, out onto the sand, exclaiming with delight at what they saw, bending to slip out of shoes, then stretching up to slip out of their dresses, pulling each other by the wrists towards the sea. Others moved towards where Danilo and his two equally good-looking assistants stood waiting for them, dressed in identical purple silk shirts with red bandannas, long black hair tied back in ponytails. Several of the girls immediately swooped up their drinks and then went plunging on into the water to join their friends and Honey and

Edouard, while at the same moment the music changed again, to a loud heavy bass.

'Who are they? How do I not know all these people?' Honey shouted, keeping her arms around his neck possessively as each wave seemed to bring with it another stunning girl determined to catch his attention. 'Where have you got them from? Have you trained them all to be like this?'

'Face it, Honey, they find me irresistible.'

She looked back up at him. 'No, you have to have paid them.'

He laughed. 'Most of them are here for the summer. They've rented a couple of big houses in Santa Agnes. I know most of them from London.'

She nodded. 'Your secret life in London.'

'Not secret,' he shouted above the noise of the music. 'You're just not interested in finding out about it.'

'I am. I want to find out now.'

'Then I'll tell you anything. Everything you want to know.'

She grinned back at him. 'So tell me if you've slept with Anna.'

'Quieter, Bee!' he exclaimed. 'And no I haven't.'

'Kissed her?'

'I meant that I'd tell you anything about my work.'

'But that's boring. Tell me if you've kissed Anna.'

'Nothing's going on.'

'Then I think that's even worse. Poor Anna, because I get the feeling she'd like it to be.'

'Not poor Anna. Perfectly fine, indestructible Anna. She's a business partner, that's all.'

She met his eye. 'I don't like her.'

'She has good ideas.'

'No, she talks rubbish. Eco this and green that without any sincerity at all. Surely you can see that?'

'She's very clever.'

'She's a fake.'

'She's been good to work with,' he said stubbornly.

'Oh, for God's sake, Edouard, please. Is that really all that counts?' She let him go. 'I don't know, why do I still care what you think, what you do? I thought I'd stopped, years ago, when you left me here and didn't even tell me why.'

'Bee, now you sound so sad. And I had to go. You know that.'

'But it hurt. I missed you.'

'Oh, darling Bee, you never said that before.'

'So I'm telling you now.' She looked around her. 'Perhaps not the best time, perhaps not a conversation to have at the top of our voices, standing in the middle of the sea with a party all around us, but let's face it, there haven't been many other opportunities this year.'

He came closer and bent his head so that his forehead was almost touching hers. 'I'm sorry.'

She looked back up at him. 'You left and for six months I didn't hear from you at all.' Then she shook her head, and pushed him away. 'But don't worry about it too much because, of course, for years now it hasn't hurt at all. For years I've hardly thought about you.' She looked around them, at the sea, the people all about. 'But now that we're here doing this again it's all coming back to me, all the fun we used to have. We're dancing in the sea and you're getting your trousers wet, and it's as if nothing's changed at all.'

In answer he took her hands and pushed her slowly backwards deeper into the water. As she walked backwards she could feel it touch the back of her knees, then her thighs, could feel it catch at the hem of her dress, and then rise up to her waist and slowly they walked further, out of the range of the flares, until only the light from the moon lit the water and the music suddenly seemed very far away and it was as if they had been left all alone.

She could feel his heart beating fast against hers.

'You've proved it now,' she heard herself say, her hands flat against his chest. 'You've shown how you can live without us all, so why don't you come back again? Loads of your old friends are coming back. Milo and

Christian and Frankie and Tina, they can't stay away. Some of them are commuting, staying her for a few months at a time. Couldn't you do that?'

'Honey, have you got the first clue what I do in London?'

'No,' she admitted, laughing into his wet T-shirt. 'Something to do with Trade Secrets?'

'Hopeless. You know nothing. So just for the record, my job isn't one that would allow me to spend a few months of every year in Ibiza. My job involves me getting on the tube at six-fifteen every morning, in a suit, to be at my desk, in Golden Square, by seven. This,' he nodded out towards the water, 'Ibiza, is my most favourite place in the world but what I had here when I was sixteen without a care in the world, couldn't be found any more.'

'Yes it can.'

He shook his head. 'We're old now. I am an old man with serious financial responsibilities.'

'You're a pompous old man. It wasn't that we were only sixteen, it was a state of mind, and we could get it again if you'd only try. Of course we could,' she insisted, 'but better. Now we know what we like we'd do it even better now.'

'Are you so certain?'

'I am, because I know I'm right. I'll show you.

Choose three places and I'll take you there again, but one of them must be Es Palmador. We have to go there.'

'Ride the horses into the sea at Cala Mastella?'

'Yes!' She took two steps back from him surprised he'd buy into the idea so easily and surprised by how much she wanted to do it too.

'Where else?'

'Santa Medea?'

She nodded again. But almost immediately thoughts started rushing in. Take up her precious time, it would mean nights away from Can Falco, how could she do it? The all-work-and-no-play Honey instinctively backed away, but only briefly because at the same time the old Honey was rising to the fore, knowing this was her chance to prove he'd been wrong, all those years ago, to leave her and Ibiza. More than anything she wanted to prove it to him, that the island he'd left was a jewel, heaven on earth, and he'd been a fool ever to have forgotten.

'Three dates,' she told him, serious now as she started to plan. 'Three weekends. We could start tomorrow evening with Es Palmador, but perhaps you shouldn't leave your friends at El Figo?'

'They wouldn't mind. Belle would certainly understand and Nancy and Paul will hardly notice I'm not there.'

'So shall we sleep the night on the beach?'

'Clay masks and hot springs.' He saw the happiness in her face. 'Bee, I hate that you think I don't remember.'

'Catch some fish for supper. We can take some mackerel lines.'

'Lie back and look at the stars.'

'Get bitten by the sandflies.'

'No, no, no!' Now it was Edouard defending the memory. 'That never ever happened on Es Palmador.'

She grinned back at him. 'Listen to you,' she teased. 'There's hope for you still.'

'So we'll do it, yes?'

She was enchanted by his enthusiasm. 'We'll do it.' She reached forwards and kissed him and he caught the back of her head with his hand and held her there, trapping her lips against his cheek.

'Bee . . .'

She broke free again. 'And now, Mr Bonnier, you should join your party and all those other girls.'

Hand in hand they waded back to shore, to Danilo's daiquiris and Mark Ure's music and a cluster of their friends waiting for them on the beach, and minutes after having left the sea the hot night air had dried her dress, and soon she was joined by Belle and Nancy, Maggie and Troy, Inca and her friends Claire and

Tony, until it seemed as if everyone from childhood and beyond was dancing on the beach, some people she hadn't seen for months, who reminded her, over and over again how little they saw of her now, how much they wished she could make more time for them all.

And when much later the sky began to lighten and the water turn to pink and gold, the drum and bass finally quietened and then the real drummers began, beating in the dawn of a new day. The fishing boats returning home to San Antonio heard their unique and wonderful sound and, as they drew nearer, picked up the smell of barbecued bacon and eggs and freshly baked bread on the air. And then, as the sun began to rise some more, some of them saw the moment when all the dancing abruptly stopped and almost as one the entire party on the beach dropped onto the sand to face the sun and sat in silence but for the beating drums, to watch its spectacular climb into the sky.

six

HONEY LAY under her sheet, feeling the weight of the sun like a bar of heat across her legs, watching through half-closed eyes as the brilliant pinpricks of light filtered through the cracks in her half-open shutters. She was thinking about boats, how a pretty sailing boat would be ideal, with a rug and a picnic already waiting for them, tucked into the locker on board. In the old days there'd been boats aplenty and no end of people to lend them to her too. Sometimes she and her friends would make their way across to the island of Es Palmador in a flotilla of dinghies and rowing boats, once even a yacht, but now that she really needed one there was only their own little fishing boat, *Baby Jane*, which had sat in the garages at Can Falco for at least ten years and was bound to be rusting and peeling, with rotten sails and a broken outboard motor. She'd go and have a look at her after breakfast, while she still had the rest of the day to come up with an alternative.

She checked her watch, stretched one last time, slid her legs off the bed and then streaked across the room to the shower. She'd ask Claudio to cover for her while she took Belle and Nancy to Las Dalias, she thought as she poured conditioner into her hair, trying to loosen the windblown tangles from last night. She'd catch him before the end of his shift.

After the shower she took a beautiful new kaftan made by an old school friend from her cupboard. It was pale pink and embroidered with translucent seed pearls and sequins and Honey was currently trying to persuade her friend to make enough to sell them in the boutique at Can Falco.

As she dressed she reminded herself that Claudio was reliable, that after a few months he knew the routines of a Can Falco day as well as she did. She told herself that she couldn't have picked a better Saturday to take off, with so few guests arriving and leaving, and that if she wanted to camp the night on Es Palmador, swim horses into the sea and sunbathe at Santa Medea, she'd only be doing what Claudio had been urging her to do for ages: take more than one day off at a time.

But first there was the class and Tora, she knew, would be utterly delighted to see her there. Tora loved getting her hands on Honey – she was, after all, her most recalcitrant, challenging pupil of all. And in return Honey enjoyed the classes, recognizing that they were the only times she'd ever felt the full focus of her mother's attention, the only times she felt Tora reaching out to her. The fact that Tora sensed Honey's *bad energy*, as she put it, but never seemed even to contemplate asking her about it had long since ceased to hurt. The fact that Can Falco had been so busy and Honey had had barely time for a cup of coffee let alone a class for the past three months had, of course, passed Tora by.

After breakfast she left Claudio manning the front desk and went to the garages to have a look at *Baby Jane*. The padlock on the garage doors was stiff and the key refused to turn until she'd split her nail to the quick, dripping blood onto her clothes, but eventually the lock clicked open and she pulled apart the heavy wooden doors and peered inside. Outside the heat was already intense and the sunshine dazzlingly bright. Inside it was cool and dark, the room smelling of wet cement and mildew, and it took some time for Honey's eyes to adjust.

Backed up against the far wall were boxes still waiting to be unpacked from almost twenty years before, enormous wooden planters from Bali, some terracotta pots, several cracked now, all of them bought while Can Falco was still being planned, and which had ultimately found no place. And in front of the boxes, sitting on a trailer with two flat tyres, was the boat.

She approached her cautiously. The last time *Baby Jane* had seen water was at least five years ago and even then anyone sailing her had known to have a bucket to hand. Never the prettiest boat, there had at least been a cheeriness to her but now she looked tired and dispirited and Honey felt terribly guilty that she'd neglected her so. *We'll clean you up darling*, she whispered, looking down into sludge at the bottom of the hull and sniffing distastefully. The holes seemed to have been plugged with dead flies, long-dead flies. She went over to the locker beside the boat and unclipped it and pulled out a little of the sail, covered in mildew now, with a two-foot long tear, and the rest felt so fragile it would no doubt rip completely at the merest hint of a breeze. Was fate telling her that her trip was doomed, a lost cause after all? She kicked shut the locker, wondering if she dared look at the outboard motor.

'Honeybee?'

She turned to see her father standing in the doorway, shielding his eyes with his hand and peering in curiously.

She clapped her hands free of dust and walked over to him. 'Hi, Dad. Just looking at *Baby Jane*.'

'Very good, very good.'

'No, not very good at all, she's a complete mess.'

He took her arm eagerly, starting to steer her away. 'Now, I was wondering what you'd think about a trip into town?'

'You mean you'd like someone to drive you in?'

Her father had given up driving a few years earlier, after he'd missed the edge of the road in a storm and had been trapped in his car for twelve hours.

'That would be marvellous.'

'I can't, Dad. Not this morning. Get Claudio to take you.' Then she remembered she needed Claudio at Can Falco.

'But I'm asking for your daughterly hand. I'd like you to come out with me. We could sit in the square and gawp at the grockles and their revolting pink legs.'

'I could do with a hand too, a fatherly hand, blowing up the tyres on that bloody trailer, emptying the gunge and the flies out of *Baby Jane*'s bottom.'

He burst into delighted guffaws of laughter. 'You're not serious?'

'Yes, I am. She'll sink if I take her to Es Palmador in the state she's in now.'

Es Palmador? he should have asked. *Darling girl, why are you sailing to Es Palmador?* And if he'd asked she'd have told him. She would have loved him to ask. Not that he'd have had the first clue how to respond. He'd have given

her a sweet smile and would have wandered away, the
thought of challenging anybody about anything utterly
alien to him. The world beyond the white walls of Can
Falco was not really his concern.

'But, Honey, I can't help you,' he cried instead.
'Look at my clothes.'

'So get out of the pouffy smock, help me clean up
Baby Jane, blow up the tyres on the trailer and in return
I'll drive you to Ibiza town. Do it while I'm at Tora's
class and then we can leave as soon as I've finished.'

He frowned down at his feet. 'I'm not sure I'd know
where to start.'

She shook her head. 'I don't believe you. You're just
saying that because you don't want to get dirty.'

'No,' he said. 'It's not that. I really wouldn't know
where to start.'

'But it's your bloody boat, Dad.'

'I know, I know. But I haven't sailed her for years.
Honey, I'm an old man who wants to spend his morning
with a beer in the square, not messing around with
boats . . .' He turned away. 'But not to worry if you're
too busy, I'll see if Maggie and Troy fancy a trip.'

She came up close to him, belatedly took in the
neatly parted grey hair, the freshly shaven jaw, the clean
pink toe-nails in his open-toed sandals.

'So what's so tempting about Ibiza town, Dad? You

hate the place in summertime. What's making you want to go in today?'

'Oh, no one, nothing at all,' he said, all of a sudden not meeting her eye. 'I need a change of beer, that's all. I felt like sitting outside Montesol, watching the world go by, just like the old days.' He turned to go.

'Dad?' He looked back at her. She waited.

'Goddammit!' He exploded into laughter. 'All right, I said I'd meet a woman.' Then he grinned at her mischievously. 'You should be proud of me, Honey. She's an absolute cracker, got the most marvellous eyes. She arrived the day before yesterday all on her own, came from Durham or Darlington or somewhere beginning with D, anyway and I feel sorry for her. I said I'd show her around.'

'You mean Marianne Darlington?'

'Perhaps.'

'Who's here checking out places for her honeymoon? Great idea to show her around, Dad. You'd be doing her such a favour.'

'Pah, of course she isn't here for her honeymoon!'

'Yes, she is.'

'If you're saying this just to upset me, it's not working. I'm telling you she watches me, Honey, all the time.'

'She'd eat you for breakfast.'

'To which I mightn't say no.'

She shook her head. 'You're impossible.'

'Come on, spoilsport,' he cajoled, 'it's just a bit of fun. It's all in my head, Honey, you know that.'

'So clean up the boat and in return I'll take you there.'

He looked back at her with the kind of wariness she saw more and more on his face these days, as if he couldn't quite believe she was his daughter, so alien was she.

'You're very tough on your old dad, you know.'

'You think so?'

'I do. And Marianne's a perfect lady.'

'I'm sure she is. I trust her completely.'

He stuck his hands on his hips and looked dispiritedly back into the darkness of the garage.

'Do I have to go in there? It really smells very damp.'

'Leave the doors open.'

'I'm sure Shimmy Roberts would lend you *Nervous Wreck*.'

'If I set off in *Nervous Wreck*, there's a good chance I'll never come back.' Then she leaned closer in to him, grinning. 'But you'd chance that wouldn't you, if it meant you didn't have to clean out *Baby Jane*?'

'Honey, there's absolutely no chance of a mere boat

getting the better of you. You're the most capable woman I know.'

It's lucky I am. It's lucky I am. She began to walk away, reached the gate in the wall that led her through to the Garden of Serenity. 'Bye-bye, Dad, I'll pick you up at three. Get those hands dirty.'

Their exchange left her feeling mean-spirited and horrible. She knew what he thought of her, how all work and no play had made Honey a very dull daughter. With her tight-lipped refusal to laugh at his jokes, cheer on his boozing, encourage his flirtations, innocent as they may be, she knew, in his eyes, she was slowly turning into a self-righteous kill-joy. And yet, honestly, she knew that she'd always treated him this way. She'd wagged her finger at him at ten years old. She'd never been the daddy's girl who'd thrown herself exuberantly into his arms. Perhaps she'd been afraid that he'd drop her, even then.

But now, as she walked towards the Garden of Serenity, she was filled with regret and a powerful longing for it to be different. This morning he'd asked her to sit with him in the square, something he hardly ever did, and she'd responded by making him pay for it first. Of course he wasn't going to relish the chance of helping her with *Baby Jane*, he was a fusspot in a new

white smock, but as usual she'd been tough on him
when, just for once, she could have been gentle. Yes,
of course Marianne Darlington was at the heart of his
request, but there was always a woman on the horizon.
The prospect of a pretty new guest was what got him up
in the morning. What was different about this morning
was that after months when they'd hardly talked at all
he'd come specially to seek her out and she realized how
pleased she was that he had. She vowed there and then
that she would surprise him, she'd join him outside
Montesol and they'd drink a beer together and she'd let
him chat, she'd let him relax.

She was the first to arrive in the Garden of Serenity,
before even Tora. She went to the fountain, bent her
head and splashed her face, then found a spot on the
grass and laid out her mat, close to where her mother
would be teaching, partly shaded by the hedge. It was
almost nine thirty – late for a yoga class, with the sun
already high and hot enough to make any movement
hard work, but she was looking forward to it even so.
She needed a channel for the restless energy that had
been building since she'd woken that morning and
wouldn't leave her until the night on Es Palmador was
over.

She lay back on the grass, shielded her eyes from the
sun with her hand and pictured the two of them,

Edouard and her, sailing across the bright blue sky on a
ship-shape *Baby Jane*.

Perhaps they should snorkel? She'd better bring kit
for Edouard. She wondered what it was that he remembered best about Es Palmador, what it was that he'd
liked best. She wished she'd thought to ask him. And
then she pushed Edouard out of her mind, telling
herself to relax, breathe and let her thoughts dissolve.
Better bring blankets too. She forced her eyes shut, breathed
slowly, in and out again, in and out, then let them flash
open again. How far she'd come from her sixteen-year-
old self! Because Es Palmador had never been about
doing something, it had been about *being* something,
being happy, being there, knowing that Paradise was a
secret beach in the warm inky dark of the night, with
a smoke and a beer in your hand and a snapping log
fire at your side, while the sight of the stars and the
sound of the waves wove their magic.

But it had also been about being sixteen. Was
Edouard really imagining she could re-create that? It
was impossible. She sat up again in a flurry of panic.
Being sixteen had been at the heart of the magic. How
could she re-create having no care in the world, with
Edouard lying beside her obsessing about the FTSE,
while she, no doubt, fussed about Can Falco? She
stretched out her legs in front of her so that the sunlight

caught the rings on her toes and she imagined him pacing the shoreline in a pinstripe suit, begging to be sailed home. In agitation she stretched and pointed her toes until she gave herself cramp. Then she shook everything loose again, smiled at the nervous wreck she'd become. Tora and her Barely Yoga class clearly couldn't begin too soon.

She lowered her head slowly down to her knees and brought her arms high over her head in a careful stretching arc then rested them on her ankles and stayed there, breathing in through her nose, out through her mouth, and finally her mind began to clear.

And then, with a jolt her eyes flew open again as she heard someone calling her name and remembered at exactly the same moment that Belle and Nancy were supposed to be joining the class. She leaped to her feet, flicking a quick glance at her watch then ran back out of the Garden of Serenity, across the gardens and into the hotel, through the big open windows that led into the main hall. There they were, mats rolled up under their arms, talking to Claudio, who was sitting in Honey's chair behind the desk, staring with rapt adoration at Nancy.

Belle came forwards and kissed Honey's cheek. A navy polka-dot scarf held back her thick chestnut hair and she was wearing baggy white cotton trousers and a white T-shirt. 'Hello. Were you hoping we'd forgotten? Tell me I'm wearing the right clothes?'

'I'd forgotten,' Honey admitted, breathing hard from her mad dash to reach them. 'My brain's closed down today. And you look great.'

'Claudio was just telling us the way to the class.' Belle grinned conspiratorially at Honey and added quietly, 'Silly me, I mean Claudio was just telling *Nancy* the way to the class.' She took Honey's arm. 'Take your time,' she called over her shoulder to Nancy and she purposefully led Honey away. 'The sparks are flying between those two. When we walked in through the doors, into the hall, he saw her and she saw him and, Honey, his face . . .' Belle shook her head wonderingly. 'There was this look of utter, complete . . . *besottedness*. I've never seen anything like it.'

'She is very pretty.'

'Yes, but even so. Perhaps that's just him. Please tell me he's not like that with all the girls.'

'No, I've never seen him like that with anybody here before. And as far as I know he hasn't got a girlfriend. So – ' she shrugged, laughing at the bemused look on Belle's face, 'why not? Perhaps that's it. Love at first sight. You should be pleased you were there to witness it.' She saw Belle's concern and stopped, surprised. 'You surely can't mind if she falls for Claudio and finally dumps Paul?'

'No. Not at all, but Nancy is . . .' she shrugged, trying to come up with the right words. 'Paul and Nancy are very complicated. I've seen other guys falling for Nancy, but it's never made any difference to her. He's bad for her, but she's been with him so long I sometimes doubt she'll ever get away.'

'How bad for her?'

Belle frowned. 'He's not violent, nothing worse than what you saw the other night, but he's a bully. You saw that too?'

They paused in the doorway of some French windows that led them out of the hall and into the gardens outside.

'I saw him push her in. Afterwards I wondered if I'd misunderstood. Edouard clearly thinks he's great.'

'No, it happened just as you saw.' Belle looked serious for a moment. 'Don't underestimate him. He's been working with Edouard over the past few months, and he's been to the flat quite often, so I've seen more of him than I've wanted to. And he's always so charming and wonderful. He'll take the trouble to remember the name of my boss, make jokes, bring bottles of champagne. And he's careful and polite and easy to have around but I look into his eyes and I know he's trouble. I wish he'd stay away.'

The warning in Belle's voice touched Honey with unease.

'But what does Edouard see in him? He's not a fool. He knows this, surely. Doesn't he?'

But now Nancy was bearing down upon them again, pushing her way between Belle and Honey and the three of them stepped outside together through the windows and both Belle and Nancy stopped and shielded their eyes from the sun.

'My God,' Nancy breathed. 'It's so beautiful.'

'Could that be Claudio or Can Falco?' teased Belle, laughing and then running forwards. 'Where do we go? Aren't we late?'

'We are late,' Honey agreed. 'And Tora does not like people to be late.'

She led them on, round another corner but then Nancy stopped again as she saw the terrace ahead of her, people sitting at the various tables and chairs, sipping coffee, eating croissants, talking and laughing, while the stunning gardens stretched away towards the pool.

'Please can I live here?' she said in wonder. 'Does anyone do that? Book in for six months? Or perhaps I should come and work here. How about it, Honey? I'm extremely efficient.' She caught the questioning look on Honey's face. 'Oh, for God's sake, not you too. I only spoke to him for about three seconds.' But she'd blushed a deep pink. 'He's very sweet. I'll admit that,'

'Everybody's in love with Claudio.'

'No, Honey, please, not me!' And there was a plea in her voice. 'You know the score.'

Now they'd left the terrace and had reached the Garden of Serenity, where they stopped beside its arched entrance cut into the hedge. Belle and Nancy looked at it, curious and impressed, trying to see inside. On the other side Honey could hear her mother chanting with her class, 'One taste, one touch, one choice, one heart, one cry, one joy, one life, one world.'

Belle, hearing it too, suppressed a quick splutter of nervous laughter and then glanced at Honey. 'I will be serious,' she told her solemnly. 'It's an honour to be here.'

Less than two minutes ago Honey had been early, now the three of them were going to have to walk into a class that had already begun. Honey stepped aside to allow Nancy to go through first and then, when Nancy didn't move, gave her an encouraging push. But instead of striding forwards, Nancy took two steps back and spun to face Honey, her eyes round with disbelief.

'When did you mention they'd be naked?' she gasped.

Belle clapped her hands over her mouth.

Naked? Honey looked through the hedge and saw her mother sitting on her mat, facing her class, and she was indeed naked as were they all.

Barely Yoga. She'd imagined it meant stripped-down yoga, yoga at its purest. But, given Tora, how ridiculous ever to have thought that.

'Good morning,' Tora said, smiling at her from her mat, but the glint in her big blue eyes said, *You're late.* 'Bring in your friends, we've just begun.'

She was sitting in the lotus position, her grey blonde hair piled up on top of her head, a few stray tendrils curling softly around her serene and beautiful face, upturned hands resting on her round brown knees, her breasts rising and falling gently with each inward and outward breath, her long legs wrapped gracefully around each other, the position of her feet and ankles, for now, leaving the rest of her to the imagination. Honey quickly looked around the class, there were about ten of them, a mixed class, all in the lotus position, following their leader, all naked. She stepped back through the hedge to Nancy and Belle.

'Did you know about this?' Nancy demanded from where she stood, pressed flat against the hedge, her yoga mat clutched tightly against her.

Honey shook her head apologetically. 'But as Tora spends most of the day naked I should have guessed . . . So, do you want to stay?'

'Of course we do,' Belle declared, bending down to take off her sandals. But Nancy suddenly crumpled to the ground in hysterical giggles.

'I can't, I can't,' she cried. 'I won't know where to look.'

'Don't be ridiculous, close your eyes,' Belle told her as she pulled her T-shirt over her head. 'Or stare straight ahead.'

'You're weird,' said Nancy. 'You shouldn't be so keen. Imagine doing the Downward Dog.'

Belle grinned up at her. 'It doesn't bother me.'

Far more confident than Nancy with her clothes on, for Belle it was just the same with them off, even if it was Nancy who had the perfect body. Belle strode through the group with her shoulders back and her head held high, apologized to Tora for being late, then unrolled her mat and took her place. Following her in, Honey sat down beside her, then came Nancy, shoulders hunched, biting her lip, looking straight ahead.

Tora sat quietly, for the moment saying nothing, a beatific smile upon her face.

The whole class must be in love with her, Honey thought. Three people down from Belle, a thick-set hairy man was sitting out of line and staring at Tora with love pouring out of his eyes. Barely Yoga, unlike some of Tora's other conceptions – such as Touch Me Yoga and Upside Down Yoga – was clearly going to run and run.

'Now, at first you might find Barely Yoga strange,' Tora said in her slightly sing-song voice that yoga classes always seemed to accentuate. 'You might find it feels funny. If you do, you are allowed to laugh.' She looked around at her class. 'Or perhaps Barely Yoga will make you want to cry?'

Nervous faces stared back at her.

'I warn you, kneeling on your pubic hair can hurt.'

Tora was not a naturally humorous person and said this rather awkwardly but the group let out a little chuckle even so, and Nancy an uncontrolled, spluttering snort. Honey, risking a glance at her, saw her cheeks were very pink and her bright eyes wide open, fixed on the fountain ahead of her. But for the rest of the group it was clearly the right thing to say. All around her Honey could feel people start to relax and shift position, this poor buttoned-up class finally feeling fresh air all over their bodies and finding it felt rather good.

'These are the bodies we've been given,' Tora reasoned earnestly. 'We should be comfortable with them. We should celebrate their unique geometries, not hide them away . . . because each fold of flesh, each line and wrinkle is as much a part of us as our thoughts and fears. Barely Yoga brings us one step closer to realizing that.'

From the corner of her eye, Honey saw Nancy give Belle a tiny, straight-faced nod.

'You will recognize many of the poses and breathing exercises from other classes,' Tora went on, 'but today you will experience them in a different way, in a naked way.'

All around Honey her class seemed to shuffle in agreement. Honey risked a second glance at Nancy and this time Nancy caught her eye, glittering with fun and barely controlled hysteria.

And yet, Honey thought, Barely Yoga could still work. Yes, the class was naked. Yes the hairy man clearly wanted Tora for his wife. But so far her mother's words were making sense, and as long as she carried on this way, practical and devoid of sexuality, as long as Tora didn't go off on one of her specials and start talking about Indian temples and tantric sex, perhaps good things could come from such a class.

'And then,' said Tora, 'when we are comfortable in our skins, we will take a journey together.'

Ah, thought Honey, remembering the last journey, the one that had led them out into the gardens to sing

to the olive trees and thank them for the joy they'd
brought to the world. She couldn't quite imagine Belle
and Nancy dancing naked through the gardens.

'But first let us stretch.' Tora paused, looking
around her pupils for one, two, three seconds, and
then she began, stretching her legs out in front of her.
'We shall bring our right knees in to our chests.' She
looked approvingly around as the class, to a person,
immediately followed her lead. 'Good, good. We shall
hold it, one, two, three, we will stretch out through our
heels, point and raise, point and raise, then lower as we
exhale again . . .'

And so they stretched and with each outward breath
the class collectively seemed to relax some more, everybody committing wholeheartedly to each pose, clearly
willing to follow inspirational Tora wherever she led
them, from sitting to lying to standing to kneeling on
all-fours, swinging arms, touching toes, legs wide apart,
bare bottoms lifting willingly to the sun, so that it was
only Honey – and perhaps Nancy – who remained
certain that Barely Yoga was heading towards more than
just a naked exercise routine.

Fifteen minutes later Tora abruptly brought the
stretching to an end. Honey, who had been waiting
for the moment, glanced up to see a definite look of
anticipation on her mother's face as she sat cross-legged

once more, waiting for the complete attention of her class. When she had it, she nodded.

'Now we are going on our journey,' she told them, eyes opening wider, 'a journey down to the ocean of our beginning, to where all our stories start.'

The class stared back with rapt attention at Tora. Honey risked another quick glance at Nancy, who nodded very solemnly back, but her eyes were on fire again and suddenly it was Honey fighting not to laugh.

'Dive deep,' Tora told them, 'clear your birthing spiral and allow your inner curiosity and delight the freedom to fly. Now that we are naked as babies, let us be reborn.' With that, she dropped her head to her knees and gracefully wrapped her arms around her body. 'We will dive deep and we will stretch to the sky.' She tipped back her face and flung her arms high above her head. 'Stretch to the sky, stretch to the sky, reach for the light. All of us, naked, let us be reborn. Let all the doubts and fears that have settled on our skin be cast away.'

'Not really yoga at all, is it?' Belle whispered to Honey out of the corner of her mouth as she reached, reached for the light.

'It's *Barely* Yoga,' Honey reminded her.

Tora threw her arms over her head again and all around Honey and Belle the rest of the class enthusiastically did the same, alternately ducking down, then lifting their heads, throwing their arms in the air and chanting with Tora. 'Let's fly, let's fly. Stretch to the sky.'

Then Tora rose to her feet and the class eagerly scrambled up after her, and now there was passion in her husky voice and her cheeks were flushed as she began a kind of breast stroke in the air. 'Come on, class,' she urged, 'chant with me the precious words and feel your rebirth begin. Stretch . . . pulse . . . undulate . . . reach for the light.'

'Stretch . . . pulse . . . undulate . . . reach for the light,' the class recited. Honey risked a quick glance down the line and saw that the hairy man had stayed sitting cross-legged on the floor and was now rocking gently with eyes wide open and a fixed blissed-out smile on his face.

'Stretch . . . pulse . . . undulate . . . reach for the light.'

And at this point the loudspeakers set into the fountain suddenly gurgled into life, filling the garden with a cacophony of flutes, drums, splashing water and calling birds. Honey, unable to risk a look at Belle, focused on the hedge in front of her and put her hands together, copying Tora. She'd never found the music funny before, but then she'd never had Belle beside her yet.

'She's hypnotized everyone,' Nancy managed to squeak out at Honey as around them the class chanted on. 'Does this happen often?'

'No, not so much. Not like this.'

'I love her. I love this class, but admit it, Honey. She's completely bonkers.'

Beside Nancy a woman was loudly chanting with Tora, 'Stretch, pulse, undulate, reach for the light.' The woman was saying it over and over again, eyes closed, building herself into a frenzy, her arms diving forwards, reaching for the light, her hair dishevelled, breasts bouncing, her cheeks flushed. 'Reach for the light,' she cried, wobbling on her feet. 'Oh, Jesus, reach for the light.'

Nancy caught Honey's eye again, struggling desperately to smother her laughter and failing completely.

'Reach for the—' And then, 'Oh—' the woman gasped. 'Oh, God.'

'Is she?' Nancy said disbelievingly. 'Oh Honey, she is, isn't she?'

'Yes,' cried the woman, 'yes, yes. Oh Jesus, yes.'

It was too much. Doubled up with laughter they dived back through the hedge, and threw themselves gratefully, giggling uncontrollably, onto the grass on the other side.

seven

LATE THE SAME morning Honey, Belle and Nancy wandered into the crowded Las Dalias market, and seeing it through Belle and Nancy's eyes, even the stalls full of tat had a magic that day. They wasted no time, swiftly plunging in, brushing their way through rails of hand-embroidered blouses and skirts, breathing in the bergamot and patchouli oil, moving from stall to stall, filling their bags not only with clothes, but also with dream-catchers, wooden toys, wind chimes and incense sticks.

'Where next?' Belle asked breathlessly when, an hour later, they'd finally completed the circuit.

'Nearly done,' Honey replied. 'And on the way out we'll pass my very favourite stall of all, but first . . . you have to meet Paris and Lucinda.'

'Is that a brand?'

'Almost,' Honey laughed. 'You'll love them. They've been here longer than anyone and they live in a white castle on a private island halfway between Ibiza and Formentera. They have elephants in their garden and they throw the most badly behaved parties ever.'

'Darling, darling,' Lucinda growled, taking a quick last drag on a Cuban cigar before tossing it away as Honey steered Belle and Nancy towards her stall. 'How absolutely marvellous to see you here.'

She prodded at the shaggy, white-haired man asleep on a deckchair beside her. 'Paris, wake up. Darling Honey's here.'

Lucinda made jewellery, *because we girls like wearing something pretty, darling.* She had dyed jet-black hair, painted eyebrows and very red lips, and mesmerizing blue eyes that now turned with interest to Nancy and Belle.

'Friends,' Honey insisted, warning her off.

'No, customers, darling, customers, how exciting.'

Tentatively Belle picked up a fine jade necklace that had a little round ceramic disc in the middle, held it up closer to see that in the middle was a tiny ceramic hairdryer, brush and a pair of scissors.

'Hairdresser's necklace, darling,' Lucinda explained. 'But that one's not selling so well. Surfers and fortune tellers sell brilliantly,' she flashed her blue eyes at Belle. 'Two-four-five-O, darling, twofourfiveoh. Say it fast and it doesn't sound so bad.'

'That's two thousand, four hundred and fifty euros,' Honey said, slowly in case Belle hadn't taken it in.

'Yes, darling,' Lucinda said, completely unabashed, 'worth every penny.'

Belle put down the necklace and picked up a silver charm bracelet strung with taps.

'Does this have a profession too?'

'No, darling, I just thought it would be fun.'

'And this?' Belle had picked up a brown leather belt with a heavy silver buckle and a fringe of little silver books.

'You must have heard of the Bible Belt?'

Nancy laughed delightedly and reached out for it.

'I want it,' said Belle, grabbing it off her.

'So do I,' protested Nancy.

'I have more, many more. I have the corn belt,' – Lucinda pulled a belt made of plaited straw out from beneath her desk – 'and Orion's Belt – that has a sword of course. And the green belt.' She held out a belt made half of what looked like real grass, and half a succession of grimy-looking tower blocks and chimney stacks. They're two-six-oh, darling, all the same price.' She flashed them both a sudden kind smile. 'But as you're friends of Honey's you can have them for fifty.'

From his chair Paris opened one eye, took in the

fact that three pretty girls had wandered in, and opened the other.

He stood up and looked at Nancy. 'Do I know you? Who are you? What time is it?'

'It's twelve,' said Belle.

'Oh, I don't recognize anyone until I've had my beer. What's your name again? Have we met before?'

A green belt, a bible belt and an invitation to one of Lucinda and Paris's infamous parties later, and the girls moved on, ambled their way back towards the exit and the main road, and then made one last stop at another of Honey's favourite stalls. This one was owned by a Spanish woman called Camila and it sold quilts and blankets, cot size to king size, cashmere and silk, fine and soft and incredibly warm, striped or checked in bright sea greens and turquoise blues then oversewn with wonderful collage-like pictures made from downy feathers or shells, scraps of velvet and taffeta, pearls and silver thread, all of them one-offs, each of them completely stunning.

Honey stood to one side, knowing Nancy and Belle were bound to love everything, and sat down in an empty deckchair just inside the stall, prepared for a long wait. And then, as she cast an idle eye around, immediately she saw what could only be *her* blanket right there in front of her, pinned to the sheet that divided the stall from the one next to it. It was big enough to cover her double bed in winter and so appropriate and so beautiful it had to have been made for her, with its aqua blues and greens like her bedroom and its picture was of her and Edouard, a boat sailing through a sunset-streaked sky, two indistinct figures sitting at the prow, gold and silver fish dancing in its wake.

She forced herself to look down at her hands instead and told herself *absolutely not*. Not only because it was far too intricate and carefully sewn to survive a trip on *Baby Jane* and then a night on Es Palmador unscathed, but probably much too expensive as well.

And she truly thought she'd convinced herself, even as she stood up and found herself interrupting a surprised Belle, mid-haggle, to ask Camila to bring the blanket down so that she might look at it more closely. And then, with just a quick glance to confirm it really was as beautiful as she thought it was and without even an attempt at a haggle herself, she heard herself interrupting Belle again to say that she would like it. Much to her own surprise, she was then quickly opening her bag with sweaty fingers and bringing out a roll of euros, counting them off, ignoring the astonished look on Belle's face and, less than two minutes later, and almost as if it hadn't happened at all, she was sitting again in the corner of the stall with the beautiful blanket now clasped safely on her lap.

Ten minutes later Belle had bought one too and only Nancy was still undecided.

'Come on, ditherer,' urged Belle, looking as if the heat and the crush had finally caught up with her. She shifted from foot to foot, rolled her eyes at Honey and mouthed bitterly, 'Paul,' and belatedly Honey understood. She stood up and went over to join Nancy, who was standing over Camila's desk, looking anxiously at the blanket spread out in front of her.

'You're not sure Paul will like it?'

Nancy's choice was of a blanket that looked like an old English garden, sewn with clusters of roses, made of silk taffeta, beautifully finished in shades from palest baby pink to dark rugosa red. There was a fat bumblebee climbing the sky, and a cup and saucer wittily sewn into the velvet green grass, but Honey resisted the desire to urge Nancy on, understanding that, however lovely it was, that was not the point.

'A bit too girly for him,' Nancy decided regretfully. She thanked Camila and turned away.

'But you don't even live with him,' Belle snapped from her place on Honey's chair. 'And it's your bedroom, your bed.' Nancy spun around and gave Belle a steely look. 'You should be able to put what you like on your own bed,' Belle insisted quietly.

'I know, but I'm not going to. Let's go.'

Belle stayed where she was, rubbed a hand across her hot forehead. 'The least you should do is buy it and stick it in a cupboard until you've got rid of him.'

'You think?'

Belle nodded and somehow managed to hold Nancy's angry stare. 'Yes, it's my bed,' Nancy said. 'But I want Paul in it too. So shut up.'

'All wrong, all wrong,' muttered Belle but she said nothing more, just pushed herself to her feet and Honey followed the two of them out of the market and back into the sunlight.

Heading towards the car, she hung back so that the other two could walk together. She watched Nancy, giggly, laughing, clearly ensuring the tension was immediately put behind the two of them. Was it lust for Paul that kept her at his side? Defiance in the face of too many people telling her to let him go? Either way Honey could no longer believe she was the defenceless little doll she'd witnessed the night before. However scary and threatening Paul had seemed, however much it had seemed she was in his thrall, Honey doubted it now.

Back at Can Falco Honey left them sitting on the

terrace with glasses of iced tea while she caught up with Claudio. They'd only been away for a couple of hours but she'd had the briefest of handover chats with him before she'd joined the Barely Yoga class and, towards the end of their tour around Las Dalias, niggles of concern had kept leaping into her mind. Ridiculous niggles: there was a couple desperate to buy the bed from their room. Could Honey sell it to them? They were checking out that afternoon and Honey had forgotten to talk to them about the bed. And a young woman who'd fallen in love with a dog she'd met on the beach. Could Honey organize its return to England? And practical niggles, too. They were running very low on charcoal for the barbecues – had she remembered to ask Claudio to order more?

Claudio had ordered the charcoal and had tried to persuade the couple to let him order them a new bed, exactly the same as the one they'd been sleeping in, but they were having none of it. He'd begun the laborious process of bringing the dog to England and two new waitresses had turned up for work the night before so coked up he'd had to fire them before they'd even started. It was a familiar enough catalogue of events, Honey hardly needed to react at all.

'And can you work the next three Saturday nights?' she asked instead.

They were standing side by side, looking at the diary open on her desk and at that he turned to her in surprise.

'Of course,' he nodded then. After all the times he'd teased her for working too hard, he was careful not to say anything else.

'And tonight too? Would you mind?'

'Absolutely not. I would be delighted.'

'Claudio?'

He turned and looked at her solemnly. 'Yes, Honey?'

'It's nothing to get excited about. I'm going out – stop acting like I've never done it before.'

At that a grin broke across his flawless honey-gold skin, his eyes with their thick fringe of black lashes laughing into hers. *Gorgeous*, she thought, startled by his beauty. *You are absolutely gorgeous. Nancy would be a fool to let you go.*

'I understand.'

She put the diary away in a drawer. 'I'm sailing to Es Palmador.'

He nodded again.

'Dad's helping me launch *Baby Jane* this afternoon.'

'Now you make me nervous.'

She laughed. 'I wondered. Do you want to come and have lunch with me and Nancy and Belle?'

'You mean now?' He looked back at her startled but, instantly, transparently keen. 'This lunch? Lunch today?'

She grinned back at him. 'Angela can watch reception. We can eat on the terrace and then she can grab us when something goes wrong.'

Honey had to bide her time, but after lunch her opportunity came. Stretching in her chair, first Belle sighed at the heat, then fanned herself with the wine list and, taking her chance, Honey bounced to her feet.

'Come for a swim?'

'No, I'd drown.'

'Belle,' she said impatiently, 'I've got half an hour, then I'm back on duty. Claudio's taking the afternoon off, so come and swim with me now.'

At Honey's words Nancy stretched back in her chair and closed her eyes, clearly in no mood to move herself, and Belle belatedly got it. 'Swimming! Of course I want to go swimming.'

Honey turned to Claudio. 'Don't go back to reception, please. Angela knows where we are. If you're covering for me tonight you must take a proper break now. I'm going to tell her to give you another hour.'

She saw that he was aware of what she was doing and

that he couldn't quite believe it. The look on his face made her laugh inside. She'd crossed a line with Claudio that day but all she could wonder was why it had taken so long. It had felt so right. They'd eaten together many times before, shared lunches, sometimes alone, other times with guests, but she'd never strayed into his personal life, certainly wouldn't have plonked the object of his affections down in front of him, actively gone out of her way to make it happen. And perhaps it had been triggered by the desire to prise Nancy away from Paul, but it was her affection for Claudio that she was aware of now. And having watched the two of them flirting over lunch, there was no doubt at all that she'd helped set something in motion between them. How far Nancy would allow it to go she'd have to wait to see.

When she arrived at the pool she found Belle already in the water doing lengths, her bag on a nearby sunbed. Honey pulled off her kaftan and sat down in a spotted blue bikini, then flipped up her legs and lay back, closing her eyes, trying to ignore the guilty voice telling her that she shouldn't be there, she should be inside, that whatever she'd said about Angela, Angela was next to useless and manning reception alone would terrify her. She closed her eyes against the sun and forced herself to lie still.

A few seconds later Belle lay down beside her,

spraying her with welcome droplets of water. 'Do you ever go topless here?'

Honey shook her head, shielding her eyes from the sun.

'Not unless you're doing a Barely Yoga class, you mean?'

Honey grinned. 'Wasn't it fun?'

'Absolutely brilliant. I'll be there again tomorrow – if you don't mind. Your mother said I was a natural. I told her I'd booked my place. You know, I wonder if I could persuade them to take it up at Esporta.' Then moments later she sighed heavily. 'My God this is bliss. How do you ever do any work?' There was the briefest of silences while Belle waited for Honey to respond and then she went straight on.

'OK, Honeybee Ballantyne, what are you up to?'

'What are you talking about?'

'I'm not talking about Nancy and Claudio. We both know the score there . . . have to cross our fingers and hope.'

Honey could think of nothing to say and so she just lay there, letting the sun beat down on her face, waiting for whatever Belle was going to say next.

'I'm talking about Edouard.'

The truth was she didn't want to talk or think about him. Edouard was about this evening. This was now.

'You'd have seduced him years ago if you'd wanted to,' Belle went on, forcing Honey to open her eyes. 'But I can't help thinking that's what you've got in mind for tonight.'

'Wrong, wrong, wrong.' She shut her eyes against Belle's inquisitive stare.

'I don't think so. You're taking him to a deserted island for the night. How romantic is that?'

'We have a history there.'

'Honey, please! Don't you think he's attractive?'

'Of course I do.' Honey sighed, took her time. 'But we've always been too close. We're like bro—'

'Oh no, don't say it.'

Now Honey turned her head back towards her. 'It sounds like a cliché but I mean it. For years he was much too important for me to think of him in any other way. Edouard and I have known each other all our lives and you have to understand how it was here. Both of us are only children. Both sets of parents lived in permanent la-la land. We only had each other. We'd spend all our time together.' Unconsciously she'd pushed herself upright in her chair as she spoke because from nowhere it was now very important that Belle understood how it had been. 'We'd go off camping, take a rucksack and come back after a couple of days and they wouldn't have realized we'd gone. Can you imagine that? How could they? We were only about ten. That's what I mean when I say we were important to each other.'

Belle didn't answer, but looked at her solemnly.

'Actually in a way it was fantastic. We used to have adventures, do amazing things.' She hesitated, wondering how bizarre her life might be sounding to Belle and how much more she wanted to tell her, after all. 'And then Edouard's parents grew up a bit, started to act more like parents, while if anything mine went even more loopy and unreliable.' She frowned. 'So what I'm saying is that if I hadn't had Edouard around I'd have become a very strange child and a completely deranged teenager.'

'And you never fancied him?'

'Probably I did. I've kissed him. I even went out with him for about a week, when we were about fourteen, until we both decided it was time we found somebody else.'

'He told me about that. Oh, I'm sorry.' Belle laughed at the surprise on Honey's face. 'Not in any detail. Just told me about the tosser you went out with next, Jerome? Was that his name?'

She giggled. 'I can't believe Edouard told you about Jerome!'

'Tell me about Edouard,' Belle insisted. 'So tonight

you'll camp together, lie on some beach together, but, just to be clear, it's only for old times' sake?'

'Exactly.' Honey carefully lay back down on her sunbed and closed her eyes once more. 'Now talk about something else.'

'Haven't you ever wondered what Edouard makes of you now?'

'No.'

Belle dropped her sunglasses back over her eyes and lay back to the sun.

'I don't believe you. And I'm sure it'll muddle you up no end but I'm going to tell you what I think even so.'

'Please don't.'

'You *have* to hear it, Honey. Because if you're not interested in him, what are you planning to do on that island? You'll sit him down on the beach, you'll talk, watch the stars, drink some wine . . . and then? What do you want to happen?'

'I suppose we'll fall asleep.'

'That's ridiculous.'

'No!'

'Be honest with yourself. Last time you were on Es Palmador you kissed him. I know because he told me.'

Honey put her hand over her mouth. 'Oh God, was it there?'

'You know it was.'

'So?' she asked defiantly. 'We were sitting by the fire. I'd split up with my boyfriend and I wanted him to see me kiss someone else. That's why it happened. Edouard kissed me as a favour. It may seem strange to you, Belle, but that's all it was.'

Belle wasn't convinced. 'So you're telling me, of all the places on the island, you two have just *happened* to choose to go back there? But it doesn't have any special significance for either of you?'

'Es Palmador is not our special place. We kissed each other, no big deal. That's what we did, that's what everybody did. I've probably kissed him on lots of other beaches too, only I can't remember doing it. So don't try and prove anything, Belle, because there's nothing to prove. Edouard thinks the same way as me. We chose Es Palmador because we had happy times there. The kissing does not come into it.'

eight

THERE WERE two very different sides to Ibiza. In the south was the clubbers' paradise, around the bay of San Antonio, twenty-four-seven music and dancing. It was easy to spend a holiday there and never venture out of town. But high in the hills, the wind in the pine forests was still the only sound you heard and the wildlife was of the natural variety. Little had changed here since Tanit, goddess of fecundity, was first worshipped and the Phoenician and Carthaginian settlers sailed past Benirras Beach and stayed for the sunset.

Little had changed for two thousand years and yet in the last few decades Ibiza's peaceful and tolerant spirit had been stirred like never before and this time the marauding pirates were the money men, Mammon colliding with Tanit, greed colliding with generosity, bulldozers churning through the almond blossom to make way for new roads, threatening the Full-Moon and Petal parties with the all-night roar of a motorway.

And for Honey, sitting on the harbour wall in her sarong, swinging her legs as she waited for Edouard and thinking about such things, the thought of Paul and Anna now also looking to make their mark on the island made her sick. Hypocritically clothed in eco-speak, it was as if Anna thought a cursory nod to the green lobby was all that was necessary to make her ideas attractive. The truth was it was the Annas and Pauls with too much money and too little sensitivity who could ruin Ibiza in the end. And where exactly did Edouard stand? Shoulder to shoulder with the two of them? Clearly there was some sort of relationship developing and she knew she wouldn't like the details if she was ever told what they were. She didn't want to doubt him, and yet wasn't that why she was here, waiting on the harbour wall for him now, knowing it was time to reimpress upon him the values that they'd grown up with? Because she did doubt him. He'd clearly been impressed with Paul and for all the brushing-Anna-aside when Honey had challenged him, Honey thought he rated her still. So taking him to Es Palmador was as much about proving how wrong he was to give Anna the time of day – let alone a free rein with his house, let alone any influence at all on Ibiza – as it was about their own past together.

With much affected grunting and groaning Hughie

had finally launched *Baby Jane* into the sea, but because he had been so slow leaving Can Falco there were now just a few minutes left before Edouard was due to join her at the harbour. As Hughie had struggled to launch the boat she'd been tight-lipped with irritation, and all her good intentions of walking with him to Montesol afterwards, to put him at his ease and spend some quality time together, had vanished in her irritation. She hadn't even told him that she might join him and, understandably, Hughie had not hung around, almost running back up the hill towards a rendezvous with Troy and Maggie and, no doubt, Marianne Darlington too, as relieved to see the back of her as he was of *Baby Jane*.

She saw Edouard before he saw her, watched him slipping purposefully between the wandering holiday-makers, making his way down the street towards her. Today he was wearing shorts and a pink T-shirt and carried with him two fishing rods, and his air of purpose made him stand out. She could see people noticing him. Slipping off the harbour wall, she stood up to meet him.

'I thought *Baby Jane* had gone to heaven,' he said, peering over the harbour wall to look down at their boat.

'She's been brought back from the dead by Dad.'

'And was I hallucinating or did you invite Shimmy Roberts to join us too? I'm sure I just saw him making his way down here.'

The throaty growl of a Harley Davidson drowned out her denial and she turned away from Edouard to see Shimmy manoeuvring carefully through the crowds of people towards them. He was wearing just a pair of scuffed black leather trousers and his bare torso was as wrinkled and brown as a dried nut. A red spotted bandanna held back his rocker-length grey hair. With a final revving of the engine he arrived beside Honey then dropped his feet to the ground to balance the bike.

'Glad I caught you,' he said, scratching an armpit, directing all his attention to Honey, ignoring Edouard completely. 'Heard you'd got no flares. Heard you'd got no boat either, but you didn't fancy *Nervous Wreck*.'

'No, I didn't fancy her at all, Shimmy,' Honey agreed.

A reluctant twinkle came into his eye. 'I suppose I don't blame you, though I can't believe *Baby Jane*'s any better.' With a lopsided grin he unflipped a saddlebag, then dropped a firework into her arms. It was a rocket – *Triple Whistling*, she read on the label – red and gold and looking big enough to reach the moon. 'Fire it if you need me. I'll come and find you if I see this in the sky.'

He spoke in a quiet drawl you had to strain to hear.

As long as she'd known him, Honey had never heard him raise his voice.

'Thank you,' she laughed. 'And of course I'll have Edouard here to help me out.'

Now that he was forced to acknowledge Edouard he gave him a dismissive nod. 'Who'd a thought it?'

'I know,' agreed Edouard cheerfully. 'Look at us two, sailing into the sunset together.'

'You take good care of her,' Shimmy glowered at Edouard, as suspicious and resentful of him now as he had always been, with no more cause now than he had had before. He turned the key to his bike and the engine roared back into life. Raising a hand in farewell to Honey and lifting his feet, they watched and waited as he wove back through the crowd and disappeared.

'You know, I'd say he likes me now,' Edouard declared as he carried the cool boxes and blankets over to the boat. 'He really seemed to care.'

Then he took a running jump and landed heavily on the bottom of *Baby Jane*, causing the boat to tip violently from side to side.

'Pinstripe arse,' said Honey.

Edouard had brought the booze and she'd brought the picnic – apricots, figs, almonds and grapes from the gardens at Can Falco, bread, sweet round potatoes to cook on the fire, packets of butter and herbs, tomatoes and freshly caught fish that tasted like heaven when barbecued on the beach. And for breakfast the next morning she'd brought orange juice and rolls, a frying pan, bacon and eggs – for all that she'd never lived in England, she was an English girl at heart.

They sailed out of the harbour, the wind strong enough to fill *Baby Jane*'s sails and lift Honey's spirits just the same. They sat on opposite sides of the boat, Edouard's face turned to the open sea, and Honey watched him close his eyes to the wind as his streaky hair blew back from his face, and she saw that he loved it already and wondered if maybe Es Palmador was about to work its magic after all.

They crossed the water without a mishap and by the time they reached Es Palmador it was six and the sky was turning pink. In the shallows they jumped off *Baby Jane* and pulled her up onto the beach. There was a place in the dunes that they had always made for, sheltered and yet open to the sky, close enough to the water to hear the shush-shush of the sea, and now, years after they'd been here last and without even needing to discuss it, this was of course where they headed for.

After several trips back to *Baby Jane* to get everything up to their camp, Honey spread the old tartan blankets on the sand and finally brought out her new blanket, parcelled up in tissue paper.

'What is that?' Edouard asked.

In answer, she ripped off the paper and shook out the blanket, then laid it carefully down upon the other blankets.

Edouard spent a few moments taking it in, then came over to Honey and slipped his arm around her shoulders. 'It's us. It's you and me!' He bent down to see her face and she nodded her agreement. 'How sweet that you brought it. It's beautiful.' She grinned back at him. 'And so is here.' He raised his eyebrows at her, making her laugh. 'And so are we, *beautiful*, and so are you,' he dropped his voice again, '*beautiful*,' he said softly.

'Shut up silly man,' she replied, laughing still.

'You know we're going to have fun?'

'More than fun. We're going to make you sixteen again.'

He nodded. 'And you too.'

He turned away from her and dropped to his knees beside the cool box. 'Beer, wine, champagne?' he asked. 'A little Vino Tinto? What did you used to like?'

'Bailey's Irish Cream,' she admitted, laughing again.

He rummaged, found a corkscrew and a bottle of wine, then sat back on his heels to open it for her, as completely at home as she'd known he would be, sand on his long brown feet and brushed up against his legs, his pink T-shirt wrapped around his strong muscular body by the breeze.

She turned back to the sea and undid her sarong. The cotton was so fine that the wind caught it and made it stream out from her like a long pink sail. Underneath she was wearing a white bikini, fifties style with a halter neck top and a big square tortoiseshell buckle between her breasts. Holding the sarong high above her head as the wind whipped against her hair, she fought it for a moment and she knew that Edouard had stopped what he was doing and was watching her. And then she let it go and the sarong dipped like a kite before the wind blew it upwards into the sky and away across the sand dunes.

'After it!' Edouard declared with a shout, dropping everything and running, racing up a sand dune, then leaping out of sight with a rush of laughter, half cry, half shout. Honey tore after him, leaping and falling, running again. They found the sarong almost immediately but in an instant they'd become children again, climbing to the tops of the sand dunes to take it in turns to wave it and let it go again, then running, leaping into the air, rolling into the sand at the bottom, so that sand went everywhere, up their noses and in their mouths, their hair, their ears, down her bikini and Edouard's shorts.

Then, exhausted, they staggered towards the sea, Edouard stripping off his T-shirt and tossing it back onto the beach before diving into the silky warm water, disappearing underneath. They ducked under and swam side by side, Honey's long hair streaming out behind her like a mermaid's, opening their eyes in the salt water to grin at each other before bursting back to the surface. She felt for the bottom with her toes, then pushed her hair back from her face, eyes shining, and Edouard took two clumsy steps towards her and pulled her under again.

As darkness fell they lit a fire and lay on the rugs, opposite each other, propped up against the old cushions they'd brought from *Baby Jane*, watching the stars and the flickering fire, smoking a little grass and drinking wine from two crystal glasses Honey had purloined from Can Falco – after all, what was the point of having such beautiful things for all the guests if they couldn't occasionally be used by her?

'Last time I was here you kissed me,' Edouard said, lifting the frying pan onto the fire. 'Right there.' He pointed to a patch of sand a few feet away from him. 'You do remember that, don't you?'

'Belle reminded me about it yesterday.'

'But you hadn't forgotten.'

'No.'

On hands and knees she crossed over to him and kissed him again but this time on the cheek, not the lips.

He touched the place with his hand. 'First time felt better, you know.'

'Too bad.'

She turned and lay down beside him and stretched out, resting her head against his bare shoulder, knowing that she was being unfair coming so close, but unable to stop herself all the same. 'Roman Castilia,' she said, remembering the name of the boyfriend she'd just split up from, who'd prompted her kiss with Edouard. 'He deserved it too. I can't even think what he was like now.'

She felt his arm pull her closer.

'Hot and sweaty,' he said.

'What?'

'That's what he was like. That's what we used to call him, me and all your friends, when we used to laugh about him behind your back.'

She looked up at him. 'No, you did not laugh. He was a God.'

'You know he couldn't swim?'

'Of course he could. He was a fine swimmer.'

Edouard shook his head. 'I remember distinctly.'

She relaxed against his shoulder, sipping at her wine. He was making her laugh, and laughing made her want to kiss him so badly it almost overwhelmed her. She wanted to stretch out on top of him and kiss him and kiss him. And she wanted to tell him too. *I can't believe how badly I want to kiss you Edouard*, she wanted to say, but of course she didn't.

Years ago, when they'd lain here before a flickering fire, their friends had been close by. She'd leaned over him, catching him completely unawares. And as she'd softly touched her lips to his, she'd seen the surprise in his face turn swiftly to pleasure and passion and abruptly she'd stopped again.

'Why?' he'd asked, lying flat on his back staring up into her face.

'Because I know Roman is watching me.'

It had been a thoughtless thing to do, even if she hadn't seen until too late how much Edouard had cared. At seventeen he hadn't been able to disguise his feelings quite so well.

Now the older Edouard, mature, grown-up Edouard, who had got so good at hiding his feelings and thoughts she hardly knew him at all, shifted comfortably beside her.

'Remember James Bream's sunburnt buttocks?'

She laughed out loud in thankful relief. 'They had a baby, didn't they?'

He nodded. 'Him and Miranda Henson.'

'And do you remember the plague of wasps?'

'That wasn't here, that was Formentera.'

He nodded. 'The jellyfish were here.'

'Stung that American guy who was allergic to sand.'

'You'd think he'd have found that out before he came here.'

'Didn't he have such a bad weekend?'

'He did.'

Edouard gently disentangled his arm and sat up, stretching forwards to flick a knob of butter into the frying pan.

Honey sniffed appreciatively. 'Even butter smells delicious here. Have we died and gone to heaven?' Then she lay back again against the cushions, watching him as he rolled the butter around the pan. 'You have to admit, Edouard . . . We've proved it already. It's as lovely as it always was.'

'I do admit.' He opened the cool box and found the fish, dropping them one by one into the sizzling butter then squirting them with lemon.

'And we've only just begun. Remember, we haven't

even touched on Cala Mastella and Santa Medea . . . So you have also to admit that you should spend some more time here, that you need to say, "Sod the job".'

'Oh, Honey,' he turned to her, shaking his head with disappointment, 'don't you realize you're going to have to try much harder than that?'

'I'm not so sure. I think Es Palmador's working its magic on you. Salt in your hair, sand between your toes, your sweet happy face . . . I'm beginning to recognize you again now.'

He sat back on his heels and looked at her with affection and amusement. 'Look who's talking, Bee Ballantyne.'

She knew what he meant. She felt different too, better, younger, sillier, ready to start again.

She looked around her, gave the sand an appreciative pat. 'It's true. I needed to come here as much as you did.'

He moved the fish off the fire and wrapped the end of a towel around the skewers and pulled their potatoes free from the fire too, then dropped them into a bowl. Honey pushed herself up and brought out the tomatoes from the cool box, chopped them roughly, then added olive oil and salt and ripped-up basil, and poured them both another glass of wine.

With their plates in their hands, they sat back against the cushions once more and Edouard gave her back his arm, eating his food one-handed.

'But what I've always wondered is why you had to go so suddenly.'

She'd started conversationally, not acknowledging that perhaps this was an area to be avoided, only realizing when the words were said and it was too late. This conversation had begun in the sea at Edouard's party, but this time there were no distractions and suddenly she wanted to know the answer, wanted to know why he'd gone, wanted him to tell her the truth.

'So why didn't you come back for nearly six years?'

'It was time to grow up.'

She frowned at him in surprise. 'You sound sad. Were you unhappy? Did something keep you away?' And as she asked she was trying to remember the last days before he'd left but those days were hazy and indistinct. All she could know for sure was that by then she'd been thrown into the struggle at home. For her the halcyon days had already gone. 'At times I wondered if you were angry with my life at Can Falco, with Tora and Hughie for keeping me there all the time, but I can't believe it was that. You knew I couldn't be anywhere else—'

'Of course I didn't mind. I was sorry for you.'

'Then explain!'

'At times I was happier in Ibiza than anywhere else.'

'So why go?'

Her words hung in the air and all the laughter had gone from his face . . .

'Why do you keep asking that question when we've both always known the answer?'

She went very still because of course he was right. Probably she'd always understood but still she didn't know what to do about it. She couldn't meet him but she couldn't turn away, and after a few long seconds it was Edouard who got to his feet and walked away, climbing up the dune with his plate in his hand. He stopped at the top and looked towards the sea and the darkening sky and something in the way he was standing – so still, so close and yet so remote – made her rise to her feet and she would have joined him but he raised a hand, warning her to stay still, and she faltered and then she heard it too, the faint buzz of a motorboat.

At first it was intermittent. The sound occasionally carried on the wind, so that for a while neither of them spoke, both desperately hoping that they were picking up sounds from the mainland or perhaps the engine of a small plane, but as the moments passed it grew louder and more insistent. It was a motorboat heading their way.

'Shimmy?' Edouard suggested, clutching at straws.

Honey shook her head. 'No chance.'

The plummeting disappointment meant that for a moment she couldn't speak. Thunder, lightning, swarms of wasps or biting sandflies, nothing could ruin the intimacy of their deserted island the way other people would. And the sound got louder and louder as the boat came in to shore and then the engine was cut and for a few last moments there was silence before the sound of the engine was replaced by wild whoops and laughter, accompanied by loud, throbbing trance music.

'They won't have seen *Baby Jane*,' he said moving on through the sand dunes to get a better look. 'They've landed around the corner. Our boat's out of sight.'

'Why does that matter?' She scrabbled after him. 'If they know we're here perhaps they'll leave.'

'No, Honey, they'll invite us to join the party.'

'And if we were sixteen again we'd probably say yes.'

'Will they notice our fire?'

'Probably not.'

As she spoke the sound crescendoed still more.

'If we were sixteen again they wouldn't be here,' he shouted back to her. 'People fucking knew not to do things like this back then. This wouldn't have happened when we were sixteen.'

'They sound as if they're coming right over. They're

going to dance straight through our camp. Can you hear them talking? Are they Brits?'

'No, they are fucking not.'

'Spanish?'

'No!' he shouted furiously. 'They're not staying here. They're not doing this. They're going to leave.'

In sudden panic she ran to catch him. 'You can't, Edouard. Don't. They're not going to go, whatever you say, and, you don't know, they might beat you up for asking. You can't confront them when there's only the two of us.'

He hesitated, knowing it was true, and looked bleakly down to the beach.

'Hey.' She caught his arm. 'I'm sorry, I'm so sorry.'

But some of her wasn't. Some of her was grateful to them for the breathing space they'd just given her because their arrival had halted Honey and Edouard's conversation just as it had begun to make her heart thump with nerves, panic, excitement, just as it had begun to get serious, and of course Edouard had known that too. He had been right: she had known why he'd left Ibiza so abruptly, six years before. He'd left because of her, because six years ago, when she'd kissed him there in the sand dunes, so close to where they were standing now, she'd had a moment of choice: to kiss him some more or to pull away.

And now six years later, here they were again, and she'd been about to be kissed again, by a different Edouard, an Edouard who'd been gone a long time and had come home a different man.

He allowed her a small smile. 'Honey, if you start dancing to this music I will never ever speak to you again.'

'It's Infected Mushroom. Don't you like them?'

She left him alone for a moment, turned and went back to their camp, picked up her beautiful new blanket and wrapped it around her shoulders, then climbed back up to join him.

Below them the group had stopped on the sand. There were about ten of them, a few already spread-eagled on the beach, two women dancing together, while back at their boat three men and another girl were bringing the last of their provisions ashore.

'Hardly anybody knows about this place . . .' She looked down at them all. 'And those that do would never vandalize it like this. Everyone agrees you don't bring music here. You're right, this would never have happened before.'

He nodded. 'It's what I was saying, isn't it? Times are changing. Nothing's the same as it was.'

For a few moments they stood side by side, watching the beach. 'So shall we fire the rocket at them? Shimmy did say it should be used in emergencies.' He looked down at her blankly. 'Perhaps it'll scare them away.'

At least she'd made him smile. 'You're not serious?'

'Yes.'

He slid back down to their camp, found the rocket, lifted it up and waved it at her. 'You realize they'll probably love it?'

'Perhaps it'll bring Shimmy. That would surely scare them off.' She looked more closely at the box, reading the instructions. 'I say fire the bloody rocket, Edouard. Teach them a lesson.'

'Oh, Bee,' he sighed, coming forwards impulsively. 'You know that I adore you, don't you?'

'I adore you too. And not up into the air either. Aim it straight at them.'

'So is our conversation over?' He was standing so close, less than an arm's length away. 'The one about you and me, is it over before it even began?'

'No,' she looked back at him. 'It's not. But we're not having that conversation here, not now tonight. We've lost our chance. This lot have made sure of that.'

She could still have moved towards him but she didn't and in the end he took the firework and ripped off the red paper it was sealed in, then jammed the launching stick into the sand, steadied it, pointed it carefully straight up to the sky and well away from the crowd on the beach, fished in his jeans for his lighter and lit it. Together they took two steps back and held their breath, waited, waited and then with an exhilarating whoosh the rocket ignited.

'Go,' Honey encouraged it, willing it on. 'Go, baby, go!'

But it didn't go anywhere, just toppled onto its side and lay in the sand, hissing half-heartedly, spouting a miserable scattering of orange stars all of six inches into the air.

'Can you believe it?' Edouard said with disgust.

'The story of our night,' Honey watched it sadly. 'Not with a bang but with a whimper.'

And as if in response the music from the beach rose in volume drowning out his answer, loud enough to reach San Antonio.

'I hate them,' he said venomously.

'Let it go. They're only having fun.' She went over to him and opened the big blanket and pulled him inside, lifting her arms around his shoulders so that the two of them were wrapped together, on the top of their sand dune, silhouetted against the sky. 'Perhaps they'll get so stoned they'll fall asleep and we'll be able to creep down and turn it all off.'

In answer he carefully settled the blanket back

around her shoulders, tucking it in around her throat, then gently turned her back towards their camp.

'You sending me off to sleep?' she asked.

'You want to try to go home?'

She shook her head. Slowly she made her way back down to their fire and sat down and waited for him to join her, but for a long time he stayed at the top of the sand dune, with his back to her, watching the party below. They'd come to the brink of the big conversation and she'd stalled and now, understandably, she could feel he was slipping away, all the intimacy that had built up between them sucked into the repetitious morphing beat that never stopped, music that made her feel as if she was spinning out of control, going mad with the sound.

Which was why when he finally came sliding back down the sand dune to join her, lay down on the blanket to face her, she felt she had to pick another subject, what felt like a safer, far less emotive subject. And so she asked him about Anna and Paul, and what were the evil plans being concocted by the three of them?

He took a long time answering, just propped his head on his hand and stared back at her for ages, so that eventually she gave up on waiting for an answer and started to study his face instead, his lashes thick as sable, his eyes so wide and serious, the skin across his cheek-bones slightly flushed from too much sun . . . and then abruptly her thoughts came back to him, and she concentrated again, as she realized that he still had not answered her.

'Paul is planning a new club for the island.' He said it very quietly but he was so close of course she heard every word. 'He'd been waiting for a site for years and finally one came up about five months ago and I'm going to help him develop it. He and Anna have worked together before, there've been a couple of places in America and Monaco, super clubs that can take five thousand people a night. Pure will be much smaller than that.' He spoke quietly but she could hear the tension in his voice, and at that moment he bore no resemblance to the Edouard who'd been sitting with her just half an hour before. Now it was as if he thought he was speaking with a stopwatch, as if he imagined he had just a certain time to make his pitch. 'Paul needed someone like me, who knew the island but also under-stood the financial implications of what he was plan-ning. You wouldn't believe his plans.' And it was then that she realized the truth of what she was hearing. It wasn't tension she was picking up in his voice. It was pure undiluted excitement. 'The returns are going to be over 800 per cent. It's a complete no-brainer.'

'A super club in Ibiza? Didn't a few others get there first?'

'Not a Privilege or even a Pacha, much smaller than both of them, but still with the best sound in the world. It'll be a club for the twenty-first century.'

'You mean it'll be green? Composting toilets and biodegradable foam parties?'

'Don't mock it, Honey.'

'I'm sorry but it sounds ridiculous.'

'You mean you've decided that already? I knew you would.'

'Why do you say that?'

Gone was the intimacy that had brought them so far. Wariness on Edouard's part and instinctive hostility on Honey's swept in to take its place.

'Because you don't like Paul,' he said. 'So you're going to hate anything he comes up with.'

'No, I don't.' She pushed herself upright so that she was sitting facing him cross-legged.

'Yes. You took one look at him, sitting there in his city-slicker pinstripes, and you decided you didn't like him before he even opened his mouth.'

'No, actually. It was when I realized he was a complete shit.'

She looked away from him finding it hard to believe he could be so ready for a fight, as if he'd been thinking and feeling all this for ages before, and was relishing the chance to say it now. She tried again. 'What are you accusing me of?'

'Being a snob.'

'No.'

'You're right about Paul,' he went on. 'But that doesn't change a thing because I'm talking about you. It started about five years ago. And since then you've got worse. It's what Ibiza's done to you, made you laugh at people who work in an office, carry a briefcase, commute, wear a suit.' She shook her head and opened her mouth to deny it, but Edouard had hit his stride and carried straight on. 'Of course you are. You think we're missing out on what's real, that we're living these shallow, two-dimensional lives. That we're all about money and greed. Come back to Ibiza and get a life, as if Ibiza's the only place where it's possible to *find yourself*. But the truth is that guys like Paul and everybody else staying in my house this weekend, they're not really any different from you. But you don't want to believe that, do you? You and your chilled-out friends want to clap around the campfires and despise everyone else, all those suits who haven't got hold of their inner rainbow. The truth is, Honey, we'd all quite like to give up our ride on the tube on a Monday morning for a life here,

banging drums, but it doesn't work like that for everyone, even if it has for you.'

He stared back at her, with a defiant look in his
eye that told her she was right. He was glad he'd said
it.

'Banging drums, I wish.'

'I'm not saying you don't work hard.'

'Longer days than you've ever managed, I'm sure.
And I never get a holiday and I never go away and, yes,
sometimes this place feels like a prison. But just because
I don't wear a suit, and I have flip-flops on my feet and
I work in the sunshine and don't live in London, Paris
or New York, you think my hard work doesn't count.
And you're saying *I'm* the snob? Paul's suit had nothing
to do with it. I disliked him because he was a violent
smartarse and I think he'd like to kill someone and I
think his weasel of a friend would probably have sat
back and watched that too. And the thought of him
getting his hands on an inch of Ibiza makes me feel
quite sick . . . And the thought that you are helping
him do it makes it even worse.'

'It's a good idea. I've seen the plans and it will be
stunning.'

'You've sold your soul to the devil.'

'Probably.'

She shrugged. 'So get building. It's your choice. You knew how I'd react. You had your speech all planned.'

He looked uncertain for the first time. 'Even so I was hoping you might be involved . . . I was dreading telling you, but I figured if in the end I persuaded you to join me it would be worth the mauling first.'

'Sorry, but you'd better count me out.'

'Wait. Listen to me first. Yes, Paul is a complete bastard, loud, aggressive, massive ego, but he's also the most effective, energetic, imaginative person I've ever worked with and perhaps you shouldn't turn your back on him and me quite so fast. He has vision, sensitivity and bucket loads of cash, and what he's planning on doing, with me or without me, with you or without you, will be knock-out spectacular. I think you'd be proud to be involved. And he wants you, Honey, when he and Anna saw Can Falco . . .'

'He came to Can Falco, with you and Anna when I wasn't there?'

He nodded. 'Don't look like I was betraying you. As you say, you weren't there. And of course he was completely stunned by what you've done. It's what he wants for Pure. And he's right. Nobody could make it as beautiful as you could. Anna doesn't know it, but Paul would hand over all the design to you. You could have a free hand to do whatever you wanted. And Honey, please . . .' now he knew she was listening all the antagonism had gone from his voice. 'Please don't reject it without giving it a chance. Come with me and meet them both, talk about it. Anna's design company Green and Pleasant is the best. Everybody wants to work with her. You shouldn't walk away without giving her a chance.'

She'd been too hasty. Edouard was right. She'd jumped at the obvious, behaved like the Ibiza snob he'd said she was, when what was wrong with another club on Ibiza, the island of clubs, especially one that at least attempted to be environmentally sympathetic? And if Paul wanted to involve her, what could she lose? Imaginative, effective, energetic businessman that Paul was, perhaps together they could make something special.

'So where's the site?' she asked.

'OK, Paul will build the club in Santa Medea.'

And instantly she was there. The pine forest rising steeply up behind her. She was standing on a rocky cliff path high above the sea, staring down at the tiny idyllic bay below her, the sliver of sand, curved like a baby's fingernail, cradling the turquoise water of the sea.

She said the first thing that came into her head. 'But it's so small and so pretty.' Her voice sounded small too, constricted by the shock. Then she came swiftly to her senses and grinned to show she hadn't been fooled. 'Where's the site, somewhere in San Antonio?'

He gave her a thin smile back. 'No, it really is Santa Medea.'

Somehow she managed to stumble out the words, 'But he can't build a club there.'

'Bee, don't get precious about it, please.'

Green and Pleasant, green and pleasant. Green pine forests, thousands of acres, stretching towards the sea, perfect in their uniformity. Didn't Edouard remember that Ibicencos shouted their news to the pine forests and would wait for the reply that would come shivering, whispering back in the breeze? Now she imagined the sound of bulldozers, the scream of chainsaws, clouds of smoke, open wounds across the hillside, huge cranes appearing on the skyline.

'There's nothing there, Honey, nothing to spoil,' Edouard insisted. 'It's not like Salinas. There's nothing to Santa Medea but a strip of beach below and the forest above.'

Who are you? She wanted to shake him. *What have you done with the real Edouard Bonnier?*

'Look at the campaign against the motorway,' she said woodenly. 'People will fight.'

He nodded. 'Yes, look at the campaign against the motorway.'

She turned away because despite the protests and the marches, the placards and the banners, the motorway had gone ahead.

'Paul's on to it,' Edouard went on. 'He knows the right people. And Bee, what's there to ruin, I don't understand? There's nothing to spoil. What's so special about Santa Medea?'

It was as if he'd been waiting for exactly this response, for she was after all the small-minded child of the island, the hippy chick, so predictable, saying everything she was programmed to say. Of course he'd known he'd shock her, that she'd wave her arms around and protest a bit – it was, after all, exactly what she'd been programmed to do. But she'd come around, he must have thought there was hope that he'd persuade her to change her mind, for him to bother to tell her at all. She wondered if, after all, this was the only reason he'd brought her here. Not to seduce her but to make money with her, out of her.

'Have you been to Santa Medea recently?' she asked. He shook his head. 'So this strip of sand and a forest, that's just a memory, and a distant one at that?'

He stiffened. 'I do know the place, Honey. I may not have been there for years but I lived here, too.'

'Don't you think you should go there and see it again before you build all over it?'

'I'm going to.'

'Oh I see! That's why you chose it for another of our dates. What did you think? That we'd pace out the plans together while we were there? Decide where to put the dance floor? And what about that annoying little problem called planning *permission*? You do realize people will feel strongly about this, there'll be marches, petitions—'

'The plans were approved six weeks ago.'

'I don't believe you!' she shouted furiously. 'We'd have known. We'd have heard something.'

He shrugged. 'I can't help it if you didn't.'

Could it really be true? Could Paul really have managed that? She thought back to the man she'd observed at the pool, remembered his bulldozing force and relentless self-interest, and thought he probably could.

'So what did he do? Backhanders wouldn't work. Not at this level.'

'Not everybody thinks like you do. Lots of people support us.'

'How did he do it?'

'By being innovative, ambitious and exciting. Pure will be like nowhere else you've ever seen. Other people recognize that.'

'And that's the name?'

He nodded. 'Because the sound will be pure – we've retained the best acoustics designer in the world. And the structure will be pure too. That's what makes it unique. Anna will make it the most ecologically advanced, environmentally friendly building ever.'

'If you want to be environmentally friendly don't build it.'

'Biodegradable foam parties.'

She laughed bitterly. 'And you're serious, aren't you?'

He nodded. 'Pure will be solar-powered, of course, and there'll be minimal light pollution and everything will be built from natural materials.'

'Composting toilets?'

'Oh, for fuck's sake. I knew you'd be like this.'

He went to stand, but she caught his arm.

'No, don't go. It's too important.'

'What's the point in talking any more? I hoped you'd understand. I suppose I knew you wouldn't.'

'Edouard, please. You must have some doubts, any doubts at all.'

'Even if I did, it's going to happen anyway.'

'So you do have doubts, a doubt, even one?'

'Isn't it better that we're involved and can help control it?'

'People used that argument to go to war.'

'Oh, Honey!' he exploded. 'You're bright, you're brilliant but you're so predictable. I thought you might just want to work with me on this. I had this silly tiny hope you'd get it. But no, it's your little island because you got here first and you can't bear anything, anything at all, to change it! But you didn't get here first, Ibicencos were here before Honeybee Ballantyne and lots of them aren't quite as sentimental as you. They see that Ibiza needs places like Pure. Tourists bring work, money, infrastructure, new hospitals and schools.'

'But you have a doubt,' she said stubbornly.

'No, I don't.'

'Then save me the spiel,' she snapped. 'I bet you love the motorway too, carving the island in half, speeding everything up for all the clubbers.'

'Yes, I do. So beat me up about that too. And we'll probably need a bigger airport, with lots more cheap flights. And lots of islanders would like that, too.'

'And I'm not against change. I wasn't even against your club until I found out where it's going to be. But Santa Medea needs protecting. Edouard, please! Don't tell me you can't see that. It's fragile and beautiful and you would never bulldoze it over if you'd spent more than three weeks a year here. You pretend it's not so but you have forgotten everything. You camped on beaches like Santa Medea, and swam with your horses in the sea. The old Edouard would have lain down in front of the bulldozers. Don't you remember how you felt?'

He stared stonily back at her. 'And then I left and got a different life.'

'And I lost you. I knew I had. I just didn't realize how completely. Or perhaps you were always like this, only seeing the worth in something you can buy and sell.'

'You're wrong.'

'So prove it.'

'But it's a good idea.'

'Not there it isn't. Listen to me. I am not against a new club in Ibiza. I am not automatically programmed to reject any change to the island. But listen to me, Santa Medea is special. Go and see for yourself. Go, go and look. You won't need me at your side to convince you, you just need to open your eyes.'

'Oh Christ, I knew you'd be like this.' Dramatically he spread out his arms then toppled backwards onto the sand and lay silently looking up at the stars and she stared down at him waiting, waiting for more.

'Do you know you drive me mad?' he said at last, talking to the sky.

'Not as mad as you make me.'

'All the time I've been working, at my desk until

midnight, night after night, taking calls from Anna, listening to Paul, meeting architects, trying to do my job, all the time you've been there, sitting on my shoulder, driving me mad.'

'Saying just what you expect me to say?'

He looked up at her. 'Yes, so why do I listen?'

'You don't listen. You've ignored every word I've said.'

He let a handful of sand run through his fingers. 'No, I've heard you say it in my head ever since Paul first approached me. You've been shouting at me all the time.'

'I'm sorry. Go and look at Santa Medea, then you won't need to listen to me any more.'

He kept his eyes on the stars far above. 'Will you come there with me?'

'We were going anyway. We were meant to be going to Santa Medea and Cala Mastella too. Remember our plan?'

'But you don't want to go any more?'

'No,' she took a deep breath. 'Not if you carry on with Paul. Not if you don't stop him building that club. If you stay involved then there's no hope for you and me.'

'But it's not so simple. I am involved now. I can't

just walk away from Paul. I'm committed financially and I still think you're wrong. But I will go to Santa Medea and I hope you'll come too.'

'No, you should see it for yourself, you know what I think.'

'Then I hope I will still meet you at Cala Mastella next weekend.'

'We'll have to talk about that another time.'

He'd surprised her again. Later she lay on the sand, rolled tight in her blanket thinking about him as he dozed beside her, staring at his sleeping form caught in the dying embers of the fire. She'd so nearly kissed him and if she had would he still have told her about Santa Medea or would he have kept quiet, preserved the magic, betrayed her with his silence?

Then just before dawn he sat up suddenly and grabbed her hand.

'I want to make it happen. You and me, we've got to make it work.'

'What are you talking about?' she asked sleepily. 'Are you dreaming?'

'I want to make you happy. That's all that matters, you do know that, Bee?' He said nothing more, slipped down until he was lying flat again, still holding on to her hand, and she lay there beside him aware of his body slipping swiftly back to sleep, but in those few dreamy half-formed words, and in the way he still had hold of her hand, he had made everything OK again.

As the sun began to climb the music finally stopped and now it was light enough to see. They gathered together everything that they'd brought, stepped tentatively past the sleeping bodies scattered across the beach, slipped back down to *Baby Jane* and sailed away.

nine

TWO EVENINGS later, Honey was at her desk when
Edouard rang from London. Ever since she'd left him
at the harbour wall in San Antonio, she'd been waiting
for his call, telling herself it was all for the sake of Santa
Medea, but knowing, of course, it was nothing of the
sort. And at times she'd found herself stopping her
work just to sit and gaze out of the window in disbelief
that it was Edouard, Edouard Bonnier, whom she
couldn't get out of her head, who'd done no more than
hold her hand as he'd fallen asleep but was now,
illogically, making her feel this way, making her want
to dance through the French windows, throw her arms
around her father, shower her guests with free drinks,
her mother with flowers. She'd rung Nancy, who had
stayed on in El Figo while Belle had had to return to
work, and invited her for supper; she'd put Claudio on
duty and bunked off for one whole morning, spending
the time shopping in Ibiza town – something she

165

realized she hadn't done for months – all because of Edoaurd, and the giddy anticipation of seeing him again the following weekend, the expectation of what was about to happen next.

But then, when he did call, he immediately asked her to hold, and he kept her waiting on the phone for a good half a minute.

'Bee!' He said finally coming back to her with a great sigh of relief. 'I thought you'd have hung up on me by now.'

'I nearly did.'

'I'm having the day from hell.' There was a pause, then, *'No!'* He said it calmly, then exploded. *'Call him back and tell him no!'* Then only slightly more gently, 'I'm sorry.'

'Sounds as if you could have picked a better time to call me.'

'Yup.' He said it through clenched teeth.

'So tell me quickly, what's going on?'

'Do you want to know about the corrupt German backers, or the psycho American ones? Or do you perhaps want to know about the ridiculous Ibicenco planning laws? Or the fact that you can't tear down a dangerous building without getting it approved by health and safety . . .' He gave a short bitter laugh. 'Or do you want to know about a shit-stirring journalist who seems to know more about what's going on in my business life than I do?'

'Sounds as if I should get off the phone.'

'Wait, I needed to talk to you about Friday night. I can't do our date at Cala Mastella. I can't come out next weekend at all. I'm really sorry.'

Disappointment dropped through her like a stone. What's more, he sounded so preoccupied she wasn't sure he even cared.

'You want to rearrange?'

'Yes, yes, of course I do.' Again he paused. 'Deutsche Bank? Is he mad?'

'Edouard? Call me some other time and we'll make another plan.'

'No, wait,' still he sounded distracted. 'I was wondering if you were free on Wednesday night instead.'

'You mean, the day after tomorrow?' Instantly she pushed herself upright in her chair. 'Do you mean you'd come out especially?'

'Don't make it sound so strange.'

'I'm just surprised you have the time—'

'I don't. But the truth is, it's dark outside and tonight I won't be home before midnight, and tomorrow two of my clients are competing to give me the biggest nervous breakdown and I'm thinking how on Wednesday night I'd much rather be galloping along a beach at Cala

Mastella with you. Crazy, isn't it? But I called Doon earlier this afternoon, because I presume that's where you'd get the horses from, and she said it would be fine, she can just as easily give us them on Wednesday night as at the weekend. So if it's all the same to you. . .' He paused. 'Excuse me, Honey . . .' There was another pause. 'Yes, if we can. Of course we'll sue.'

Her spirits raised, she waited patiently.

'Honey?'

'I'm still here. Sue who?'

He heaved a great sigh. 'Anyone who prints lies. Anyone who makes things worse than they already are. Anyone who gives me a hard time.'

'You sound so scary when you say that.'

'Good. So, how about Wednesday?'

'Wednesday would be fine . . . Edouard, can you tell me what's going on, with your work? I'd like to know.'

'It would be a long and complicated explanation and you probably wouldn't find it very interesting anyway.'

'It's interesting if you're in trouble.'

He didn't laugh. 'Then I'll tell you about it on Wednesday.' She could hear the weariness in his voice. 'When perhaps it will all be over. But you know, right now, Bee darling, I have to go.'

'You sure you don't want to leave the riding for

another week, perhaps when you have more time? You might find you're tied to your desk – that you don't want to make a special trip here.'

'Erm . . .' Another pause. 'No. I won't be. I'll be in Ibiza already.'

She flushed with embarrassment. Why had she ever imagined he'd fly all the way from England just to go riding with her?

'I have to be honest with you, Honey, Paul's arranged a meeting about the club and I've committed to being there. I'm meeting him in San Antonio. I could be with you afterwards, about seven thirty.'

She jumped at the snap of tension still there in his voice.

'Good!' she said hastily. 'I mean, good you can kill two birds with one stone. You'll be here anyway with Paul, so good you can fit in the riding with me at the same time. Although, I have to wonder why you're bothering meeting me at all if you're going ahead with Paul.'

'Honey, I can hear in your voice you think I should apologize for something and I'm not going to. I told you I'd listened about Santa Medea and I meant it, but right now I've got a lot on.' She felt her heart miss a beat. Edouard just didn't speak to her like that. 'And you should know that Pure is not going to go away simply on the strength of a couple of conversations with you.'

'I've hardly had a chance to say a word.'

'I know what you're thinking.'

'What I'm thinking is that you should call me back when you're feeling less bloody bad-tempered.'

He sighed. 'I'm sorry. And I'd like to ride on the beach with you on Wednesday. Will you still come?'

'No, I've got better things to do.'

She cut him off and pushed the phone away from her in disgust.

She'd hated the disappointment. She hated how he'd just spoken to her, the awful condescending tone, the unwillingness to try to explain, the implication that terribly important multimillion-pound meetings were taking place, way, way over her head. *So we need to shift the pony ride to Wednesday, Honey, surely you understand?* OK, he hadn't actually said that, but it had been there in the tone of his voice. As if the ride to Cala Mastella had been her treat, as if he hadn't talked her into taking him out in the first place. As if she cared whether they went on the sodding ride, and as if she gave a flying fuck about him and his bloody club that was so clearly still on course.

Resisting the urge to hurl the phone across the

room, she pushed herself away from her desk. Thank God she'd got Nancy arriving for supper, thank God she'd got something to do, someone else to see. Nancy, who perhaps might not yet know about the disastrous project her boyfriend was involved in, who might find she was taken on a quick introductory visit to Santa Medea herself. Not that Honey had any faith in Nancy's ability to change Paul's mind.

All day Tuesday Honey wondered if Edouard would call back. Then on Wednesday morning, when she still hadn't heard from him, she rang Doon at the stable yard and found that he had called that morning to confirm that two horses would still be available.

'Benjamin and Sabrina,' Doon told her. 'He said you're taking them swimming so do make sure you dry them off before you bring them back.'

'Did he mention my name?' Honey couldn't believe his nerve. 'Edouard definitely said we were riding?'

'Honey, I wouldn't let them out with anybody else.'

She rang him on his mobile as soon as she'd put down the phone to Doon.

'I hoped you'd still come,' he said before she could say a word.

But he didn't elaborate. Clearly he wasn't about to apologize and he still wasn't about to give her an explanation and yet she had to hope that the problems

at work were to do with cancelling the project at Santa
Medea. Was it naïve to hope she was right?

She let a moment's silence hang between them.
'Then I'll be there at seven.'

'Thank you.'

'And when I see you, you can give me that huge
apology you owe me.'

And so there she was a few hours later, loitering
against a stable door watching dust boiling and building
along the dirt track below, as Edouard's old jeep made
its way at breakneck pace towards her.

'Bee, I'm sorry. I'm very, very sorry.' It was the first
thing he said before he'd even slammed shut the door.
'I'm sorry, I'm sorry, I'm sorry.' He walked towards her.
'I was bad-tempered, I was rude. Work got to me badly
last week. There.' He grinned at her. 'Good enough?'

She kissed him politely. 'Thank you. And did today's
meeting go well?'

'It's too early to know.'

'Was Anna there?'

'Yes.'

'And was she bursting with great green ideas?'

'Please don't do this to me, Bee.'

'Then tell me: it's not going ahead. You've managed
to stop it. Tell me.'

'Paul is absolutely sure of Santa Medea. Getting him to change his mind is harder than you could imagine.'

'You probably put the idea there in the first place.'

He didn't deny it.

'So what next?' she asked.

'The three of us, Anna, Paul and I, are flying back to London together tonight. Bee, I'm still trying to work it out.'

'Nice of him to wait for you to finish your ride,' she snapped back.

She didn't want to be sarcastic, petulant. She didn't want to burst into tears, but Edouard was so frustrating, standing in front of her so calm, refusing to rise to her barbed comments, deliberately being obtuse, skirting around the issue of Santa Medea and still holding back from telling her exactly what was going on.

They tacked up the horses and Honey called goodbye to Doon and then led the way out of the gateway and into the setting sun, turning immediately off the road and up a steep sandy path that cut towards the pine forests and took them straight into the hills.

She was on Sabrina, a pale grey mare who picked her way carefully along the rocky path, forcing Edouard – on Benjamin, a tall black horse – to walk slowly behind, and his horse plunged and fussed at the indignity. Then as they entered the first forest and the path levelled out and widened, Edouard let Benjamin go and for a while the two horses raced side by side, splitting the pine needles that carpeted the ground beneath their flying hooves and filling the air with a wonderful scent, before Benjamin, bigger and stronger, passed Sabrina and streaked away. Honey pulled her mare back to a canter and then to a trot, patted her sweaty neck and laughed when ahead of her Edouard came to an abrupt halt at a fork in the forest path as he realized he didn't know which way to turn.

As she walked slowly up to them, he turned in the saddle with a grin, and she managed a tight-lipped smile in response and then they were leaving the forest behind, Honey leading them once more. They clattered down the rocky paths to the beach, the horses moving eagerly down over the stones as they realized where they were going.

Down by the sea, dusk had begun to fall and lights from the restaurants made the night sky feel darker. There were already people sitting outside at the bars and restaurants and they stopped talking and looked on in interest as she and Edouard came riding past silently.

They kicked on, ignoring the people and each other, straight out into the sea, threading their way carefully in single file through the rocks, the water rising to the horses' shoulders as they made their way around the side of the bay, then on to another tiny empty cove on the other side. Just a rock fall separated them from the restaurants and people on the other side. They could hear the laughter of children playing on the low walls outside the restaurants, but here their cove was empty of people and they were unobserved.

On the beach they both jumped off their horses. They undid the girths and slipped off the saddles and then the bridles too, following a time-honoured tradition, still neither of them speaking. Under her T-shirt Honey was wearing no bra, and under her jeans just a pair of skimpy green bikini bottoms. She glanced over to Edouard and saw that he'd stripped off down to a pair of boxer shorts. She kept on her bikini bottoms but took off everything else, then guided Sabrina towards a rock, slipped a leg over the horse's soft warm back then turned to see Edouard vault back up onto Benjamin. She leaned forwards, whispering into Sabrina's ears, guiding her towards the sea, and immediately the horse bounced forwards in an uncomfortable trot, Honey gripping on tightly with her knees, her back to Edouard as she and her horse plunged and splashed into the black water. Sabrina snorted as the sea-spray caught her nostrils, then struck gamely out from shore. And then Edouard was alongside her, his horse prancing as the water swirled beneath him. As they came alongside Honey, Benjamin curled his top lip comically at the taste of the sea-spray.

'He's expressing how I feel about you.' And then despite herself she caught his eye and started to laugh.

'I said I'm sorry. Let it go,' he demanded. 'There's nothing I wanted to do more than be with you tonight. And Bee, as far as the club goes, you have to trust me when I say I did listen to you. And I went there and now I'm doing what I can.'

'Do you mind me asking what you're discussing with Paul?'

'Think in the region of five, six million quid.' He nodded at the surprise on her face. 'You see now? Why it's not so easy to just walk away. I have a responsibility to him and to all my staff too. I'm on dangerous ground, Bee. I must tread carefully. So tell me, what do you make of Pineapple Beach?'

'I think it's the biggest dive on the island, why?'

Pineapple Beach was a battered, faded club facing a car park in San Antonio. Hip in the seventies, with each decade since it had gone further and further downhill and it was now, in Honey's opinion at least, Ibiza at its vomit-splattered, drug-infested, drunken worst and that was just in the daytime. At night she would think twice of walking within a few blocks of its open doors and the rare times she had been forced to pass by at night, she'd felt threatened like nowhere else on the island.

'That's what I thought,' said Edouard in relief. 'I was walking by earlier today and I looked up at it and suddenly it struck me, here it is. I thought *this* is Honey's kind of place. The problem with it is that the surrounding area is just as bad.'

'But we're not talking about Pineapple Beach, we're talking about Pure,' argued Honey. 'And we're not thinking about the rough edges of San Antonio, we're talking about the unspoilt perfection that is Santa Medea.'

He stretched out towards her with his hand. 'I know. And you find it very hard to understand and harder still to forgive me, I know that too. And I'm so glad you still came tonight, and if there was a neat explanation about what I'm going to do now you could have it, but there isn't. When Paul Dix put his business plan on my desk I thought it was fantastic. I listened to Anna and I thought she was fantastic too. I even bought into the idea that Pure could benefit Santa Medea, that the club would ensure developers didn't cover it in tacky hotels and golf courses, one little club open just four months of the year, it really didn't sound so bad to me.'

'You're not still trying to persuade me?'

'Not since I went back.'

It was good to hear. 'And now how do you feel?'

'Even worse.' He threw back his head and looked up at the sky. 'Now for once I don't know what the fuck to do.'

She came up alongside him. 'Yes you do. Because you're smart and you're savvy and you can run rings around Paul when you put your mind to it. I know you can.'

He smiled at that and took her hand and gripped it hard while below them the sea bed dropped away and the two horses breasted the water and started to swim.

'Can we forget about Santa Medea for the rest of tonight?'

'Thank God,' he laughed. 'Thank you.'

Now they leaned forwards and half floated, half sat on their horses' backs, hands buried in their manes, feeling the wonderful power and strength of the horses kicking out beneath them, their coats soft and slick with water, their eyes bright, nostrils wide. Without reins to guide them, they let the horses go their own way and for a few wonderful moments they struck out further and further from shore. Then, just as Honey was beginning to wonder if they shouldn't head back the horses turned together, snorting and blowing with exertion, and stopped where it was shallow enough for them to stand once more.

As soon as she felt the sea bed beneath her, Sabrina started to paw at the water and Honey shrieked and quickly slipped off her back and swam away, knowing just what the horse was planning. Edouard swam away too and came to join her and they floated out to deeper water while nearer the beach the two horses both began to paw insistently at the water and then, almost simultaneously, eight legs buckled and they went down, rolling luxuriously.

Further out to sea, Honey and Edouard stood neck-deep, keeping balance with their hands. From where they were they could see both sides of the beach. To the right-hand side of the rocks the horses were making their riderless way out of the water to stand and wait quietly, but on the other side of the rocks, to the left, the restaurants were now even busier. They could see children balancing on the walls that divided one restaurant from another, could clearly hear guests talking and laughing.

'Is the chef the same as last year?' someone asked, and Honey snorted at the well-heeled English drawl. It was as if this man was staking his claim. I've been here before, he was announcing. I do know the island. Please don't take me for a tourist, whatever you do. 'And do you recommend the sea-urchin?'

'Oh, absolutely,' Edouard replied in a perfect imitation of his voice, 'and you must swallow the spines, every one.'

He held out his hands and instantly she swam forwards and took them, just managing to dance on the bottom with the tips of her toes. He drew her closer, bending his arms so that he brought her body right up against his, and then as she struggled, laughing at her inability to stand still, he slipped his hands beneath her bottom to help her and instantly, without any thought of the consequences, her legs wound themselves around his waist and gripped him hard.

'Sorry,' she said, half embarrassed, relaxing her grip a little. But she was laughing too, at finding herself cradled so close, laughing at the wave of excitement that was building up inside her just from staring at his face, his perfect mouth, his perfect lips.

'Don't mention it,' said the lips.

And his shoulders, how brawny they were. How could she not have noticed before? How satiny smooth and brown his skin.

'So where were we, Bee, when we were so rudely interrupted in Es Palmador? Do you remember? You were about to tell me something, I think.' He came even closer and she stared into his eyes, his gold-flecked, warm brown eyes.

He bent and kissed her shoulder and she flinched, startled that he could be so sure of her. 'What were you going to tell me?'

'Why you went away,' she said nervously, unable to look away from him. This moment was upon her so fast, and yet she'd known it was coming, from the night on Es Palmador, she'd known what would happen this night, she'd been waiting for it.

'Tell me why I left Ibiza.'

His voice sounded husky and raw and she swayed towards him. She felt his lips brush her cheeks as he spoke. It's happening, she found herself thinking. Can I believe this is happening?

'You went because I didn't kiss you. Because I stopped . . .'

'That's right.'

Still he hesitated as if he wanted to be absolutely sure she knew what was about to happen. And then, at last, he bent his head and she heard her own muffled little cry as his mouth met hers and this time she clung to him and kissed him back.

Kissing her, kissing her all the time, he waded to

where the water was shallower and he could stand more steadily and when they stopped she stroked his face, reached for him again.

'Oh my God,' she whispered, 'Edouard. Oh my God!' She had to break free to tell him, couldn't breathe or think. She put her hands on his chest to push him away, but found she couldn't bear to let him go and instead let herself fall against him again and for a moment he held her tight and they were still but for the gentle sway of the sea. Then she raised her head once more and he was ready for her, caught her mouth with his own, slipped his hand around the back of her head and kissed her back so blissfully that she had to put her arms around his neck to stop herself from sinking down into the sea.

'I can't believe this is you,' she muttered as he moved from her lips to kiss her neck and then her collarbone.

'I know. That's been my problem for a very long time.' Then he stroked the palm of one hand against her breast, against her cold, hard nipple, making her arch her back and bite back a cry. 'How am I going to convince you?'

'You've done it.' She covered his face with kisses. 'I'm sorry it's so easy but I think I'm convinced already.' She ran her hands down his big strong arms that held her against him so lightly then let her teeth graze against his shoulder. 'Or maybe I'm not, what else will you try?'

He slipped his fingers inside her bikini bottoms and at his touch she cried out in shock.

'Edouard!' It was all she could say. At his touch her voice had gone, her mouth could speak no more words, it could only kiss and be kissed now her body had become so heavy she could barely hold herself upright. She felt his hand tugging down her bikini and she wriggled herself free letting it float away, then wound her legs higher around his waist as he pulled his own shorts clear, giggling as he lurched awkwardly forwards almost pushing her under, even as the passion built inside her, making her reach for him again, desperate not to let him go. Then his hands were holding her bottom again and this time she let herself lean backwards, away from him, far back until she was floating on the water with her legs still wrapped around his waist, keeping afloat with her hands. He stroked the flat of her stomach in idle circles, kissed her stomach until she felt she would dissolve with lust, holding out a hand to steady her when she thought she might go under the water, and not even care. She gripped his hand hard and immediately his other hand moved back into position once more, then stretched lower down her belly, then between her legs, touching her so that the spiral of lust and desire instantly began to build again, out of control. She felt him hold her hips steady, then slide inside her, making her gasp at the wonderful heat of him after the coldness of the water and then she felt his hands reach for hers and he held her tight as he began to move more quickly, sending them both spinning away together, both of them racing towards their moment, yet willing it never to end.

Afterwards they lay on the beach, their legs tangled together, waves lapping gently at their feet, Edouard with his arms around her, their faces inches apart, neither of them able to look away. And they'd probably have stayed there all night if Benjamin, bolder than Sabrina and growing restless at the lack of attention, hadn't finally come stepping down the beach to find them, hadn't dropped his huge head between them and blown a long impatient horsy breath straight into their faces, telling them in no uncertain terms that it was time to go home.

ten

HONEY MISSED Edouard terribly the next day. She stood in the shade of the olive trees, watching her guests at Can Falco out by the pool, her father swimming among them, and wished savagely that she didn't have to be there; that just for once Hughie could get out of the ancient red swimming trunks, put on some clothes and settle down behind the desk to help her. It was his desk, his house, and yet she could count on one hand the times he'd done it. And she wanted help now, more than ever before. She wanted to sprint to her car, drive to the airport, catch the first plane to London, just to be near Edouard, for now, having found him, to lose him again so soon felt as if it might rip her in half.

She watched her father as he made his way to the edge of the pool, the strut in his stride telling her he was about to do something stupid. He was performing for someone and she cast a glance around the guests, spread out on the sunbeds, and saw Marianne Darlington facing the water, wearing a pair of Jackie O glasses, with a paperback in one hand. And then Honey's eyes flashed back to her father, and with a terrible shudder of fear, she saw him teetering on the edge of the shallow end, saw the stupid, crazy thing he was about to do. And so she began to run forwards, just as he leaped, into the air, into his dive.

Everyone says they hate hospitals. Honey loved them, white and quiet, orderly and calm, clean antiseptic corners, confident-looking nurses moving through the corridors on silent rubber-soled feet, patients all behaving themselves, keeping out of sight. She sometimes wished Can Falco could be more like a hospital.

She asked at reception and was given directions towards her father's ward and now, as she turned the last corner, she could see him, sharing a room with a couple of other men, both sleeping quietly while he lay back against his pillows in a pair of pale blue hospital pyjamas, with swollen, blackening eyes.

She walked on into the room and over to his bed. He turned and looked up at her and she caught the guarded, almost fearful look on his poor battered face. Her heart burst inside her and she sat down wordlessly beside him and took his hand, stroked the fingers and the shiny pink nails.

'Damned idiot, wasn't I?' he said sheepishly.

'You were showing off for Marianne Darlington, weren't you?' He nodded. 'I'm sure you impressed her. There was an awful lot of blood.'

'Don't,' he touched his nose gently with his finger-tips. 'Aaaggh.' He closed his eyes.

'What did the doctors say?'

He kept his eyes shut. 'That I'm a lucky old fool.'

'Your skull's still in one piece?'

'Just about.'

'Tora did say you had a very thick one.'

He gave a tiny grin. 'She should know.'

She sighed. 'Glad to see you've still got your sense of humour.'

'I don't know how, Honey. I don't know how.'

She took his hand. 'Who's Rachel?'

She waited but he didn't answer, didn't open his eyes, appeared not to breathe.

'Dad?'

'I don't know,' he muttered but his fingers twitched briefly in her hand. Then as if he knew they'd given him away, he pulled his hand free and rested it on the sheet beside him.

'I don't know either, but you talked about her at the pool. You thought I was her.'

'Never heard of her before in my life.'

'Dad? I don't think that's true.'

With his other hand he moved his fingers to the bridge of his nose and touched gingerly. 'Aaaggh.'

But she wasn't distracted. 'If you wanted to tell me, you know you could. I wouldn't tell Tora, I wouldn't judge you.' She was stroking his arm gently as she spoke, feeling more tender and protective towards him than she'd ever felt before. 'I know you think I disapprove of everything you do, but it's not true. If she's someone you care about, someone you'd like to talk about, I'd like to listen. Perhaps it might help if you told me about her . . .'

He lay there motionless but she noticed that two fat tears had collected under his eyes, and as she watched they began to race each other down his cheeks.

'I can't believe I said her name.'

'Who is she?' His eyes opened again and he wiped the tears impatiently away. 'Tell me.' Confide in me, please. Here's our chance.

'She's an old girlfriend,' he told the ceiling. 'Someone I knew before I met your mother.'

Honey couldn't understand why this was such a big deal to him. He was talking thirty years ago, after all.

'So you still think about her, do you?' He nodded. 'You've kept in touch? Have you seen her?'

Hughie shook his head, then clutched at it, screwing up his face with pain. 'Aaaggh.'

'Do you think you're still in love with her?'

His face cleared instantly. 'I was never in love with her.'

Relief poured through Honey. 'Then why do you still care? Why did you say her name?'

Hughie finally looked at her. 'I was concussed. I thought you were her.'

'Thirty years on?'

Now his look turned mutinous but she waited patiently, not about to give up, and eventually he went on. 'I feel bad about her even now. I buggered off. Left her.'

'So, who was she?'

'She was . . . she is Rachel. And we lived together.' He paused, picked at his sheet, and she could see how uncomfortable he was, frown lines etched into his forehead and cheeks. 'In Ladbroke Grove. We lived there for four years until I came here for the weekend and met your mother.'

'And then?'

'And then I behaved like a complete shit. Rachel

loved me and I didn't love her and I stayed here and never told her I wasn't coming home.'

'You bastard!'

'Yes.'

'You didn't even call?'

'I never spoke to her again.'

'Dad! How could you?'

'Easily. It's the kind of man I am.' Hughie closed his eyes again, switching off the accusation in her eyes.

'But Rachel,' Honey said, 'she knew where to find you? She could have come here?'

Now Hughie was biting on his knuckles, fighting off more tears and she knew this time it was genuine and she shouldn't be pressing him. But if she didn't persist she'd never have another chance like this one.

'Why would she do that when it was so obvious I didn't want to be with her?' he croaked. 'You wouldn't do that, not if you had any pride at all. And my behaviour made it pretty clear I didn't want to be with her any more.'

His voice had broken, he'd had to force out the last words and now he lay back against the pillows looking exhausted. Honey gently stroked his hair, guessing that the concussion was making him all the more emotional. She'd come to the hospital determined to ask him about Rachel, knowing her one chance to get the truth out of him was while he was in this vulnerable state. But now, seeing him so upset, she wondered why it had felt so important to her. What exactly had she thought would be gained from pushing him? What was it she'd wanted him to say?

I've been looking for something that would help me understand you and me, she thought sadly, watching the tears seep again beneath his eyelashes – something that would tell me why we've never been close.

His plane touches down at Ibiza airport. He makes his way to the arrivals hall, knowing how out of place he looks in a dark suit, a briefcase in his hand, among the baggy shorts and the espadrilles. He's itching to get through the airport and out the other side, picks up the pace, leaving his friends momentarily behind. And then he sees her. She's standing directly ahead of him, a vision in flip-flops and a long lime-green skirt, sunglasses in her blonde hair, and he stops dead because she's so beautiful — more beautiful than he ever imagined any woman could be. Completely entranced, he finds himself staring at her as all around them there are happy reunions, tears, hugs and kisses. He's dimly aware of his two friends coming up to join him but then she starts to smile at him and all at once she's full of mischief, daring him on, and he finds himself doing the bravest and simplest thing he's ever done in his life. Dropping his briefcase, he walks forwards and without saying a word opens his arms and pulls her towards him. He remembers the narrowness of her, the neatness of her head resting below his chin, her shiny hair, the madness in his heart.

'Who are you?' she asks, looking up at him, blushing and laughing.

And he remembers how he bent his head and kissed her before she even knew his name.

Hughie slowly opened his eyes again and the vision receded as he caught all the love and concern on his daughter's face. He found he couldn't bear to see it, looked down at his old man's hands instead and forced himself to let go of the sheet clasped between his fingers, then touched again his poor broken nose, felt the ache behind his bruised eyes and closed them once more.

And Honey looked back at him, saw the ageing hippy, weak and sentimental and yet still her lovely dad. She sensed his grief and the pain of a guilty conscience and felt protectiveness rising up inside her.

'If you want to apologize to her, to Rachel, you could still do that.' His eyes flashed open again but he said nothing. 'Would that make you feel better? If you knew that she'd forgiven you?'

'I would like to know what happened after I'd gone,' he conceded. 'I'd like to know that she's happy now.'

'Then why not write to her?'

'I did. I have done, on and off for the last twenty-five years. And she's never replied.'

'So go and find her.'

But even as she said it, Honey knew it was a fanciful thought. Her father could barely navigate the length of Ibiza, let alone fly back to England and find this Rachel. As if he knew it too, and was embarrassed, Hughie turned his face to the wall.

'And there's your mother,' he said quietly. 'I never told her. I certainly wouldn't want to hurt her now.'

Honey pictured Tora sitting cross-legged with her class in the Garden of Serenity, isolated from it all.

'I think it was what I first loved about Tora,' Hughie went on. 'How she could live entirely in the present – she was completely disinterested in what I'd left behind. And I was scared. I thought that if I confessed my regret about Rachel it would sound so bourgeois. I was in awe of Tora, intimidated even. I thought it would spoil what was happening between us. And you know what? In thirty years, she's never asked me anything about my life before I met her. And so I've never told her.'

It was the most intimate thing he'd ever told Honey and yet it was to Tora that Honey turned in her mind – how much easier it is to live in the present when you're young and beautiful and having the time of your life.

Why did she think her mother was looking back to the past now?

She thought back to herself as a little girl, to the cliché-ridden sun-soaked days and her mother smiling and laughing, catching her hands and dancing her through Can Falco, fun, exuberant, wonderful. And she wondered when exactly it had all changed. Was Hughie wrong to think Tora knew nothing and didn't care?

'I could find her for you.' There was no sign of any reaction from Hughie. 'Perhaps it would be good for all of us if you had a chance to apologize? Because you never had a chance to let her go, Dad, and perhaps even after all this time you still need to?'

'Edouard's parents, Delphine and Tom, I think they kept in touch with her for a while.'

'Then I can ask them for you.' He nodded. 'Would you like me to do that?'

'You could go,' he said quietly.

'Leave the hospital? You want me to go?'

'Go from here, Can Falco, Ibiza. I know you should.'

She let his words hang in the air for a few seconds, but she didn't register them at all.

'You should have gone years ago.'

'Don't say that, Dad.'

'But it's true.'

'I love it here. This is my home.'

'It's your cosy, familiar cage. I don't need Maggie and Troy to tell me that.'

'Why are you saying this to me now?'

His eyes suddenly beamed into hers. 'Because when else have we had the chance to talk? Every time I try, you slip away.'

'I didn't know you felt like this. I had no idea.'

Now it was Honey who was fighting not to cry, simply and pathetically grateful that he wasn't as oblivious to her as she'd always believed, that he had thought about her, once in a while.

Hughie took her hand and held it between his own and they sat there quietly for a moment.

'Talking about Rachel makes me weep for England too,' her father said eventually. 'I haven't been back for thirty years. I don't think I'll ever see it again and I wish so much that I had taken you back to meet my family, to see what a glorious place it is. Why haven't we done that, you and me?'

'I thought it wasn't important to you. You hardly ever mention England. I used to think how I'd like to have met your parents . . . got to know some cousins, that kind of thing.'

'Poor lonely little Honey.' His face screwed up in pain. 'I was so ashamed of what I'd done. I wanted to blank it out of my mind.'

'But it's never been something I've worried much about,' she said, trying to reassure him now. 'England doesn't feel part of me at all.'

He shook his head. 'That's terrible.'

'So you'd like me to go? Pay a visit to your parents?' Find Rachel for you? The question was there, clearer than anything she'd said out loud, and even though the idea had only just occurred to her she was already feeling the anticipation, a tiny little seed, dividing and growing, blossoming inside her. Edouard, England. She could fly to him, be with him. He could help her find Rachel. With him she could go to Wiltshire, stay with her grandparents. She pictured Hughie's mother and father, ruddy-cheeked and windblown, standing in front of some cold, old manor house. Then she pictured herself walking hand in hand with Edouard through the London streets, him showing her his house, his life that she knew so little about.

'Oh no, you couldn't go to London.' Hughie had read her mind. 'Far too dangerous, chock-a-block with lunatics. It's not like here, you know. You'd be a fish out of water. You'd be like Crocodile Dundee.' He loved Crocodile Dundee, and stopped for a moment to savour the thought, distracted like a child.

'Dad, I have been away from here, remember? I'm not such an Ibiza bumpkin. I'd love to go, the season here is winding down and I could be back before you'd even known I'd gone. I could go for the weekend.'

'Don't go on my account. You don't have to do that for me. Not travel all that way, a telephone call's all you'd need to do. Go to England, but go for yourself, not for me.'

And she knew instantly that she would do it, of course she would. The idea had already seeded, blossomed in her mind. She didn't know when, but soon, and Hughie knew it. And when she was there she'd contact Rachel, and Hughie knew that too.

eleven

BACK AT HER desk she jumped at the sound of glass hitting the stone floor of the hall just out of sight.

'We are under control,' a loud and imperious voice insisted. 'Stay where you are.'

Heart sinking because, much as she loved them, she really hadn't got the energy for them now, she looked up to see Maggie and Troy standing in the doorway. Domineering, sentimental Maggie, her Pekinese cradled tight against her chest, and just behind her, dapper cherubic Troy, with an overstacked tray wobbling in his arms.

Having stepped aside for Claudio, who'd appeared at their side with a dustpan and brush almost before the glass had finished shattering, Troy then came forwards once more. On his tray were three glasses, a bottle of sparkling rosé, tapas and a plate of lemon meringue pies, and Honey watched as they all made their slow hazardous journey towards her. Arriving safely, Troy dropped the tea tray onto the table with a crash and immediately took Honey in his arms.

'Oh my girl, what a super-hero you were.' He immediately jumped back from her, wiping at his spotless white linen shirt.

Honey kissed his soft cheek. 'You were watching, were you?'

'We were indeed.'

He pulled out a chair for her and pushed her gently down into it, and then Maggie arrived at Honey's side, dropping the little dog straight into her lap. Meanwhile Claudio replaced the broken third glass as Maggie took the bottle of wine and started to pour, giving Honey a close-up of her spectacular mahogany cleavage as she did so.

'Now I know you don't like it but just this once – I promise, Honey, just this once – I told the girls to prepare me a tray because I think, in the circumstances, we all need a little drink.'

'They wouldn't mind if you occasionally paid for it,' Troy suggested mildly, helping himself to a slice of salami.

Maggie stopped mid-pour and gave him a contemptuous stare. Today she was dressed in a white turban and long white dress with a gold coiled snake entwined around her outstretched arm.

'I've had a horrible, stressful morning. I think they

were pleased to help out. I thought Hughie had died. Honey flinging herself into the water like that was very alarming.' She placed a glass in front of Honey, then settled back into her chair.

'No, I can't stay,' Honey said. She lifted the dog off her lap and deposited him straight back into Maggie's, 'I'm off . . . Got to find Tora.'

Maggie took a careful bite of lemon meringue pie, then dabbed at her lips with a napkin. 'Such a good idea these are, darling, mops up all the alcohol and everybody absolutely adores them. They're a little taste of England, aren't they?' She went on without a pause, 'Honey, your father's such an old fool. You know not to listen to a word he says.'

Honey stared back at her. 'Did you know who he was talking about?'

'I'm sure there's nothing to know.'

'Oh yes there is, there's a great deal!'

'So.' Maggie stopped stroking her dog and laid her hand upon Honey's. 'I did wonder if he'd tell you.'

Honey sat back in her chair and took a sip of wine. 'What do you know?'

'I'm sure nothing more than your father's already said.'

'I wouldn't be so sure. I want to find her, Maggie. Do you know how I can do that?'

'Leave it be, darling. It happened thirty years ago.'

'Did you know her?'

'A little, back in London. Remember we all came out here at about the same time.'

'He left Rachel behind.'

Maggie nodded. 'Of course, I remember that.' She glanced at Honey uncomfortably. 'Oh, sweetie . . . I don't know what to say!'

'Now you're making me nervous.' Honey turned to Troy. 'Do you know Rachel too?'

He shook his head.

'Your mother is the love of your father's life,' Maggie said in a rush. 'Always has been, always will be.'

'Your father stopped thinking straight the moment he met her, and, as we know, has never managed to think straight again,' said Troy.

Honey reached forwards for a lemon meringue pie and nibbled it carefully around the edges. 'I'm thinking of going to England.'

Now there was a gleam in Maggie's eye.

'I'm not surprised. So tell us, we want to know all about him. And first of all, darling Honey,' she leaned forwards, 'we want to know why the hell it took you so long!'

'What!'

'Then we want to know *everything* you've been getting up to.'

Honey started to laugh. She was just so incredulous that Maggie could know anything, when it had only happened the night before and neither of them had had a chance to tell a soul.

'How do you know?'

'We're so happy for you, darling,' Maggie went on in a rush, hardly pausing for breath. 'You know, Troy and I, we adore him, we always have. We've always hoped this would happen, everybody has, Edouard's parents, Tora and Hughie. Have you told them yet?'

'No, I bloody haven't. And I want to know what you know and how you know it too!'

'I was there!' Maggie cried. 'Last night. I was there on the beach! I saw you.'

'You didn't,' Honey gasped.

'You went riding past me, straight into the sea,' Maggie went on blithely. 'It looked absolutely marvellous. She turned to her husband and took his hand affectionately. 'And I thought why didn't we ever do anything like that?'

'You saw we went riding,' Honey repeated in relief, grinning at them. 'Yes, we did, it was fun.'

'And what about the plans for his new nightclub?' Maggie asked. 'I must say that sounds like a very good idea. Pure.' She rolled the sound on her tongue. 'There was somebody telling us about it at Edouard's party, a very charming young man . . . what was his name?'

'Paul Dix,' offered Troy.

'That's right. He was telling us how Edouard's helping him put it all together.'

'No.' Honey said with complete finality. 'Edouard's not involved with that any more.'

'Oh, what a shame! Are you sure?'

'Don't look so crestfallen, they were going to build the club at Santa Medea.'

Abruptly she slid her drink into the middle of the table and pushed back her chair. 'But, you know, I can't talk about it now. Do you mind – I've got to go.'

She wanted to hear Edouard's voice. She wanted to tell him about Rachel, right then. Too much had happened that day for Edouard not to know about it all. She needed to get away.

Maggie looked at her sympathetically. 'Darling, of course. Send him our love. And come back for dinner. We're staying tonight so you should join us. We wanted to have Paloma's baby pig. What's the difference, do you think, between piglet and baby pig?'

'For God's sake, Maggie, let the dear girl go,' Troy finally interrupted. 'Go, Honey, go.'

'Thank you, Troy.' Honey smiled back at the two of

them. 'I don't think there is a difference between piglet and baby pig,' she said. 'It's just Paloma's English.'

'But baby pig makes me feel so guilty. Perhaps you should change it?'

'Perhaps I should.'

'We've booked for nine thirty,' Maggie called after her as Honey turned for the open floor-length windows running along the side of the room. 'And, Honey, why don't you ask Edouard to join us?'

Outside, she could hear chanting coming from the Garden of Serenity, and rising above it, the sound of her mother's gravely rock-chick voice singing *Om shanthi, shanthi shanthi* could clearly now be heard.

'Because he flew back to England last night,' she told Maggie from the open doorway.

'No, darling, he's here!' Maggie replied in surprise. 'I saw him just ten minutes ago. I thought you knew.'

Dappled sunlight poured through the almond and orange trees, and as she turned the corner to her cottage she saw him, dark against the light, leaning against the rounded whitewashed wall, in a well-cut suit that made her ache with wanting him, and with a mug of tea in his hand.

'I missed you,' he said, dropping the mug on the ground as she hurtled into his arms.

'You aren't meant to be here!' she cried, her voice muffled against his chest. 'But I am so incredibly pleased that you are.'

She lifted her face to his kiss.

'But you *are* going again aren't you? Now? You look as if you're dressed for work and I know you shouldn't be here at all.'

He nodded. 'I haven't got long, but I had to say goodbye. After last night I couldn't bear to go without seeing you again. They flew back without me. I got as far as the car to the airport but not the plane.'

'And, darling Edouard, you know I am so pleased you did.' She kept her arms tight around his waist. 'Until this moment today's been a spectacularly bad day. Everyone's gone mad.'

He stroked her hair sympathetically. 'I thought that happened years ago.'

She looked back at him. 'Oh yes!' She smiled up into his face. 'So it did.'

A soft look passed across his face. 'Poor Bee. Sometimes I forget what a hard time you have.' He kissed her again. 'What happened?'

'Dad hit the bottom of the pool . . . with his head.' Edouard winced. 'But he's fine – hallucinating, spouting gibberish, same as ever.'

'He'll be OK, then?'

She was outraged to see he was starting to laugh.

'It was bad!' she insisted. 'Lots of blood . . . And then we had a conversation in the hospital. And, oh God . . .' Suddenly the need to talk about her father was stronger than anything else and she slumped down on the ground and leaned back against the wall of her cottage and immediately Edouard did the same.

'Dad told me about a girl called Rachel, someone he knew a long time ago. I wonder if your parents ever mentioned her? Because they knew Dad in those days, didn't they, before he came out here?' She rubbed at her eyes and then let her chin drop down to her chest. 'He left Rachel behind in England when he first came over here,' she said, looking down at the ground through her knees. 'And I'd like to know more about her. But I'm not sure I have the energy to deal with all that now.'

He slipped his arm around her shoulders. 'Rachel the old girlfriend?'

'So you do know about her!' She looked up at him in surprise.

'I presumed you did too. She lived in London with your father, didn't she? And then he came over here for a weekend and met Tora and *Ka-Boom!* Mum and Dad were with him in the airport when it happened.

And they were the ones who went back to London and had to go and tell Rachel he wasn't coming home again.'

'Yes,' Honey whispered, 'that's her. How did I not know anything about her at all?'

'I always thought you did. Just one look at Tora and he was completely, desperately in love. I grew up on that story.'

'And I didn't. I never heard a word of it until today.' She looked at him helplessly. 'Of course I'm happy to know they were in love, but why am I so shocked?'

'You mustn't mind too much. Remember your mother's the one he wanted, she's the one he fell in love with.'

'I know, I know,' she laughed sadly. 'You'd think with all that love they might have made a better job of being together.'

'They're not so bad.' He stretched out his legs on the dusty ground. 'I remember how besotted they were when we were very young. I remember how your dad was always picking her up. She was always in his arms.'

Honey shrugged dismissively, such images of her parents' happy early life somehow didn't touch her at all. 'Do you think your mother maybe kept in touch with Rachel? Might she know where she lives and what happened to her? Because if I could tell Dad I think it would transform him. All his life he's been wanting to say sorry.'

'I could ask them. I haven't heard her name for years so I guess they're not great friends.'

'Would you, please?' She waited, looking at him expectantly and belatedly he got it.

'You mean you want me to ask her *now*?'

She nodded, allowed him the smallest smile. 'Right now. Get out your phone, please, Edouard. Do it now.'

He dutifully reached inside his jacket pocket and brought out his phone. She watched him press in numbers, bit at her nails while she waited as he waited, flinched when he nodded to her as the phone was answered, waited again as he talked and listened, her heart banging in her chest as he then finished the call, said goodbye and snapped shut the phone.

'OK, Rachel got married about a year after Hughie left,' he said rapidly, getting the facts out while they were still fresh in his mind. 'She became Rachel Paget. She and my mother kept in touch for a while and the last my mother heard she was living in Oxfordshire, in a village called Lingcott.'

'Anything else?'

He shook his head. 'They've lost touch.'

She clenched her fists in agitation.

'Honey, what are you planning? What are you going to do?'

'Call directory enquiries and get her number.'

He looked back at her amused. 'You can't just barge into her house.'

'Of course I wouldn't! I don't know if I'll get in touch with her at all but I wouldn't mind the option. I'd like to have her number. I'm going to ring directory enquiries and when I've got the number I might call it. And I might speak to her and if that goes well, I might even see her when I'm next in London.'

'You're planning on being in London soon?'

She grinned, fell against him affectionately. 'Very soon. How does this weekend suit you?'

She saw the answer immediately and she pulled herself free in surprise and sat back. 'It doesn't suit?'

'Please don't look so sad.'

'But I'm right? You don't want me to come?'

'Of course I do. But what I *want* doesn't come into it.'

'You couldn't see me at all? Not even for half an hour?'

'I'll be in Paris. But if you came *next* weekend I could see you. Please . . .' He kissed her cheek. 'Come next weekend. This weekend I have work that will eat me alive if I don't take care of it. Please, darling Bee, understand. You surely see it crucifies me to say that, knowing that I could be spending the time with you.'

So cancel the work. However important it was, surely it couldn't be as important as her? She knew it was childish to think it. She knew of course she couldn't expect his life to stop just because she'd decided to come to London. That of course he had a world that currently didn't involve her at all . . . But they had only just found each other, and so she wanted him to prove, with one sentence, that she was the only thing that mattered. She wanted him to sod his plans and his office. She wanted to be irresistible. But she wasn't.

'Next weekend,' he insisted.

'Perhaps.'

'Bee?'

'I do understand. I do. I can't expect you to drop everything just for me.'

'But you can and I would. Any other time.'

She didn't ask him what was happening in Paris. At that moment it didn't even occur to her that his work there could be connected to Santa Medea, and Paul Dix, and Pure. *Edouard's work* was a phrase, an explanation for why he wasn't in Ibiza, or for how he could afford to run such an expensive house as El Figo. In Honey's head, *Edouard's work* was still a vague world of black-suited men and ringing telephones, plush office suites and huge sums of money. But if anybody had asked her what he did there she wouldn't have a clue. She knew he was good at it, knew that he moved rather effortlessly through his days, rarely saw the stresses and tensions in him that she so often experienced herself, but the details had always escaped her. And even now that she'd been given a glimpse into the world through the possibility of Pure; even though she had, for the first time ever, been shown the levels of money he worked with, the kinds of people he had to endure, still it didn't occur to her to open the door wider and walk on in, to ask him questions, look around, even to wonder if perhaps there was any practical way she could help.

He kissed her again, and she opened her mouth and kissed him back but almost immediately he was stopping her, taking her hands in his. 'I have to go now.' He kissed her hands held in front of him, then reached forwards, and kissed her mouth, her nose, her cheeks, her hair. 'I'm sorry. I'll miss the plane. I held on because I couldn't bear to leave without seeing you again. I've been here all morning waiting for you. I was just about to give up and then you appeared, and now I have to go.'

'I had to go to the hospital with Hughie. Did nobody tell you what had happened?'

'I sat here with the laptop and my phone and didn't see a soul.'

'And I'm sure the hours flew by.' She couldn't help herself saying it, even though she knew she shouldn't. 'Go. You'll miss your plane.'

She kissed him again quickly, then watched as he walked away, turning all the time to blow her kisses as he went. She watched him until he walked out of sight, disappeared around the side of Can Falco and out towards his car and then she ran after him.

She caught up with him at the front door. 'I can take you to the airport.' And she led the way out to her car and he got in beside her. 'How long before your plane leaves?' She put her key into the ignition but he reached across and turned it off again then lifted her hand to his mouth and kissed her fingers.

'Bee,' he managed to mutter before she found his mouth with hers, kissing him desperately, winding her arms around his neck.

'Please don't leave me,' she said. 'I don't want you to go. Not yet. You can come back to my house, now. You have to.'

He kissed her lips, her cheeks, her hair. 'I could . . . You know I think I must do that.'

'Quickly before someone sees us, before someone catches me.'

hippy chick

They both got out of the car, looked around guiltily, but the car park was deserted. Then Edouard took her hand and led her stealthily along the drive then back towards the main house.

'No, not that way!' Honey hissed seeing Maggie and Troy emerging through another doorway and turning straight towards them.

'Why does it matter? Tell them you're busy.'

'It's not just them,' she whispered back. 'It's everyone else.' She grinned at him. 'So keep quiet.'

They slipped along a pathway that took them around the side of the hotel and met nobody. But then ahead of them was the terrace full of guests taking their late-morning coffees and early lunches, all just waiting to tell her about their day so far and she knew there was no alternative but to make her way straight through them.

'I'm not going to speak to anyone. Keep your head down,' she told Edouard, 'whatever they might say.'

'Honey, darling,' cried the first voice, a woman calling from the nearest table they passed. 'Come and join us, we'd like to take a boat to Formentera today, could you recommend a skipper?'

But she ran on.

'Honey!' called someone else, another woman. 'Could we have a word? Our room smells of—'

She didn't wait to hear what.

Then, seconds later it was a man's voice, the sexy, well-bred voice of Oscar-winning actor Damian Grant. 'Honeybee Ballantyne, stop right there. I need you.'

But she ignored him too, and ran on.

'Now I see,' said Edouard catching her up as they left the terrace and the guests and could finally slow to a walk. 'I had no idea. They want every bit of you, don't they? Tell me it's not like that every day.'

'It's worse,' she agreed laughing and breathing hard because now they had reached the front door of her little house, her haven and she was free. 'And I am on duty, and they are used to me always stopping and talking and listening to them. I don't usually have such a distraction as you.' She leaned back against her door. 'So, do you want to come inside?'

Once behind the door they fell upon each other, unbuttoning each other's clothes, pulling themselves free, then Honey led him into her bedroom, jumped onto her bed, then pulled him roughly down on top of her.

'I'm so glad you're here,' she whispered, giggling at his kisses. 'Now when you've gone at least I'll be able to remember you here, in my bed.'

She spread open her arms as he bent his head to kiss her again, tracing the line of her jaw down her neck with kisses, burying his face in the curve of her shoulder.

Afterwards he lay still as she sat up beside him.

'Bee?'

She looked down at him.

'We should go away. Go somewhere new for both of us, don't you think?' She ran her hand slowly down his bare smooth chest, loving the fact that she could. 'It's not that it matters that I've only ever seen you here because of course I'd feel the same wherever we were.'

'But I know what you mean about going away . . . Before us.' She stopped again because *Before Us* and *After Us* felt like two separate worlds. 'Before us I wanted to go away all the time. I thought I'd go mad with how much I wanted to leave. I think that was why I was angry with you – for being able to go so easily and leave me here. I think that's why I didn't want to know what you did when you were away, why I've never asked you . . . It was never that I didn't care, and now,' she let herself fall against his chest, 'I want to know everything, about your house and your office, who works there, who's left, I want to know about Paul Dix and what's happening with Pure. I want to know if you're happy there or if you're going to run away with me and build a new hotel somewhere else . . .'

'We could do that.' He took her hand. 'I always hated leaving you and yet for years I hated being here too, being so near you and yet so far away.'

Sadness crossed her face and abruptly she pushed herself off him again. 'And still it's just the same, isn't it? Because now you must go and I must stay. Better get dressed or you'll miss your plane.'

'Stop that.' He kissed her. 'Don't try to punish me. Everything has changed now. Don't be sad.'

But it was impossible to smile, the thought of losing him harder than it had ever been before.

She began to pick up her clothes, dress herself again, then stood in the doorway to her bedroom as he redid the laces to his shoes, slung his jacket over his shoulder.

'You don't have to come to the airport.'

'I want every last second.' She pulled herself together, made herself smile at him. 'Now, remember to ignore the guests on the way back, OK?'

When she got back home again she went straight back to her cottage, shut her bedroom door, sat down on her bed, picked up her phone and with the names *Paget* and *Lingcott* on a piece of paper in her lap, she rang international directory enquiries. And she did it at least partly because it was easier than thinking about

Edouard, easier than acknowledging the pain she felt at him going, at the thought that it would now be almost ten days before she saw him again.

She wanted time to talk to him without looking at a clock. She wanted to sit in a restaurant late into the night and talk and talk about what had happened, how it could be that they'd taken so long to find each other and how perfect it was now they had. She wanted to hear him say everything out loud that he'd still not said. She wanted to hear from his lips that this monumental, life-changing event had been just the same for him. She wanted to hear him say it aloud, again and again, how now that he'd found her, he would never let her go. But he hadn't. He'd talked about taking her away and then he'd run to catch his plane, and had disappeared again without her, out of her life, just as he had always done before.

There was a Paget listed in Lingcott, a village in Oxfordshire, a Banbury code, and after the briefest of waits they smoothly gave her the number and she wrote it down. Just like that.

She sat some more, looking at her whitewashed walls, trying to collect her thoughts. She had the number in her hand. Edouard was making his way to London. And somewhere else in England, there was Rachel and bizarrely it was as if Rachel was suddenly the means of connecting with him again. Her head was full of images of him but there too was this woman whom she'd never met, but whom she could picture so clearly it was as if she was looking at her – the woman whom Hughie had abandoned, and in so doing he had changed her life and his, and Tora's and hers too. And she lived in England, pulling Honey towards her, to where Edouard was too.

For a couple of minutes more Honey sat on her bed, holding the piece of paper, telling herself how ridiculous it would be to dial the number now. That she needed to go back to her desk, back to work, that right now she wasn't thinking rationally, that she needed to give herself time to plan what she would say if the phone was answered.

She carefully and slowly pressed in the numbers, still telling herself she could hang up before anyone answered if she changed her mind but after just three rings the call was answered and a man's voice said, 'Nick Paget.'

It gave her such a shock the phone dropped out of her hand and onto her lap and she had to scramble to pick it up again and get it back against her ear. He'd said it like a question and of course he needed an answer.

hippy chick

'You don't know me. I expect I'm mad to be calling. But don't worry—' she could hear the shake in her voice and she was babbling because she was nervous and hadn't planned what she was going to say – 'it's nothing awful, nothing scary.'

At that, the man on the other end of the phone laughed a pleasant reassuring laugh. 'Go on then.'

And she responded to the friendliness in his voice, slowing down. 'I have this number for Rachel Paget . . . And you're Nick Paget.' She hesitated. How old was the voice? Was he her son, her husband, her brother? She was trembling with the need to get this right. 'I was wondering if perhaps I might speak to her.'

'Do you mind telling me who you are?' He didn't sound confrontational, only interested.

'She wouldn't know me. I'm ringing on behalf of my father.' Did she dare to say his name? 'Hughie Ballantyne,' she blurted out.

'He's your father?'

'Yes.' She waited but Nick Paget said nothing, and yet she was sure he knew the name. 'I know it is thirty years since they last saw each other, and it's probably a ridiculous thought. She probably doesn't remember him at all . . .' Nick Paget was quiet on the other end of the phone. 'But my father has been speaking of her.'

She hesitated. 'If you think it's better not to tell her I called, then I understand. It was just a thought—'

'Rachel died just over eight years ago,' Nick Paget told her carefully and Honey's heart turned over. 'She was my wife.'

twelve

'EDOUARD. I AM coming to England this weekend!' She knew she was loud with excitement and had consciously to think herself quiet. She'd caught Edouard still in the airport, about to make his way to his plane. 'I'm meeting the Pagets,' she explained. 'One phone call was all it took.'

'Bee,' said Edouard. 'I think you're crazy.'

'Yes!' she laughed. 'Maybe I am. I spoke to Rachel's husband, Nick Paget. He suggested lunch.'

'Oh, then you must go,' he said sarcastically.

'He said there was something I should know.'

'Then you definitely mustn't go! Please, Honey, can't you see? He wants you there but he knows if he tells you why you won't come!'

'He didn't say it in an ominous way. I think it's exciting, scary. I can't believe it would be dangerous to meet him.' She rushed on before he could answer. 'And whatever it is he wants to tell me, I'm ready and

I want to hear it now – I can't wait another whole week.'

'Bee, you know nothing about him apart from the fact that he married the woman your father dumped thirty years ago. He could be a nutter, out for revenge. *She* could be out for revenge. Of course that's it, Bee! This is how to get back at Hughie, after all this time.'

'Rachel is dead,' Honey said flatly. 'She died eight years ago. And her husband sounded extremely sane, rather kind actually. And it may be impulsive, it may be crazy, but you're away and I'm going to do it. I'm going to meet him this weekend.' She walked out of her cottage as she spoke to Edouard, the phone pressed hard against her ear, then while she waited for him to reply she strode off down the paths towards the main house. 'And I know you'd like me to wait so that you could be there too, but they want to meet me not you . . . And I have to do this, whatever you say.'

She'd reached the path leading to the pool, where there were guests, a couple floating on lilos in the water, others sprawled on the sunbeds. She'd been about to stride straight through them all as she talked and she hadn't even realized it. She stopped abruptly, then spun on her heel and turned back, repeating her strides, length for length, back along the paths, back to her cottage.

'He wouldn't tell me over the phone, but I'm guessing it'll be about Dad. I'm prepared for it to be something I won't like, but I'll be fine and I'm used to it. What could he tell me that could be so awful?'

Edouard's silence told her that he had lots of ideas.

'Listen.' She walked away from the cottage once more, this time finding her own path through the trees, moving forwards swiftly, not wanting Edouard's caution and reluctance to put her off her stride. 'Don't feel bad about not being there. I'll be gone for most of Saturday now, meeting Nick Paget in Oxfordshire and then on Sunday evening, I'll be flying back here.'

She was wearing a pair of leather flip-flops and she'd lost the path now, but still she strode on, scratching her feet on the thorns and the thistles.

He gave a short hopeless laugh. 'What a fucking joke. I've been waiting years for you to say you want to come to England and now you're coming and I'll be in Paris.'

Then cancel your plans.

'But Belle will be home.' At the thought he sounded almost buoyant again. 'You could stay with her. If you insist on coming at least *she'll* be there to keep you company.'

'I'd catch the train back to London soon after lunch. Nick Paget has agreed to pick me up from the station. And then perhaps you'd be back in time for us to spend the evening together?' She could hear the roar of a jet engine coming through his phone. 'Could you do that? Show me your street?' She shouted the question above the noise. 'And your house, and your bedroom. And of course I wish we had more time, but this weekend isn't about us it's about the Pagets. It's so important that I can tell Dad I've met Rachel's family, especially when I have to break the news that she has died. And I can't keep them, or her, a secret from Dad for long . . . I feel I have to go this weekend and for once I don't even care if Claudio can't cope without me, if the bookings are cocked up, if the sheets don't get changed and nobody gets paid.' She looked back to her cottage, to her little terrace, the pots full of geraniums, the pretty pergola, the hammock swinging merrily in the breeze. 'I have to get away from here and it's one weekend. Surely this place can survive without me?'

She really couldn't express it properly, the sense of urgency making her want to drive to the airport in the clothes she was wearing and jump on the first plane with a spare seat. Did she hope that, by finding Rachel's family for her father, somehow she'd break through to him herself? Or was it nervousness at what Nick Paget might have to say? Or was it simply pure excitement at the prospect of spending even the littlest bit of time in England, even without Edouard there, but seeing his kitchen and bedroom, his bed, the whole of the rest of his life that for much too long she'd had no sense of at all?

'Dad and I got close this evening in the hospital, better than we've been for years.' The sound of the plane was dying away now and she dropped her voice, speaking more softly. 'I have such hopes for England. The way Hughie described it, he loves it so much and, although he didn't say so, he's desperate for me to go and see his family too – and I never even knew he still thought about them. And when I suggested coming to England it made me feel I was connecting with him for the first time in years. If I go, I know everything will be better between us . . . And Claudio can look after Can Falco, he only needs me to brief him and he could do it standing on his head. I think he'll be relieved to see the back of me.'

'Bee,' Edouard said shortly, grabbing a chance to speak before she began again, 'that was the last call for my plane.'

Belatedly she caught the strain in his voice. 'I'm sorry, please. Surely you can't be too cross with me? I'll come next weekend too. You know I only want to be with you, if you were anywhere I could get to, I'd do it.'

'It's nothing to do with you. I got a call just before you from Paul, that's all.' And now she heard the tiredness and defeat in his voice as he spoke. 'It's not important. Concentrate on Hughie now.'

She would have asked more. It occurred to her that she had to quiz him when he returned from Paris, find out what he'd been doing, make sure he didn't palm her off with the usual vague responses that it was work, it wasn't important. But still it didn't occur to her that he could be in any serious trouble, that the stakes could be sky high. It didn't occur to her that any of the strain she heard in his voice could be justified. When he'd first raised the question of Pure the weekend before, she misunderstood how advanced the project was, thought it was just that, a question, and so she had no idea how complicated and well advanced the plans were, just how many different developers and backers were already involved, how many thousands of drawings, hundreds of plans had been sketched and how much money had already been spent. Edouard's rather cautious descriptions had given her the impression Pure was just a thought, a fantasy castle based on air, but if she'd thought about it some more, she'd have known that it wasn't.

thirteen

england

HONEY WAS on a train from Paddington, looking out of the window at England.

She'd arrived at lunchtime the day before, after just one day of planning and packing, bringing Hughie home from hospital, convincing them all – and herself – that Can Falco could carry on without her. Then she'd found her way to Edouard's Islington townhouse and even though she'd been told where to look for a key, that there'd be nobody there in the middle of the day, Belle herself had opened the door and surprised her, throwing out her arms in welcome.

'I know all about you and Edouard and it's brilliant,' was the first thing she'd said.

Then she had led Honey through the door and into a wide, white-painted hall with a creamy limestone floor that led them on through an archway and down a couple of steps into a light-flooded square-shaped drawing room with floor-to-ceiling windows looking out onto a leafy communal garden. Two squashy sofas faced a flat-screen TV, the bookshelves were crammed with books. There were interesting paintings on the walls and rugs on the floor and a Ganesh – the elephant head of Lord Ganesha, master of intelligence and wisdom, a favourite of Ibiza – up on one wall. She smiled at that, touched to see him there.

Altogether the house was uncannily similar to El Figo in feel, the two drawing rooms, at least before Anna got to work on the one in El Figo, were almost identical. Honey had looked around, greedily drinking in the signs of Edouard and his life in England as Belle gave her the quick tour, pointing out the sweet little private terrace, pots overflowing with flowers, the kitchen, *too much chrome but we haven't had a chance to change it yet*, and the three en-suite bathrooms, *gold plate and marble, aren't we so lucky.* She showed Honey the spare bedrooms, white-painted and innocuous, immaculately tidy, then slipped past her to open the door to Edouard's bedroom and Honey looked in, saw a pair of his battered navy Converse trainers lying on the floor and wished Belle would leave her alone to think about him.

Because surely Belle didn't know how it felt to see this empty space that still seemed so full of Edouard.

She wasn't to know that by showing her his room, Belle was making Honey long for him so badly she wanted to climb on the bed to hold his pillows against her cheek. She nearly did it anyway.

After that, as they made their way back down to the ground floor, Honey saw him everywhere. In her imagination she was resting her hands on his shoulders as he sat at the breakfast table, bending down to kiss his head as he stared out of the window.

That Friday afternoon she and Belle spent shopping around London, using the open-topped tourist buses to link up their wanderings, sitting on the top decks, in the dusty August heat, breathing in the city fumes and ticking off the sights: the London Eye, St Paul's, the Houses of Parliament, Trafalgar Square. Then in the late afternoon they'd wandered down the Portobello Road Market, London's response to Las Dalias, and Honey had bought six Coalport china cups and saucers, hand-painted with roses and butterflies, and a rose quartz massage wand for Tora. And then, at the end of the day they'd returned to the flat and Honey had had a bath, soaking in the water with a glass of wine in her hand, as Belle had cooked in the kitchen downstairs, sending wafts of delicious Bolognese sauce up to greet her.

'He's still worried Nick Paget is planning a terrible revenge,' Belle had called to her up the stairs at one point.

'Don't sound so happy about it,' Honey had shouted back. 'Seriously, do you think I'm mad to be going there?'

'If you have to make a run for it, keep your head down and don't look back.'

'Shut up. I'm having lunch with him, that's all.'

'Still, charge up your mobile and call me if you need help. I could be there in a couple of hours. I'm not joking now.'

'Thank you.'

'I hope it works out for you.'

'Thank you, again.'

'Although – don't bite my head off for saying this – if Rachel's died, I'm not sure why you're still going.'

'I'm going because I can. And because Nick Paget is as curious to meet me as I am to meet him.'

And all the time, through every doubt Belle had raised, every second thought Honey had had, there'd been the anticipation of this morning, this journey that was now sending her flying through the fields and through the cities and towns ever nearer to the village of Lingcott.

It was as simple as that. She was going on a whim but it didn't stop the weight of expectation growing heavier with every mile, making her twitch in her seat, enjoy the sight of the countryside flashing past her window while not really taking it in at all.

Back in London, Honey had still been enjoying her bath when the doorbell had rung. Irrationally think-ing it was Edouard, she'd leaped from the water then stood at the top of the stairs and watched Paul Dix stride confidently into the hall and then disappear into the kitchen, Belle frosty-faced just behind him.

She'd dressed quickly and had walked downstairs, filled with misgivings and Paul had turned delightedly at the sound of her approach. Clearly it was she who he'd come to see. Belle, now silently standing behind him, just didn't figure at all.

He'd come forwards with a broad smile and a kiss she didn't have a chance to decline. He'd looked glossy and smooth and expensive, his soft dark hair shining in the hall lights. At the sight of Honey his eyes had gleamed with satisfaction.

'I have something to show you.'

Without asking, he'd cleared the table of the newly

laid knives and forks, mats and glasses that had been put ready for her and Belle's supper and placed first a bottle of champagne, dripping with cold, then a large brown leather folder onto the table instead.

'The champagne is for you if you get all the answers right.' He'd turned from Honey to Belle. 'Any chance of some glasses?'

And he had then sat down without an answer, smoothing his hair back from his head, unzipping the brown leather folder and taking out a sheaf of papers and some photographs, either disregarding or completely oblivious to Honey's continued silence.

'Now Edouard tells me you've been having second thoughts.' He scratched his head, studying the pictures as he spoke. 'So which one to show you first?' He looked up at her. 'I can understand why, don't get me wrong, I can see what a special place it is, of course you're concerned.' He rifled through some more pictures, thinking aloud as he did so, '. . . so I thought, I'd come and see you. Find out a little more.' He looked back at her again. 'Santa Medea – it's not spectacular, not even particularly beautiful, but it's got that special something, hasn't it?'

'What is that?' asked Honey politely.

'Oh I don't know . . . Its loneliness? Its calm?'

He doesn't have a clue, she realized. He can't see

what makes me want to protect it, so he's having a guess, calling up the adjectives in the hope that one of them hits home.

'The place gives me goosebumps,' Paul tried again. 'Isn't it completely unique? You stand there on the cliff, you look out at the sea, and you want to protect it, keep it safe for ever. Not just for our pleasure but for future generations too.'

Couldn't he have come up with even one original line?

'And you think Pure can do that, do you?'

'Of course.' His eyes gleamed. 'Because the consortium that will own Pure will hold on to the surrounding land too, I think we're going for about sixty, seventy acres, and they will therefore ensure that the rest of that coastline never gets developed. If Pure buys the land around Santa Medea, you will never get those ruined hillsides, crammed full of identikit villas. You may hate the idea of anything there at all, but think about it, Honey, if we don't do it, surely someone else will. And if it's not Pure, how do you know it's not going to be several high-rise blocks of flats?'

He'd got a point. What she didn't know and wished she did was who actually owned Santa Medea and what sort of protection was offered to such coastlines and forest and how it was that Paul had managed to circumvent them. She would find out. But for now she knew she'd get much more out of the conversation if she sat back and listened.

'Look,' Paul went on again. 'When Edouard told you about Pure he had nothing to show you but the ideas in his head. No wonder you couldn't make real sense of what he was saying, but I have plans, detailed drawings and photographs, wonderful examples of the kinds of things Anna's been involved with in the past. And I promise you, Honey, when you see them you'll change your mind.'

She picked a photograph off the table. It was of a swimming pool, built in some sort of neo-classical style, rectangular and very plain with a column at each corner and flat stone edges and dark blue water.

Gently he took it out of her hand, pushed it out of reach. 'Don't look at that one, look at these.'

'Where will the swimming pool be?'

'It doesn't matter, it's got nothing to do with Pure.'

'It looked stunning.'

'Oh, did it?' He laughed, surprised. 'Then I'll tell you we're putting up a little boutique hotel alongside the club. Pure will be so beautifully soundproofed you won't even hear the music unless you want to. Isn't that amazing that they could exist side by side?' He went swiftly on. 'But what I want you to see first is the dance space.'

She let him hand her another photograph. 'By night mind-blowing,' he said and she looked and saw a huge round dance floor crammed full of people, arms above their heads. She caught a glimpse of a palm tree, half lost in the corner of the picture, and what looked like a series of billowing white sails strung across the roof.

She shrugged and handed the picture back to him.

'Exactly,' Paul cried delightedly. 'That's exactly how I wanted you to react. That's why your touch would be so vital, why I have to have you on board! It's nothing now but when you've waved your magic wand it will be mind-blowing.' He poked at another picture with his finger. 'Look at this. This is it by daytime, this is the broad canvas you'd have to work on. Look at that, isn't it utterly magnificent? That's what our guests will see first when they arrive. Now try and tell us what we're doing wrong.'

She saw a gigantic staircase, steps carved into what looked like rock, leading down and down to where the rock opened out onto the sand, and built there at the bottom was the most enormous glass-enclosed space, and what looked like the sea, spread out beyond the windows. And then with a start she saw that it *was* rock, that she was looking at the rocky hillside of Santa Medea; that the photograph was an artist's impression to show how Pure would look. The rocky flight of steps was genuinely carved out of the rocks, the gigantic dance floor, covered in glass, really would be built on the sand, on the beach, just a few laps away from the sea.

She couldn't hide her stunned, awestruck reaction and Paul saw it immediately and pounced upon it.

'You love it! I can see you do and why not? It's the most spectacular idea. We've mocked these pictures up. This is what it will be like, exactly how it will look. And there's nothing wrong, there is not a single thing you can pick out and say *change it*. That's the fucking beauty of this place, nature has done it all for us. Imagine it Honey. You will walk down the steps, down through those cliffs, a lemon vodka in your hand, and you will be transported to heaven.' He spread out his arms. 'Heaven! You will see the sun rising in the morning, you will look through the glass walls and on the other side of the glass will be the sea, right there, close enough to touch it. It will be the most beautiful club in the world.'

He was right. It would be absolutely incredible. She scraped back her chair and stood up.

'Paul, is everything in place? You have the permissions? And I presume you've overcome the tree-huggers, the protesters. It's just I'm surprised there's been none of the fuss and publicity that you might have expected, nothing like the kinds of protests we saw for the motorway.'

For the first time she thought she saw a flicker of annoyance in his face.

'The motorway was an abomination. This will be nothing like the motorway. I don't appreciate you suggesting any comparison at all.'

'I'm sorry. And you have the bay, Santa Medea is yours?'

He didn't say yes and he hesitated briefly, just long enough for her to see there was a hitch.

'We have ninety-five per cent of what we want. To have you on board can only help us with the last five.'

She took a deep breath. 'But of course I can't be on board Paul, you know that. I'll fight to stop you developing Santa Medea with everything I have.'

He slapped his hand on the wooden table with a crack of sound.

'Don't mock it, Honey.'

'I don't. Pure would have been a stunning club, but people like you can't be left to rampage through places like Santa Medea. There has to be a point of control. Build your club in San Antonio, leave Santa Medea alone.'

'Edouard will be ruined if Pure fails.'

'No he won't be, because he'll have nothing to do with it.'

It was a mistake to say so. She knew it as soon as the words had left her mouth. But the need to shut Paul up, puncture his huge smug ego, had been irresistible.

In response Paul gathered up his papers and slipped them back into his case and stood up. And then at the doorway he paused once more and turned back.

'You might like to think you own Edouard, that because of your shared history you can persuade him to do or not do whatever you like, but unfortunately for you, and rather conveniently for me, Edouard pays less attention to you than you think. We are opening in a couple of years and Edouard had just agreed to take full financial responsibility for the next stage of development. Full steam ahead! Keep the champagne, you might find you need it.'

And then he'd walked out, shutting the door quietly behind him, and Honey had sat heavily down in a chair, thinking she should call Edouard.

Now, looking out at the fat hedges and steep wooded hillsides speeding past, the grass bright green even in a drought-ridden August, the ancient churches and old red-brick farmhouses, she felt as if she was fleeing the lot of them, fleeing Paul Dix and fleeing Edouard too, fleeing her anger with him. A superclub, Edouard had told her back in the sand dunes on Es Palmador, one that would take up to five thousand people in a night. Different zones for different music, different nights for different music, rock, house, hip hop and pop, funky Balearic house, electro and trance, but listening to him then she'd thought he was talking about a castle in the sky, a proposal, nothing more, that could be over just as fast. She hadn't understood how determined Paul would be. And when, as they'd ridden the horses into the sea in Cala Mastella, she'd asked Edouard what had happened to the plans he had let her think he was in control. He hadn't deliberately misled her but he'd let her think the crisis was over and clearly it wasn't.

And now, remembering again the moment when Paul left the house in London, she felt the same sense of frustration with Edouard that he could get involved in the first place with a thug like Paul, frustrated that he chose not to tell her everything when she might have had a chance to help. And frustration that he would let her think he was extricating himself, when now she knew he was still involved and becoming more so with every day that followed.

After Paul had left the flat Honey had called Edouard's mobile and caught him in the middle of a dinner in Paris. He'd left the table to take the call, and she'd explained calmly enough what Paul had said, at that stage still expecting he would have an explanation she could live with. But there'd been none. Instead all he could tell her was that everything Paul had said had been true. He was still involved. He was still trying to come up with a way to get out. And she'd hardly listened to any more, so that in the end he'd sharply told her that he'd been away from his table too long and had to go. She hadn't spoken to him since.

Now the train slowed again and she stood up and made her way towards the door, smoothing her skirt down with her hands, nervously shaking her hair back into place, tucking a strand behind her ear. She took her sunglasses off and put them in her shoulder bag so that Nick Paget would be able to see her properly.

In her head she heard Belle's warning once more. *He's looking for revenge*, and at the same time the train came to a slow, screeching stop.

The doors opened and a push of people began to flow through the doors.

She jumped off too, hiding behind the other passengers as she walked towards the exits, wanting a first glimpse of Nick Paget before he saw her.

She immediately knew it was him, standing near the steps that led to a bridge over the track, the only man waiting to meet someone. He was scanning the crowd with the intensity of a customs official with a tip-off and she checked her pace, not quite ready for him to see her. Up closer, she saw he was tall with short dark hair, grey at the temples, attractive in an open-shirted, burnt orange-corduroyed English kind of a way, and she found herself smiling with relief because she thought he looked nice, the right sort of stranger to have waiting to pick you up.

She strode towards him, waiting for his reaction to confirm she'd got the right man but, when he did catch sight of her, his look of complete surprise made her stop in her tracks. Then, he quickly recovered himself and came striding towards her with a big smile of welcome.

She took his hand. 'Hi, Nick Paget!' she said shyly.

'Hello, Honeybee Ballantyne,' he said solemnly back but there was a twinkle in his eye and immediately she thought *I like you*. 'You must call me Nick, and may I call you Honey? I must say I think you're very brave to come.'

'Everyone keeps telling me that,' she agreed. 'But I have left letters to be opened if I don't return by nightfall.'

A quick flash of a grin. 'Very wise.'

He steered her towards a flight of steps that took them across the tracks.

'Everybody's dying to meet you as I'm sure you can imagine. I only just managed to persuade them all not to come with me.'

'So who are they all?'

'I have a son, Nat, and two daughters, Beth and Julia.'

'And who else?' she said suspiciously.

He laughed, looking at her approvingly. 'You're going to do just fine.'

Charming and confident, he had the manner of someone who found people generally behaved as he wanted. She'd bet that he was practical, resourceful and successful and always made things happen the way he wanted them to. Right now, today, he'd wanted to tell her something, he'd wanted to do it on home turf, he'd wanted his family to meet her so he was bringing her to them, brushing her fears aside. Tomorrow, no doubt, the focus of his attention would be on someone or something completely different.

'There are two others at home. There's my aunt, who we call Lettuce, and who is blind and ninety-two and lives at Lingcott. And there's my younger daughter Julia's boyfriend, Pete, who is a therapeutic masseur and who thankfully does not.' His eyes twinkled into hers. 'You're probably used to therapeutic masseurs in Ibiza?'

They walked across the bridge and came down the steps on the other side, walked out through the station doors and into the car park where a very clean, very speedy-looking vintage sports car sat waiting for them. He opened the door for her and helped her inside.

'Julia, the daughter with the boyfriend, is so very much in love we'll probably hardly see her,' he said as he walked around to his side and got in. 'The other one, Beth, will probably not leave you alone but don't worry, she's lovely. Lettuce will hardly realize you're there and Nat is extremely charming and will be delighted to meet you. They all will be. They're all so grateful you took the time and the trouble to come. OK?' He looked across at her, checking she'd done up her belt. 'Let's go.'

He drove like a bat out of hell, whipping them along the narrow lanes, through avenues of tall trees that dappled the light suddenly, and then they burst back out again, back into the brilliant sunshine. The wind tore at her hair, slapping it across her mouth as she tried to answer Nick's continuous stream of questions about her life, her family, growing up in Ibiza, running Can Falco.

'I must stop,' he said finally. 'I promised the girls I wouldn't quiz you until they could hear it all too. You'll have to tell them everything all over again.' But then, moments later, he started again. 'What does your mother look like? I imagine like you? In my head, I'll admit, I think of her as a siren, calling your helpless father to her island with her beautiful song, breaking my poor wife's heart.'

She looked at him lost as to how to respond.

'I'm sorry.'

'Oh, Honey, *I'm* sorry. I don't want to embarrass you. I'm very grateful to your father for giving me a chance. But I am glad if your mother is beautiful because I don't know why but it makes everything fit together better.'

She turned away from his piercing stare.

'How far from Lingcott are we now?' she asked instead, a nice bland question that might just keep him on track until they got back to the house and his family.

'About five minutes.'

They managed a minute more in silence.

'What was it you wanted to tell me?' she asked then.

He gave her another quick appraising look. 'If you don't mind I'd like you to wait for that until we get home, after lunch even, when you've met everybody . . . Then I have something to show you.' And he moved immediately on before she could argue. 'Does it ever get boring, living on Ibiza all of the time?'

'How do you know that I do?'

He laughed. 'Looked you up on the internet. Read some article in a magazine called *Red*. It was interesting. I got to see your wonderful hotel, all the bedrooms, the gardens, the Garden of Serenity – where your mother practises her yoga.'

She didn't know what to make of him. Did she like him? She wasn't so sure now. He was almost too confident, bowling her along in his vintage car. She felt uneasy knowing that he'd been reading about her and yet, wasn't it rather enterprising of him, and the article was there after all for all the world to see. She decided, for now, to give him the benefit of the doubt.

'I used to think I'd never leave but recently . . . I don't know.' She let her hand trail out of the window as the car sped smoothly on. 'I've discovered how lovely it is to do what I like, just for a little while, every now and then.'

'So you're having fun in England?'

'Oh yes, I'm loving England even though I've only been here a couple of days.'

'You realize you're seeing it at its very best. It doesn't get more perfect than a day like today. The sun is hot. At Lingcott everybody will be out, lying by the pool.' He gave her another grin. 'Home from home.'

She shook her head. 'Nothing like home. I can hardly believe it's the same sun, the same sky.' She turned away from him, looking out of her window. 'Here there's such a lovely wash over everything. In Ibiza the sun's so bright and fierce. It makes all the colours seem sharper: peppermint-white houses, bright red soil, sharp blue sky . . .'

'You make it sound captivating. Tell me more,' he insisted, 'more about Can Falco and who lives there. Do you have sisters and brothers?'

'No, it's just me. And Can Falco's a finca, a farmhouse, very old. It was derelict when my parents found it, about thirty years ago.' She stopped abruptly. 'Of course,' she said quietly, 'you know when.'

'You don't have to choose your words so carefully. It all happened a long, long time ago, and you and I weren't involved. We didn't make their choices, even though we are here because of them. That's why I asked you to come. That's why you're here.'

She coloured and looked down at her skirt. 'Thank you.'

'So how did you find us?'

Just saying Edouard's surname aloud made her stomach lurch with anxiety and dismay. So many times she'd been on the verge of calling him again but she hadn't done it.

Minutes later they drove into the village of Lingcott, full of sleepy medieval-looking cottages built from a crumbling golden stone. The village was tiny and picture-postcard beautiful, with a pub and a village green, and even ducks swimming on a pond. She'd never quite trusted such places truly existed.

Off the village green, they passed through wrought-iron gates, 'LINGCOTT FARM' discreetly etched into a stone pillar on one side, then through more open fields and across a rattling cattle grid, a kink in the road and they were there in a beautiful hidden landscape where fat white sheep grazed upon gently rolling hills and, in the middle of it all, stood a square stone house.

They drove around to the back. It was less manicured here than she'd expected, a proper farmyard with a couple of barns in an 'L' shape ahead and to the right of them, built in the same warm stone, and cobblestones on the ground. There was straw blowing out of an open stable door and hens scratching in the dirt. In the field beyond the barns were two ponies with their heads stuck through the fence stretching for the grass on the other side, and everything looked lived-in and English and welcoming. Then the kitchen door opened and two women came out, arms wide to welcome her. There was no question of awkwardness, it was as if they'd known her all their lives – which, after all, in a way they had.

The first sister to appear had shoulder-length strawberry-blonde hair caught up in a flower clip and a sweet freckled face and Honey saw with a start that her hands were covered in what looked like blood.

'It's all right, it's summer pudding,' she called, seeing Honey's shock. 'What a start! Silly me! I'm so sorry. I was just trying to put it together before you arrived.' She gave her hands a half-hearted shake then wiped them down the back of her jeans and stepped forwards again. 'Hi, Honey,' she said, her eyes shining and now Honey thought she might be crying a little. 'I can't tell you how much we were looking forward to meeting you.'

'Me too,' Honey said, smiling back at her.

The other sister had dark shiny hair cut very close to her beautifully shaped head. She had fine features, delicately arched eyebrows and brown, almost black eyes. She was wearing rolled-up baggy jeans and a scoop-neck white T-shirt and she had bare brown feet. She stepped from behind her sister and hopped gingerly towards Honey across the cobbles, went to take her hand and then said, 'Sod it' and caught her in a bony, heartfelt hug. 'I'm Julia. We're so glad you came.'

And then last out of the doorway came Nat, tall and dark as his sister Julia, in a pair of khaki shorts with a lovely lean face and eyes the colour of the sky. He broke into a delighted smile at the sight of Honey, came forwards to shake her hand and then, like his sister, changed his mind and kissed her cheek instead.

With Nat leading the way, the four of them took her into the house, through a messy farmhouse kitchen, washing-up piling several feet out of the sink, a chopping board covered in strawberries dripping juice onto the terracotta-tiled floor, and then on into a long low drawing room, which in contrast was tidy and quiet, serene and beautiful, where the mellow morning sun flooded across the bare brown floorboards and two squashy-looking sofas called out to them to come and sit down.

The dark-haired girl, Julia, did just that, flinging herself down, then turning back to Honey with an expectant smile.

'Do make yourself comfortable, Julia,' said the other sister waspishly and she gave Honey a quick flash of a smile. 'Now,' she announced with a flourish, 'I'm just going to wash my hands and fetch some drinks.'

'Nat will do that,' Julia called after her. 'Won't you, Nat?' she asked, turning back to her brother.

Nat nodded, walked back to the open doorway. 'Where's Pete, by the way?' he asked over his shoulder.

'Still in bed.'

'Good,' said Nick.

'He knows we don't want him around,' Julia told Honey. 'I said we'd call him down for lunch.'

Nat reappeared with a bottle of champagne and five glasses.

'Lamb for lunch,' Nick told her with hearty relish. 'Does your father still enjoy a Sunday roast? If it was me, it's the kind of tradition I'd insist upon.'

'Insist upon what?' asked Beth back in the doorway again.

'Insist on my Sunday roast,' said Nick. 'Right from the moment I arrived in Ibiza I think I'd insist upon that.'

Honey looked to the doorway and seeing the way Beth was waiting so avidly for her reply, she faltered. I'm sure they're broadminded, she thought. I know they're grown-up, but what can I say about a Sunday roast? Imagine Nick's face if I told him that in those days, when Dad first arrived, he was sometimes tripping for several days at a time, and in any case he never got up before three. Or that my mother usually spent her Sunday lunchtimes feeding milk and honey to the spirits she imagined lived in our well. They'll be horrified or they'll laugh and either way they'll switch off from me and I don't want them to. And yet she could see from their expectant faces that she wasn't going to get away without saying something.

'Well,' she began cautiously, 'for a start everything in Ibiza happens a lot later than it does here. And so at lunchtime usually it's a question of finding my parents first. When it was hot we would quite often have slept the night before in the garden . . .'

'In tents?' Beth asked innocently, still standing in the doorway.

'No. I don't think we ever bothered with a tent. It's so warm.'

'But don't you get bitten?'

'You soon become immune. And sometimes we'd hitch mosquito nets up between the olive trees, kind of like a tent.'

'It sounds lovely,' Beth said wistfully.

'Yes, it was. Other times we'd have ended up by the sea the night before and the mosquitoes aren't so bad there. When I was a child we'd often go to parties together, all of us, all the parents and the kids, and we'd build fires and camp and dance on the beach . . .'

She could feel the conflict bubbling inside her, half of her wanting to play it down, remembering that English girls and boys went to bed saying their prayers and surely long before sunrise, while the other half of her wanted to tell them exactly how she remembered it, idyllic, vibrant, eccentric, the whole island pulsing with its own hypnotic beat.

'When Tora and Dad were first in Ibiza, before I was born, there'd be wild parties but they've tamed down a bit now. There used to be animals wandering around the dance floor at Ku – Ku was the most famous nightclub in the world – and everyone would dance and dress up in fabulous costumes and parade down the streets before . . .' She tailed off, still not wanting to let it go, wanting to tell them *I'm not ashamed of him, I know he hurt your mother, your wife. But he's my father and I understand how intoxicating it was to be in Ibiza, experiencing it all. I don't blame him for being too weak to turn away.* 'But it's not like that now, everybody's far too responsible.'

Julia sighed, stretching back against the sofa.

'I'm so jealous. Meanwhile Beth and I were at Pony Club camp and Nat was in the Beavers. Or was it the Cubs, Nat? Do you think you'd become a Cub by then?'

'You know,' Nat laughed, 'I think I had.'

Finally Beth came on into the room and sat down on the floor, leaning back against the sofa. 'It does sound spectacular, Honey.'

While Julia sounded as if she genuinely wished she'd tasted that life too, Beth seemed rather relieved that she hadn't. 'And we know it still is, of course. I've not been there yet but even I know about Manumission and Cream and Oblivious.'

'Amnesia?' Nat asked.

'Exactly,' Beth agreed.

Honey looked at Beth, at her clothes so co-ordinated and freshly pressed and old-fashioned English, her flyaway hair clamped down tightly against her head with a checked blue hair clip that carefully matched her blue T-shirt. But the fun in Beth's face told Honey that she'd love Ibiza. She was just waiting for her chance.

Nat worked the cork out of the bottle with a practised hand.

'Champagne, Honey?' Beth asked, eagerly fetching her a glass.

'Thank you,' said Honey, 'how generous of you.'

Nat leaned forwards and kissed her cheek. 'You're a good reason to celebrate.' He held up his glass to her then sat down on the sofa next to Julia.

'Here's to Honey,' Julia and Beth added their toasts. Then Beth leaned back against Nat's legs.

'I've been thinking what I'd have done if I were you,' she said, 'and I'm sure I wouldn't have come.' She had the same direct way of speaking as Nat but without his confidence, and even she could hear her words had sounded awkward. 'But I'm so glad you did,' she added hastily, blushing pink. 'Dad promised not to ask you too much in the car because we all wanted to hear everything you said.' She looked up at her father as she spoke and he gave her an affectionate smile. 'And you're just like we hoped you'd be, not that we hoped you'd be anything particular. We just wanted to meet you.'

Honey looked at the four of them, all watching her intently, and felt that although it was friendly, it was an inquisition all the same.

'You wanted to meet me out of curiosity and of course I was curious to meet you, but actually I think there is something you could help me with too.' Instantly she had their attention. 'Until last week, when my father had a fall and concussed himself, I didn't know about your mother.' She glanced up at Nick, '. . . About your wife. I hardly knew anything about my father's life in England, but suddenly he started talking about her and it was clear that there was a whole world he'd left behind here. He hasn't forgotten her and he hasn't forgiven himself for leaving her the way he did. And I came here to ask you just that, to forgive him.'

In her mind's eye she saw her father, back by the pool at Can Falco, talking too loudly, laughing and joking as he always did, a sunhat perhaps the only concession to his accident, with this secret of his still clutched tightly to his chest after so long. And suddenly it was unbearably poignant to be thinking of him back there in Ibiza as she sat here in England, in this house, on this sofa, telling his story to Rachel's husband and children, her spirit all around them.

'I think the memory of what he did has stayed with him all his life.' Honey frowned as she felt tears gathering behind her eyes. 'And when I realized that, I said I thought I might come and find you and tell you, on his behalf, how sorry he was.'

From his place in the corner of the room Nick came forwards and gently touched Honey's hand, and Honey saw tears in his eyes too.

'He shouldn't be sorry. You should tell him that Rachel was very happy. You might even say that during her life here your father was the last thing on her mind.' He smiled gently as he said it. 'And you could say that she forgave him a long time ago, because after all, she married me instead. She died too young and we miss her unbearably, but her whole life here at Lingcott was busy and happy and fulfilled, and if it helps to go home and tell your father that, tell him – it's the truth.'

Honey nodded. 'Thank you. I know it will mean everything to him.'

She looked at all three of the children in turn and Beth and Julia immediately wiped at their eyes, laughing as they did so.

'More drinks before we all start crying,' said Nat, standing up and quickly turning his back on them.

Beth got up off the floor and came to sit beside Honey. 'Please be OK,' she told her, slipping her arm around her shoulders and hugging her close. 'Nothing but good can come of you being here now.'

Honey looked back up at Nick. 'It's a very personal question . . . But do you mind me asking how long it was before Rachel met you?'

'She'd known me for a long while,' said Nick, 'but we started going out together about six months after your father left and we were married shortly after. We lived in London for a while and then came here.'

'And when did Rachel die?'

'It was eight years ago this summer. She was fifty-four.'

Abruptly Nick turned on his heel and walked out of the room.

'Don't worry,' Nat reassured her. 'He wouldn't have minded you asking. He likes to talk about her but, even so, sometimes it can still upset him.'

Now she felt responsible for his sadness. Facing these three siblings, so united and strong, so blameless, she still felt responsible for Hughie whatever they said about their mother's happy life. Suddenly her own life in Ibiza felt flimsy and insubstantial by comparison. At that moment, looking at them grouped together, so mutually supportive, she felt alone and envious of their love for each other, envious of their big happy family and their lovely shambolic house, envious even of the grief they all shared. She looked uncertainly towards the doorway, wishing she knew Nick Paget well enough to go after him, to try to explain, but explain what she didn't know.

'Now, I'd like to know more about Ibiza,' said Beth.

'Half of Britain's thrown up on the streets of San Antonio,' said Nat. 'I can't imagine Honey's very impressed with us Brits.'

'Remember, I'm half Brit, too,' Honey insisted. She pulled herself together, forced out a smile.

'Nah,' Julia joked, 'you look nothing like a Brit.'

'WHY?' protested Honey. 'What do you mean?'

Julia pretended to consider the question and Honey looked self-consciously down at her feet, unpolished toenails, flat silver sandals. She was wearing a long olive-green skirt that had been in her cupboard for years and could have been bought anywhere, and a long-sleeved white shirt made out of very fine cotton and lace, which had, admittedly, been hand-made in Ibiza.

'Don't think it's a criticism, please,' Julia said. 'It's a compliment, you look gorgeous. British girls spend their lives trying to look like you.'

Honey shook her head. 'You can't say that.'

'Oh, she can, because it's true,' Beth agreed. 'It's the way you're put together, look at you and look at me.' As she spoke she looked down at her own very white legs, freshly shaved, the pink nail polish on her toes peeping out of her flowery flip-flops, and sighed. 'I tried, I really did, but I grew up in Banbury and it shows. Even though I live in London now, and I've got bloody hundreds of boho-boutiques to choose from, I still wouldn't know where to start. If I put some little plaits in my hair like you've done, I'd look like a fool.' She brushed at her hair with her fingers and laughed again.

'Whereas Honey's clearly spent her life running bare-foot through the trees picking ripe figs,' said Nat.

Both Julia and Beth stared at him. 'How the hell did you work that out?' asked Julia.

'And I'm not sure it sounded very nice, Nat,' said Beth.

'She's a hippy chick, that's all I meant,' Nat defended himself laughing, pushing himself back on the sofa and grinning at Honey, then he raised his glass to her once more. 'She's beautiful.'

At that moment the door to the drawing room opened slowly and an old Labrador with milky blind eyes came stiffly walking in.

Nat immediately jumped to his feet. 'Lettuce, Pete,' he called towards the open door, 'we're in here. Come and have some champagne. Come and meet Honey.'

fourteen

AFTER LUNCH, Honey, Beth, Julia and Nat spread out around the pool outside.

While Nat, Julia and Pete immediately stripped off and stretched out on the sunbeds, side by side, facing the pool and calling for Honey to join them, Beth went instead to the shade of a big white sun umbrella, open above a wooden table and chairs. She sat down, kicked off her flip-flops and fanned her pink face.

For a moment Honey hesitated, then went to join her and sat down and Beth grinned up at her with pleasure and surprise.

'Don't you want to swim?'

'Not yet.'

'It's too hot for me,' said Beth. 'The whole summer long and I'm still not used to it. I'd never survive Ibiza.'

'Oh, you would, you would, you'd love it, and you know lots of people don't go into the sun at all.' Honey squinted out towards the pool to where Julia was now sliding slowly into the water and into Pete's arms. Inevitably it reminded her of Edouard and at that moment all the new hostility she felt about him dissolved away and she thought only how she missed him, so much. 'We have houses made of stone six feet thick, they're beautifully cool inside all through the summer. Some days I don't go out at all.'

'I'd like to come to Ibiza some time.'

'Then you should!' She turned back to Beth. 'Come and stay with me.' It was so easy to offer it to Beth. There was something so sweet and undemanding about her compared to the angularity of her sister and brother.

'That would be wonderful and I could even put it down to research.'

'Why? What do you do?' Honey asked.

'I work for a wine merchant in London. Spanish wine is a speciality.'

'Oh, my father would love you,' Honey laughed. 'Spanish wine's his speciality too.' And as she said it she thought how for the first time it felt OK to be talking about him, especially to Beth. 'He has certain old friends he brings to Can Falco and they sit in the gardens under great big parasols, and I bring them the wine, and they sit there, and they research. They take it very seriously.'

'The best bit of the job.'

'Or, in his case, the only bit of the job.'

But Beth didn't laugh. 'Is it hard, living and breathing Can Falco while your parents have all the fun?'

'Oh no! Did I say that?'

'It's not what you say. It's the disapproving look when you say it.'

'That's really bad,' Honey winced. 'I thought I was making a joke.'

'But is that how it is?'

'A little, if I'm honest . . . but it's my own fault. It's easy to blame Can Falco and my parents, but nobody *makes* me work the way I do.'

'You should find someone to give you a hand.'

'I do. I have gorgeous Claudio to help me. He's looking after everything now. And certainly, coming to England again has made me ashamed at how little I've been here. I suppose, through the guests we have, I've always felt in touch with England, even though I've hardly been here myself.' She stretched out on her chair. 'It's also made me see how it is possible to get away for a weekend. I'm surprised how little I'm thinking about them all, how little I worry what I'll find when I go back.'

'Honey, you've come here for one weekend, not even a proper holiday.'

'I know. I've been programmed to think I'm essential, and I'm probably not at all.'

'So do you ever think of going anywhere else? Doing something different?'

'One of the guests, a rather rich guest, has a plantation in a place called Hue, somewhere on the Perfume River in Vietnam. I know nothing about it at all, but it sounded so beautiful that I thought I would like to go there one day, set up another Can Falco.' She laughed. 'His idea not mine.'

I want to go with Edouard, she thought privately, not elaborating to Beth. *That's what I'd thought, that we'd go there together.*

Out of the corner of her eye Honey could see that Pete was now lying along the diving board, stretching down to Julia, who was in the water below him holding on to his arms. Their heads were close together, noses touching as they talked.

Beth followed her gaze. 'Well, that certainly puts me off swimming. Do you want to go in? I'll tell them to stop if you do.'

'No,' Honey laughed. 'You can't do that.'

She stretched out her legs to the sun, slipped her feet out of her sandals and pulled her skirt up to her thighs and sat back and thought how ironic it was that she'd flown to England only to end up beside a swimming pool in the hot, hot sun. And yet how right it felt to be here with them all, how welcoming they'd been, how glad she was that she'd made the decision to come. She wondered if she'd ever see them again after this day.

In front of her the gardens spread out from the pool. Patches of the lawn were burnt and brown but the deep borders and beds were still full of colour, and roses and clematis in full flower climbed the old stone walls of the house. And there were so many wonderful trees, hundreds of feet high, bigger than any she could remember seeing before, beautiful bluey-green, their branches widely spread, elegant and symmetrical, casting long shadows across the lawn, the grass beneath them still spongy and green. She thought how perfect it would be to sit there and practise her chakras and how funny that she'd thought such a thing, how fitting that here in England she felt so much more her mother's daughter, whereas in Ibiza she behaved, at least in her mother's eyes, like the archetypal uptight Brit.

'OK?' Julia called to her from the pool, arms around Pete's neck.

'Perfect,' Honey told her. 'I might borrow something to wear and come and join you.'

In answer Julia gave her a thumbs up then swam over to the side, resting her arms on the stone slabs that surrounded the pool and looked up at Honey.

'You know, it's so great to have you here.'

'That's very nice of you to say.'

'Exactly what I've been telling her,' said Beth, reappearing beside her and dropping a swimming costume onto her lap.

'Exactly what I've been telling her too,' Nat said from his sunbed. 'Don't leave me out.'

'Thank you, Nat. Thank you, Julia, thank you, Beth. You are all being extremely nice.' She got off her sunbed and picked up Beth's offer of a costume. It was pink and white gingham with a little frilly skirt.

'Oh, I get it,' she grinned at them. 'Now you're going to have a laugh.'

'No, not at all. You don't have to wear it,' Beth said anxiously. 'I had it when I was about twelve, but I don't think anything else of mine now will fit you.'

'Beth, how could you?' Julia giggled.

'You're right,' Beth was now acutely embarrassed. 'What was I thinking? Of course Honey can't wear it.' She looked pleadingly at Julia. 'I'm such a fool. I should have got her one of yours.'

Honey wished she hadn't made the joke. Standing in

her own tight, white, rather see-through costume, Beth looked as if she was about to run away and cry.

'Honey will look sweet and she's certainly thin enough to get it on,' Julia comforted Beth.

'I love it,' Honey confirmed forcefully.

With the costume on she sat down beside Nat, then lay back and through half-closed eyes watched Beth swimming a length, moving powerfully up the pool. Upon reaching the far end, she turned immediately for another. Meanwhile Julia had slipped away.

'I should go soon,' Honey said to Nat, 'even though I don't want to.'

He looked over to her, shielding his eyes from the sun. 'Can't you stay this evening?'

She shook her head.

Beth climbed out of the pool and made her way over to the diving board.

'Got better plans?'

She grinned back at him. 'Maybe.'

'Where are you staying?'

'London, Islington.'

'With your boyfriend?'

'None of your business.'

Up on the diving board Beth walked to the edge and held her arms up high.

Nat stretched in his chair, brought his arms above his head and sighed. 'I didn't mean to be nosy.'

But Honey wasn't listening, wasn't really aware that he'd spoken at all, because up on the board, gripping the edge with her toes, Beth was getting ready to dive. She thrust out her chest, her hands pointed up to the sky then she bounced once and spread out her arms and was launched up, up into a perfect swallow dive.

And for a moment Beth seemed to freeze in mid-air, held by invisible lines in the perfect blue while Honey gripped the sides of the sunbed, feeling as if it was she who had been tossed high into the sky . . . There was no doubt at all that she'd seen that dive before, back by the pool at Can Falco. Beth was her father's daughter from her freckled face and strawberry-blonde hair to the way she'd flexed her fingers and tipped up her nose as she prepared for take-off.

Beside her she felt Nat touch her and she turned to him blindly, unable to breathe for the shock.

'Honey,' he said, gripping her wrist tightly as he spoke, 'it's all right. We know.'

fifteen

BETH'S DIVE made hardly a splash and now she was swimming the length underwater, her disjointed, rippling body moving her swiftly towards the shallow end, every stroke bringing her closer to the moment when she would burst free of the water and Honey would have to react . . . but she didn't know how, she really didn't know how.

Nat still had his hand gripped tightly around her wrist as if he was physically holding her together. 'Honey, it's OK.' She couldn't speak. 'We didn't know how to tell you.'

'My father doesn't know,' she managed to stumble out.

'No, of course.'

'She's my sister.'

'Yes.'

She pushed free of Nat's hand and walked stiffly towards the shallow end of the pool, but Beth got there first and rose to the surface in a shower of glittering water. She pushed her wet hair back from her face and swung around and Honey thought again, *this is my sister*. She felt her knees give way and she sat down heavily at the edge of the pool.

Beth sprang out of the water and was there at her side, slipping a wet arm around her neck and hugging her close.

'Oh what a shock,' she breathed as Honey stayed stiff and unresponsive. 'I've known about you most of my life. You're not the surprise I am to you. But how must it be for you, coming here, walking straight in among us all, with no idea?'

Still Honey couldn't make her brain move beyond the one thought, *she's my sister*. Before Nat had spoken there'd been a few panic-stricken moments when her mind had moved shot ahead in urgent leaps and bounds. *Tell them or not? How can I? How could I not? If I tell Beth, would she want to meet Dad? Of course she would. How would he cope? And what about Tora? What would she make of a step-daughter she didn't know she had? Am I wrong to guess she wouldn't like it at all?* All these thoughts had tumbled over themselves in their struggle to be heard. But then as soon as she realized Nat already knew about Beth and that Julia knew too, all the questions in her head abruptly stopped and everything went quiet. It was as if her brain acknowledged she didn't have to take control and as a consequence could no longer move at all.

Beth kept her arm around Honey. 'Ever since you got in touch with Dad, I've known I was about to meet you. I've had time to prepare, whereas you've had none at all.'

No time to prepare, Honey thought, watching the drops of water from Beth's wet body find the cracks between the slabs of stone and race away. *I've had a whole lifetime of not preparing.*

'We, Nat, Julia and me, we couldn't say anything on the telephone. Once we knew you were coming here we were so delighted. It felt as if everything was falling so perfectly into place. But since you've been here there's been no time to tell you properly. I nearly did, that moment when we all started to cry, but then Lettuce walked in and then it was lunchtime and . . . I hope you don't mind.'

Honey was aware it was funny. Not, *I hope you don't mind you have a new sister* but *I hope you don't mind I waited until after lunch to tell you.*

'And then,' Beth went on, 'sitting out here with you just now, talking about Ibiza and your dad, I knew it was the right time to say something.' She bit her lip. 'But I was just so scared . . .'

Beth's admission made Honey lift her head in

surprise. In the brief few moments she'd had to think, it hadn't occurred to her that Beth could be scared.

'When you dived it was as if I was watching him,' she told her. 'You look very like him, you know.' It was the only thing she could think of to say.

'What will he think when he meets me?'

'I don't understand. When do you mean?'

'I'm sorry, I'm sorry, I shouldn't have said that.'

But she had and immediately a surge of protectiveness swept through Honey, making her want to stamp down on Beth straight away, leave her in no doubt that Beth might be her sister but she could not simply invade her life, Hughie's life, Tora's life too.

'Of course I'll do whatever you think is best.' Beth lifted her arm from around Honey's shoulders and sat back on the stone. 'I've been waiting for this day for so long, and it's turned out so brilliantly. I'm sorry if I'm getting bits wrong, rushing you, saying the wrong things. You have to understand it's only because I'm so happy to meet you, to know you. I'll do whatever you want, of course I will.'

Honey nodded.

'When you arrived, when you got out of the car, I couldn't help crying. I know you noticed but of course I couldn't tell you why.' She stared at Honey, eyes shining again. 'I was so proud of you. It was the first thing I thought, before you'd even said a word.'

'I thought you were crying because of your mother.'

'No, only you.'

She was being generous and sweet and the fact that Honey couldn't respond in the same way didn't seem to matter to her.

'It's always been Nat and Julia, Nat and Julia,' Beth continued. 'You can see what they're like, how close they are. They look the same, sound the same, whereas I don't at all. But I've always known that somewhere there's you: there's Nat and Julia, but there's Beth and Honeybee, too.'

'You even knew my name?'

She nodded. 'I've always known your name.'

'I suppose your mother would have heard from the Bonniers. You know them? They're a family on Ibiza your mother kept in touch with. Their son is a friend of mine . . .'

And I wish he could be here right now helping me hear all this.

Beth shook her head. 'My mother told me about you when she was ill. She thought I might have wanted to find you one day, you and your dad.' Beth stopped abruptly. 'I would like him to know about me.'

'Of course.'

'I mean soon. I've waited so long.' Beth bit her lip, eyes wide. 'I don't mean this very moment, but, yes, I'd like you to tell him where you are. Tell him about me.'

'No!' she said it sharply but then some instinct told her to play along, not belittle Beth or her idea. 'I understand why you want him to know now, but you see, the problem is he's just been in hospital and perhaps it would be better if—'

'He's been in hospital!' Beth cried in horror. 'Why? What happened to him?'

'He had a little fall, he hit his head.'

Beth leaped to her feet. 'Oh my God, but that's terrible.'

'No, no. It really wasn't so bad. He dived into the shallow end of the pool. It's the sort of mad thing he does quite often.'

She took Beth's hand trying to persuade her back to the ground.

'Please, Honey, no!' Beth insisted. 'He could have broken his neck, fractured his spine. When did he do this, did you say?'

'On Thursday.'

'And you're here!' Now she was incredulous. 'He's only just out of hospital, with concussion and you've come here?' Now she shivered uncontrollably. 'Perhaps you think I'm getting all hysterical, over-reacting, but

what if he dies? Now I'm having this terrible thought
that I'm never going to meet him. I've waited so long,
all my life and you tell me he's in hospital.' She clutched
at her head, gave Honey a wobbly helpless smile and
then her eyes abruptly filled with tears. 'Now you're
telling me he's had an accident and wouldn't it be such
a perfect bloody tragedy. I can see it happening. He's
going to die and I'll never meet him.'

'No!' Honey got to her feet and pushed Beth back
down so that she was sitting beside her once more.
'Listen to me. I promise you it was not bad. Do you
seriously think I'd have left him if I'd thought it was?'

Beth wiped at her eyes, and sniffed. 'I'm sorry,
probably not, of course you wouldn't.'

She sniffed again. 'It's just I'm furious with myself
for not thinking this could have happened years before
now. He might have died, mightn't he? After all you
came to find my mother and she's not alive. It would
only have taken one accident, one illness, in all the
years I've been waiting to meet him, all those years
while I've been listening to everybody telling me to wait.
*It's too soon after my mother's death, don't go now. Finish university,
don't go now.* I've been waiting all the time for Nat or
Julia or my father to give me the go-ahead. Why did I
do that? Why should they make the decisions? I've hated
it. And then, last week, Dad said you were coming . . .

It was as if you were his gift to me, when I'd always wanted to find you for myself.' She paused for a shaking, wobbling breath, and Honey held tightly to her hand, waiting while Beth slowly brought herself back under control.

'I used to imagine coming to Can Falco to stay, walking around as a guest with none of you knowing who I was. It's all right, I wouldn't have really done that,' she added hastily, seeing the look of alarm on Honey's face. 'It was much too devious for me, not how I wanted to do it at all. And when Mum was alive you and your father were out of bounds. She'd done such a good job of forgetting. I always felt it would be a betrayal of her and Dad to come looking for you both and I suppose, even after her death, that's what stopped me. That and knowing what it would do to Dad. But then out of the blue you called us, and now, having met you, it changes everything, doesn't it?' She sniffed again. 'And all I have been able to think about, apart from the fact that I was about to meet you, was that also I'd meet him.'

Come to Ibiza, come to Can Falco, Beth. Come to the home of the wonderful, the incomparable, Mr Ballantyne, thought Honey sadly. *Watch him split his skull on swimming pool floors, watch him fight with his neighbours, fall off harbour walls into the sea, or through the roof of someone's gazebo, or out of a car window. Watch him trip over someone's chair in the restaurant and land face-first in their food.*

'When I go home I'll talk to him,' Honey promised. 'I think it's best if I tell him about you first. But you should meet him as soon as you can. And then, there's my mother, Tora, too . . .' who could either scoop Beth up in her arms with cries of joy or ignore her completely.

'Oh, of course,' Beth exclaimed. Honey's concern was understandable, but not putting her off her stride in the slightest. 'I didn't think I could just walk into Can Falco, catch them at the bar. *Hi, Stepmom! Hi, Dad!*'

At that Honey let out a splutter of appalled laughter. 'He'd know straight away you were serious, too.'

'I could give him a heart attack to go with the concussion.' Now she was joking, trying to reassure. 'Look, it's too soon for you to trust me, I can see that, but all I want is to be your friend, as good a friend as you'll let me be. I know I might have freaked you out then, saying I had to meet him straight away; of course I don't. I'll meet him whenever you want to introduce me. He's your dad in a way he'll never be mine. I've never known him and, back there in the house, I already have a father who's looked after me and loved me all my life, and whatever I say about feeling different from Nat and Julia, I know they're still my family and I do adore them too. And so the last thing I want to do is take anything away from you. I want to add to it, that's all.'

She had moved in seconds from bordering on hysterical to being reassuring and calm.

'For a while Mum said she had to fight the urge to go out to Ibiza to find Hughie and try to persuade him to come home,' Beth went on. 'She was sure he would have done if he'd known about me, but the truth was that their relationship was falling apart months before and she knew it would never work.'

And Honey thought, already she's calling him Hughie. She has a 'Dad' and now she has a 'Hughie'.

'I don't know why they let me happen at all but they did.' Beth shrugged. 'Anyway, she never did tell him.'

And so Beth talked on, telling Honey how her mother and Nick Paget had married very quickly, that Beth had been born only a few weeks after their wedding, but every time Honey took a breath to respond, to say something caring and kind, instead the mean, vicious fears circled overhead making her hesitate. She worried that Beth would come to meet Hughie and he would break down or even reject Beth completely. How shattered Beth would be if he did. There she was, sitting on the stones, bravely facing Honey, telling her over and over again how she expected nothing and could cope with anything and Honey knew it wasn't true. Of course

Beth was looking for something, just as Honey had always done herself.

And she saw too, that it was more complicated still, that alongside the genuine worry for Beth, there was also a desperate reluctance to give up her own roles as only child, only daughter. Even if it was a role she'd always complained about, it was *her* role all the same, it was what made her who she was.

Honey met Beth's eye, really focused on her for the first time, and prepared her words, thinking how to say the right things, whatever they might be, but all she saw was Hughie staring back at her with the same wide-eyed, pale blue eyes, a little bit hurt, a little bit wary. Seeing him and Beth all mixed up, so familiar and yet so new too, she didn't say a word but burst into tears instead.

'I'm happy,' she insisted as Beth immediately threw her arm back around her. 'I am. You mustn't think I'm not.'

'It's OK,' Beth soothed again. 'Second by second, minute by minute, hour by hour, you'll get a little bit more used to me. That's all you have to do.'

With Beth's arm around her, she looked out at the great gardens of the house, shadows from the trees lengthening along the beautiful soft curves of the lawns. She breathed in the sense of calm serenity, along with the excitement and expectation that her visit had brought to this thriving family, and among all the tumble of emotions there was fear for all of them, fear that by becoming involved with the Ballantynes, not just Beth but all of them would lose so much more than they'd gain. Because it seemed to Honey that they already had it all, everything that they could possibly want, apart from Rachel, of course.

'I wonder if the Bonniers knew about you,' she said through her tears, 'they were her friends.'

Beth shook her head. 'Nobody knew. My mother left London very quickly and moved back in with her parents. She went to ground. Granny and Grandpa were very supportive, although they hardly approved, and then she found Dad. And very soon after I was born they moved here and had Nat and Julia. Nat's just eighteen months younger than me, Julia came along a couple of years after him. And so to most people I'm one hundred per cent Paget too. I've grown up knowing that Dad isn't my father but I've got his name and, to be honest, for years I hardly thought about it at all.' She grinned. 'But I did think about you.'

'And then, suddenly, here I am, walking into your house with absolutely no idea what I'm about to find.'

'Not too horrible a surprise, I hope.' Beth laughed.

She's so in control, Honey thought. She's planned for this and now, after that one understandable outburst of panic, she's dignified and warm and happy about it too.

Honey sat back uncomfortably and looked around to find that they were still alone, then turned back to Beth. She knew what she wanted to do. She wanted to leave here, have a chance to think and take it all in before she made the wrong move she knew was just waiting to happen. She wanted to be back home in Ibiza, working out how best to break the news to her father, and most of all she wanted Edouard beside her.

'It's time for me to go, you know. I should get Nat to take me to the station.'

'Honey, you're not serious!' Beth looked at her with disbelief and hurt. 'I've only just found you. Please, please don't go.'

But I want to. I want to be with Edouard. I'm all over the place, can't you see? I'm in shock. I want to run away from you all, find somewhere to hide and go over everything that's happened this day, think how best to deal with it. She remembered a little phrase of Tora's: Let me find my moment of stillness. *That's what I need.*

But here beside her was Beth, expectant, saying nothing but clearly desperate for Honey to stay and Honey knew she couldn't refuse her, that if she rejected Beth's plea, her sister's plea, that she'd never be able to make things right again.

So she made herself smile warmly and say that she'd love to stay.

'But I should call my boyfriend, Edouard, and let him know I'm not coming back. He was expecting me tonight.'

She pushed herself to her feet.

'Are you going to tell him your news?' asked Beth, following as Honey walked back to the sunbed and found her handbag underneath her clothes, waiting expectantly as Honey took out her phone.

She swung away from her not answering, wishing that Beth might understand she wanted to make the call alone.

'Bee, I've been trying to reach you all day,' Edouard said straight away.

'Why, what's wrong?'

'Nothing! Everything's right. I'm home, I'm waiting for you.'

She felt her cheeks burn. Hearing that lovely familiar voice, it didn't matter now that they'd spent the last conversation shouting at each other, that they'd allowed Paul Dix to shove his way between them. It didn't even matter if Paul had won. All she knew was that she wanted Edouard there beside her so badly. And she knew that if she only asked him, he would come straight away . . . and she couldn't do it.

She half-turned away, knowing that Beth was listening still.

'I want to tell you about my day. And why I have to stay here tonight.'

At that Beth immediately held up her hand in apology but still didn't leave her alone.

Honey started to walk slowly across the lawn.

'No, Bee!' he laughed. 'Don't say that.' He wasn't being serious. She could hear from his voice that he didn't actually believe her.

And then, when she didn't deny it, he spoke again more quietly, his voice full of disbelief.

'You'd rather stay with *them*? I've worked day and night to finish early and you're staying with them?'

'I have to.'

'Why?'

She told him why.

sixteen

IT WAS AS if Beth had privately had a word with Julia and Nat, even though Honey knew that she hadn't had the chance. When the four of them met again just inside the house – Honey still in the ridiculous pink swimming costume – thankfully neither Nat nor Julia chose to fall upon her in floods of tears. Instead Julia immediately suggested she would take Honey upstairs and show her where she would sleep and seemed instinctively to understand that Honey could do with some time alone and was certainly not in the mood for another big heart to heart.

They passed a landing on the first floor and climbed the stairs again, Julia scampering ahead in her bikini bottoms and a little T-shirt, and eventually the staircase opened out onto a second floor just like the first, their bare feet soundless on the oak floor boards. First Julia led her to her own bedroom, which was a large square room painted white, with more bare floorboards, a big rumpled, unmade bed, and a green velvet chair piled high with what were presumably Pete's clothes. There was lots of oak furniture, and gauzy white curtains blowing at the window and a glass vase crammed with blowsy pink roses, their petals blown to the floor by the breeze.

Julia ran across the room and shut the window, picked up the vase and gave it to Honey.

'Here. Let's take them for your room.'

Honey, still standing in the doorway, took them carefully from her. She felt very close to tears now, knew that once she was alone, in her own bedroom with the door shut, she would succumb.

'Sit on the bed while I find you some things.' Julia moved to her chest of drawers, opened a drawer and tipped out a pile of clothes onto the floor and Honey did as she was told, moving to the bed and putting the flowers carefully on the bedside table before sitting down.

On the floor Julia shook out a round-necked grey T-shirt. 'You can sleep in this.' Then she opened a smaller drawer at the top and with a grin swung a tiny lace thong around her index finger. 'And you can wear this tomorrow. It was a Christmas present, I never wore it. It's all I've got.'

'Better than nothing.'

She threw it across the room and Honey caught it one-handed.

'Toothpaste and brush,' Julia said next, disappearing through a doorway and then reappearing with Colgate and a toothbrush in her hand. 'Now, what else do you need?' She paused, looking wonderingly at the pink swimming costume. 'What was Beth thinking?'

She jumped up beside Honey on the bed so that they were sitting side by side, four brown legs in a row. 'Your clothes are still by the pool but you can borrow something of mine if you like, but you don't have to,' she added hastily. 'You're not on show and tonight we'll all watch telly together and hardly talk at all, I promise.' She gave Honey a sympathetic smile. 'We must remember we don't have to cram in every important conversation into this very first afternoon.'

Honey nodded and allowed herself to fall back against the mattress. She felt exhausted. Sinking back into the soft squashy mattress, she'd have been happy not to move again.

Julia looked down at her. 'I could leave you here? I could cover you up with a blanket? You could have a sleep?'

Honey gave her a grateful smile back. 'Not such a bad idea.'

She didn't want to admit to Julia that actually it was someone else, completely unrelated to all of them, who was taking up most of her thoughts right then.

Julia tucked a stray strand of black hair behind her ear and put her head on one side like a bright-eyed blackbird. 'I keep wondering what you're making of us. I can't imagine how strange it must be for you.' She shifted on the bed so that she could see Honey properly. 'I hope when you've got used to the idea, you'll be pleased to have us around.'

'Of course, I am already.'

'But how can you know?' she looked at Honey seriously. 'It's time that will tell how close we're going to get. We're grown-ups, we're not kids who are going to be forced to live with each other. No one will judge how much time you spend with us, how much of your life changes because we're around.'

'Yours will change too.'

'Of course, but let's not pretend we're as affected by this as much as you are.' She smiled suddenly. 'That sounded nothing like I wanted it to.' Then she surprised Honey by falling down on the bed beside her. 'The truth is that Nat and I are just as pleased about you as Beth is. You do know that, don't you? We have all lost our mother, and I think we're all closer to you because of that. I suddenly listened to myself and sounded rather detached, but that's not how I feel at all.' She shrugged then gave Honey a wide easy smile. 'I want to welcome you but I don't want to swamp you.'

'You're not at all.'

'So what did your mum make of your coming here?'

'She said may the rainbow of truth and love bring me home again soon.'

'You're joking?'

'No!'

'I mean it's as if she knew,' Julia said delightedly. 'How absolutely brilliant of her.'

Honey shook her head. 'She didn't know. She wouldn't have kept quiet about it if she had done. Tora doesn't believe in secrets.'

'So what will she make of Beth?'

'I really don't know.'

'Here are your clothes,' said Beth from the doorway and Honey quickly pushed herself back upright to see her sister standing there with an armful of clothes and Honey's handbag clutched between two fingers. The look on Beth's face made Honey feel as if she'd been caught out. She immediately jumped off the bed and took them from her.

'Honey,' Beth said, now looking determinedly down

at the floor. 'I was wondering if you'd like a cup of tea?'

'Sure,' Honey tried very hard not to let on how uncomfortable Beth was making her feel. 'Julia was just going to show me my room and then I'll come down.'

Beth nodded. 'That's fine then. I'll see you downstairs.'

'Thanks so much,' Honey called after her as Beth ran back down the stairs.

'Oh, dear Beth,' Julia sighed. She pushed herself upright and looked at Honey. 'You see how careful you're going to have to be?'

'So far she's been amazing, very sweet and only concerned about me.'

Julia nodded. 'That sounds like Beth.'

'What do you mean?'

'It's just she can be a bit intense. And she's been fixated about this day . . . and you. Not in an unnatural way,' she added hastily, 'in a perfectly understandable way.' Abruptly she bounced back off the bed. 'We'd better go back, they'll be wondering what's happened to you. The best thing you could do right now is go and drink her cup of tea, reassure her that she's your number one.' She looked at Honey and smiled. 'Sorry, but that time on your own we were talking about? Forget it. I think my father's waiting to talk to you too . . . But wait! I nearly forgot. Let me quickly show you your room.'

Honey's room, very similar to Julia's in the way it was laid out, was two doors down and was next to the bathroom. It had one window that looked out across the gardens, and another to the right of the bed that looked down to the farmyard below. They looked in for just long enough for Honey to place the vase of flowers on her bedside table then strip off the un-swum-in swimming costume and replace her T-shirt and skirt. As an afterthought she picked up her phone and dropped it into the deep pockets of her skirt.

Outside again Julia pointed out Nat's bedroom, which was opposite Honey's, and the one next door to that belonged to Beth. Down on the first floor, Julia explained, all the rooms were laid out in exactly the same way and housed Nick's bedroom and one for Aunt Lettuce.

When they got back down to the kitchen it was to find Beth making tea. Everybody but Nick had re-emerged to join Nat and Beth in the kitchen. Honey was appalled to see blind Aunt Lettuce standing at the table carving large pieces of fruit cake for everybody with a bread knife while beside her Nat and Pete sat reading the papers, oblivious.

'Don't worry, Honey. I do it by touch,' she told Honey, passing her a slice, then she took her own plate and a cup of tea and went to sit down at the other end of the table.

'Honey!' Nat looked up at her.

'Hello, Nat.'

'Edouard Bonnier?' he demanded. 'Who is that? Did you say you knew him?'

Honey froze. 'What about him?' She saw Nat was reading the business pages of the *Saturday Telegraph*.

'Does he run a management company called Masterplan?'

'Yes he does.'

He nodded, turned back to the paper. 'Spells his name with "ou" not "w."'

Beth came across the kitchen, passed her a mug of tea. 'Have this.'

Honey took it from her. Now the kitchen was suddenly stifling and she felt sweaty and hot. She crossed the room to join Nat.

'His mother's French. Why, what does it say? If it is *my* Edouard Bonnier, you'd better tell me what you've read about him.'

'It's only some mucky gossip columnist stirring up trouble,' said Nat. 'Nothing important. You haven't heard of a guy called Paul Dix?'

'Yes I have.' She leaned over his shoulder to read the paragraph he was highlighting with his finger.

Edouard Bonnier says it is business as usual, but Paul Dix would have it otherwise. Word has it another major player will desert Masterplan on Monday. Business as usual perhaps, but right now that's hardly reassuring news for the shareholders.

'Don't take this journalist seriously,' Nat said. 'I'm sure Edouard Bonnier doesn't.'

'Honeybee!' said Nick, walking into the kitchen and straight up to her. He patted her gently on the shoulder. 'Tell me you've survived.' He picked up a mug of tea for himself. 'Shall we take a walk around the garden while we drink these? Would you mind?'

'I need to make a call.' She touched a hand to her hot cheeks.

He looked surprised at her abruptness. 'Are you all right? Do you want to use my study?'

She pulled herself together. 'I'll go outside. Then I'd like to walk with you.'

She held out her phone in front of her without waiting for his answer and keyed in the numbers, then took it out into the yard outside, willing Edouard to pick up.

It went straight to answerphone.

'I wish you were here,' she said rapidly. 'I wish I was with you. What cheap stunt has Paul Dix pulled now? Are you OK? Are you surviving?' She hesitated, looked out across the sunlit peaceful hills. 'I don't even know where you are. In Paris? Did you come home? Perhaps you're in Ibiza. Let him build all over it if it means he will leave you alone. I just care about you.'

She went back to the kitchen and picked up Nick and they walked together across the front lawn, Honey grateful to be outside, then gingerly made their way one by one across the cattle grid that divided the garden from the fields, Honey following him as he led them along a little track close to a high hawthorn hedge and then immediately over an old wooden stile.

'I want to show it off to you,' he told her with a smile. 'I want you to see how perfect England can be.'

It was a golden early evening with just enough of a breeze to cool the air, the sun still warm, casting everything in a beautiful light. In the distance Honey could see the rooftops of the village, the spire of the church, heard the distant whinny of a horse, while alongside the path they were following, the hedges were unexpectedly full of movement and sound. A blackbird sitting on a bramble, belting out its full-throated song, staying put as she walked quietly by, while all around her she could hear the rustle and snap of twigs as other animals and birds, hiding in the undergrowth dived back to safety at the sound of her passing feet. She looked down at her feet covered in dust, at her white shirt now grey, a day's worth of dirt. She felt battle-worn, vulnerable in her grimy clothes, wary of Nick as he led her on, aware that he'd brought her outside to talk some more and too tired to want to hear it.

'First, an apology,' Nick said, 'for bringing you here under false pretences, for no doubt giving you the shock of your life.'

She gave him a shaky smile. 'Tell me Beth *was* the something you should know? Tell me there are no more secrets still to come out.'

'She was my secret and I'm very sorry I couldn't be clearer, but I thought it was the best way. I thought it was wise to allow you to have a chance to get to know Beth and see what a sweetie she was before we spilled the beans. I'm presuming, I mean I suppose I'm hoping, that she was a good surprise?' He broke off a dark gold ear of wheat, broke it open and passed Honey a single kernel. 'Try it.' Honey bit hard and it split open,

the floury texture familiar and yet it was sweet as a nut.
'That's perfectly ripe. They should be harvesting here
tomorrow. I always love watching them, don't you?' He
gestured to the second tyre track running alongside her.
'Come and walk beside me.'

They reached a five-bar gate that led them out into
a grassy meadow, this time full of buttercups blowing
in the breeze, another archetypically English scene, and
Nick stopped, leaning over the gate and sipping his tea.

'I'm still shocked,' admitted Honey. 'But Beth is so
sweet and kind. I could see that straight away. I'm lucky
to have found her. I know we'll be good friends.'

He smiled in relief. 'Good for you, Honey.' They
walked on. 'You saw that Beth's got a great deal resting
on meeting her father?'

At his words Honey looked at the baked and cracked
ground under her feet, knowing that she wanted to be
loyal and faithful and true, wanted to champion Hughie
not tear him down but that she wanted to be honest
too.

'I don't know if he'll live up to expectations.'

'Did you ever think you might have had a sister or
a brother?'

She glanced at him in surprise. It seemed such a
strange response.

'Of course not. I didn't know anything about any of

you until last week,' Honey answered. 'My father never said anything to lead me to suspect . . .'

'And your mother? Did Tora say nothing either?'

'I don't think she knew any more than I did. Why do you ask?'

'I fear that perhaps Beth won't be such a surprise to your father.'

'He definitely didn't know,' Honey said vehemently. 'He would never have left her if he had.'

That had to be true, didn't it? Please? Hughie wouldn't have been so cowardly as to run away knowing Rachel was carrying his child. 'Why do you say that to me?' She didn't want to believe it, but already she was starting to. 'Don't tell me that he knew. Did Rachel tell you that? Did she say so?'

'She said she never did tell him. But seeing her pregnant with our other two children I can't believe he wouldn't have known. I'm sorry, Honeybee, but I'm telling you that because I want you to help me keep Beth safe. In good time she will meet your father, but before she does you must make sure that he understands it would be devastating for her ever to learn he abandoned her.'

Loyalty made her not want to admit to Nick Paget that it could be true and yet the knowledge fitted everything she knew of her father, not just in the way he had always run away when things got tough, but in his uselessness, as if he'd always hated himself as a consequence. And telling Beth was the kind of impulsive thing he would do. Catch him off guard and he might admit it to her in their very first conversation.

'I know you've misjudged him but even so I'll make sure I talk to him, find out what he means to say.'

'Thank you.'

He opened the gate and they walked on, along a tiny path that led them down to a stream where a couple of sleepers and a guard rail stretched across as a footbridge, and here Nick came to a halt again, leaning over the rail and catching his breath, looking down at the running stream below.

'Rachel and I would often come here.'

Honey leaned her arms over the wooden guard rail and watched the journey of the water flowing below. In places it sped past, splashing over the pebbles and rocks, nearer the bank it pooled, moving so slowly that long-legged insects were sitting on its surface, splayed on the water, their feelers gently testing the air.

'She needs you to keep Beth safe.'

'I will,' Honey insisted. 'Know that I wouldn't take a chance on something so important.'

At her words his ready tears plopped down into the stream below. 'I must sound so desperate, but I feel as if I'm handing her over. She's my daughter, Honeybee. She's never been anything else. But in this I have to let her go with you.'

She put out a hand and touched his. It felt a curiously intimate yet very natural thing to do. The confident almost abrasive man who'd met her at the station was unrecognizable now.

'I'm repeating myself, I know, but you have to watch her,' Nick went on. 'She's vulnerable. She's told me already how Julia has tried to lend you clothes, how she's found you in Julia's bedroom having a chat and hated it so. You can see she wants you all to herself.'

'We've only just begun,' said Honey. 'She can't outguess me. She has to learn to trust me . . . I'm sure it's been hard living with the pair of them, always that little bit happier, that little bit different to her, but she has to let me spend time with them, laugh and joke with them too. It would be unnatural if I didn't. I have to be free to sit on Julia's bed and I want to be able to have a drink with Nat without guiltily looking over my shoulder in case she's watching. She's got to learn to have faith in me.'

'I know, I'm just telling you how it is.'

He led the way back off the footbridge, back into the wheat field and this time Honey stayed behind him and they walked in single file back towards the house.

hippy chick

Once inside Honey desperately needed some time alone. She motioned to Beth that she was going upstairs, slipped through the kitchen door and up the stairs, opened her bedroom door and flung herself upon her bed, filled with pain at the thought that Hughie could have known about Beth all along.

Much later, long after suppertime, long after the house had gone to bed, she was still thinking about it, puzzling over everything she knew, all the time edging closer to the knowledge that of course Hughie had known about Beth. She sat in her bedroom, looking through the open window, and held out her arm to the night, feeling the air cool against her skin, there was none of the heat of an Ibiza night. She thought how back at Can Falco at eleven o'clock people would be beginning to stir and think about dinner. But here it was very much time to sleep, around her the whole house was falling asleep, and she too was so very tired. She drew the curtains and returned to her bed, sank wearily down onto the old bouncy mattress and pulled the sheets around her.

Her head started spinning as soon as she closed her eyes. Whether it was because of the wine or tiredness or confusion or a combination of all three, she was immediately awake again. And thinking of Can Falco had made her sad. She'd been gone two days, it felt like years. But somehow, now that it was night time, it was easier to accept that not so far away the same moon was shining down on her hotel and on Hughie and Tora, and for all the sadness suddenly she felt a huge pang of missing them too, a massive love for them, just as they were, and a longing for nothing to have changed after all. She feared the future. She felt cold at the responsibility now not just to them but to Beth too. It was no longer going to be enough to be a good daughter, now she had to be a good sister too.

Lying in her bed with eyes wide open, now she longed for Edouard, who expected nothing from her at all. She rolled against the pillows burying her face, then twisted again, lying on her back, staring up into the darkness.

Suddenly she sat up in the bed, finding the walls of the bedroom claustrophobic. She wanted to get outside, to walk in the moonlight, pace the gardens and think what to do, and once the idea had come to her she couldn't stay in bed any longer.

Quietly she opened her door and walked out into the shadowy hall. She slipped along the corridor and then down the main hall stairs. At the bottom she felt her way towards a doorway and to where she imagined there would be a light switch, patted blindly around the walls but found nothing. She stood in the silence, listening for clues but there was no sound at all. She moved on into the darkness, and slowly her eyes adjusted to the light. Then she was in a hall that she thought had the kitchen at its far end and once she decided that it did she walked boldly down the length of it and opened the door at the far end, to find herself not in the kitchen at all but in another hallway that seemed exactly like the first. Now she looked back the way she'd come, then forwards once more and it felt as if she was in a dream, that if she walked on she would find another door and another hallway, and then another and another and another. So she turned back the way she'd come, paced back the length of the first hall and then stopped because she'd passed a window sill, waist-high, the moon bright and hanging low in the sky, three-quarters full. She opened the window wide, breathed in the soft cool darkness of the beautiful gardens outside, grey in the moonlight, where nothing moved at all, then sank down cross-legged on the stone floor, tucked her T-shirt beneath her, held her hands together in her lap and tipped up her face to the light. She closed her eyes, rested her hands on her knees and imagined the moon's delicate silvery light bathing her face, its warmth gently slipping through her body. She breathed slowly, in and out, thinking only of its light and its gentleness and gradually she felt its peace settle upon her shoulders.

She stayed there for about five minutes and when she opened her eyes again it was because she could hear someone breathing. And then a side door squeaked open halfway down the hall, and suddenly there was Beth peering through it.

Honey stayed where she was, waiting for her and she came cautiously through the door. When Honey didn't rise to her feet at the sight of her, Beth hesitated and then sat carefully and silently down opposite her.

'For a moment I thought you were a ghost,' she whispered. 'You looked so pale, with your hair and your grey T-shirt. I'm sorry. I didn't mean to interrupt you.'

Honey shook her head, wondering if she was in the middle of a dream, It all seemed so strange.

Beth nodded towards the open window. 'You're watching the moon?'

'Yes.' She smiled, amused by Beth's chatty tone.

'I can see why, it's magical isn't it? Sometimes at night, when I can't sleep, I go out into the gardens and I lie under the cedars and I watch the light through the branches. Have you ever done that?'

'Never,' said Honey, thinking how in Tora, Beth might find a kindred spirit after all. 'One day you'll have to let my mother get her hands on you. She has excellent tricks for getting to sleep.' Honey scrambled back to her feet, hesitated a moment. 'I couldn't sleep either. I thought I might have gone for a wander outside but I couldn't find the door.'

'Easily lost and I've lived here all my life.' Beth rose back to her feet. 'I'll show you if you want. Can I come with you?'

'I'd like you to.'

Beth reached behind her and pressed a switch and immediately the hall was bathed in light, and Honey saw the grey stone floor she'd been sitting on, the heavy curtains on either side of the open window and further down an oak-studded door. Beth went over to the door and carefully turned its iron key, opened the door. And the two of them stepped outside into the wonderful night, the sky packed with stars.

'Come on,' Beth said, dropping her voice to a whisper.

Barefoot they padded across the garden. In the moonlight Honey could see the way towards the cattle grid and on to the path she'd taken with Nick that afternoon. Now it seemed a completely different place, the garden grass slightly damp and soft and springy between her toes. They walked on towards the tall dark trees. Cedars of Lebanon, Beth had said. They moved between them, pacing deliberately, hardly needing to speak and yet here in the darkness, with each unspoken word, she felt closer to Beth than she ever had in the daylight.

Beth walked to one of the tallest trees and laid her hands flat against its trunk, then pressed her cheek against its scratchy bark.

'I lie beneath it like this . . .' She sank down to the ground, then lay on her back looking up into the dark branches. 'I love the balance of the earth beneath me and the weightlessness of the night above.'

Her clear musical voice was loud in the silence of the night. Tora will work on you, thought Honey, lying down beside her. She will mould you and guide you, lead you down the pathways to fulfilment and inner joy. Perhaps of the two of her parents, it would be Tora who'd influence her most. You will love her. And you'll love Ibiza too.

'Beth?' she whispered a couple of minutes later, when the grass had become a little colder and the sky had begun to lose its attraction. There was no reply. 'Beth?'

Honey shook her awake.

'Honey!' She opened her eyes. 'Did you feel it too? Wasn't it great?'

'You were asleep, Beth.'

She stood up first then helped Beth onto her feet

and together they walked back across the lawns to the house.

Back inside at the top of the stairs Honey paused to say goodnight, leaned in to kiss her, when Beth caught hold of her arm.

'Forgive me if I make life difficult for you.'

Honey shook her head. 'Of course you don't.'

'No,' said Beth, 'I don't mean now, I mean later.'

Honey slept late the next morning, had a lazy bath. Then, wrapped in a towel, she found her way to Beth's bedroom to ask for some clothes to borrow. When there was no response to her knock, she quietly opened the door expecting to find her still asleep, but the bed was made, and even before she logged that the room was completely empty, no sign of Beth at all, she heard voices downstairs calling her name and Beth's too and she knew something was wrong.

She left the room, crossed the hall and stopped at the top of the stairs. She could hear Nat and Nick at the bottom and she leaned over the banisters to see what was going on. Below her she could see Nick looking vainly out through the open front door.

'Has her car gone?' As he spoke he moved towards the window to see.

'I don't know.' Nat came into view, moving closer, to look out of the window too.

'I think it has,' said Nick quietly. 'She's left without a word. So why would Beth do that, Nat? Where could she possibly have gone? And why wouldn't she want to tell us first?'

At his words Honey flew back to her bedroom, and dressed in the same dirty clothes that she had worn the day before, then came back to the top of the stairs, took a deep breath and began to walk down.

Below her Nick was now sitting in a hall chair with his head in his hands.

'She wouldn't want to tell us because she'd know we'd try to stop her.'

He looked up to where Honey was standing halfway down the stairs and stared at her in horrible surprise.

'What can you mean? Where is she Honey, do you know? Is she safe? Is she in trouble?'

'I think she's on her way to Ibiza.'

Honey stepped forwards down the last stairs and stopped to face the two of them. 'Yesterday, beside the pool, all she could think about was meeting my father . . . Hughie.'

'Her father,' said Nick.

'She wanted me to call him straight away to tell him that she was here, who she was, and I didn't want to brush her aside. I didn't want her thinking she didn't have a right to see him as soon as she wanted to, but I wanted time to prepare the way, so I told her how Hughie had been in hospital. I thought it would make her see she shouldn't rush him, but it did the opposite. She couldn't bear it. For a while nothing I said made the slightest bit of difference and then suddenly she calmed down again, apologized even, and so we stopped talking about him, about when she'd meet him and I forgot about it. Perhaps she sensed that if it was left to me, it would be a while because I wanted him to be well again, I wanted to prepare him. Perhaps it was wrong of me to think I had any right to do that. Perhaps she knew even then what she'd do this morning. And then later last night she asked me to forgive her if she made life difficult for me and again it makes me think she had to have been planning this. We were up at two or three in the morning, we'd been walking in the garden. Perhaps she even left last night, after she said goodbye to me. Two, three o'clock in the morning, she could be there already.'

Nick looked back at her uncomprehending.

'Dad,' Nat said awkwardly, clutching his arm, but Nicholas immediately shook him off.

'And will Hughie tell her?' he demanded, rising from his chair and striding up the stairs to face Honey, all hostility now. 'Will he tell her that he knew about her before she was born?'

Honey looked him in the eye. 'I don't know. Why would he want to hurt her? He's not that kind of man, but if she surprises him, perhaps. I don't know.'

'I think he is that kind of man.' Nick laid his hand against his chest. He was a strong, confident, vital man but now his hand trembled uncontrollably and he crumpled down onto the stair below Honey. 'My poor little Beth.' He looked down to where Nat waited silently. 'Please find her,' he begged him. 'Please don't let her be hurt.'

Nat nodded. 'I'll make some calls.' And immediately he left the room, leaving Honey alone with Nick.

'You promised me you'd keep her safe. Oh this might not seem so important to you, but Beth is so uncertain, so unsure of herself. You have no idea how she's blossomed already in your company because you've never seen her any other way, but she's not strong, Honey, and I dread her meeting him, blurting out everything without you at her side to stop him rejecting her again.' He closed his eyes. 'Oh, Honey, what did I do bringing you into our lives? Did I make the most terrible mistake?'

'She's my sister. And it was the only thing you could do. Secrets have a way of getting told.'

'It's true. I know and I'm sorry. Lashing out at you doesn't help anyone.'

'I want to look after her too, I want to help her, make her happy.'

As she said that he dropped his head back in his hands.

'If she's gone to Ibiza I must go too.'

'Let me take you to London,' said Nat, returning to the room. 'I'll drive you. And Dad?' Nick turned agonized eyes towards him. 'Beth will be fine. You know she will be. You're acting as if she's in terrible danger, but you must know she's more likely to be sitting in her car in a traffic jam on the M40 or perhaps she has no intention of going to Ibiza. And, Dad, she's not so fragile either. Stop making out that she can't stand up to anything without one of us at her side.'

'I know,' he whispered. 'I know you're right but I have to look after her for your mother, that's why I worry so.'

'And you must stop blaming Honey for what happened to Mum. Don't turn this little family drama into something that's her fault. Blame Hughie Ballantyne if you have to, but don't even think of blaming Honey.'

'I don't!' he cried defensively. 'I was the one who brought her here.'

'But she's his daughter, and now you're terrified that he's about to take Beth away from you.'

Nick couldn't reply. For a moment Nat looked at him, as he slumped to sit down on the bottom stair, then awkwardly dropped his hand on his father's shoulder.

'We'll follow her, Dad, and you'll see everything will be fine.' He turned to Honey. 'Cup of coffee, then pick up your bag and we could leave straight away, yes? We can call from the car and find out where she is.'

Julia and Pete had joined Nat when she returned from her bedroom and Nick had disappeared. She stopped, looking at Julia from the third from bottom stair, wondering if she felt the same way, whether secretly all of them blamed her for what had happened. But in answer Julia took one look at Honey's face and ran up the last few stairs to meet her.

'Poor Honey. You know, she does this sometimes. She likes to watch us run around after her, prove how much we love her.'

'I'm ringing her,' Nat told Honey, phone against his ear. 'She might answer and tell us where she is.' He grinned. 'Then we could stay for breakfast.'

He waited, waited, but got no reply and eventually he put away the phone. 'It's gone straight to answer. She's not picking up.'

'She's such an awful drama queen,' said Julia, leaning back against the wall and addressing her comment to her father, who'd reappeared from the kitchen. 'She'll know exactly what she's doing to us all, running away like a kid. I'm cross with her Dad, not particularly worried, I'm pissed off.'

Nick looked back to her. 'I don't want to know.'

'She won't have gone to Ibiza. She's gone back to London. She's got the day off tomorrow so she can do what she likes. Tuesday morning she'll be back at work and we'll all be expected to forget all about it.'

'Beth wouldn't have left Honey here without a good reason.'

'And if she has gone?' Julia challenged him. 'So what if she does make it to Ibiza? Whatever she hears from her father, she'll get over it.'

'Stop it, Julia,' said Nat ending the conversation sharply. He nodded to them all. 'I'll take Honey with me now. I'll drop her off and then I'll go on to Beth's flat, find her, or at least see if she's been there.'

'And if she hasn't?' asked Julia.

'Then we talk and we decide what to do next.'

Nat put his arm around Honey's shoulder. 'OK?' he asked her. 'I'm very sorry your first visit here is ending this way, but you know this is a hitch, that's all, and when we've got her back then we can begin again.'

Nick bit his lip at his son's words, but as they passed him by on their way to the front door he turned and she moved stiffly towards him before he caught her by the shoulders and held her still.

'I'm ashamed to say I'm still furious with your father. I have been angry with him for thirty years, but that's no justification for lashing out at you. You couldn't have handled this weekend better than you did.'

Then he moved aside for the two of them and Nat took her hand and ushered her through the door.

When they moved out onto the drive and to Nat's car, she turned to see Nick standing in the open doorway to watch them go, and as the car leaped into life and Nat pointed it towards the drive, saw him raise his arm in sad farewell.

seventeen

BACK AT EDOUARD'S flat Belle was waiting for Honey. Tight-lipped and hardly meeting her eye she was a different person from the woman Honey had said goodbye to only the day before. And still feeling buffeted from the fears about Beth, at first Honey thought it had to do with the Pagets and what had just happened, that somehow Belle had heard about it all and also blamed Honey for Beth's flight.

She let Honey into the house and then stalked back into the sitting room, leaving her alone in the hall. So seconds later Honey stalked in after her. After everything that had already happened that morning, she was in no mood for Belle's unexpected and completely inexplicable bad temper.

'You need to tell me what's going on,' said Belle.

'So do you,' retorted Honey.

Belle cleared the long brown leather sofa clear of newspapers and magazines to make a space, throwing them in a big pile onto the carpet, then she sat down, crossed her legs and waited.

'No,' Honey said flatly. 'First you tell me what's pissing you off.'

'Absolutely I will. Edouard's in trouble, but you know that, don't you, you just don't care that much. You worry about Santa Medea, what happens to darling Ibiza and all your new friends, the Pagets, but it doesn't cross your mind to worry about what could be happening to Edouard.'

'Belle, what's wrong?'

'When Paul threatened Edouard, here in this house, did it occur to you that he was powerful and dangerous and that if things didn't go his way he could make trouble?'

'Of course it did.'

'So what did you do about it?'

'Nothing.' Honey shrugged helplessly. 'What did you have in mind?'

'Anything at all. Because you've let Edouard run around after you, watching out for you, understanding, putting up with you. Six days he's gone without sleep. He's flown all over Europe, he's been sweating in his office, twenty-hour days, trying to pull this around, trying not to lose El Figo, trying to pacify Paul, trying to find him some other place to build on. And you haven't even thought about it, have you? You certainly didn't mention it to me yesterday. I don't think you even realized there was a problem until Paul came marching in here. Honey, as Edouard's friend, I'm saying it's not good enough.'

'I don't care what you think.'

'You have to because it's true! You just presumed that Edouard had sorted the whole Pure fiasco out for you, didn't you?'

'No. I knew it was worse than that. And I read something in the newspaper today . . .'

'Oh, well done.'

'No, don't. I've explained to him, we've talked about this.'

'You didn't know!' Belle exploded. 'And I'm so angry with you on his behalf because Edouard's never going to be angry with you himself. Before we came out to stay with Edouard last weekend, Nancy and I knew about every last detail of Can Falco. We knew the grass seed you use on the lawns because Edouard told us, we knew about the wild asparagus you gather in the hills and serve in the restaurant and what date your mother's birthday is. We knew you liked quince jelly with your Ibicenco lamb and that your friend Hayley Boston makes jewellery for Barneys in New York. He cares about you so much he can be *that* boring about you. He knows the date of your anniversary of when you opened Can Falco, and you have to admit he always remembers it too. But, Honey, you didn't even know his address. You tell him all your thoughts, your hurts, he cares about every one of them, but what do you know about him?'

She hadn't finished.

'You know Edouard considered opening a club with Paul Dix, but only because he told you, because he had to tell you, because he wanted you to become involved. But you didn't know about it because you were interested in finding out about *Edouard*. It wasn't as if you'd asked him one question ever about what he does here, what his world is about when it's not to do with you. For all your life, Honey, as far as I can tell, Edouard has been there for you and you haven't even noticed. What do you give him in return? Not your time, your concern, not a single thought when it's not directly related to you. What's his middle name, for example?' Belle demanded.

'Fabien.'

'Where did he go to school?'

'At home until the sixth form . . .' Honey faltered. 'Then a boarding school in England. I don't know its name.'

'What was his first job?'

'I don't know.'

'Where did he live before we moved here?'

'I don't know.'

'You see?' Belle asked more gently. 'You can do his life up to when he left Ibiza and then it's as if he only existed when he was there on the island in front of your eyes.'

'But that's not true! And in any case this is nothing to do with you. I don't need you to tell me how to behave around him, I know it for myself. And we're happy Belle, really happy. Perhaps that's your problem with me?'

'Don't even think it's like that. You're only together because of me, because I suggested he could trigger some reaction from you if he took you back to Es Palmador, and Cala Mastella and Santa Medea and I was right.'

'But we chose those places. I can't believe you think you had anything to do with it.'

'I've worked with Edouard for the last five years, and all I've heard about is you. I've seen girlfriends come and go, other women try to get his attraction, but it was always you. And so finally I persuaded him to invite me to Ibiza to meet you. We talked, remember that day when we were lying out by the pool and I was asking you what you thought? The night before you went to Es Palmador? Even then you weren't having it, even then you weren't ready to see him for what he was.'

'So what's it to do with you?'

'Honey! I loved you, everything about you, you know I did. Everything but how you were behaving around Edouard. And he's my friend.'

'And Nancy? Did Nancy know what was going on too? Did she feel the same way?'

'No, she knew nothing about you at all. She had no idea what she was getting into. And oh, by the way, you'll have to talk to Nancy.'

'Why? What's happened?'

'Let her tell you.' Belle nodded. 'Although you can probably guess.'

Angry as she was with Belle, still she cared enough about Nancy to keep talking. 'Claudio?'

'Something like that.' Then Belle smiled for the first time. 'Paul's lost her, anyway.'

Honey nodded. 'Good for her.' She stood up, started pacing the room. 'Where is Edouard now? Do you know?'

'He's flying back from Paris. You'll see him soon.'

Honey dropped her head in her hands. 'It's none of your business, but I'll tell you anyway. He's all I've been thinking about. Everything else that's happened and he's all I care about.' She looked up at Belle. 'Once I deserved what you said but I don't any more. I saw it myself without you saying a word. Everything's changed.' She wasn't angry with Belle now. In the scheme of everything else, what did it matter what Belle thought of her anyway?

Her mobile rang and she saw that it was Nat, picked up the phone and closed her eyes, waiting for his news.

'Beth has gone to Can Falco,' Nat told her and Honey felt the floor drop away beneath her. 'Julia's just spoken to Beth's flatmate. Apparently she came home to pick up some clothes and her passport. Her phone's switched off, she's had too much of a head start for me to be able to catch her now. I can only say that she's a good person and she won't be looking to hurt anybody. And I hope when she tells your father who she is that he'll be a good person too.'

'Let me go. Put down the phone and think what to do. Then I'll call you back.'

She dropped her phone and turned back to Belle, having to fill her in on the whole story but struggling to find the words to explain, whilst at the same time driving forwards, knowing that she wanted to be there, supporting them both, Beth and her father, but at the

same time knowing too that her place wasn't at Can
Falco. It was here in London, waiting for Edouard to
join her.

'She'll walk into Can Falco. What will she say to
them, how will they cope?'

'You can catch a plane home, right now.'

'I can do that, I know.' Honey looked back at Belle
wide-eyed. 'But I'm not going to. They're not my
priority any more. I've always presumed Edouard would
be able to sort anything out in the world, given a
chance, because that's how he's always been and I'm
sure he'd understand if I left for Ibiza now. But I'm
not going to presume that. I want to be with him now.'

'You know he'd understand.'

Honey shook her head. 'Yes, he would, but I'll wait
even so.' She rang him straight away, caught his answerphone again and this time she took the plunge.

'Edouard. It's Honey. I want to tell you again.' She
swallowed, suddenly overcome with what she wanted to
say. 'Actually, I want to tell you for the *first* time that
I love you. I really do.' She laughed, suddenly light-
hearted. 'And there's a message you don't get every day
. . . And I'm here with Belle, and I'm waiting for you.
I want to see you very much. So where are you right
now?' She could feel herself reaching for him, willing

him to be nearly home. 'Call me please and let me know how close you are.'

She put down the phone and looked back at Belle and Belle grinned back at her.

'You're doing the right thing.'

'Belle.' Honey leaned closer towards her. 'Don't you see? I don't care what you think.'

Belle laughed. 'Yes, you do.'

Then her phone rang again and this time she saw that it was Edouard, and she fell back onto the sofa with relief and told him everything that had happened.

'Get the train to Gatwick,' he insisted. 'You'll have most chance of a flight from there. I'll come and find you, I'll be right behind you. Don't wait for me at the flat, I'll catch you up.'

'No, I want to stay. I'm not leaving you again.'

'But I'll be there too.'

'I won't catch a flight without you.'

'I'll be there.'

'You have to go,' said Belle, coming back into the room as soon as Honey put down the telephone.

'You were listening!'

'Just a little. Get a cab to Victoria. I'd call you one but I think you'll be quicker getting one off the street.'

'I'm saying thank you even though I think I'm still rather angry with you,' Honey said against her hair.

'I thought you didn't care. You're so lucky.' Belle pushed her away.

Belle grabbed her keys and they left the house together, running out onto the empty road.

'This way,' Belle insisted. 'I know where to find one,' and she took Honey's hand and ran with her, turning left and right, until she brought her out onto a wide main road, and a black cab slid to a halt right beside them.

'Got cash?' Belle called as Honey jumped in. Then she waved her away.

On the journey to Victoria Honey managed to get hold of easyJet and then her knowledge from Can Falco became priceless. It was a Sunday afternoon, August, she could name the flight numbers and times in her head. There was the six o'clock from Gatwick with spare seats, which taking into account the hour difference would get her in to the airport at about nine. She should be back at Can Falco by ten. She booked it and, afterwards, having quickly called Nat to tell him what she'd decided to do, sat back in her seat and fell back to worrying again as the cab made its painfully slow way through the London traffic. She worried about whether to call Hughie and Tora to warn them that Beth was on her way, but what could she say? Beth hadn't said a word about who she was, and then Honey would have plunged in with the news herself.

And then she had to wonder whether she was wrong to be charging straight back to Can Falco. How much was it about her wanting to take control, when in fact, wasn't she being presented with one occasion when she should be willing to step back? Perhaps Beth had a right to tell her own father who she was, without Honey's interference, and perhaps Hughie still had a right to hear it first hand from Beth and show them all that he could behave with a dignity she knew was there somewhere.

At Gatwick she joined the queue for easyJet's check-in, slipped through easily with hand luggage only, and then found herself on the other side with time on her hands and nothing to do but wait.

She made her way to a half-empty café, bought a plastic-looking cheese and tomato sandwich and a cup of coffee and sat down, took one sip of the coffee and realized she couldn't physically bear the sensation of anything passing her lips even though she'd eaten nothing all day.

'Hi,' said a voice.

It was Edouard, looking so dear and so familiar, the old trusty flight bag slung around his shoulder.

She jumped up and straight into his arms, hugging him close.

'So what's been going on in your life today?'

'Oh,' she cried with pleasure and relief, 'just a bit too much.'

He laid down his passport on the table in front of her, his boarding pass slipped inside.

'You're not coming on this plane?' She laughed. 'Are you? With Masterplan falling down around your ears and you having just flown home from Paris? Tell me. Are you getting on this plane with me now and coming back to Ibiza?'

'I surely am.' He bent and kissed her lips, held her face in his hands and kissed her again.

'Belle told me,' she said, pushing him away so she could tell him, 'how desperate it's been for you, how hard it's been to pull out of the Santa Medea project without Paul Dix crucifying you.'

'I had to stop him building it without me. That was what was so difficult to arrange. I knew I had to find him something else . . .' He grinned at her. 'But you have to admit, Bee, Santa Medea would have made a fantastic site. No wonder he wouldn't let it go.'

'Absolutely right.' She laughed. 'Of course it would have done. When he showed me the plans it was the first thing I thought too. Nowhere could beat it.'

'Then I went there, the morning after Es Palmador, early morning, before I came to find you. I parked the jeep and walked down through the cliffs to the beach, and then I sat on the sand and of course I knew it couldn't happen. And then I thought how I loved you and how I mustn't leave Ibiza without telling you. And then I did just that.'

'Oh,' she cried in surprise. 'I think that's the nicest thing I've ever heard.' She waited. 'So? You could tell me now.'

He laughed. 'I love you, I love you. I love you.'

'And I love you, love you too. I always did.' She stroked his face. 'I always will.' She kissed him then rested her head against his shoulder. 'So then what happened? What did you do next?'

He hugged her tightly as he spoke. 'Next I had to find Paul a new site, very, very quickly. And not just any site, it had to be one that we didn't mind him having and one he would want to have, which is where Pineapple Beach comes into play.'

'But how? Paul couldn't possibly think Pineapple Beach is a fair swap for Santa Medea? It's the grottiest place on earth, and even if he tore it down, the whole area around it is a wreck.'

'Which means there are grants to help him pull it around. It was obvious that's what he should do, the problem was convincing him. But he's going to do it, Bee. He's going to redevelop the whole sordid, sleazy area, miles of it. He's pulling down the Pineapple Beach and putting up Pure in its place, not with quite such a sea view, but as he said, people have always had trouble when they try to build on sand. He's ripping down whole streets of hotels.' He laughed. 'Can you imagine anyone else doing it quite so thoroughly as Paul? Don't you think it's a spectacular solution? Take one seedy bloke with too much money, point him towards the dodgiest, dirtiest spot we can find for him and let him clean it up. Give it five years and that part of San Antonio will be like Notting Hill.'

'But how did you steer him away from Santa Medea?'

'He still needed me. He needed me to make the Santa Medea project work and when I wouldn't he tried to make life hard. First he pushed, bullied, called up my backers and my other clients, dropped hints to City editors, tried his hardest to make me crack. And definitely there were times when I thought he might win, not that he'd persuade me but that he'd pull Masterplan under as he tried. It was only in Paris that I knew he wasn't going to pull it off.'

'He came around to your house to see me. He seemed very confident of you, but he was threatening too, and angry when I wouldn't cooperate.'

'On Saturday morning – yesterday, it was only yesterday – I went to him with the ideas for the Pineapple Beach project. And ultimately he realized he had to change tack, that he couldn't have Santa Medea and that he needed me to help make it happen somewhere else. In the end he knew he had far less of a choice. But you were his last attempt, his last way to change my mind.'

'He barely tried. I think I said *no* and that was it. He was out through the door. A couple of lies about you but he didn't even hang around long enough to see if they'd had any impact. Perhaps even then he was starting to see that things were going very wrong.'

eighteen

Ibiza

THEIR PLANE was full of partygoers heading straight for the clubs. Honey, secure beside him, fell asleep on Edouard's shoulder before the plane took off and woke again as they began their descent, to find his coat and his arm around her, while the other arm wrote notes in a big black leather book which he snapped shut as soon as he saw that she was awake.

'Hello.'

She took his hand, thinking this was the first time in ages that she'd woken without an instant lurch of worry.

He brought his face down close to hers and kissed her gently on the lips. 'When we arrive I'm going to put you in a cab and then I'll go back to El Figo and I'll come and find you in the morning. This evening is about you and Beth and your father, much as I'd like to be there. But then, first thing in the morning I'll be back, and I'm not leaving your side again.'

Gratefully she shifted beneath his arm and he looked back at her steadily, then bent his head and gently kissed her again, so softly, so deliciously, and it seemed he thought so too because he lifted his coat over their heads and kissed her again as the landing lights were dimmed and the reverse throttles roared, and he carried on kissing her all the way down to the ground.

She was sped out from the airport, the roads thankfully clear until they hit the heavy traffic around Ibiza town that slowed her taxi down to a crawl. She gritted her teeth as they crept along, even though she knew she'd be too late to stop anything now. What she was expecting to see and hear she didn't know. Shouts? Screams and cries? The sight of Beth weeping, devastated, her father out of control, Tova chanting furiously, blocking out the sound.

When her taxi finally drew up outside Can Falco her first reaction was relief that the hotel was still standing, as calm and white and reassuringly immaculate as it always had been. Then the front door opened and Claudio came striding out, at first looking confused because of course he knew just which guests to be expecting and he certainly wasn't expecting her.

'Honey, why are you back?' he cried out in surprise. 'You've only been gone for two days. You are home too soon.'

'Is she here?' she asked urgently.

He picked up her case, looking decidedly shifty. 'How did you know? I thought perhaps, Belle said she wouldn't tell you.'

'Claudio!' Despite her fear of what she was about to find once she got inside she had to smile. 'Who did you think I was talking about?'

'She's staying in my room. She's not taking a guest bedroom, so we didn't think you would mind.'

She laughed and walked ahead of him, pushing open the front door.

'Honey!' Nancy rose to greet her as she appeared in the hall on the other side. She'd been sitting on a chair beside Claudio's desk. 'Please don't mind! Remember you kind of set us up, so you really can't.' She was laughing as she said it, but was so self-conscious too, walking towards Honey in a new, very floating, very Ibicenco kaftan, the sun already evident on her skin, everything glowing about her. 'Claudio would have told you, but he hadn't a chance and we didn't want to interrupt your time in England.'

Honey took her hands and kissed her cheeks enthusiastically. 'You know I think it's perfect.' As she said it she was looking towards the doorway towards the bar. It was just past midnight, it would be astonishing if Hughie wasn't sitting somewhere there.

'Claudio, let me see the book,' she said, turning back to him. 'I was talking about another girl. I'm looking for someone who may have checked in. A girl, on her own, she might have arrived tonight.'

'I know exactly the one!' Claudio declared. 'Elizabeth Paget. She has taken the single room. She rang earlier on today and she was very lucky because we had just had a cancellation. She arrived a couple of hours ago. I think she is even sitting with your father now, in the bar. Do you want to join them? Would you like me to take your bag to your house while you go and say hello?'

And even as Claudio was speaking, Honey could see Beth sitting in the bar, facing the door. She was at a little table, with her father sitting opposite her. If she looked up now she would catch Honey's eye, but she didn't look up. She was speaking rapidly, concentrating hard, eyes clearly fixed on Hughie.

'Remember your friend Lucinda?' Nancy came up and slipped her arm through Honey's. 'Remember how after we'd bought the belts she invited us to a party? Do you remember?' Honey could hear Nancy talking but she wasn't listening to a word she said. 'Well, the party was last night. Even though you hadn't mentioned it again, I took my courage in my hands and I came back for it. I stood up Paul and I bought a ticket in the airport and I flew over. I've never done anything like that before in my life. But there's something about this place that makes you so spontaneous. And then I got here and you'd gone. It never occurred to me that you might not be here. But oh, Honey, Claudio was. And the party . . . we went together, and there was an island in the middle of her swimming pool with a man playing the piano. And so many of your friends were there, Maggie and Troy, Claire and Tony, Inca and Nash, Victoria and Hilly, they were all so kind I wanted to stay here for ever. And you know your mother looked after the hotel while we went. And she was marvellous at it, everybody loved her . . .'

'Nancy, wait a moment,' Honey said. She walked away, towards the doorway, keeping close to the wall.

Hughie and Beth were sitting opposite each other at a table, with half a bottle of red wine and two half-full glasses in front of them. Hughie with a bandage on his head that had slipped over one eye – or had he pulled it down deliberately? And as she watched, he said something and Beth immediately laughed, a proper, delighted, open-mouthed laugh that immediately had Hughie roaring with laughter too, clearly very chuffed to be so entertaining.

She watched Beth pick up her glass, swirl around the wine expertly and then swallow a mouthful. Then she put down her glass and said something to him and in return he promptly downed the rest of his glass and clapped both hands down on his knees delightedly.

Honey looked at their two heads, close together, their two pairs of hands on the table between them, and then, as she watched, Hughie lifted one hand and rested it gently on Beth's shoulder and, seeing that, Honey had to hang on to herself not to burst into tears, because how come he could laugh so easily with Beth but never with her? And why, despite all the time and the attention and the love, did she never merit such an affectionate touch?

As to whether Beth had told Hughie who she was, she didn't know, and there was now just one way to find out.

Honey moved forwards into the room, then hesitantly towards their table.

Beth saw her first and Honey saw the look of fear upon her face before her father turned in curiosity and then exclaimed 'Honey!' loud enough to be heard above the noise of the bar.

In response the bar went quiet and then immediately surged loud with sound again as the room seemed to repeat after him, *Honey!* Familiar faces, affectionate voices calling out, *we missed you. Thank God you're back. The place has collapsed, look at us, no food, nothing to drink!* Any other time she'd have loved such a welcome, this time

331

she took it all in only dimly, while all the time her gaze was fixed on Beth, who was staring back at her, and slowly shaking her head.

'This is Elizabeth and she is quite the most marvellous girl,' Hughie declared, looking back at Beth enthusiastically. He brought Honey quickly up to speed. 'She's staying just one night. She's got a sister on the island – she hopes she's going to see her tomorrow. The sister's coming here in the morning.'

'But then perhaps she might surprise you and arrive tonight,' said Honey tightly, looking at Beth.

'I doubt it darling,' said Hughie. 'It's getting rather late.' He rubbed his hands together gleefully. 'Whatever, in the meantime, I've promised to look after Beth.' Belatedly something then occurred to him and he frowned. 'But why are *you* here, Honeybee? Surely you shouldn't be back yet.' He leaned in and kissed her cheek. 'Welcome home.' Then he added in a whisper, 'And of course I'm on tenterhooks wondering what happened in England.'

'So why are you here?' he repeated more loudly, smiling and including Beth in the question. 'Honey's been on a weekend away,' he explained to Beth, 'seems to have ended rather sooner than expected. I know, let me get you a drink and then you can tell me properly.'

He rose to his feet, adjusted his bandage and set off for the bar, and as soon as he was gone Honey dragged a chair from a nearby table and sat down opposite Beth.

'What the hell do you think you are doing?' She wanted to slap Beth.

Beth looked back at her unflinchingly. 'I haven't told him.'

'But you're going to? I presume that's why you're here? And yes, I would if I was you, or you might find he starts flirting even more than he is already.'

'Don't say that.'

'It's true.'

'You should be pleased we've been getting on so well.'

'You have a right to be here, a right to tell Hughie exactly what you want to tell him, you even had a right to leave Lingcott without telling anyone where you were going.' Honey glanced quickly to the bar, desperate to finish before her father returned. 'But what you can't do is pretend you're not looking to provoke a reaction because of course you are, you *know* you are . . . And here I am, provoked.' She again looked to the bar but thankfully Hughie had been caught in a conversation. 'You knew by leaving like you did that everybody would wonder. You must have known you'd get me on the next flight back. What I don't understand, if you don't feel the need to punish me, is why you had to put me through today!'

At that Beth looked stricken, appalled. 'But of course I don't want to punish you.' She shook her head. 'It was the last thing I wanted to do. Of course it's not like that.' She glanced over to Hughie then back to Honey, pleading with her to understand. 'I don't want to punish him either. I wanted him to know who I am but I don't even dare tell him. He's such a wonderful man.' She shook suddenly, her hands trembling violently on the table in front of her. 'I don't know what to do. I don't want to upset him but I know I will. But you tell him, Honey, if you think it's right. I'll leave it to you to decide. Please,' she pleaded. 'None of this was meant to hurt you. I just couldn't stand the thought of waiting any more. I felt as if I'd been stalled, over and over again and that I had to take charge of my life, stop letting everybody else make the important decisions on my behalf. He's my father, Honey, and he could have died too, here on Ibiza, before I'd had a chance to tell him who I was, before I'd had a chance to meet him.'

Honey was still not quite ready to let her off the hook. 'You should have told me where you were going. Why you needed to run away. Can you imagine how it was when we couldn't find you, how worried everybody was?'

And for the first time Honey saw something in Beth's stare that admitted, of course she'd known a little of what she was doing to her family. She stuck out her jaw. 'Yes, I suppose I was proving something to them. I thought why not let them worry. I was sick of being so predictable, following everybody else's lead, *don't try to find him*.' She nodded to the bar. '*Don't try to find you*. Nat and Julia always had an opinion and so I waited. I've been waiting to meet you and Hughie for the last four bloody years! And they've always stopped me, always told me later would be better. And then you walk into the house, and you're wonderful, everything I could possibly have hoped you'd be. But still everything goes on exactly the same. We'd come to this monumental turning point and nobody was turning, everything was exactly the same.'

'You hardly gave us a chance.' Honey had to laugh at Beth's nerve, her lack of logic. 'Remember, I'd only just met you. I'd only been at Lingcott one day!'

'I know.' Beth had the grace to look contrite. 'It wasn't a question of time. It was a question of attitude. And yes it was selfish of me because I knew I'd scare you and I knew it would make you run back here. But you know what.' She laughed, looking embarrassed. 'When I did it, I didn't care. So what if I did spoil your trip to England, you'd already done the most important bit, you'd come to find us, all I was doing was hastening your return.'

'You think? Actually it was all more complicated than that.'

Then Hughie left the bar and they had to stop speaking. The two of them watched him make his way back to their table. He passed Honey a vodka and tonic, and then placed another bottle of red wine into Beth's hands.

'Ribera del Duero, 1997. See what you make of it.'

'Corkscrew please,' she said and stuck out her hand.

'Girl after my own heart.' He handed her one with a smile then sat heavily back down in his chair, and turned to Honey.

'Not even a long weekend? Was it so hard to stay away?' He was joking for Beth's benefit but she could see the question in his eyes. *What went wrong?* But of course he couldn't ask.

'I'll tell you what,' he went on. 'We've been having rather a hoot while you've been away.' Honey waited, looking back at him, seeing the traces of his two black eyes still there in the bags beneath his eyes. 'Can you believe Tora and I even did the washing-up after lunch today? Granted we broke a few plates and Tora ended up twisting her ankle, floor got rather bloody slippery . . . but the truth is, we did a very good job. We *marched* to the kitchens. We said, "*Paloma we insist you take the afternoon off.*" We shooed her out and we took control. And then,' he went on with great satisfaction, 'then I got Claudio to show me how to clean the pool with that marvellous sucking thing.' He turned to Beth, 'Finally got a chance to have a go,' then he boomed with sudden laughter. 'When the cat's away, that's what they say . . . But you know what?' He turned back to Honey and started to guffaw with laughter, 'I think I hoovered up somebody's specs.'

'Great,' she said.

'Not that anybody complained.' He beamed back at her, then clearly decided he'd been getting it wrong. 'Not that we didn't miss you, darling,' he said in a rush. 'Did you have a good time? Did you have an *interesting* time?'

'How much have you given him to drink tonight?' Honey asked Beth, wondering whether this wasn't perhaps the moment to tell him. Whenever she did it, it would be the same monumental shock, and at least tonight, now, he had the two of them there together.

They were planning on telling him the truth, no secrets, and in his own roundabout way that's what he was asking, so what was the point in holding anything back?

The point was it was very difficult to find the right words. It was, without a doubt, the hardest thing she'd ever had to do.

'Dad,' she said, in a voice that caught his attention.

'What's wrong?' he demanded immediately. He hastily took an almighty swig of wine and grabbed hold of one of Honey's hands. 'What is it?' he asked in alarm, and then he threw a glance to Beth, who smiled a wobbly smile back at him and at that something fearful passed across his face. Honey waited until she was sure he'd finished the mouthful of wine and then she took Beth's hand with her other hand.

'This is Rachel's daughter.'

At that Hughie inhaled deeply and held his breath and the grip on her hand tightened. Honey looked to Beth, sitting now so still and so upright, staring straight at her father.

'But more than that, Dad. Beth is your daughter too.'

His eyes darted swiftly to Beth then back to Honey, where they locked on, and he stared at her imploringly. She didn't say anything, just held his gaze until eventually he broke the stare and slowly turned to Beth.

'Perhaps I should have written first?' She smiled at him weakly.

'We met each other yesterday, I didn't know before.' Honey knew that Hughie wouldn't be hearing a word she said, but hoped that the sound of her voice might just ground him, help him, while he tried to take it in. His hand was still gripping tightly on to hers. He'd still not said a word. 'Yesterday, I can't believe I've only known her a day. It feels like years.' She glanced at Beth as she said it, tightened the grip on her hand. 'Beth's known about you all her life, Dad. She's known about me too, and our life here, and Can Falco. She's been brought up in England. She's got a brother and a sister and a stepfather called Nick.'

'But what about Rachel?' Hughie asked in a broken whisper. 'Does she? Does she forgive this horrible wretch of a man for leaving you both? I didn't know,' he said pleadingly to Beth. 'You have to believe that I didn't know.'

'Of course she forgives you,' Beth told him. 'Never ever did she think you hadn't made the right decision for both of you.'

Hughie nodded. 'That's very generous of you to say so.' Then he put his head in his hands and started to cry. 'No, I'm telling a lie and I can't do that any more. I feel that I've been lying all my life and I have to stop now.' He looked up and held Beth's kind, questioning gaze, then turned to Honey, who threw everything she had back into her stare, willing him to stop, shut up, to understand that a lie isn't a lie if it's never said. 'I . . .' he stumbled, then glanced to Honey again, while Beth waited, sitting very still. 'If I'd been kinder . . . if I'd taken more trouble over Rachel, if I'd been more in tune with her, I might have realized that she was carrying our child, you, our baby girl.'

He'd realized, he'd stopped himself in time, even if it had been Honey who'd made the decision for him that Beth shouldn't know, that there was no benefit and only harm for her to learn now that Hughie had knowingly left her behind; that he had known all along that Beth was out there somewhere, that some part of him, deep inside had been waiting for this day, but that he'd never gone to look himself.

'I want to speak to your mother,' he told Beth, and looked at his watch. 'Now that I've met you it can't wait any longer. It's two o'clock in the morning. Do you think she'd mind if I woke her up?'

Honey closed her eyes, swallowed, wondering how she was going to be able to do it, this third revelation.

'You can't do that,' she began.

'Rachel is dead.' Beth said it for her. 'My mother is dead. She died eight years ago.'

'She's dead?' Hughie started weeping properly now. 'She's dead. I can never say sorry?'

'Don't think like that,' Beth tried to comfort him. Two days, two bombshells to deliver. Beth had had to give an awful lot of herself away and she'd done it brilliantly well. 'She forgave you a long time ago,' she told Hughie gently. 'She married my father, who loved her very much. She had a good life.'

'But she's died. Oh, God, oh God, she died.' He cried it out loudly, pulling his hands free of the two of them, attracting attention from the guests and friends standing at the bar. 'Rachel has died,' he told them all standing up, wringing his hands. 'None of you knew her, but I'm telling you even so. Rachel has died.'

The fact that there'd been another even more dramatic aspect to the revelations had been momentarily forgotten, but that was Hughie through and through, not that Beth was to know it. 'She's died,' he cried again. 'Oh God, she's died.'

From the throng of people standing speechless at the bar came a dear, familiar face. It was Maggie, marching purposefully towards Hughie, and gathering him up in her arms.

'Darling girls,' she told Honey and Beth, patting Hughie soothingly on the back. 'I'll take him home and put him to bed. Honey, why don't you find your mother?' Honey nodded, speechless. 'Of course it's all the most terrible shock. And getting him pissed doesn't help either.' Maggie rolled her eyes at Beth, while Hughie stayed sobbing against her chest. 'I watched you two all evening, knocking back the bottles. I knew exactly who you were and I thought, she's getting him pissed, doesn't she realize? She's about to tell him this monumental news and she has got him completely blotto? No wonder it's all ended in tears.'

'How did you know who I was?' Beth asked timidly.

'Spitting image of him, you are, my darling.' She looked at Beth kindly. 'I'm very pleased to meet you.'

With Maggie helping them and Troy bringing up the rear, they shepherded Hughie out of the bar, then through the hall of the hotel and out into the gardens, following the pathways to his cottage. Inside there were still lights on and as they approached the door, it opened to reveal Tora waiting to greet them, dressed in a bejewelled bikini and a shimmering gold housecoat, busily mashing herbs with a pestle and mortar, producing a noxious stench of fennel and bergamot.

'Good evening, Honey,' she said calmly at the sight of her daughter, missing Hughie's distraught manner altogether. 'My darling, I had no idea I'd miss you so.' She kissed the top of her head then stroked her cheeks. 'Why are you home so soon?' She looked into Honey's troubled face and shook her head. 'Naughty girl, you were meant to stay away. Did you not think we could survive without you?' Belatedly she took in her husband shuffling on past her through another doorway, Maggie supporting him. When he disappeared into the bed-room and shut the door she turned back to Honey, and only then noticed Beth.

'Beth's come from England,' said Honey.

'Oh yes?' Immediately she was suspicious. 'Is that why Hughie's crying?'

And the way that she asked made Honey suddenly certain that she knew the truth, understood who Beth was.

'He's crying because she's his daughter,' Maggie said from the doorway and Tora spun around, stared at her imperiously for a long moment and then swivelled her attention back to Beth, who in return cowered in trepidation at the force of her stare.

But there was no need to be afraid.

'So, you're not a girlfriend,' Tora breathed. 'You are his daughter.'

She stretched out a slim hand and shook Beth's. And Beth wasn't to know that Tora had never shaken hands with anybody in the whole of Honey's life; and that if ever there was a sign of her discomfort, that was prob-ably as obvious as it was going to get.

'I'm sure I'm a terrible shock. I've been so worried what you might think,' Beth started to confess shyly, trying to hold herself straight. 'All day, I've been wondering desperately how to tell you.'

And simply by uttering those words, *terrible*, *worried*, *desperately*, Honey saw her transform in Tora's mind, no longer the potential threat, no longer even the stepchild, but simply someone in need, and therefore potentially the new disciple. Raw, uncertain, hurt, vulnerable, Beth was perfect.

Gracefully Tora stepped forwards and took Beth's hands, held them out in front of her, then threaded her fingers through Beth's and said, 'I am so charmed to meet you.'

'Oh,' Beth stuttered. 'That's very kind.'

And because Tora was so ethereally beautiful, so charismatic, so certain of what she was doing, Honey saw that Beth was falling instantly under her spell.

In her wonderful husky voice, still holding on to Beth's hands, Tora whispered.

> 'As gentle as the rain at the window,
> As soft as the whisper of the trees,
> As joyful as the sun,
> As it breaks a new dawn . . .
> You shall dance little angel on the breeze.'

Completely transfixed, Beth stared back at her. 'That's beautiful,' she breathed, and with thankfulness and delight Tora stepped forwards and folded Beth against her. 'And so are you, my dear, so are you. Welcome to Can Falco.' Then she looked up at Honey and said in a far more businesslike voice, 'Did you catch the six-fifteen tonight?'

'Yes we both did.'

'Tora, she's your stepdaughter,' Hughie bellowed from the doorway, making everybody start. 'React like a normal human being, please!'

Tora turned and a look of mild disdain crossed her face at the sight of him.

'But, Hughie dear, I think she's delightful.'

'Oh, Tora!' he groaned.

Now she seemed genuinely confused. 'How would you like me to be? I don't understand.'

'What don't you understand? That I left another woman for you? Left her pregnant? Is it not the most terrible shock that I have a child?'

'A terrible shock? No.' Tora looked back at him with a kindly smile, now falling completely into her earth mother role. 'For in this world we are *all* one family and through our new love for Beth we shall feel her joy. We shall comfort and protect her and through our love we shall set her free. We shall let her spirit fly.' She looked carefully at Beth as she spoke and despite Honey's own certainty that her mother always spoke the first words that entered her head, whatever they might be, still she couldn't deny that this time Tora's choices had been rather good ones.

'In this world we are all one family,' Tora repeated, then walked over to Hughie and kissed his cheek affectionately. 'Aren't we, darling? I welcome the chance to know Beth. I am happy that she is here.'

'Either you are amazing or you are completely nuts,' said Hughie, coming forwards and kissing her back. 'Thirty years and I still haven't worked out which it is.'

Tenderly Tora pushed his bandage further up his forehead. 'You worry too much.' She pulled on his arm. 'Now come to bed. Leave them until the morning. You need to sleep.'

'It's a bit of both, I think,' Maggie told Beth as Tora and Hughie disappeared into their bedroom. 'Tora's an exquisite mix of the nutty and the sane. You'll see.'

Beth looked after them rather longingly as the door shut quietly behind them.

'Come with me,' said Honey as Beth then started to sway on her feet. 'I'll take her to the cottage,' she told Maggie. 'Thank you,' she added. 'You sorted them out beautifully. We'll find you in the morning.'

hippy chick

So Honey took Beth by the hand and led her away and Maggie came out after them, muttering and laughing to herself, to pick up Troy, who was patiently waiting for her in the garden outside.

nineteen

IN THE MORNING Honey brought Beth a cup of tea to her bedroom and gently called her name. She put the tea down beside her bed and went to the window opening the shutters and letting the bright Ibiza sun fall straight across Beth's face.

Predictably Beth stirred and sat up, rubbing her eyes.

'It's early but I thought you'd want to be awake.' She turned to look out of the window. 'You never know, something unexpected might happen today.'

At that Beth groaned and let herself fall back among the pillows, then she looked back at Honey and started to smile. 'Was it really all as mad and as wonderful as I remember?'

'Yes, it was.' Honey grinned at Beth. She felt so happy. Grab hold of the moment, she thought fleetingly, remember this time.

Beth took a deep, wobbly breath. 'You've forgiven

me then? I promise I won't ever scare you again. I know I won't because even though I've just arrived here, and I can hardly explain how it felt to meet Hughie, I know already that something has settled inside me. I feel this joy, this peace. It's hard to explain.'

'Talk to Tora about it.' Honey grinned. 'I'm sure she'll know just what you mean.' She got up off the bed. 'We should call Nat and Julia, let them know you're OK.'

'And Dad . . . Oh God,' Beth shook her head. 'I do feel very awful about running away from him.'

'I think he understood better than the rest of us did. Call him while I find you some clothes, then you can come back to the hotel and we can have breakfast. Find Tora and Hughie and see how they are this morning.'

While Beth called her father and dressed, Honey left her and went back to her own bedroom, opened her suitcase and methodically started sorting it out. One weekend, it was all she'd been away. Still less than a week had passed since her father had dived into the pool and blurted out Rachel's name, just ten days since she'd climbed the hills to El Figo and joined Edouard's party.

She came back into Beth's room with an armful of clothes. 'Sort through these, borrow anything you like. I should go over to reception to see Claudio. Come for breakfast when you're ready.' She blew her a kiss.

'Honey,' said Claudio when he saw her. His eyes were twinkling and bright, a smile refusing to disappear even though he was trying to look serious. 'I knew you wouldn't mind.'

'You are such a devilishly fast mover.'

He leaned forwards, shaking his head. 'It was Nancy, not me. I was *"No, no. Go away from me."* ' He shushed his hands theatrically, 'I kept telling her, *"Honey wouldn't approve, we're not meant to have a relationship with the guests,"* but she was having none of it. "I'm not a guest," she kept telling me. "I've never slept a night here in my life." Anyway,' he smiled happily, 'she has now. She's asleep in my bed.' He laughed. 'My lovely Nancy is asleep in my bed and I am very happy about it and nothing you can do will change my mind.'

'I don't want to,' she told him. 'I said so last night. I think it's brilliant. You know I do.'

'She would like to stay. Decide what she wants to do. Perhaps she might find a job, somewhere nearby. Perhaps you might like the two of us to run Can Falco together, give you some proper time away? You know what Ibiza does to people, how it grabs hold of them and they never leave?' He nodded. 'I think that must be happening to Nancy. And Tora—' His eyes widened, 'Tora loves her. Nancy's been to every one of her classes. Apart from the Barely Yoga. Nancy says she must wait for you before she does that class again, but she's doing all the others, can you believe it?'

'Never,' Honey insisted. 'Everything else you've told me sounds absolutely believable, but don't tell me Nancy will ever do another Barely Yoga class.'

She could hear a car making its way up the drive towards Can Falco and she spun around.

'Claudio,' she said quickly, '. . . even though I'm back, and of course I'll be around to help you out tonight, would you mind if I kept today free?'

'Honey!' he exclaimed, outraged. 'I would mind if you didn't. Please, you must take four days off, even if you don't leave the island at all.'

'Four days?'

'I mean *any* number of days, as many as you want. Four was just the first number that came into my head. Because you see Honey, how I can cope when you're not here? You see that Can Falco is not a smouldering ruin, it's still standing, even without you here to prop it up?'

'Yes, it's great to see.' Just how great he wasn't yet to know.

Now the car was pulling up outside Can Falco and immediately she left Claudio and ran towards the door thinking that it had to be Edouard, even though logically she knew that it couldn't be – he had an old jeep that certainly didn't sound like that.

It was a taxi, pulling up in a cloud of dust, the doors opening even before it had come to a halt and she stopped shocked to a standstill to see it was Julia and Nat who were climbing out.

'We had to come!' Julia cried. As soon as she was free of the car she started running towards Honey. 'When we heard where she was and what she'd done. We caught the first flight this morning. Are we too late? What's happened?'

'She's fine. She's here. Everything's good, everybody knows everything, and we've all survived!'

Then Nat came around from the other side of the taxi, didn't need to say anything, just enveloped her in a huge hug. 'Thank God, you found her.'

'Thank God Honey hasn't killed her, you mean,' Julia corrected him.

'No. I haven't killed her. You must come and see her,' Honey told them, laughing. 'She's in my cottage, she's still in bed.' A bemused Claudio had come out to take their bags and Honey turned back to him, still laughing. 'I'm not sure they're moving in, Claudio. I don't know if we have any room.' She looked to Nat and Julia. 'Are you staying?' she asked them. 'Do you want to stay?'

Claudio shook his head to Honey. 'We are completely full.'

She grinned at them broadly. 'If you want to you can have my cottage, move in with Beth and catch up on all her news. I have somewhere else I can go to. Go and find Beth,' she said again. 'Let Claudio show you the way.'

And so Honey stayed at reception, where she could hear Edouard's car when it finally arrived. But then she found she couldn't do that either; couldn't stand to be inside, and so she wandered out and stood, leaning against the whitewashed wall, until finally she heard the sound of an engine, saw the dust building on the track below.

When finally his jeep pulled to a halt on the gravel outside she ran to greet him, didn't stop as he got out of the car, just ran straight into his arms.

'Thank you for bringing me back,' she told him. 'Did I say that last night?'

'No.' He laughed.

'Did I say anything at all? There were so many things I wanted to say.'

He dropped his head and kissed her and she closed her eyes and kissed him back. 'Like what?'

'Like take me away, now, without telling anybody where we are going, just take me away.'

'You realize we've still got a date to go on?'

'Santa Medea?'

'Of course.'

She turned briefly back to Can Falco. Through the windows she could see Nat and Julia making their way down the pathways towards her cottage. She knew that any moment Beth would open the door to them. She knew that back in Angel's Wings, Hughie and Tora were waking up to a new day, and she saw – finally – that they would and could all get on just fine without her; all of them apart from Edouard, and that the only place she needed and wanted to be was with him.

She ran around to the side of his jeep and jumped in. He started the engine, turned the car and then they were out on the road, twisting down to the coast, the wind in her hair.

They flew along the cliff road and then began to climb again, up through the pine forests and then down again the other side until the road narrowed and became nothing more than a bouncing, stone-covered track.

'You remember where it is?' she asked him.

'Of course I do. I told you I came here on my own, like I said I would.'

'I'm sorry.' She looked at him shamefaced. 'How could I ever have doubted you?'

'Oh, you were right to doubt.' He grinned, the wind blowing his hair back from his face, and he looked completely, wonderfully carefree. 'I deserved every doubt.'

'But Belle told me you were never so keen on Pure as you made out.'

'A grotty club in San Antonio is being demolished to make way for it. I've been very keen on Pure. And I spoke to Paul again this morning. He's delighted, I've saved him a fortune.'

'Oh great that we've made life so easy for him!' She laughed. 'At least he lost Nancy.' She took his hand. 'Do you think we can lose that tacky pink glass from the front door of your house?'

'But then I won't be able to look through it to see when you're coming.'

'Then I'll stay with you, safe inside, and you'll know just where I am. How about it? I do need somewhere to stay for the next few nights. Would you mind?'

'Stay for ever.' He looked back at her. 'Not just in El Figo but all over the world. Come with me, let's run away and explore.'

'I want to build a hotel on the Perfume River.'

He laughed. 'Then we'll do it.'

He tucked the jeep up against the side of the track and turned off the engine, then lifted their picnic from the back seat and led her by the hand, carefully, slowly, down a sand-covered path to where the ground opened out onto a little clearing and the cliffs dropped away below to the sea. This was where the cliff jumpers came, she'd told Belle, the daredevil ones who liked to leap forty or fifty feet down into the sea. As teenagers she and Edouard used to come by dinghy, to sit in the water and watch them.

Sheltered from the wind, he spread their blanket out on the sand.

'I stole it,' he admitted. 'You didn't notice, did you, how it never came back with you from Es Palmador? It's been on my bed ever since. But today I thought it should come for the picnic and give us something soft to lie on.'

In answer she came forwards, grabbed hold of him and kissed him hard on the mouth and in answer he dropped the picnic basket and crushed her into his arms, falling with her back to the ground, to pin her down on the rug and stare down into her face.

'Shall we do it?' he whispered and she looked back at him with bright eyes, understanding immediately.

'Do you dare?'

'I've always been too scared.'

'Not with me.'

'No, not with you. Let's do it.'

'Will we die?' she asked, stepping out of her shoes, while still tightly gripping his hand.

'I don't think so.' He had to let go of her to pull off his T-shirt.

'Kiss me again in case we do,' she told him, laughing and terrified at the same time. 'It would be such a bad ending otherwise.'

They kissed hurriedly, laughing with fear, finding it unbearable to let each other go and yet at the same time knowing that to jump would be their perfect ending and their perfect beginning, daring each other on.

'Shall we do it?' Edouard asked again.

'Yes.'

'Shall we run, or shall we go to the edge and look first?'

'We must run.'

'OK. We must run.'

'Kiss me again.'

He kissed her again, clashing his teeth against hers and she kissed him back, scratching her fingers down his back, tangling his hair in her hands. And then they broke free from each other once more, and this time they ran, hands held fast, and with a shout of exultation leaped off the cliff and high out above the sea.